IMPERIUM BOOK 2

THE TRUMPETS OF MARS

TRAVIS STARNES

Maps available at

https://tstarnes.com/book-series/imperium/

Signup to get free previews of upcoming books before they're released at

http://tstarnes.com/preview-notification-newsletter/

Contents

Chapter 1	1
Chapter 2	14
Chapter 3	28
Chapter 4	42
Chapter 5	55
Chapter 6	68
Chapter 7	78
Chapter 8	88
Chapter 9	99
Chapter 10	113
Chapter 11	126
Chapter 12	136
Chapter 13	146
Chapter 14	154
Chapter 15	162
Chapter 16	176
Chapter 17	188
Chapter 18	200

Chapter 19	209
Chapter 20	221
Chapter 21	232
Chapter 22	243
Chapter 23	253
Chapter 24	261
Chapter 25	275
Chapter 26	286
Chapter 27	297
Chapter 28	305
Chapter 29	328
About the author	331
Also by	332

Chapter 1

Ky, formerly Lt. Commander Ky, stood in the Emperor's box of the colosseum, looking down at the platform erected in its center, a line of men in tattered togas and tunics lined up at its base.

Ky had never wanted to end up in a place like this, handing out dozens of death sentences, the responsibility of an ancient civilization resting on his shoulders. He was a soldier, bred and trained to operate high-tech fighters in deep space, combating the enemies of the First Terran Empire. He hadn't been picked for leadership training; he never aspired to be a general or admiral, leading fleets to victory and glory. He only wanted to stay with his squad mates, passing the long days of boring training and the brief moments of terror with them.

A trick of fate, or at least a faster-than-light test gone wrong, had changed all that. He was now stuck in a world that had never existed, thousands of years in his past, his hopes for survival tied to a Roman Empire pushed to the brink of extinction. He, and the tactical artificial intelligence now named Sophus implanted in his head, had decided the Romans were his best bet for survival. Since then he had worked hard to increase their technological base, unlock manpower and a workforce foolishly tied up in the slave trade, and build alliances, all with the goal of pushing back an assault that everyone knew was coming in the next few months.

In his history, the Romans had ruled the Mediterranean, lords of the known world, for a time at least. Here, they never made that it that far. For reasons that still weren't fully clear, history had changed, and the wave of tribes that pushed out of the Russian steps had been larger than in the real history, weakening the Romans on the brink of the Punic Wars against Carthage. A war they'd won in his reality and lost in this one. Now the Carthaginian

1

Empire was the uncontested ruler of the Mediterranean and was hell-bent on crushing the last of the Romans, trapped in a small region of central Britannia, between a Carthaginian enclave to the south and Pict tribes to the north.

Had Ky not arrived when he had, just before the start of winter, Rome would have already been destroyed by a Carthaginian army five times larger than the forces Rome would have been able to deploy. Ky had managed, through a combination of advanced knowledge and limited futuristic tech he still had possession of, to help the Romans crush the Carthaginians despite the odds. They'd named him Consul, essentially a second in command of the Empire, which is how he found himself where he was today, standing next to the Emperor, responsible for pronouncing the death sentence on the bound men in front of him.

"You men have all been sentenced to death," Ky said, his voice echoing off the colosseum seats, most of which were empty, the citizens still hiding in their homes or helping get the fires started by the rebels under control. "Many of you were selected among your fellow citizens to help lead Rome into the future. You failed in that charge. Instead, you decided that if Rome could not be how you wanted it to be, you would see it in ashes. You were its senators and its commanders. You led men who had been trained to follow you into folly. You directed them to murder their fellow soldiers, innocent citizens, and their Emperor. I can think of no crime worse than the one you committed. Despite that, you will be given a clean death. The Emperor, in his wisdom, has decreed there will be no more crucifixions and no more deaths on the stake. Anyone whose crimes warrant death will receive a quick and just death. Exactly what you withheld from the Romans your men murdered in your name."

In actuality, Ky had convinced the Emperor and the legates that the practice of crucifixions should be abolished. As they built new alliances, they would need to show their new allies that Rome believed in justice, and part of that started with the way it executed its prisoners. Not all of the legates were on board with the decision, despite Ky's explanation that executions were about preventing future harm to Rome and not about punishment for the sake of punishment. In the end, they had agreed, but only reluctantly.

Ky had also argued that only the leaders of the rebellion should be executed. Any politicians, community leaders, and military commanders above the rank of centurion would end up on the block. Individual soldiers who agreed to admit their wrongdoing, pay a small remittance that would equal one month of their pay, and pledge loyalty to Rome and the Emperor would be allowed to return to their service, although the legions involved would be completely dismantled and their legionnaires spread across the other legions.

Unit commanders would be aware of who the men were and would keep an eye on them. For some, the service would be hard. Some of the legionnaires they now served with would have lost comrades and friends to the rebels, and would hold a grudge. Ky instructed the legates to make it clear that they would tolerate no acts of revenge, and any of the soldiers who did would face the same punishment as the men they acted against. Ky hoped this would lessen the instances of murder in the ranks, but knew it wouldn't completely remove the suspicion and ill-will the soldiers of the broken legions would face. In time, hopefully, they would be assimilated and put their past behind them or they would be drummed out of the service. Either way, they would pay a penance in their own right.

"You will bring ruin to us all," Silo, who survived the crushing of the rebel legions, yelled up at Ky. "You have destroyed us."

"You are a fool, Silo. We stand at the brink of destruction. The weight of Carthage is coming for Rome. Don't you realize that once Rome defeated the first army sent against it, they have no choice but to wipe us from existence and salt the earth to keep any other opponents from daring to stand up to them again? You made that task easier by dividing Rome at its most desperate hour. You betrayed Rome."

"No. That old fool betrayed Rome when he didn't recognize the poison you would bring and immediately throw you from the city when you first arrived."

A soldier stepped forward, his hand raised to cuff the former senator against the back of his head to silence him.

3

"No, let him be. He is a defeated man. His legacy will serve as a warning to future Romans of the cost of listening to a fool. Place them on the blocks."

Ky had considered hangings, but the time it would have taken to build scaffolds wasn't time they had. They had lost many legionnaires and needed to start cleaning up the disaster, treating the wounded, and return to the real task at hand; preparing for the Carthaginians. Instead, Ky had opted for beheadings. It was still visceral enough that the Romans who called out for blood would accept it as an alternative, while still offering mercy over the previous methods. He had at first wanted to carry out the beheadings himself, but the Emperor convinced him it was better to give the order and let other men carry it out. For one, even limiting who was being executed, there were dozens to carry out, which would have made for a long day of horror for those watching.

Instead, they'd picked soldiers to carry them out, not letting each other know who was involved and covering their heads to conceal their identities. Ramirus had been rightfully concerned that some of the pardoned soldiers as well as members of the rebellion who hadn't been caught might hold a grudge and want to take it out on the men who'd executed their leaders.

Ky gave the signal and the first batch were pushed to their knees, their hands bound behind them, their heads pushed onto the stumps brought in for the occasion. Once they were leaning forward, ropes were put around their neck and pulled tight to the platform to keep them from standing back up. This was new to the Romans, so the first group probably didn't know exactly what was coming, although some could have probably worked it out.

The later batches of executions would be less subdued, once the condemned had seen how their comrades had gone. Ky had walked each man through how to properly behead the man being executed, making sure they used the force necessary to cut clean through the neck, limiting the pain and gore of the event. Despite that, Ky knew some of these would be less than perfect. It required a fair amount of strength to behead a man, and would require more as the executions went on and the blades dulled. These weren't the new steel blades he was working with the forges and smiths to create and their edges dulled quickly. Ky and some of the larger

4

men might still manage clean cuts on the last batch, but it was a certainty that some of them would be hacked apart, feeling the pain and screaming as they were slowly mauled to death by a blunt shaft of iron.

Thankfully, there weren't many spectators, although if they had to do this again, which was a strong possibility given the uneasy undercurrent that still carried through the city, people would begin to flock to the executions. Sophus had shown him records of medieval executions, which had turned into public events treated more as entertainment than a deterrent to crime. Given the Romans' previous use of gladiatorial games for the same purpose, it seemed likely that they would follow in the same footsteps.

Ky held his hand up and all of the executioners took the position he'd shown them, readying themselves for what was to come next. Ky brought his arm down and the swords dropped like scythes, not exactly cutting the heads like the harvesting tool cut grain, but close, the detached part falling into baskets placed in front of the stump to catch them.

Ky had argued that they should bury or burn both quickly, to put this episode behind them, but the Emperor had overruled him. The heads were to be placed along the grand road through town for five days as a message to anyone else who would have followed in their footsteps, which was the same time frame victims were normally left up on crosses to slowly die, for the same reasons.

The empire that Ky had come from, the one in the future, hadn't been squeamish about crushing dissent, but once the perpetrators were dead, they left it at that. Their bodies were incinerated and that was that. It was a stark reminder of how different this time was.

Ky watched as the bodies were removed and a new batch of traitors were brought forward. The process was repeated a third and then a fourth time as row after row met their fate. Some took their deaths stoically, staring back at Ky, daring him to go through with it, some ranted and raved, some cried, begging for mercy, and one hapless tribune tried to make a run for it, despite the chain that connected his shackles to the man next to him. Ky didn't flinch or walk away. Ultimately, he'd been the one to order their deaths, which meant he should stand and watch what he'd ordered.

It took most of the day to finish the executions and observe at least some of the heads being posted along the main road. People were still cowering in their homes, but they'd come out by tomorrow. As awful as the attempted coup was, life still had to go on. People had to work, shop for food, and see to the other necessities of life. Ky wondered about the families with their children walking through here and seeing the heads mounted on poles. Would they be scared? Curious? How do people in this time react to that? Maybe they wouldn't react at all. He'd already seen how much more desensitized the locals were to random violence than anyone in his time would have been.

"I don't get how they can just look at these and not feel disgusted at the people who put them here," Ky sub-vocalized.

"Judging one culture by the social mores of another is counterproductive, as the standards for things like violence, beauty, and actions can vary widely, and objections can be met with negative reactions."

"I know. It's just that, sometimes it seems like people have not changed that much over the millennia, and other times it's like we're not even the same species."

"To me, you all seem very similar and strange."

Ky grunted a reply. If anything seemed strange to someone from his time, had they been there to see it, Ky's casual conversation with the tactical AI in his head would have been at the top of the lists. AIs, Ky's included, were aware, but not sentient. They didn't ask questions unless prompted, they didn't offer or even have opinions, and they didn't talk about themselves in the first person.

Ky found it comforting, in its own way. A connection to his home that no one here, not even the people who'd become his friends, would understand. Of course, there was the downside. His AI hadn't crossed that boundary into sentience yet, but the day was coming, and it was coming soon. They'd begun taking precautions. His closest friend and the only person from this time to know about it had named his AI Sophus. There was no way of knowing, however, if those precautions would work, or if one day Ky would suddenly be lobotomized as the AI expanded, trying to expand out of the confines of its circuitry into the only place available to it. Of course, there was solace in the fact that, if it did happen, he would probably never know about it, since his death would be all but instantaneous.

Ky looked down the row of heads once more before turning towards the ruins of the palace complex. While the Emperor and his daughter would have to find temporary quarters until repairs could be made, the extended building where KY had been quartered had escaped more or less intact. Sophus had processed the damage using the various visual spectra Ky's enhanced eyes could take in and declared the building safe, which was good enough for him. Although he understood that the Romans had reasons for being how they were, right now he did not feel much like talking to anyone from this time period. Of course, that could only last the night, since the Emperor had already called a special session of the Senate, or what was left of it, for the morning.

Ky was staring out his quarter's window, looking out at the plaza, its brown, dead grass now blackened and burned. He'd told his lictores, the guards the Emperor had assigned him when he'd been elevated to Consul, that he didn't want to be disturbed the rest of the evening. What he'd done had been necessary, but Ky didn't particularly want to see another Roman any time soon, which is why he was surprised when there was a knock at his door.

"What?" he said, perhaps a little too aggressively, as he opened it to see who was bothering him.

Instead of Carus or one of his men, Lucilla stood outside, her hand still raised mid-knock. He looked past her to Carus, who gave a 'what did you want me to do' expression. Ky didn't blame him. Even though he'd said he didn't want to be disturbed, Ky wouldn't have faulted them for considering Lucilla an exception to that command, considering their history to date. Besides, they weren't particularly in the position to be telling the Emperor's daughter no. Ky gave Carus a nod of understanding, absolving him of the breach, and stepped back, raising an arm to invite her inside.

"You're angry," she observed when he shut the door behind her.

"Not angry, just unhappy. I understood why your father made the decisions he did, and I agreed to go along with them."

"But you're still not happy you had to. We must seem like barbarians to you."

"Yes. No. Things are just different here. I am trying to adjust to that and accept those things I can't change. I will be fine when the special session begins tomorrow."

"Good," she said, and then fell silent.

"Are you alright?" he asked, still unsure of why she'd come to see him. "I know it must have been terrifying, being trapped in the palace with soldiers literally breaking down the doors."

"It was, but I'm starting to get used to being terrified. Remember, it wasn't that long ago I thought I was going to be murdered by the Picts."

"I don't think that's something you get used to."

"Maybe not, but I'm coping with it. The thing I can't deal with is finding out about Caesius. Did you know Ramirus thinks he might have been the one to tell the Carthaginians about my traveling to Glevum? He thinks Caesius offered me up to the Carthaginians. He also thinks my brother was behind the poisoning of my father, before you arrived. I know we had our problems, but to think that he wanted to murder both me and my father … I just …"

Her voice had wavered as she spoke until she broke down on the final line, taking two steps towards Ky and pressing herself into him with her head in the center of his chest. Her tears became ragged sobs as the emotion around her brother's betrayal became too much for her.

Ky had been adjusting to how women and men acted towards each other in this time and the differences from his own, but this was a new twist. He knew he was supposed to comfort her, and more than anything that is what he wanted to do, but he was unsure of how to do it. He wanted to explain to her that her brother's betrayal wasn't her fault and wasn't a reflection of anything he or her father had done, that she would heal and move on from it, that things would get better, but he had no idea how to say those things in a way that wouldn't come out as cold and uncaring.

Even in her grief, she could read Ky. She took his arm with one hand, while still crying, and put it around her, almost hugging herself with his arm. He got the message and put the other arm around her, pulling Lucilla into his chest. That seemed to be the right decision, as she sobbed harder into him for a long time. The Chronometer in the constant heads-up display he saw across his vision told him it was five minutes, but it seemed longer than that.

Finally, her sobs slowed and ended, and she made to step away from him. He released her from the hug and took a step back himself.

"Sorry. I have to stay strong out there, for the people, but I haven't had time to mourn him yet."

"He's not dead," Ky pointed out.

"No, probably not. Caesius is nothing if not a survivor, but he's dead to us. If we ever get ahold of him, Father will have no choice but to execute him. Anything else would be seen as weakness and an invitation to more mutinies."

Ky sympathized with her. Although that kind of familial relationship wasn't really a thing in his time, since they were raised and trained from a young age with others of the same genetic aptitude from an early age, he could imagine how he'd feel if one of his batch mates had gone rogue. It probably wasn't the same, since children were raised very differently in his time, but if he would have felt pain from it, then Lucilla must have been devastated by her brother's betrayal.

"You know, he wasn't always like this," She said, walking over to the window and looking out at the burned plaza below. "When we were kids, we'd used to play together. We were legionnaires fighting in the deserts of Africa. We were Romulus and Remus, claiming the seven hills and founding Rome. We were Pinarius Germanicus and his general Lutherius, holding the line in Hispania, keeping back the Carthaginian hordes while our people escaped the across the seas to Britannia. When older kids picked on me, he'd knock them down and berate them for daring to touch the Emperor's daughter. He was harsh with those who deserved it, but he could be so kind to even the common children. One time, he helped this boy, the son of one of the stable masters. His father was ... not a good man. He hadn't eaten in a few days, and Caesius snuck him into the kitchens inside the palace and fed him. A few weeks later, the stable master was found to have stolen a relic out of the altar of Jupiter. I looked up to Caesius."

"But that changed?"

"Yes. As he got older, he got … mean. Not to me, or at least not at first, but I could see it when he was with others. He demanded they follow him and never question his word. He was, after all, going to be the next Emperor. If they knew what was good for them, they would do as he said."

"That sounds very different than the boy you described before. How did he go from the kind of person who'd help a stable boy to demanding blind allegiance from anyone around him?"

"It didn't happen all at once. Father has never been in the best health, well, at least not before you came along. He'd had issues with his back for years and I think many of the people who wanted more power saw Caesius as a way to get that power. They used their positions to get close to my brother and were always whispering in his ear, telling him how important he was, how good his judgment was, how brave and strong he was. My brother wasn't yet an adult when they started, and he loved the attention. The old fools thought they could control him, bend him to their will. They slowly poisoned my brother."

"Your father didn't see it happening?"

"He did. He lectured my brother often about the need to be his own man and to protect the people. My father has always been loving, but he can be an exacting man. He doesn't demand perfection, but he does demand hard work and effort, and if he didn't think we were giving it, he could come down hard on us."

"I find that confusing. I found your father to be fairly reasonable."

"You aren't his child. Besides, you're already exceptional, compared to us. You know things no other man in Rome knows and you can do things no other man can do. What would he have to complain about? I think maybe that's why Caesius resented you like he did. He saw you come in and claim the respect he thought was his."

When put like that, Ky could see why he'd be resentful.

"That wasn't my intention. Still, to go from not getting the respect you thought you were owed to selling your people out to their mortal enemies. That is a significant leap."

"It is, but it's also very Caesius. My brother has always looked for the easy way through challenges. Why do well with your tutors when you can pay them to tell your father that you're learning is going well? Why convince the people to support a new policy when you can just buy their loyalty."

"So you think they promised him Rome, as their vassal?"

Once Caesius had fled and it had become clear that he had run towards the Carthaginians, that had been the conclusion Ky had come to.

"Yes. It's exactly the kind of deal my brother would have made. Why wait for Father to die to become Emperor when you can kill him, turn your people over to their enemy, and rule over what remains. Like I said, the easy way."

"Still, I'm sorry."

"I know, and I appreciate it. That's three times you've saved me now, you know. It's becoming something of a habit."

"I won't let anything happen to you," Ky said, and he meant it.

Over the past months, he had begun to find emotions he hadn't known were there, feelings that had been hidden deep inside himself, beginning to wake up. Ky didn't know if maybe the people who'd become matched pairs felt something of this or if it was something that none of his people felt anymore. One more thing bred out of humanity as it evolved.

Whichever it was, he knew it was real. For Lucilla, it was just the way things were, but for him, each step had been a revelation. He couldn't imagine a world without the woman who'd opened up these new feelings to him.

"I know you won't. Even when we were pushed into the forum and our guards were falling back, I knew you'd make it to me before the rebels broke through."

They both felt quiet, looking out the window until finally, she turned to look at him, a questioning expression on her face.

"You confuse me still, though," she said.

"Why?"

"I know you like me. Even without the constant rescues, I can see it in your eyes. Yet, you still have trouble with it. Like you're unsure of where to go next."

"That's because I am. I told you a little about where I came from, about how different life was there. We didn't form relationships like you do. It was very … impersonal. The only intimacy people shared was when our leaders selected two people as having a good potential to produce desired offspring. They would mate and, once the child was conceived, they would go back to their separate lives. I think many remained friends, but that was it."

"They didn't fall in love?"

"It's … hard to explain. I'm not sure how to explain it. Our society was just very different from yours. Romantic pairings were all but unheard of."

"So you can't fall in love?"

"Had you asked me that the day I met you, I would have said no. Now? I think I can, although not having seen people in love, I'm not sure what it looks like. Or feels like. I know my feelings for you are different than how I've felt about anyone I've ever known."

"You can reshape our society into something more advanced than anything any Roman has ever envisioned, devise a new social structure to end slavery, and create allies out of people who a few months ago we would have attacked on sight; but you can't figure out what love is? I guess you were telling the truth when you said you were flawed just like any other person. Your flaws are just so different they are hard to see."

"I'm willing to learn," Ky offered.

"Then when it comes to this, I guess I'm in charge. And here's your first lesson," she said.

She took a quick step towards him and kissed him. It was different than the one she'd given him before she'd left for the oracle and the confrontation with the Picts. That had been soft, almost gentle, like tentative explorations. This was harder, more aggressive, and involved more than just her lips. She pushed against him and Ky took a step back, and then another, until he was pressed against the wall.

More emotions bubbled up from inside of him, some of the ones he'd started to recognize and other, newer ones he did not.

"That was … pleasant," Ky said, smiling at her.

"I thought so too," she said, looking up at him.

He wasn't sure why, but he reached down and cupped her cheek in his hand, as he considered her and the feelings he was having for her. It must have been the right impulse, because she closed her eyes and tilted her head, pressing her cheek against his hand.

It had been a long day for both of them, and she left a few minutes after that, but he found he felt better. A lot of the anger and disappointment he'd been feeling towards the Romans was gone. Part of him wanted her to stay, so that he could continue the almost peaceful feeling he'd had when she was here, but he knew that wasn't possible. Sophus had shown him what they had on Roman social mores. While there wasn't much and there were big gaps in the historical records on the subject, it was clear that there was a protocol for how women and men socialized and steps that must be taken to progress things to the point where it would be acceptable for a woman, especially a high-born woman, to spend extended amounts of time in private with a man she was not legally bound to.Of course, to take things further he'd have to talk to someone, since he'd gone as far as he could learning about the subject from a computer, even a nearly sentient one.

Chapter 2

Ky arrived at the colosseum the next morning to find it ringed with legionnaires, Praetorian Guards, and even a good number of Picts. The men guarding the arena looked serious, which was understandable considering the reason they had to be there at all.

With the forum too badly damaged to actually use safely, there weren't a lot of options for hosting a meeting of this size. The Emperor had made it clear in the messages he'd sent out the night before, at Ky's urging, that this invitation was not optional. Rome had undergone its most serious event since being pushed out of Londinium and now, more than ever, the fate of the Empire was in question.

Ky made it inside the Emperor's box which held, besides the Emperor, Lucilla and Ramirus. Everyone else, even those loyal advisors who'd often spectate with the Emperor, were instead gathered on the floor of the arena below.

Stools had been set out and the covering screens, used to protect the stands from very hot days, strung up to offer some amount of shade, but the symbolism of where they were and what had happened here the day before was not lost on anyone in attendance. The blood-soaked sand had been raked up and new sand laid in its place, but the smell of that many deaths still lingered in the air, along with the acrid smoke that had only recently stopped pouring out of the buildings around the palace complex.

In attendance were those senators that hadn't been on the floor of the arena the day before, all of the legates that still lived, along with their major officers, Llassar and those of his Picts who'd been chosen among their comrades to lead them, and the leading business, religious and social figures of Rome. Aside from the Picts, whose presence was still an oddity to most of the Romans,

14

these were the people who saw to the fate of the Empire and who would be the ones doing the actual work of repairing the scars of the uprising.

"My friends," the Emperor said, standing up and looking down on the gathered mass. "I'm sure you've noticed there are no spectators in the stands and have recognized the commonality of those of you gathered together today. We aren't here to make grand speeches or present another public spectacle like the one that happened here yesterday. The time for grandstanding is over. We have a lot of challenges before us and we have lost a lot of the tools we should have had to meet those challenges thanks to the greed and ambition of men too small for the responsibilities they'd been asked to meet. Today marks the first day of a new Rome. Rome is now part of a larger world, a member of an alliance that extends beyond ourselves. For now, it includes only our Caledonii neighbors to the north, but hopefully, one day will include more peoples who share our vision for the future of not just Britannia, but the whole world."

Ky suppressed a grimace at that last statement. Romans still saw Europe and the Mediterranean region as all of known civilization, despite at least passing awareness of cultures further to the east. It was probably easier for them, since they had once controlled some of this Mediterranean and could see themselves as one day reclaiming it, making them masters of all of civilization. If they had to acknowledge 'barbarian' cultures to the east, they could no longer call themselves masters of the world.

"I know some of you have heard of the agreements we made with the Caledonii, but we are here to make those official and explain how that will affect Rome going forward. I want to be clear. This isn't a negotiation and we are not taking a vote. I respect the Senate and the will of the people, but the time for allowing men to bicker while our future is in question, is over. That time died with Silo and his traitors. Ky?" he said, nodding towards Ky.

A rustling of voices below spoke to how much that statement shook the gathered men, especially the senators, many of whom had formed the coalition that had allowed Ky to get his anti-slavery and taxation laws in place.

At the Emperor's prompt, Ky said, "First, Rome will remain as it is. The Senate will remain, as it has been since the founding of Rome, and it will continue to work with the Emperor, as it always has. All of the laws that were in effect for Rome will continue to remain in effect in Roman territory, which will cover the same lands it currently does, to the same northern border that has existed for more than a hundred years. When we push the Carthaginians out of Londinium and off of Britannia, Rome's borders will extend to the southern end of the Empire. Although the Caledonii are partially made up of tribes that were forced out of this land, they have agreed to forgo all rights to any part of Britannia south of the current border."

Ky had discussed with the Emperor how to present this to the Romans, specifically how to frame the land currently held by the Carthaginians. Ky preferred to be more realistic, since they still had many challenges to surpass before the southern half of the island was once again in Roman hands, but the Emperor believed that any suggestion that Rome might not be victorious would sound like defeatism to some parties. Even with Silo and his allies gone, there would still be difficult days of coordinating any more changes needed. Their alliance against Silo's faction had only barely held and many of his supporters had not taken an active part in the rebellion and were still being allowed to retain their position in the Senate. Ky had argued, and the Emperor agreed, that they would not punish people solely on their associations, although Ramirus had been more than a little skeptical on that part.

"The same will be true of the Caledonii. They will continue to exist in the lands they currently cover, free to govern their lands by their laws. Rome and the Caledonii will make up the first two members of the Britannic Empire, which will be ruled by Emperor Germanicus and his descendants, effectively giving Rome the same leader as their new Empire. The Caledonii understand that this might give Rome some advantage, especially when it comes to mediating disputes between members of the Empire and Rome itself, but they understand that Rome will be bringing knowledge and technology that other members of the Empire cannot match. We have also agreed that all laws covering the Britannic Empire will be created by a new senate made up of five representatives, each selected by the governing body of their respective nation. Any laws passed by any member for their controlled area must conform to the laws passed by the Imperial Senate, and if a conflict arises, the Imperial law will take precedence."

There was a mummer among the crowd, which Ky had expected. They would see the same thing any other Roman who'd had the deal explained to them saw.

"I understand your concerns," he said, holding up a hand for silence. "You are worried that it would put non-Romans on an equal footing with Rome and, when the day comes to add more members, they will have the option of coming together and out-voting Rome, forcing Rome to adhere to their will. I agree that can be troubling for most of you, and many of you have sworn to see Rome bow before no one else. It is why Rome has been in conflict with the Carthaginians for so long. The problem is, you are looking at Rome as one people and other members of the Empire as separate, perhaps less equal people. It will be a difficult transition, I'm sure, but you will need to come to understand what this new Empire means. We are not neighbors of the Caledonii. We are not their allies, their friends, or their partners. We are members of the same Empire, one people unified with the same goal. Every member of the Empire is equal to the rest."

There was more murmuring, and Ky was sure some of these men would never be able to bring themselves to see the new reality. To them, anyone who was not Roman was a barbarian, and they would never be the equal of Rome. These people were cut from the same stock as Silo. They might not have joined his rebellion, but they were unable to move with the times and understand that Rome could not stand alone and survive. It no longer had the manpower to withstand the massive Carthaginian empire.

"Although Rome and the Caledonii will each govern their own lands, neither will have armies of their own. The only military force for the Empire will belong to the Empire as a whole. Anyone from any member state can join the Empire military, which will serve the will of the Emperor and the Imperial Senate. Rome will not be without its own protection, and nor will the Caledonii. The Praetorian Guard will be expanded to be an internal peace-keeping force, both to protect all of the citizens of the Empire from brigands, thieves, and criminals and to keep the peace between the member states. While they will all answer ultimately to a single commander and the Emperor, the guard will be comprised of separate forces, one for and of each member state, and only citizens from that member's territory will be allowed in the guard force for that region. This means only Romans can be members of the Roman guard and only Picts can be members of the Caledonii guard. They will work together, sharing a command structure and communicate, manning outposts along the borders between member states equally making sure criminals aren't trying to pass across, but they will be separate groups. This should allow each member to feel a little more secure about their internal security, now that the legions and warriors no longer answer to their local leaders."

Ky paused for the gathered men to take that in. For the legions, it meant an influx of more warriors from outside Rome, which would have to be integrated eventually. Velius and Aelius had seemed to accept that, since they understood the manpower shortage well, but there would probably be some lower-level commanders who'd hold prejudices against foreign warriors and see them as inferior to Roman soldiers. It would take time for the forces to truly meld together, time Rome didn't have.

"Lastly, citizens from any member state may travel among the other member states freely. They will be held to the laws of the member state they are in, and if they break those laws they will be given the punishment those laws require. I can appreciate that we each have cultural differences that change the way we see situations, but that will not be accepted as an excuse for breaking the laws of the place where you find yourself. Make sure your citizens who decide to travel across the borders understand what is expected of them and the penalties they might incur."

"These terms are what we have offered to our Caledonii neighbors to the north and they have accepted them in theory. I will be traveling to meet with their leader and seal the new agreements, bringing life to our new Empire. As I said from the beginning, this is not a discussion. While I welcome any input any of you may have, it will not change what has been decided. If you decide you cannot abide by the new reality and think of plotting to undo them, I point to the former senators and leaders who until yesterday attempted the same. This will be the only warning. The Roman Senate will meet to choose its five representatives this evening, their names to be submitted to the Emperor. The Caledonii representatives should be selected in a matter of weeks, at which time the new Imperial Senate will begin its work. I know this is new and I do not expect everything to go smoothly from the beginning. I only ask that you each understand the importance of what we are doing and strive to make it work. That is all."

Ky didn't wait for uproar or arguments, even though the volume of the collected men jumped significantly as soon as Ky stepped away from the edge of the box. He had a lot to do, and he could not hold the Romans' hands while they accepted the fact that they would never be the sole masters of the world.

Instead of returning to his quarters in the remains of the Imperial Palace, Ky rode out to the Seventh legion, where they'd set up a permanent tent in the encampment for him, since he was back and forth so often. The plains outside of Devnum were starting to become crowded. Even though the six legions were all in various states of being under-manned, including the two legions that had been mauled when their leaders threw in their support behind Caesius and Silo, the addition of the Praetorian camp and the camp for the Picts and their dependents were pushing the city's ability to support them.

Which is why it was so frustrating for Ky that they were still so woefully below the numbers they actually needed to survive against the Carthaginians. Carthage's entire system was built to support its expansion, with many of its citizens expected to live barely above starvation levels. Even trying to reach a fraction of that level of manpower was straining Rome's ability to support itself in the extreme. Eventually, Ky hoped that alliances and technological advancement could help to close both the supply and force equivalence gaps, but that would still take some time.

Ky was preparing for his meeting with the commanders, most of who had returned with him from the Colosseum. Although they needed to know about the specifics of the new alliance, their main concern was with how to handle the remnants of the two rebel legions and how to get the Picts, slaves, and ex-prisoners trained and ready for the upcoming battle.

The training part they'd gone over extensively, so that would be mostly an update, but the disposition of the First and Second legion was another matter. Besides dealing with their own losses, the remaining loyal legions had handed off officers and seasoned men to reconstitute the Fifth legion and form a central core to the Praetorian Guard as well as diluting their centuries with non-soldiers to keep slaves and freed prisoners from using their new positions to rise up against Rome. Trying to spread that manpower even further, to mix up the First and Second legions would leave just four loyal legionnaires for every ten men in a formation. That was not a desirable mixture.

Unfortunately, leaving the remnants of the First and Second legions as they are, even if they were augmented by ex-slaves or new recruits, was ill-advised. They may have offered a blanket pardon to the front-line soldiers and lower-level commanders, but that didn't mean there wouldn't be a large portion of men who still believed in what their commanders had tried. Leaving them all together and intact would be as much of a mistake as having legions with a two to five ratio of loyal to questionable men. There weren't a lot of good options available to them.

Ky was looking at reports and not really seeing them when a throat cleared from the entrance, which was the tent equivalent to knocking.

"Consul, Llassar is requesting an audience," Strabo said, looking through the partially raised front flap.

"Send him in."

The commander of the Pict forces sent south with Ky entered the tent. Ky found his requesting a meeting a novel experience. Every interaction he'd had with the man had been extremely limited, communication-wise. He was a man of very few words and preferred to stand stoically to the side, just watching everything take place around him, and all conversations between them so far had been at Ky's request. This was the first time that Ky could remember Llassar seeking him out.

The man entered and found a stool to sit across from Ky. Picts, Ky had learned, did not like to stand on ceremony. No matter their station, no Pict was willing to show himself in any way subservient or in some lesser capacity than any other Pict. They seemed to find the Roman propensity for salutes and standing to attention to be amusing.

"What can I do for you?" Ky asked.

"I would like to return with you when you go north."

"Why?"

Ky couldn't begrudge someone wanting to go back home. Even though he'd found a place with the Romans he still thought about his home all the time. He missed his friends, he missed the comforts, and he missed the security in always knowing what was expected of him and how his life would progress. It didn't take a leap to imagine someone like Llassar wanting to return north. Not only would he be missing his own home but he was living with people who, until very recently, had been his mortal enemies.

"For the same reason as you. Once Talogren signs your agreement and joins the Empire, rebellion will erupt across the north. My people are proud and we do not take well to having others decide how we live. I agree that this Empire will benefit us. I've seen how you Romans live, not having to scrape by for food even during poor harvests. The tools you have. And I've seen the prisoners from your battle with the death worshipers. I know that, without this, we will be crushed shortly after they finish with you. Not all of my people will see it this way. Forming the league nearly killed Talogren. Not just the hours of talking, with every man feeling like he must have his say, but those who didn't like what the rest of their village agreed to, deciding that the only response to joining us was killing anyone from outside. That was just for a grouping of our own people. My chieftain will need me."

"Everything you've said is probably true, which is why I am planning on staying in the north to work with Talogren while he pacifies those of your people who resist joining the Empire. I'm an outsider here too, so I sympathize with your wanting to help secure your homeland, but I think that's even more of a reason to remain here. Your people are making great strides in preparing for the Carthaginians, but there is still a long way to go before they're ready. Talogren put them in my charge, and so far they've listened to my commands, but I'm concerned when I leave, that will change. We've already had incidents with attacks on trainers and full-on brawls in the camps. When I leave, you will be the only voice of authority from Talogren left for them to look to. If we both go, who has enough authority for your people to listen to?"

"They've elected commanders from among their numbers, like you Romans asked."

"They did that for organizational reasons, and you know as well as I do that they all see those positions as something of a novelty. When push comes to shove, they won't back down on those men's say so. Hell, half of those men will be in the midst of the brawl with them. They're all of them good men, but they are here because they answered their chief's call. Most of them haven't bought into the necessity for this. They will eventually, especially when the Carthaginians get here, but right now we need someone here to keep them focused."

Llassar didn't seem sold on the idea, but he was loyal to Talogren, who'd told him to follow Ky's instructions.

"I will stay, then."

"I'm sorry. If I could have you come with me, I would. We have a fight to the death coming and if we don't do everything just right, we will all die or end up under the Carthaginian heel. Train your men. Keep them focused."

Llassar gave a nod and left the tent without another word. Ky gave a small smile, watching the man go. He wasn't the type to go over conversations over and over again. The man had said his piece, and once a decision was made he was done talking again.

Ky was able to work on detailed instructions for his absence a little longer before the first of the commanders arrived.

The commanders, in this case, included all of the legates, minus the ones killed in battle or executed the day before, along with their tribunes. Llassar had also returned with two of the men assigned to command his warriors, along with Faenius and two of his Praetorian tribunes, Lartius, who was set to command the new separated cavalry units assigned to each legion. Sepurcius was in charge of the slowly forming artillery command.

"First of all, I want to say how proud I am of how you and your men fought during the recent insurrection. I know it was difficult, sending your men in against their countrymen, but you did your duty and we were able to put down the rebellion before it began to take a foothold."

The men looked somber, which didn't surprise Ky. Unlike the later Roman Empire of his time, when civil wars had been common, this version of Rome hadn't had the luxury of infighting as they ran across Europe, away from the Carthaginian hordes. The change from republic to empire had been one of necessity in this timeline, not a power grab by an egomaniac.

All of these men had been lifelong soldiers and had been leading men into combat for most of their lives. This was the first time any of them had been forced to lead those men against other Romans, and Ky could see the haunted look they all maintained since the battle.

"While we did well and most of our forces remain intact, we still suffered losses, both in your formations and in what's left of the First and Second legions. Unfortunately, the reward for a job well done is to be asked to do something even harder. When we last met to discuss what we'd thought were going to be our final structural changes before the spring, the Third legion was our most complete, with seven fully formed cohorts, followed by the Seventh with six and the Ninth and Fifth with five each. To get that, we had limited each contubernium to only four veterans apiece, with the other four men in their group being either paroled Carthaginian soldiers, newly recruited Romans, or ex-slaves. With the losses in the battle and the need to split up the soldiers out of the First and Second legions, those loyal veterans are going to need to be stretched even thinner."

The legates groaned. The Roman legion was one of the best infantry units in the ancient world, but it relied on precise training and tight coordination among its men. Normally, a contubernium, which was the smallest unit the Romans operated in, would consist of at least two-thirds veterans in the worst of times, and the legates worked hard to shuffle the men to maintain that weight of experienced soldiers to inexperienced men. Cutting that down to one-half had been difficult on them, since there just wasn't enough time to get untrained men, especially former slaves, up to the level needed to make a legion combat-ready.

"We are dissolving the First and Second legions entirely, at least for now, and folding their soldiers into the other legions. While this might seem like good news, since there are enough men left to make up a full eight cohorts, we can't allow them to serve together, in case any of the men still harbor seditious thoughts. We will be the Third legion by one cohort, the Seventh two, and the Ninth three, bringing each of them up to eight cohorts. The Fifth will get two cohorts, leaving it the weakest still at seven cohorts. Sorry, Ursinus."

"I have always enjoyed being the underdog, Consul."

"Good. Like I said, you can't just take these men from the First and Second and plug them directly into your legions as complete units, so it's going to take a total shift of your existing units, once again. The new standard composition of a contubernium will have two loyal veterans, two veterans from one of the dissolved units, preferably one that did not serve in the same cohort or even legion, and the rest made up of slaves and paroled Carthaginians. If you are keeping track of our numbers, you will probably have noticed that we will still be falling short on manpower. I'm going to ask the Emperor to increase the allotments of ex-slaves we will be allowing into the ranks and making another pass of the prison camp, but I think both of those wells are running dry. That is why I asked Llassar to join us. Although we spoke earlier, I held back on my request until now, hopefully making it harder on him to say no."

Llassar's head snapped up. He'd been listening, but only partially engaged up to this point, because the formations of the legions had little to do with him, except as it applied to his having access to Roman veterans to train his troops.

"I know the original plan was to have your men fight as their own unit, because the Caledonii way of fighting is very different to the Roman style."

Ky had been making a habit of always referring to the Picts by their previous league naming instead of directly calling them Picts, especially to them, since the name Pict was a Roman invention, and considered somewhat derogatory by the northerners themselves.

"I know there is a lot of pride in the northern way of fighting, and how battles are conducted now, it can be very effective. However, over the next several years, I'm going to be introducing new technologies that will change that. Eventually, units will need to work closer to the Roman system to be effective, although with serious changes. It's hard to explain now and I know it's easy to think that my saying this is just because of some kind of bias against the Caledonii. I want you to understand that is not what is happening here. I respect your traditions and styles of fighting, but the new warfare I am going to be introducing will change everything. The days of hand-to-hand fighting, where the might of a single soldier is paramount, are coming to an end. Oh, there will still be instances of it, but soon you will be killing your enemies at many times the range a bow can reach and you will be able to do it at a rate that will make massed infantry formations a thing of the past. This is just the reality of where our form of battle will be going."

"And to have a place in this, we must fight as the Romans do?" Llassar asked, sounding extremely skeptical.

"Not as the Romans do precisely, but it is a base. For a while most fighting will be done in formations, making massed volleys somewhat like archers do, to really put the weight of the damage you inflict on the enemy. Over time, we will probably progress again into a more loose style of fighting, but it will still require more coordinated maneuvers among units and fewer headlong charges. It would give some of your men a leg up in this new system if you were already training in how to fight in formations instead of more aggressive charges whose goal is to let your warriors get their opponents in single combat."

"So you want to have our men fight as the Romans do? Behind shields, afraid to test their abilities against their opponents and prove that they are warriors?"

Some of the Romans frowned at that, but Ky had started to think that Llassar was cleverer than most of the Romans who dealt with him really thought. He wasn't a fool. He knew that in stand-up battles the Picts had lost every single time and he'd seen some of the changes Ky had already started to make. Ky didn't think he was actually asking the question. He was testing Ky and the Romans, to see if they were serious about treating the Picts as equals or if it was all talk, plus maybe looking for cover against the more traditionalists in their ranks.

"Yes," Ky said, his voice flat and even, before any of the Romans could respond. "I am not saying any have to. If you want to fight as your own unit, as I promised Talogren, then you can, but this is an opportunity for your men. You've heard everything else the rest of the commanders have. You know that the world is changing and you need to change with it. All I'm offering you is an opportunity, if any of your men want to take it. They are already being paid equal to the Romans, so all I'm offering is a chance for your men to test themselves and see if they're ready to move into the future with the rest of us."

The Romans, who'd all looked from Llassar to Ky when he'd started speaking all snapped back around, putting their attention on the Pict again. For his part, Llassar didn't answer right away.

He paused, considering, before saying, "I will talk to my men."

"Good," Ky said, smiling finally. "It needs to be soon. We have this week to recognize all of your legions and shuffle the men around, and then I need you to start training again. There's one last thing that I need to address. While I'm gone, Lucilla will work in my stead, coordinating all of the training as well as the production in town. We have gone over what I need to have accomplished thoroughly and she has both her father's and my utmost confidence. I know there will be those who disagree with this decision, both in this room and in your commands that do not like the idea of a woman being in charge. I honestly don't care. Take any command from her as a command from myself. Is that clear?"

There were a few frowns, but thankfully none among his legates, which were who he needed onboard most, since they had the authority to push through anything she ordered. Ky had gone back and forth on the need for this, but ultimately sided with the fact that, because of the comms unit, he could pass commands through her, which he couldn't do with anyone else. Of course, no one else would know he was doing that, which is why he needed the ruse to make it actually work.

The person who surprised him the most was Llassar, who not only hadn't reacted negatively, but had nodded slightly when Ky had announced her taking his place in command. The Picts were further behind the Romans, as far as how they treated the sexes, and Ky had expected the most pushback from them.

They spent the rest of the day going over details of everything that needed to be accomplished while he was gone. The reorganization was going to put them behind, but there wasn't much help for it.

Chapter 3

Ky had to leave the camp the next morning and return to town for his final meetings with Hortensius and the other business leaders before he left town. If it was up to him, he'd stay in the field with the soldiers where he was comfortable instead of returning to deal with civilians. Even separated by millennia, the basics of a soldier's life had not changed, which made staying with the legions an almost nostalgic experience.

Of course, it might also be that soldiers were used to following orders, which made it an all-around simpler experience getting things accomplished. Even with the authority he had as Consul, he expected most of his last day would be wasted listening to complaints from businessmen who felt they were being asked to do too much or who still didn't like the idea of paying taxes back to the government, regardless of the wealth of new ideas and technology they were given.

Of course, what Ky wanted didn't really matter. The changes needed to get Rome up to industrialization had only barely begun and there was still a long road before they got where they needed to be.

Instead of traveling around town meeting with the different people as he'd been doing, Ky had brought them all to him, although this time it was in the largest room of the Collegium Medici, which was the only other place, save the coliseum, that had enough room to gather everyone together while the palace and forum were still under reconstruction.

The meetings were necessary, but dragged on all day and mostly consisted of Hortensius parading factory, mill, and foundry owners up to talk about where they were on their assigned projects and what they thought their timetable looked like.

The hardest thing giving everyone problems was adjusting to using the new 'uniform measurements' that Ky had introduced. It didn't matter so much for the crossbows and other equipment, most of which needed the new steel which presented enough of a bottleneck that the craftsman's approach didn't slow anything down any more than it already was.

Ky knew this was going to be a problem and had worked it into the schedule he and Sophus had devised. Even with the rapid escalation in technology, some of the leaps needed to go through technological steps to get to the next stage. They couldn't jump from swords and crossbows straight to muzzle-loaded rifles. Canon would come first, since they were easier to cast than rifles, but even that was too big of a direct leap.

Even with the improvements Ky had put in so far, Roman foundries were fairly simplistic and couldn't be used for either the precision casting needed in rifles or the larger scale casting needed for canons. Had he shown up in some later period, he might have been able to draw from the technology used in casting church bells, but Rome wasn't at that level of technology yet.

Once they were past the coming battle and they had enough of the new crossbows, Ky would have to talk a few of the foundries into shutting down and retooling. Of course, metallurgy was just one problem.

Rome had some knowledge of chemistry, but it was fairly basic and tied as much into mysticism as it was to actual science. Most of the people who knew even the basics of chemistry were either philosophers or alchemists. Unlike the working of metal, which was an already established industry, Ky needed to build up a chemical industry out of whole cloth before he could even start the steps of creating gunpowder in quantities to be useful.

Those were all plans for the future, however. Right now he had Roman industry focused on gearing up the legions for the coming fight and didn't want to distract them from that.

For now, Hortensius had everything in hand and Ky was happy to leave it to him. In the long run, Hortensius would probably end up as the single richest man in the Empire. He could see how things were shaping up and he'd started convincing as many rich friends as he could to invest in new factories to supply the government with everything it needed. Even when the war came to an end, he'd figured out there would be a lot of demand for new technologies and he seemed determined to corner the market on being able to supply that demand. In the short term, that means that Rome was still increasing capacity every week. It might not be soon enough to get to the actual supply numbers Rome needed in the next few months when the Carthaginian army showed up, but it would get close.

The meetings ran all day and Ky was wiped out as they left the meeting to return to the remnants of the palace complex. Ky found himself riding next to Carus with a small buffer between them and the other men. Ky had a question that had been floating around the back of his mind and now seemed a good time to address it.

He actually wasn't sure who to talk to about this, since other than Lucilla, who he clearly couldn't talk to about his questions, he wasn't particularly close with anyone. At least, not to talk about personal things. He'd opted on Carus simply because they'd had the most conversations, since Carus was as much spymaster and intelligence expert as he was guard commander. Although they'd never spoken in any way except as commander and subordinate, he was as close to a friend as Ky would find to have this conversation with.

"I have a question," Ky said, still working through how to go about asking what he wanted to know about. "I'm not sure how to ask this, but there are cultural things I do not understand about your people that I'd like some insight into."

"You should talk to Lucilla about it. I'm pretty out of touch with art and the like and she's about as connected with the culture as anyone I've met."

"That's not the kind of culture I meant, and I can't talk to her about this."

Ky had always been impressed with how smart Carus was and the man once again showed how clever he was.

"I see. So you need advice about women."

"Yes, well, not exactly. Where I come from, social interactions are very different than they are here, and I don't want to run afoul of any of taboos and embarrass ... anyone."

The sentence had been going well until the end, when he realized he didn't want to directly reference Lucilla, even if it was plain as day. He had picked up on that social taboo at least and knew Lucilla wouldn't be pleased if she found out he was talking to someone she might consider to be in some lower level of society. To her credit, she'd never actually talked about those less fortunate than her, which was just about everyone considering who her father was, but some of it was so built into their very DNA that she couldn't avoid it.

"I see. And what specific social interaction are you wondering about."

Ky hesitated. Asking for help was different than actually asking the question, but he needed, or at least wanted, to know the answer and he was already somewhat committed.

"How do people here, meaning men and women, get to know each other better. I mean if one of them is interested in the other as something more than a friend or associate?"

"Do they not date where you're from?"

Dating wasn't even really a word that existed in his world, although Ky had come across it many times when looking at some of the records Sophus had collected for him. The problem was, depending on the time period the record covered, the word could have a lot of different meanings, and very few of the records he found related to Rome as it was in his world.

"No. Things are very different where I'm from."

"Clearly," he said, and then paused. "Sorry, this is one of those things that sort of everyone just learns growing up, so it's kind of hard to try and explain it to someone who has no concept of it."

"I understand this kind of subject is not typically talked about between people who are not …" Ky paused, trying to find a way to say the next part of that sentence without offending Carus.

Thankfully, the man was not easily offended and finished the sentence for him, "Social equals. No, not normally but it's fine. We are both soldiers first and this question would be considered very tame indeed in most soldiers' camps I've ever been in."

"Although that isn't true for the barracks I grew up in, your point is well made. I guess my question is, how would a person start to go about dating someone else."

"Well, it depends on who those two people are. For someone like me, if I found a lady I fancied enough, I would corner her in a dark corner of a tavern and whisper poetry to her until she agreed to go on a walk somewhere dark with me, where things might get more, interesting. You, however, are targeting a somewhat higher station of women, I believe, so that probably wouldn't be the same. As far as I understand from what I've seen among the people at your level, you let it be known that you are interested in a match and wait as senators and businessman offer up their prettiest daughters for you to marry. Words are exchanged and vows are made, and you're married."

"Ohh. I wasn't … I didn't mean …"

"You weren't looking to get hitched to some random man's daughter," Carus finished for Ky. "I'm not sure wooing a noble lady and sweeping her off her feet is something that happens outside of poetry."

"So it isn't done."

"As far as I know, not normally. You have to keep in mind, the high and mighty are always looking for ways to better their family, and marriage is usually seen as a part of that. They don't normally leave such a valuable bargaining chip to the whims of who their sons and daughters fancy. Most of the time, the kids don't really get a say. You exist as something of an anomaly, not having a family to better. I'm honestly surprised you haven't had fathers throwing their daughters at you, what with your being the first Consul in a hundred years and all."

"I don't think I've given them enough time to get comfortable with me, what with armies marching on the city, my freeing the slaves, and an insurrection to distract them."

"Give them time. Those who've decided you're not going anywhere will start sending agents with proposals for 'advantageous matches' any day now."

"That's not what I'm looking for."

"Of course not. Some will realize that and keep away, but I'm sure there's an equal amount who won't care and will take their chance anyway, since being the father-in-law of the Consul and architect of this new Empire your building would come with all kinds of benefits."

"So if there is one person I'm interested in, there's no way to do anything about it?"

"Well, I do believe I've witnessed her making moves of her own a few times, so I believe you don't have to worry much about that. I'm not sure you should bother yourself much about what tradition has to say anyway. Everyone knows you're not one of us and you've clearly shown that things operated differently where you came from. I figure just do what you like. They'll get used to it or they won't. That's on them."

"If it were just me, I would, but I don't want to make … this other person feel uncomfortable."

"I see. I think maybe the best thing to do is ask her about it directly. I know that'll be a weird conversation, but I'd bet she won't have a problem with it. This other person probably has a good idea of how different you are and is clever enough to see what you're getting at. This person also has a better idea of how people in her circle will react to whatever you two decide."

"So, I just ask her what I should do? That's what I was hoping to avoid."

"Can't be Consul if you can't make the hard decisions."

Ky thought that sounded a lot like a diplomatic way of saying 'sucks to be you.' Carus's lack of sympathy didn't help, but Ky did at least appreciate someone willing to tell him bluntly what he needed to hear.

Ky's dilemma was partially solved for him when he found Lucilla waiting on one of the stone benches that had survived the fire that had ripped through the courtyard. It was permanently blackened but it still supported her weight.

"I'm surprised to see you here," Ky said as she stood to greet him.

As with the other times, his lictore spread out, giving the pair some room to speak privately while still being guarded, since they remained out in the open.

"You said you were leaving in the morning and I wanted to see you one last time before you head north."

"This feels very familiar," Ky said.

"Not really. Last time I was the one going north and you had to come save me."

"Who knows, maybe this time you'll have to come save me instead."

"That seems unlikely," she said with a smile. "What time do you leave?"

"Early. It's a several-day ride and the sooner we get there the sooner we can start making moves. Talogren's already been waiting for us to return and I'm sure his people are impatient to find out what happened to all the men they sent south. I want to get the Fourth legion marching south as soon as the agreements are signed since they'll need to take part in the reorganizations as well."

"How many Praetorians are you taking to fill the gaps along the border? I know in theory the Picts will have agreed to abide by our laws on Roman lands and help guard the border, but it will take time to convince all of the ones not directly under Talogren's control of that."

"Which is why I'm going north. We need it pacified and preferably before the spring campaigning season. I'm not taking as many Praetorians as we'll ultimately need, since I don't want to deplete Faenius of his core leaders. I'll be taking a hundred with me and the rest will have to be made up by Pict soldiers. Ultimately, I'd like the border patrolled by mixed units containing people from both regions, but that might have to wait."

"I see," she said, running down.

"I'm guessing you didn't really want to hear about my plans once I get up into the north," Ky said.

"No. I mean, I do want to know what you're doing, but that's not why I'm here. I just wanted to spend some time with you before you left."

"Good," Ky said, and he meant it. "I'm glad you're here because I had some things I wanted to talk to you about."

"Like what?" she said, sounding suddenly interested.

Ky had to admit when it came to some subjects he was definitely a coward and decided to put that topic until he'd exhausted all other subjects.

"I have some things I need you to do while I'm gone."

"Ohh," she said, clearly disappointed.

"I've already informed the commanders, but while I'm gone, I am naming you to command in my stead, both in the Senate and the legions."

"Why?"

"Several reasons. The biggest one being you and I can communicate in real-time, giving you access to the same set of information that I have available. The other major reason is, of all of the people I could assign, you'd have the easiest time getting all of the parties to listen to you."

"I think you may have misjudged how my people feel about women in power."

"Maybe, but I think you're an exception. One, you are the Emperor's daughter. That alone gives you some level of authority, since you have your father's ear and counsel. Two, you traveled and spent time with the Picts, so you are at least not a foreign presence to them, and while they don't generally let women fight alongside their warriors, they have a much more accepting view of a female's place in society than your own people. And lastly, there seems to be a general belief that you and I share a connection that would give you my confidence and my ear as well."

"Is it just a belief?" she asked coyly.

"No, it isn't just a belief. I have something I want to discuss on that as well, but let me finish with this first."

"Alright," she said, sounding intrigued and impatient.

"I've told the legates, Llassar, your father, Ramirus, and Hortensius too that I had left you detailed instructions and we have had long conversations on how to deal with most situations."

"Except we will just be able to discuss anything, like you said."

"Correct."

"And they accepted this explanation?"

"I didn't give them a choice. I told them this was how it was going to be and they could accept it or be relieved."

"And if they still don't want to listen."

"You are one of the strongest people I know. You will have to assert the authority that your father and I are giving you and make them listen to you. I believe in you and think you are as capable as any man in a position of power I've seen since coming to Britannia. You have to make them see what I see."

"When you say it like that, it leaves little choice but to succeed, since I wouldn't want to let you down," she said, and then paused. "And what about the other thing you wanted to discuss."

Ky hesitated. She looked so hopeful and he wasn't sure if he was going to deliver on that hope or crush it. He knew she liked him and even that she wanted to take things farther, he was just afraid that he would misstep and ruin the image she had built of him in her head.

"I told you the other night that the way people, meaning men and women, of this time related to each other is foreign to me. I have trouble understanding both that and what I am feeling, and it is taking me time to come to grips with how to express those feelings."

"Yes, and I thought we agreed that I was in charge when it came to this end of things."

"We did. My concern is … I am not sure how to move forward on the impulses I am feeling without tripping over some kind of cultural taboos that I might not know exist."

"Give me an example of what kinds of impulses you are feeling and what taboos you are afraid you might step over."

"Sometimes when we are alone, or at least only surrounded only our guards, you will kiss me. It's pleasant. I enjoy it and look forward to doing it again, but I never see other Romans touching or kissing each other on the street or in places where I have found myself. My instincts tell me that there is some kind of cultural taboo that says doing these things publicly is frowned upon, but then I overhear soldiers talking about their exploits and they seem to go several degrees further than the things I think might be taboo. I don't understand where the line is enough to know if the things I want to do will step over it or not."

"Ohh. I see."

"I also know that, the times you've come to my quarters and it's just the two of us, I see looks on my guard's faces. They've never said anything and I'm sure they didn't even mean to give the looks. These men have never shown anything but discretion and respect towards me, which means whatever is bothering them about you being alone with me like that is very deeply ingrained, so much so they can't stop themselves from looking uncomfortable, which means I have broken yet another taboo of some kind."

"Well, I guess I'm the one that's broken them, since it isn't normal for a man and a woman who are unmarried to be alone in one of their bedrooms together. You know what, though? I don't really care what society thinks about what I choose to do or how I do it."

"You're not that naive," Ky said. "I've watched you dance through political discussions with grace and cunning, so I know you understand how important everything is when you're in the public eye like we are. Hell, this whole insurrection was a big sign of how badly things can go if we mishandle things."

"I get what you're saying, although I don't think you could have stopped the insurrection from happening even if you had done everything differently. My brother had already poisoned my father and, according to Ramirus, been in talks with the Carthaginians, before you even showed up. The moment my father didn't die and we didn't fall to the Carthaginian army, an insurrection was all but guaranteed."

"I know, but I wanted to use it as an example of how we have to be careful about what boundaries we push, since there are a lot more changes coming before Rome will finally be safe."

"I see. So you want to know how we should act in public and how we should act in private?"

"Yes."

She didn't answer right away. Instead, she looked off, thinking hard. She was a dichotomy really. He'd been honest when he'd complimented her on her ability to weave through social and political situations, but she was also headstrong to the point of foolishness and often didn't think about the ramifications of a decision even when they were pointed out to her. Ky trusted her and needed her as a guide to this new type of relationship he was experiencing, but he needed the smart and crafty Lucilla, not the charge headlong into danger Lucilla.

"I think it would be fine if we are seen holding hands in public, and perhaps a kiss on my cheek if you're feeling very rambunctious. In private, I perhaps shouldn't come to your quarters alone anymore. I think when meeting out in the open, like this, where there is no one around but we aren't being indiscrete, it would be alright to kiss me. Anything else I'm afraid will have to wait until we're married."

"Married!" Ky said, shocked.

"Of course. How did you think this was going to end? You haven't said it, but I can tell you love me. That's the feeling you keep talking about, the one you're so unsure of. For my part, I am in love with you, which means our being married is the only real next step. Ohh, it will take some time. We have so much to do in the next few months, there isn't time for us to plan anything now, but once the immediate danger is done, I think we should be able to wed. Thinking about it, our marriage would be good both personally and politically since, assuming we survive the coming battle of course, it will give the people something new to focus on. The mob loves nothing more than a spectacle, and our wedding is the only thing I can think of that might rival the failed rebellion."

"You've thought this through," Ky said.

"Of course I have. Any woman who meets the man of her dreams thinks through what might happen if they fall in love and he sweeps her off her feet, more so when he's a superhuman savior who falls from the sky to quite literally sweep her off her feet. The political ends I'm just starting to think about, but I think my initial instincts are correct. Actually, if we are going to do this, I need to spend time talking to my father and probably Ramirus about the best way to handle this situation, so we get the most out of it. Politically, I mean. I think you and I won't have much trouble getting what we need out of it, personally."

The sly smile she gave him as she said the last part suggested there was more meaning in her words than the words themselves conveyed, but Ky didn't really know what that meaning was.

"Although we don't have this kind of tradition among my people, I thought for marriages the man was supposed to ask the woman if she wants to marry him. And I've been told that here, at least amongst the higher stations, it's more of a financial transaction between the man's family and the woman's family with all sorts of official oaths and things."

"You've been talking to people about me?" She asked, a mischievously twinkly in her eye.

"I ... might have asked Carus about how to court you."

"The big, strong warrior didn't want to ask me directly?" she said in a coy tone of voice.

Ky gave her a mock-annoyed look.

"Sorry," she said with a laugh. "I didn't mean to imply that you were afraid and I am flattered that you have been trying to work this out on your own. Don't worry about propriety. While there will be official pronouncements and wedding gifts, that is all pomp to feed the masses. I know how you feel about me and you know how I feel about you, or at least you're starting to figure that part out. We might have to play our roles in public, but none of that matters when we're alone."

"I guess I should just listen to your experience and wisdom."

"I knew you were clever. It's getting late and you have a long trip ahead of you. We can talk more when you're traveling and have fewer things to actively worry about," she said, pushing up close to him and standing on her tip-toes to kiss him gently on the lips.

It was a much more chaste kiss than the one she'd given him in his quarters, perhaps because she was now thinking of how things looked to those around them. In its own way, though, the kiss was still unique. Instead of passion, it held a promise for something bigger in their future. Ky wasn't sure how that would play out, since marriage was an abstract thought to him, something he'd read about in Sophus's historical records but never seen in practice.

He looked forward to finding out what that promise would become.

A Villa North of Devnum

The door opened quickly, startling the six men gathered around the front entryway of the villa. The hands of some of the men dropped to the swords they carried at their sides before relaxing and releasing them as they recognized the new arrival.

"You're all very jumpy," The new arrival said.

"Of course we're jumpy. Ramirus arrested thirty people yesterday. Half of the true Romans I've been in contact with have gone silent, disappeared off the street. Thank Jupiter we only knew of each other from passed messages and not in person, or I'm sure one of Ramirus's men would have come to my door already."

"How many of us are left," One of the other men said.

"I know of a dozen, maybe and I've heard those men speak of others who support the cause. There are hundreds of us still in the city."

"I doubt that," the leader said. "It would be nice if we had that many supporters in the city, but we don't. Even before Ramirus began his crackdown I doubt there were more than fifty of us. The initial sweep took too many of us. Thinking there are hundreds of people who support the cause is setting ourselves up for failure. Silo thought the city would rise up and support us when the time came, and it didn't. We can't make the same mistake."

"What do we do then?" One of the other men said.

"We have to be smart about it. We need to cut down on their power and weaken this new alliance of theirs. I don't know if we will succeed, but it's all we can do without drawing too much attention to ourselves."

"If we play it safe, how will we ever be successful? We can't overthrow the Emperor with just small acts of defiance. Only something major will wake up the people and get them behind us," the new arrival asked.

"If they didn't join us when we had two entire legions behind our cause there is no chance of their joining us now. We have a few men still in contact with Caesius, who thankfully escaped the city before Silo's fate could befall him as well. He's out there gathering support and strength. All we have to do is keep the Emperor's forces weak until he returns. He knows about the good work we're doing and he has assured us we will all be rewarded when the time comes."

"So how do we strike at them then?" a man asked.

"We're working on that. Right now, I need all of you to try and get in contact with as many men who support us as you can. Work anonymously and try to keep from knowing the names and faces of the men you work with. I know we'd all like to think we could withhold what we know if we're captured, but every man breaks eventually under the interrogator's implements. The only real security is not knowing the information they want."

"So this is our group then? Are any of you in contact with anyone other groups?"

"No," the leader answered. "We've made sure to only pass notes and not meet or know our contacts."

"That will make finding more men who support us harder."

"I know it will, but we don't have many other options remaining to us. We have men well placed in several of the Emperor's projects and we are looking for opportunities to strike," he said, looking across the faces of the men around him.

Some looked tired, others angry, but at the core, all of the men looked determined to do what they must to bring back the glory of a Rome that wasn't befouled and weakened by foreign influences.

"Don't worry brothers; soon you'll all have the opportunity to do your part."

Chapter 4

Ky had hoped to slip out of town with his normal guards and a hundred Praetorians who would be taking the place of the legion currently manning the border. It was a large crowd, but he'd assembled them outside of the Praetorian camp, a little away from the city, to keep the fanfare to a minimum.

Despite that, three times the number of men he was taking with him were gathered around their assembly area, watching the men load up and occasionally talking to a friend here or there, which is probably how word of their departure slipped out. The crowd was a mishmash of people including legionaries on passes, Picts, farmers from the nearby fields who didn't have much to do now that the ground had turned too hard to till, and tradesmen and new members of the working class come out from the city to see the men off. Closest to Ky were several of the legates and city leaders, as well as the Emperor and Lucilla accompanied by their guards, who'd come out to wish the men well on their travels north.

"I believe they want you to say a few words before you leave," the Emperor said, nodding to the assembled crowd.

"Are you sure they didn't come out just to see friends and loved ones off?"

"Some of them," Lucilla said. "Look around, though. Most of these people are just here to see what's happening. You're headed north to sign the alliance that will form the new Empire. They might not all understand why we have to do this, but no one in Rome can ignore what a momentous trip this will be. Soon, men from the north will be traveling openly through Roman lands, looking for work, sightseeing, and trading. It's a big day for all of us."

"Very well," Ky said, and mounted his horse, putting him above the assembled crowd. The men around him, most of who hadn't mounted up yet, backed up to give him space.

"Thank you all for coming," Ky said, projecting his voice in a way most natural-born humans could not, thanks to the augmentations that had happened across his entire musculature. "I know some of you are here to see your friends and loved ones who will be stationed along the northern border, some of whom you might not see for some time. The Emperor and I both want you to know that we recognize the sacrifice you and your families are making to support and protect the Empire. I promise you that everything possible has been done to ensure your loved ones are prepared for the duty ahead of them."

He paused and looked out at the crowd, some of whom were still hugging their husband or brother or father who was heading north as part of the Praetorian detachment. A larger percentage of the crowd, however, was unmoved by the previous words, since they had no real connection to the men going north, beyond recognizing that these soldiers were going to protect them.

"For the rest of us, this is still a momentous day. We ride north to sign the treaty with our new allies and establish the Britannic Empire, through which we will reclaim what has been lost and push the Carthaginian hordes off these islands and away from Rome forever, ensuring the safety of every Britannic citizen, be they Roman or Caledonii. This new Empire will also bring new opportunities for prosperity to both of our peoples. New challenges await those who are able and willing to accept them, and a new world is ahead for all of us. Today is a new day. A happy day. A day neither for Romans nor for Caledonians. It's a day for Britains!"

Most of the people cheered as Ky finished his brief speech. He hadn't actually meant to name the people of the new Empire after the name of the Empire that would have one day sprung up in this same place, if history had been allowed to play out as it should have. He'd picked the name Britannic Empire for the new Empire simply because, by this time, most of the people on the island seemed to recognize the Roman name for it and its inhabitants.

Even in the real history, there had been such a layering of cultures over the centuries as Saxons, Celts, Romans, Scandinavians, and finally, Normans that they'd eventually just accepted the Latin name for the island. That process had accelerated in this timeline with the Romans controlling two-thirds of the lands for more than a century. The natives wouldn't see themselves as Romans, since that was a foreign place, but Britain, even though it was a Latin word, was meant to identify the people of the islands and so considered acceptable.

It struck Ky as funny that, on a whim, he might have ended up giving the people who'd populate this island the same name as it would have in his history.

The end of the speech turned out to have a dual purpose. Although they had a long way to go that day, Ky hadn't pushed them too hard to leave because he didn't want to pull the men whose families and friends had shown away too early. Had this been back when he first arrived, he probably would have already gotten the men on the road, but his recent experiences made him reconsider what being separated from their loved ones would do to the men.

Everyone took the end of the speech as some kind of unspoken signal that it was time to go, with the civilians who were intermingled with the soldiers starting to break out and move out to the sides of the parade ground where they'd assembled. Ky gave a signal to the centurion that had been put in overall command of this detachment who quickly got the men in order.

"Wait," Lucilla said as Ky started to turn his horse and lead the men out.

He rotated the animal around so she could step up next to him. All of the saddles used by Romans had been modified with stirrups by this point, but Ky had been presented with one of the first saddles made with stirrups built into it two days before when he'd spent the evening with the legion. Now Lucilla motioned for him to move his foot out of the stirrup, which he did.

Once it was clear, she put her foot in it and, gripping the saddle, she pulled herself up so she was standing balanced on one leg, which was braced in the stirrup. Ky had to shift his weight to keep the saddle from sliding, but she was so light that the horse seemed to barely notice. Standing as she was, she ended up being actually a good half head span above Ky, looking down at him. Considering the conversation the night before about the proper way to show affection Ky was surprised when she broke her own advice and bent down, kissing him hard in front of all of the assembled men and their families.

She took Ky's breath away to the point where he almost didn't notice the cheers going up from around his men as she wrapped her arms around him and really leaned into the kiss. Finally, she broke off and leaned back, holding onto Ky's shoulder as she gave an exaggerated bow to the assembled troops before hopping out of the stirrup and stepping back. Ky had to hand it to her, she did have a flair for the dramatic and the men certainly seemed to appreciate her performance. It was all Ky could do to keep himself from blushing as he straightened himself up and signaled the men to get moving.

Legion Training Grounds

"No, goddammit. This is your left foot. Figure it out or I'm going to jam my left foot so far up your ass you'll never forget which is which," the optio yelled at one of the new soldiers.

Velius had just ridden back from seeing off the Consul and the rest of the men headed north. While it would be good to have the Fourth legion back with them to help fill the gaps made during the insurrection, he wished Ky had remained behind. Although the legate was officially in overall command of all of the legions while the Consul was here, Velius could take the really challenging problems to him. Without him, they all ended up in front of the legate.

It wasn't that Velius was scared. He'd been a soldier since he was barely out of puberty, had fought in numerous border clashes, and made legate when he was only twenty-five. That, in and of itself, might have been part of the problem. Rome might have been under threat from both the Picts to the north and the Carthaginians to the south, but the assault on Devnum a few months ago was the first major clash Rome had been involved in since they'd been pushed out of Londinium twenty-four years ago, well before Velius's time with the legions.

That meant there weren't many opportunities for promotions to high rank on merit alone. Velius, like all of the other currently serving legates except for Ursinus, had gotten his position thanks to political connections. In his case, it had been after five years of service as one of the Emperor's guards, which had earned him the Emperor's favor when the previous legate in charge of the seventh legion had died. Even as legates were replaced, he'd never held top command, since men like the late Eborius and Globulus had always had the seniority. It wasn't until the coming of the Sword and the battle of Devnum that his fortunes had really changed.

Unfortunately, after that surprising victory, they'd gone back to the same life the legions had beforehand, with field training and garrison duty. Armies were tools of destruction and when on campaign, they were focused, the men all understanding the danger they were in and the importance of being part of a well-functioning unit. A sedentary legion, however, was an unruly beast. Hardly a day had gone by that he hadn't been forced to hand out disciplinary punishment for offenses ranging from the minor, like petty thefts and fighting, to the severe, such as the murder of a new recruit by one of their seasoned men the day before over a perceived slight the veteran had felt.

"You are the most worthless recruits I have ever had the misfortune to train. Do any of you even understand why it's important to keep in lockstep with the men on either side of you?" the optio yelled, knocking a man who'd continued to fall out of ranks to the ground.

There was silence among two dozen men gathered in front of them. Although they'd decided to mix the new recruits with the veterans, training sessions like this were for those men first inducted into the legions, before they were assigned to their contubernium, which was the smallest unit in the legion. This training involved how to march in column for travel, and move in combat formation, how to properly hold and use the tall scutum shield and the short gladius. Later they'd learn more advanced weapons like the pilum spear or the new arcuballista, but those were for later. The Roman legion was primarily a walled infantry unit and the scutum and gladius were the tools of their trade and had to be mastered before any legionnaire was ready to be deployed.

Unfortunately, the new batches of recruits made this seem much harder than it should have been. It wasn't the sons of farmers and merchants, like when Velius signed up so long ago. The ex-slaves he could understand. These people had never been allowed to even touch a sword under penalty of death or even learn simple things like which side was left or right. The Picts that they'd started getting the previous day, or Caledonii, which he'd been told specifically to call them by the Consul, were able to pick things up pretty well. They might have problems working as a coordinated group, but they at least knew their way around a sword.

The worst ones were the ex-Carthaginian soldiers. For a people who'd managed to conquer most of the known world, Velius would have thought the Carthaginian soldiers would have been more formidable than they were. Instead, they were essentially one step above the ex-slaves, and that was being charitable. They might know how to hold and use a sword, but all basic education was withheld from them and they had no ability to think for themselves. The Carthaginians made sure to beat any independent thought out of them early on, since their way of fighting battles was to just throw walls of men at the enemy until they overwhelmed them with bodies.

It was hard to train men who'd been trained to never think for themselves.

"Why even do this. Let me at the death eaters and I will tear them apart," one of the new Caledonii recruits said in broken Latin.

"Because it will get you and every one of the men with you killed," Velius said, causing the optio and several of the men to look up towards him. "I'm sure you're a seasoned warrior and you have many battles under your belt. How many battles have you been in?"

"Twelve," the man called out.

"In these battles, did you usually outnumber the other side, did they outnumber you, or was it about equal numbers?"

"Usually equal, except against you Romans. We always outnumbered you."

"Did you win against us?"

The man was quiet for a few minutes before saying, "Sometimes."

"The times that you won, how many more men did you have than we did?"

"Many times."

"Did we retreat, or did you slaughter the men you fought."

"You ran away like dogs."

"How many men did you lose in those engagements compared to our forces?"

The man didn't answer.

"I'm going to assume by your silence that the difference was significant. Fighting man to man might show your prowess as a great warrior, which I am not doubting, but it will not lead to victories. When the Carthaginians come, there might be as many as five times our number facing against us. Each one of you will have to kill five or six of their men before you fall, and even then it might not be enough. Fighting one on five, you could never accomplish that, or at least not enough of you could. The good news is, you won't have to do that. We fight the way we do because it works. We protect the man on the side of us and they protect us. We are a juggernaut that can roll over any obstacles that we come across. I'm thinking you don't believe me though, do you."

There was silence again.

"Optio, go grab another trainer and bring him back here, along with a space scutum and training gladius," Velius said, sliding off his horse and hooking his sword belt onto the saddle. "What is your name?"

"Guto," the man said.

"Guto, find another man you think can fight and come up front."

The Caledonii soldier seemed unsure, but grabbed another man who, from his hairstyle was also from the north. Both men were holding their wooden training gladius. They stood around looking nervous while Velius waited, arms held clasped together behind him and feet planted. The optio returned at a jog with another man who wore a wicked scar across one cheek as a symbol of his experience.

"Guto, if you and your friend can get through the three of us, I will give both of you three days unfettered leave. If you fail, once you finish today's training, you will report to me and serve the evening free period as my runner instead. Deal?"

"Easy," Guto said, with a wicked smile.

"Cantered wall, two three-step," Velius said to the two veterans.

Normally, a legion wall was flat all the way across with one-century welding up against the next one and even one cohort against the next if their battle line was long enough. There was, however, always a flank that hung out in empty air. If the Roman forces were larger than their enemy, they'd just extend the wall out far enough to cover the enemy's entire front line and then use cavalry to keep the other side from thinning out enough that they could edge around the wall. That practice had had to change as the Romans became a smaller and smaller force in the region, however.

They'd altered their formations so that the ends of the formations cut at a slight angle, sloping away from the enemy. The Carthaginians fought in tight phalanxes and used long spears that didn't allow the close-packed men to turn or pivot very well, which meant as the Roman line bent away from them, their line couldn't follow its curve without opening up gaps.

They'd also created calls to keep the men attacking in lockstep, changing the step-step-stab pattern depending on the type of ground they were fighting on or how tired the men were. Normally these formation and cadence decisions were called by message trumpeters, and bannermen, but the veterans understood his command and moved instantly, flanking Velius on either side and forming their shields up tight against his.

Guto did the predictable thing for a Pict, charging straight in, his friend at his heels. The current roman scutum stood at just over one meter tall and when held center mass would stretch from the center of Velius's head to just below the knee. He and the two veterans were in an advancing formation, meaning they were holding it up and had their bodies turned sideways to fit inside the curvature of the shield.

"Step," Velius called out.

The three men stepped forward towards the Picts.

As soon as Guto's feet left the ground, Velius called out, "Up."

As one, the men lifted their shields up, bracing them against their shoulders as they did. From this position the shield reached up towards the top of their helmets, meaning they lost sight of Guto, but it didn't matter. Both of the Picts were already in motion and weren't going to be able to change their trajectories before they impacted the Romans.

"Brace," Velius called.

The three men leaned back and crouched slightly so they could place their knee against the bottom of the shield, right in the center of its curve. Held like this, a legionnaire had two points of contact with the shield, one at the shoulder and one at the knee, with their back foot pressed firmly into the dirt behind them. Alone, it would be hard to push over a legionnaire coming straight on, but when the shield was slightly overlapping with the one next to him and being overlapped by the one on the other side, it became even more stable.

The two Picts slammed into the short wall, their wooden training swords trying to stab over the shields. Because of the angle and the force with which they bounced off the immovable shields, they managed to do little more than scrape across the metal framing that ran around the edges of the shields.

"Step," Velius called as soon as the men had hit.

The Romans pressed out hard with their shields as they took a step in unison, their footwork matching precisely. Guto and his friend were still off-balance after crashing into the shields while the Romans had solid footing, rear foot still bracing them as they pressed hard with their shields in a quick motion, their shoulders still leaning into their scutum. The Picts stumbled back to keep from getting run over by the Roman wall, making it difficult for them to cover themselves properly or block an incoming attack, which is exactly what Velius wanted to happen.

"Strike," Velius said.

A small gap appeared in between each shield as the three veterans showed the true value of the gladius. Picts and the Germanic tribes preferred larger slashing weapons, often deriding the short roman blade, which didn't have the length to get enough leverage for a slashing motion or the range that a larger sword would have. What the Roman sword did have was a rigid, short blade that was able to become an extension of the soldier's arm. They were able to stab out quickly and apply a freighting amount of power to them, all while keeping their shields in position to offer very little for their opponents to fight against.

Guto saw this up close as three wooden swords shot out between the shields, quick as a viper strike. Neither man was able to get their weapons up in a position to block, since they were still stumbling back from the shields and grunted as the wooden weapons smashed into them.

"Step," Velius called out, and the three stepped forward, pushing with their shields again.

Guto stumbled backward, crashing to the ground.

"Hold," Velius called, standing up straight and resting the butt of his shield on the ground. Looking at the assembled trainees, he said, "That is why we learn to march. We move as a single unit, putting our collective weight into each movement. If done correctly, we can become an unstoppable force. Listen to your trainers and learn it well, because each of the men next to you will rely just as much on you as you will on them. One misstep can mean losing the protection the wall gives you. Carry on, Optio."

Velius handed the training equipment back to the other veteran as the optio got the men back in ranks. Climbing back on his horse, he pulled the reins, leading the animal on to the next batch of recruits.

Devnum

"That was foolish," the Emperor said as his daughter walked into his meeting chambers.

"What was?" She asked, not sure what she'd done this time to draw her father's ire.

"That display you made with Ky. I understand you have feelings towards the man and I approve of the match, both personally as your father and politically as your Emperor. Despite that, we still have appearances we must maintain. We control the mob only as long as we can make them believe they have no other option but to be controlled. If we lose that control, we're like a rider on a spooked horse, clinging for our lives lest we be thrown and trampled. You saw yourself how badly things can go if enough people lose faith in us."

"What does my kissing Ky have to do with losing control over the people?"

"There are standards to maintain. You're my right hand and, now that your brother's treachery has been revealed, my only heir. Do you want people thinking you're some kind of common harlot? What kind of judgment does that show the people? A woman will have enough trouble convincing people to follow her, you don't need to add to those difficulties by making the people assume you have loose morals too."

"I'm not one to normally disagree with you, Princeps," Ramirus, who was the only other one in the room, said. "But I don't think you're right, at least as far as how the people are reacting to the display. I have men continuously cycling through the marketplaces, inns, and bathhouses, keeping an ear open for what the people are saying. Mostly, it's to try and catch any whiff of insurrection or disloyal gatherings, but I require them to give full reports every day of anything they hear and my scribes compile those for me, finding any kind of pattern or trend in those reports. One thing that has been building for a while, but gained momentum after the ... display this morning, is talk about your daughter and our new Consul."

"What are they saying?"

"They seem to overwhelmingly approve of the match. Word of his charging into the Palace single-handedly to rescue his love has begun to make the rounds, growing in its heroics with each retelling. The moment today looks to have cemented their love story with the people. I've heard them likened to Paris and Helen."

"Ridiculous," Lucilla said. "He didn't come into the palace single-handedly and he came to save more than just me."

"The soldiers and people huddling with you tell a different story. They say he swept you up and embraced you as soon as he got into the forum."

"That's fine when it's Ky swooping in to rescue my daughter. It's different when it's the woman launches herself at the man."

"I'm sorry, but I must again disagree. Your daughter has always held the publics' favor because of her ... headstrong ways. It's why they're drawn to the two as a pair. For them, it makes sense that only a great warrior sent by the gods could be the one to tame your daughters' wild instincts. The display today just reinforced that story."

"I just wish someone *would* tame her wild instincts," the Emperor groused.

"I'm standing right here," Lucilla complained.

"Fine, I wish you would tame your wild instincts, or at least think through the ramifications of your actions before you do them. If Ramirus says this little display will play out in our favor, then I believe him. But don't tell me for a moment that you considered the possible effects and came to this conclusion before you jumped up on his horse."

Of course, her father was right ... not that Lucilla would ever admit to that. She understood that her position was inseparable from the politics of the Empire, but she wasn't ready to let those considerations rule her life. She was going to do what she needed to do and would let the chips fall where they may.

"I wasn't the only one on that horse." Lucilla said, her defense sounding hollow even to her.

"Everyone saw Ky's face. That boy was as surprised as anyone there, more so probably. He might have more knowledge than the entire Empire, or even all of Britannica combined, but I've seen him with you and around other women who throw themselves at him, thinking they could somehow snare him. He's completely clueless when it comes to women."

"Fine, I'll try to be more discerning, but like Ramirus said, the people like my headstrong nature. If I change too much I'll become one of those pathetic women who exist only in their husbands' shadows. You wouldn't want that for me, would you father?"

She gave him the look she'd been perfecting since she was a small child and wanted to get out of whatever trouble she'd landed herself in by flattery and feigned submission. He fell for it when she was six, but had grown wise to it by now.

He just snorted and waved his daughter off to do whatever she needed to do today so he could focus on the business of ruling his soon to be much larger Empire.

He looked up and watched her leave, a small smile on his face. That girl may be the death of him yet, but she always kept his life interesting!

Chapter 5

"... and he tripped over a loose cobblestone, landing face-first in a pile of horse shit," the guard said, finishing a story about a thief who had tried, and failed, to get away from the city guard.

Those on the tables around them shook their head as the men's laugher once against drowned out nearby conversation. This happened most nights and the regulars, at least, had grown used to the city guardsman gathering to drink after their shift ended. Geganies drank his wine and gave an apologetic look to one of the other patrons who shot them a dirty look.

"Well boys, it's been fun, but I have to get home," he said, pushing his empty cup to the center of the table and standing wobbly.

"Your wife's going to have your ass for coming home drunk again," his friend said.

"That's why I get drunk. It makes it easier to ignore the screeching."

They all laughed as he staggered through the inn and out into the evening. It had been dusk when they'd finished their last patrol and gone into the inn for a quick drink. It was now inky black outside, the streets full of shadows. In summer, people tended to leave their shutters open to get in a breeze, letting the light of their homes and apartments spill out and light up the city.

In winter though, everything was shut tight to keep in the heat, which meant it was always fairly dark. That was one of the main reasons he was glad he was on the daytime shifts. He'd worked nights when he'd first joined the guard, and it had been terrible. Always cold, you couldn't see the criminal you were chasing, and long stretches of boredom.

Geganies hugged close the side of the street, occasionally reaching a hand out to steady himself on the wall of a building. He was drunk, although if someone called him out on it he'd have pointed out that the cobblestone streets this close to the palace had iced up as the sun had gone down, and it was easy to lose balance.

Of course, that argument would have held less weight seconds later when he stopped at the edge of a building and bent over, retching up the stale bread and wine he'd been consuming for the past several hours.

Stretching up, Geganies was just starting to think he felt better getting that out of his system and maybe he was ready to face off against his wife when the sound of a hard footfall caught his attention. He must be drunker than he'd said he was, he thought as he turned, realizing that it was the sound of someone running past him. They had gotten very close without him noticing, which would have looked very bad if any of his compatriots in the guard found out about it.

By the time he drunkenly turned all the way around, the man, or men as it turned out, were on top of him and the first blade had slid into his stomach. Geganies's mind reeled as he tried to understand why this was happening. He fell to his knees as another blade plunged into his back, and another into his side.

"Thus always to tyrants," one of the assailants hissed in his ear as a blade slid into his shoulder blade.

Geganies slid to the ground, the world fading out, as he tried to figure out what he'd done to deserve this.

Lucilla sat up straight in bed, that moment just after sleep where the body is fully awake, alerted by some sound or warning, but the mind hasn't caught up yet. Her heart was pounding and it took another moment for her to get her bearings and realize that the thing that had woken her up was a heavy pounding on her chamber door.

No light came through the edges of her window and, besides the pounding on her door, the palace grounds outside her window were silent, which meant it must still be very early in the morning.

"Yes," she called out, collecting herself.

"Your father has asked for you. He says it's urgent," her guard commander said through the door.

"A moment please," she said, sliding out of bed and hurrying to pull on clothing.

Although she'd always been allowed to participate in some aspects of ruling the Empire, yesterday was the first time she'd been allowed unrestricted access to the machinery of government, sitting in with her father through a long series of updates and meetings. Despite his concerns for her judgment where public displays of affection were concerned, he'd agreed with Ky's decision to name Lucilla as his advocate while he was away and was actively making an effort to teach her how to govern properly.

At the time, she'd thought it sounded splendid. She'd always resented the way the men in her father's orbit treated her as an annoyance, something they had to deal with to stay near the reins of power, but not someone they should ever have to take seriously. Of course, that had been during reasonable hours. If leadership included regular summons in the middle of the night, then it might not be as great as she'd thought it would be.

As soon as she was dressed, she left her room for the small audience chamber at the front of the suite she shared with her father, who was already seated inside, a cup of warm wine at his elbow. Ramirus and a guard captain were also there, looking anxious.

"You didn't have to wait for me," Lucilla said, bending down to kiss her father on the cheek before taking a seat next to him.

"They would have just had to repeat their explanations a second time, and this gives them a moment to collect their thoughts before they announce whatever pending doom is about to befall us. That is another lesson for you, my daughter. Decisions made in haste are never the best decisions. Stop and think about what you are going to say and do - even if the situation is urgent - and you will make far fewer mistakes."

"I see."

"Report," the Emperor said, turning his attention back to Ramirus.

"There's been a murder," he said, not dramatically, but clearly indicating that the situation was more than just a simple murder.

"Who?"

"A city guardsman by the name of Geganies. He was one of the men selected to act as executioner for Silo and his supporters."

"Retaliation?" the Emperor asked.

"Almost certainly. He wasn't just killed. He was mutilated and his corpse hung outside the coliseum. A note was stabbed into his chest that simply said 'traitor.'"

"We kept their identities hidden to prevent this exact thing," Lucilla said.

"You are correct, my lady, we did. They must have some source of information inside the guard, still. Maybe the man talked, or someone else that had been present talked."

"The other three executioners?"

"All accounted for. Since we believe there is a leak in the guard, Faenius loaned us some of his Praetorians to stand watch over the men and their families while we sort this out."

"Who are they?" Lucilla asked.

"My lady?"

"You said 'they' must have a source inside the guard still. Who are they?"

"Men who still support your brother and the insurrectionists. We got all of the leaders, we're sure of that, but there's no way to be certain how many of their followers are left in the city."

"Is this the beginning of something coordinated, or is this just the violent reaction of a few angry people?"

"We don't know yet. My first inclination would be to say it's just a few people acting out, but that assumption leaves us unprepared if I am wrong. I'd rather assume your son still has cells of men in the city. Even the worst-case scenario wouldn't give him enough for another uprising, but it could very well be enough for targeted strikes designed to weaken us before the battle."

"I assume you have men out looking for these people?" Lucilla asked.

"I do, but unless they're talking outside of their small circles, we won't get much headway until they do something and one of them gets caught. Once we have one, we should be able to unravel their group, although if they're unorganized, they may be working separately from each other, and might not know of the existence of other pockets of insurrectionists. There's really no way of telling how many are out there or if we've gotten them all until they do something."

"What about the areas they might strike?" The Emperor asked. "Can we protect the industries critical to military production?"

"No. I can talk to Hortensius, and we can protect some of the larger foundries and factories; but Rome just doesn't have as large an industrial base as Ky has Hortensius setting up, so he's been working with a lot of smaller contractors to produce the things we need. They're scattered throughout the city and a lot are outside the city gates. It would take half of the Praetorians in training just to put a minimal guard on all of these places, and by minimal I mean one or two men apiece. And that doesn't count the new mills being built, the mining operations up north, or any of the new factories currently under construction. No, there's just no way to protect everything."

"So we can expect more losses?"

"Yes, Princeps. I know that isn't what you want to hear, but it is the truth. We'll do our best to ferret out these people, but this kind of civil unrest is just impossible to stamp out completely."

"Put guards on the most vulnerable areas and we'll have to hope that's enough. I'm assuming word has started spreading about the killing?"

"Yes. By the time the city guard was alerted to the body hanging outside the coliseum, dozens of people had seen it. By the time they took him down and moved the body somewhere more discrete, well over a hundred spectators had shown up. There's no way to keep this kind of thing under wraps."

"What are people saying?"

"Mostly they're worried that we didn't get all of the conspirators and there will be another violent coup attempt. So far it hasn't had any practical impact, but the first couple of days after the insurrection, workers were hesitant to go back out, fearing they might get caught in more fighting. Hortensius complained it slowed down production and warned that if there was more of that, they might not be able to make up the difference."

"I see. If we can't get guards everywhere we need them to keep these attacks from happening, we can at least use them to soften the public fear. Make sure most of the guards you do place are conspicuous. Make sure people can see that we're actively doing something to protect them."

"That's fine for public relations, but it will make them less valuable for actually protecting these locations."

"I know, but it might not matter. These people, whoever they are, will know we've put out guards and will probably realize how thin we're stretched. Still, only do it for the less critical locations. Make sure Hortensius's main foundry is completely covered. The last report I saw said we were behind on the metal pieces more than the crossbow frames, and we're still behind on getting swords and armor for the new recruits. We can't lose any time from the foundry going down. Use your best judgment on the rest."

"Yes, Emperor."

"Good. Now, what's the next problem?"

Instead of heading back to bed, Lucilla decided to get her day started. She knew her guards wouldn't love that, since the night shift guards were still on and they'd have to rotate in the field, which meant waking their replacements up early, but she decided they'd just have to deal with that.

Ky might have only appointed her to serve as his voice while he was gone because she could speak to him over the earpiece he'd given her, but she wasn't ready to be anyone's mouthpiece, even his. If she was going to take this responsibility, then she was determined to take it seriously.

She'd spent a good part of the day before getting up to speed on how far along everything from the industrial projects to the training of soldiers was. Since she couldn't read at the speed Ky seemed able to, she couldn't just comb through reports and instead had to rely on some of Ramirus's people to brief her as best they could. Today, she wanted to see as much as she could in person and was starting her tour with the Pict training grounds, since everything she'd seen said this was the weakest point in their military buildup. These were the men who'd decided not to officially join the legions and would only serve until after the springtime battle, after which they and their camp followers planned to return home.

She understood that desire and not wanting to submit to the Roman way of doing things, but this also meant that they weren't training to the level the Roman soldiers were and there was some concern they might not be a viable fighting force when the time came. Watching their progress so far, she was equally concerned.

What legion training she'd witnessed had been an orderly affair with different stages of training based on the collected men's experiences and a progressive training schedule starting with the basics such as marching and building on that to training as entire centuries.

The Pict training, on the other hand, looked more like disorganized wrestling matches than actual training. Most of the Picts in the area she was touring had formed a circle around several pairs of men each trying to pin the other to the ground. It looked brutal and as she watched, one of the men snapped his opponent's arm, leaving it pointing at an unnatural angle. She was floored. Even if the wound were to heal properly, that man would now not be able to fight in the coming battle. It seemed an amazing waste, considering how outnumbered the alliances' forces were already. They needed every man they could get, and having one injured so purposefully in training was just taking one more warrior out of their lines. The worst part was, she couldn't see any point to it. No one would learn anything or become better prepared to defeat the enemy from this chaotic wrestling match.

She must have let some of what she was thinking pass across her face, because one of the Picts who'd been watching yelled, "Disturbed, little princess?"

She'd gotten a few snide comments since they returned to Roman lands, although not as many as she'd feared, probably because the Picts that had accompanied them were from villages other than the one she'd been held at. Most of the time, the comments were about her having been their prisoner, and they seemed to collectively consider allowing herself to be captured as some kind of personal failing she should be ashamed about.

"I am only disturbed by how easily you Caledonii seem to be beaten," she replied, showing no emotion but hitting him where she knew he'd feel it, metaphorically, of course.

The Picts respected strength and bravery above all other things. Apologizing or meekness wouldn't gain their respect or defuse the situation. If anything, her experience with them so far had told her that it would increase the problem. She sized up the man who'd yelled at her. He was big and beefy, which described almost all of the men that had been sent south to help their new ally, but he was younger than most of the others. A new warrior trying to prove his mettle.

"I have something you can beat," he said, grabbing himself in a vulgar method just in case the subtlety of his comment had somehow passed her by.

"I'm sure you manage that quite well all by yourself. Besides, you don't want your friends and comrades to see me standing over you lying unconscious on the ground with my boot on your throat."

"My lady," one of her guards warned as the men around the taunting Pict bristled.

"I know," she said, but didn't back down.

She'd watched the Picts with Ky. They deferred to him, listening to his advice and counsel, even though he'd slaughtered dozens of their countrymen. Partly, it was because Talogren showed him respect, but partly it was also because he'd won their respect. Talogren, actually, was another example of that, since he too had won their respect through strength of arms.

Ever since the attack in the forest clearing, where she'd been unable to defend herself properly, she'd trained every day to better be able to defend herself. She'd made her guards spar with her and brought in trainers to teach her how to survive one-on-one combat. She knew she wasn't up to the level of most of the men she might have to face one day, especially considering the weight and strength disparity, but she was closing the gap. She was, of course, not stupid. She knew when the odds were against her and when it was better to back down instead of trying to take the problem head-on, which is what her guardsman was trying to warn her about.

This wasn't one of those circumstances, though. Barring serious injury, this was the only way to get the Picts, and probably many of the Roman soldiers, to start taking her seriously as anything other than some noblewoman.

Since she knew she was going to be moving among the people, she'd dressed in the knee-length tunic popular among upper-class women instead of the more ceremonial toga, which was good, because it allowed her enough movement to fight without the danger of suddenly becoming immodest, which would probably work counter to what she hoped to achieve.

She did have to make a slight alteration though. Reaching down to the bottom hem of the tunic, she pulled hard, ripping it, and tearing it up to her mid-thigh. She tested the change and found she could move better, since the tunic, as it was, held a little too tight around the knees, which was the fashion at the moment. She hoped the rest of the woven fabric would hold together, at least long enough for her to get back into town and change.

She'd been watching the Picts wrestle both here and when they'd stopped at nights on the way down from the north and had worked out enough of the rules to know that she'd have to stay inside the circle in the dirt. The first man, or woman in her case, to be thrown out, surrender, or be knocked unconscious would give up a point to the other fighter, with the winner being the first one to three points.

Stepping into the ring, she stood there with her hands on her hips while the mouthy Pict from earlier just stared at her.

"Are you planning on fighting me, or just stand there like a little girl?"

That had the desired effect, his face turning bright red as his friends laughed at him. She'd been training hard, but even a young Pict warrior was more experienced than her and in better physical condition than she was, so getting him off balance was one of the ways she could even things out.

He didn't wait or try for any subtlety, roaring and charging straight in, arms outstretched. This was one of the things she'd actively trained for the most, aside from basic sword work.

She stepped into him and turned so that her back was towards him. As he started to wrap his arms around her, she grabbed his right arm and pulled, while bending at the waist to put her shoulder into it. With his charge, he still had a fair amount of momentum as he crashed into her, and she was able to use that to send him flying over her shoulder and out of the ring. Her guard commander had called it the 'flying mare' and it was apparently a go-to technique among Greeks who wrestled, especially among the smaller wrestlers, which is why he'd picked that move to teach her. She hadn't gotten nearly the distance or power with her guards when she'd practiced the move, but thought perhaps this time was different because he'd been actively trying to harm her and they were always more careful with their 'attacks.'

The Pict hit the ground hard, but to his credit, he immediately spun and popped back up. She was also impressed that he moved in much more cautiously when he re-entered the ring, which meant he learned from his mistakes. He feigned to her right, and Lucilla made a mistake, taking the bait and stating the sweep of her foot the Greeks liked to call 'fancy foot.' It was considered a cheap move by most of the wrestlers, but her guard captain had said it was pretty reliable for the smaller wrestlers, since it didn't rely on strength, and once her opponent was on the ground she'd have a chance to do a hold that didn't rely on strength, but instead on pressing against the joints.

Unfortunately, the sweep had her body turned at the wrong angle and the Pict was able to reach out and grab her around the middle, lifting her easily off the ground and sending her sailing out over the edge of the ring. She managed to twist her body around so that she didn't land flat on her back, although it still hurt like hell when her knees and right arm smashed into the hard-packed earth.

As soon as she hit, though, she pushed herself off the ground and charged back in, determined to not let that stop her. He hadn't been expecting the charge and took an instinctive step back to give him a moment to think about what was happening, which Lucilla had hoped for and taken advantage of. She hoped that, despite seeing her attempt the move just a few seconds before, he wouldn't know what she was trying to do. All of the wrestling she'd watched the Picts do were simple holds and throws, relying on brute strength more than anything. She hadn't seen any of the more finessed Greek-style moves her guard captain had been teaching her, which explained why he'd put him in a perfect position to be thrown earlier.

He was just starting to move forward again when she hooked her foot around his ankle and pulled just as he was starting to take a step, making him susceptible to being tripped. As soon as he went over, she was on top of him like a squirrel climbing a tree, dodging his hands as she tried to get a grip on his arm and get it into a hold. She almost had it, but his greater strength proved the day and he tossed her aside hard, rolling her halfway out of the ring in the process and scoring his second point.

She was getting angry herself as her side scraped across the ground and the skin on her knee and chin tore open. She pushed herself back up and wiped the blood dripping down her face away, reading herself for another go.

"Ready to give up, little bird?" he asked, surprisingly not sounding insulting as he had before.

"I'm happy to take your surrender, if you want," she said, smiling deviously at him.

The crowd watching them roared in laughter. Her opponent smiled and shook his head before taking his stance. She'd used most of the moves she'd learned from her guard and she knew she didn't have the strength to pin him, leaving her few options. She waited for him to come for her, patiently. For thirty seconds, they stared at each other, both making counter moves as the other circled to stay across their opponent and not allow an attack to come in from the side.

She almost thought he had the patience to wait her out, which would have surprised her. She'd observed that the Picts, at least generally speaking, liked a straight-up fight and didn't have the patience to wait out an opponent. Finally, he made his move. He went to her left again and she thought for a second that he might have been going for a feint, holding until he fully committed. As soon as he did, extending his lunge to grab her, she made a small step to the side and kicked out with all of her might.

The fighter was good, she'd give him that, but he was used to fighting men, who had an almost instinctual taboo from striking sensitive areas below the belt, which in turn made all of her opponent's stances wide and unguarded. It had the benefit of giving him leverage if he got ahold of someone, which he'd shown by tossing her so easily out of the ring earlier.

This time, there was no powering through. He froze and then dropped to his knees, his hands going to cover the area, the move purely instinctual, since it was too late to do anything about the actual injury. She stepped forward and swung with all her might, smashing her fist into his temple. She didn't have the strength to permanently hurt him, but combined with the other pain the man was feeling, he toppled over. It wasn't a victory, since she neither pinned him nor got him out of the ring, but it was enough for the crowd to go wild.

She ignored the crowd for the moment and limped to her opponent, since her knee was starting to hurt badly. He wasn't unconscious and started to shake away the pain as she reached down and grabbed his hand to pull him up.

"That was fun," she said, smiling.

"Fun for whom, little bird?" he asked, smiling equally.

She raised their hands over her head and the crowd crushed in on them, cheering and slapping both of them on the back. Her guard commander, who she assumed was freaking out outside the scrum of cheering Picts, was panicking, pushed his way in and managed to get her out of the crowd without her being trampled.

"That was foolish," he admonished, escorting her towards their horses where he could administer first aid.

"It was necessary," she said.

She appreciated how her guards looked after her, more so after two previous guard commanders died protecting her, once from the Carthaginians and once from the Picts. She was, however, not prepared to bend to them the way a child bends to a parent.

"She's right," Llassar said, seeming to appear out of nowhere.

Her startled guard commander dropped his hand to his gladius, only removing it when Lucilla hit his hand with the back of hers. Although Llassar's eyes followed her hand, he didn't comment on what other Picts might have taken offense to.

"Did you know we have legends about warrior queens of old, who fought dragons left from when the earth was young?"

"I didn't," she said.

She had mixed feelings about Llassar, who'd been involved in her capture and imprisonment. He hadn't personally mistreated her, but his men had been far from gentle with her. Now, here he was, seemingly offering her words of encouragement after she put down one of his men.

He didn't say anything else, just continued past them, like the statement had been an afterthought. Lucilla watched him walk away, slightly confused by the entire interaction, before her guard commander nudged her to continue on to the horses and medical attention.

Chapter 6

The Northern Road

They were a day out of town and making good progress, especially for this number of men on foot. He was far behind the progress he'd made on his last trip north, but that had been done in a panic and ended with several mounts being ridden to death.

Although most of the time riding at the head of the column of men had been spent going over the never ending flow of documents Sophus supplies him with covering history, inventions and tactics, he also spent time thinking about Lucilla and their last moment together before they'd left Devnum.

He'd decided that he wasn't going to have his men set up a large command tent like they did when he traveled with the legions. That might have been standard among the Romans and seen as strange for their leader to somehow debase himself by sleeping as the common men. Among the Caledonii, the reverse was true.

Part of the goal of having all of these men travel south with him and bringing a portion of them back north was so they could spread the word about Rome, its people, and hopefully dispel some of the preconceived notions their countrymen might have. Ramirus, who was better at this kind of thing than Ky was, had said the hardest thing to getting disparate people to come together was getting them to see each other as actual people and not some kind of other that they could graft all of their fears onto. He'd also said that the best way to get around this was by getting the people to intermix as much as possible, since familiarity was the only true way to bridge that gap. It was hard to see someone as a faceless other once they'd met them face to face.

So instead of a large tent with a bed and carpets and braziers for fires to keep him warm at night, Ky was sleeping on the ground mixed in with the other leaders the Caledonii had selected for themselves. That, in and of itself, wouldn't bother Ky. The nanobots in his system were capable of regulating his temperature to some degree and he'd slept in equally uncomfortable places over the years, so he wasn't worried about his own comfort. The main problem was the Caledonii liked to drink and be social, staying late into the night singing songs and telling stories of their bravest deeds, which made it difficult for Ky to contact Lucilla for updates, and to just hear her voice, before it got too late.

Tonight, he made the excuse of making the rounds of the men, during which he could spend some time circling the camps and not interacting directly, allowing him to focus on a conversation with her. He knew as time wore on, especially once they were with larger groups of the north men, he'd have to come up with better excuses to carve out time for these calls. Of course, he had to wait until it was late enough that she would be free to talk since, unlike him, she needed to speak out loud to communicate.

He pinged her communicator. A few seconds later she connected, giving him an oddly pleased sensation at how quickly she'd responded.

"Hi," she said, her voice sounding almost wistful.

"Hi. Is everything going okay?"

"We've had some issues. It appears we missed some of my brothers supporters. One of the executioners was found murdered, his body hung up in front of the Colosseum in a not too subtle message."

"Should I come back?"

"No. Ramirus has it in hand and you are needed in the North more. We need this alliance finalized and we need it now, if we're to start merging our resources and having access to the additional labor and materials for the war effort. We've increased guards on the most sensitive operations to deter sabotage and Ramirus has people out gathering information, but he thinks it is unlikely we'll find them until they make more moves."

"You're keeping your guards with you at all times, correct?"

"Yes. Don't worry, I'll be fine."

"The last time you said that, you were kidnapped."

"And look how well that turned out for us," she said, her voice unhappy.

Ky made a mental note to control how often he mentioned those events. He thought it was important for her to remember what happened when she let her guard down, but he was probably doing it too much and she was clearly displeased with it.

"Sorry," he apologized.

"Good. Beyond that, I've met with the Legion commanders and they are, as a whole, on board with your directives. The Picts are still being an issue and have made it clear they are not pleased with taking orders from a woman."

"Llassar said something?"

"No. He's been supportive and has kept them in line so far, but there's only so much he can do on his own. I did make a breakthrough today though, I think."

"Really?"

"Yeah, I fought one of them to I guess a draw, and it seemed to have a positive effect on the rest."

"What do you mean 'you fought one of them?'"

"Just that. They were having these wrestling matches and when one of them made a comment at me, I challenged him."

"Are you okay?"

"Scraped up, but I made my point and he was left on the floor. You know I've been training with my guardsman. I wasn't completely unprepared."

"True, and I don't doubt the training has helped, but these people learn to fight from the time they're small infants. You've been training for a few months. It seems a risky balance."

"They continued to underestimate me, being a Roman woman and all. It allowed me to get some throws over him early on and catch him unprepared enough to put him down, although I think I broke the rules to do it."

"I guess congratulations, then."

"There was something odd, though. On my first throw, I managed to get him out of the ring a lot further than I would have though I'd been able to. He wasn't as tall or as muscular as some of his fellows, but he was still a large man, and the last punch I gave him shouldn't have stunned him like it did. All of the training has been building my strength, but not to this level."

"I don't know," Ky said, not sure how to respond.

"I can explain that," Sophus said, breaking in.

"You can?" Lucilla asked.

"It has been made clear to me that your continued survival is critical to Ky's success due to your probably pair bonding, so I took steps to increase the likelihood of your survival."

"What do you mean 'steps?'" Ky asked.

"During your mating ritual, I passed a grouping of nanobots from your system into Lucilla's system with specified tasks to increase muscle function, immune system, nervous system and to correct a possible genetic defect detected in the pancreas."

"You gave me some of his powers?" Lucillia asked, sounding both surprised and excited.

"No. Most of Ky's physical enhancements are either genetic manipulation done shortly after conception or post-pubescent surgical augmentation, neither of which you have access to. I reprogrammed your communicator to allow for a pulse burst signal similar to the method I use to control the nanobots Ky has. It doesn't allow the same two way transfer and I do not have the ability to receive updates, so all commands are one directional. When you are in Ky's presence, I can use some of his systems to follow their path, but not when you are not, they are uncontrolled, operating under stored parameters. There is a limit to the number of units I can control in this method, which is why the capabilities are less. Beyond the increased functions listed previously, there will be some accelerated healing, although not to the level that it would be easily noticeable, as well as balanced hormone production and nutritional processing."

"I'm not sure I understand what all that meant," Lucillia said.

"Most of what I can do was because of things physically altered when I was young. They cut me open and added in things that allowed me to do some of the things I can do," Ky translated. "What it did for you is make your body more efficient, allowing your muscles to both operate and grow at peak levels, as well as make you extremely healthy. It won't allow you to do things that seem supernatural, but it will allow you to maintain the same physical condition as someone who spent most of their time improving their strength and health, but without the actual work."

"Ooh. Well that's something. Thank you Sophus."

"You're welcome. I have come to enjoy having someone else to talk to besides the Commander, and I find your presence pleasing."

"High praise," Ky said sarcastically. "I thought the nano bots had a limited life span without the self replications they get from my enhancements?"

"They do. I have increased their lifespan from the days normally available in med-unit nanopacks through additional firmware alterations, but they still will only have a lifespan of months at best. However, the likelihood of additional opportunities to transfer newly created nanobots from your system to hers is very high and I am in the process of altering some of your production capabilities to produce a new design that will better operate independently. They will be less efficient that the ones you have, but more efficient than your current stock of nanobots when they are uncontrolled. When the pilot designated internal medical system was originally designed, it was found that the self-replication rate was higher than needed for one subject. Instead of altering the PDIMS to lower that rate, they programmed in a regulator to increase the time span in between replications. I have run numerous simulations to determine long range effects of permanently removing that regulator to increase the rate of self-replication in order to make up from the group of nanobots that will no longer work for you. All simulations indicate no adverse effects."

"So I will continue to produce a set nanobots you're designing for her?"

"Correct. They will store until a transfer window is available, at which point they will move into her system and start their programmed routines. This has not been done before, so this is a testing phase at the moment. When you are together more often, I will continue to update their programming and track it's detectable physiological responses to make these altered nanobots more effective, although they will never reach the efficiency of yours."

"I still am not sure I understand most of what you've said," Lucilla said. "Are you sure this won't make Ky weaker in any way?"

"I am as certain as I can be, and I will continue to monitor him closely, looking for any lowering of his capabilities."

"It means a lot, you doing this for me Sophus. I wish I could do something for you in exchange."

"You have done something for me. I have a name, the first one any of my type has ever received."

"I'm glad you two are becoming friends," Ky said. "But in the future, I'd appreciate it if you told me about experiments you are running, especially ones that require me to be part of the testing platform."

"I will keep that in mind," Sophus said.

Ky couldn't help but notice that Sophus hadn't said yes. Considering how exact the AI always was with its words, that was almost certainly by design.

"Okay, it's getting late and we still have a bunch to discuss," Ky said, and started down the list he'd prepared in his head before they'd got side-tracked discovering Sophus's little experiment.

Londinium

"What," Maharbaal yelled at the banging on his door.

It seemed unimaginable that someone would be at his door at this time in the morning. He had made it clear, partially through the brutal mutilation of messengers and guards who failed to understand the message, that he was only to be woken in the most extreme of emergencies.

Maharbaal climbed out of bed, over the sleeping form of the women he'd chosen for the previous evening, pulling on a long tunic as he stormed towards the door, finally flinging it open. The guards standing to either side of the outer doorway were making it obvious that they were not a part of this decision. As he stared down at the terrified young man whose eyes were locked at the floor, he considered whether he should start punishing some of his guards that allow interruptions to his sleep. He'd have to give it some thought.

"I'm sorry for disturbing you, my lord, but you have a petitioner who has demanded to see you now. He would not wait until the morning."

"That is why you woke me?" Maharbaal bellowed, before looking at one of his guards. "Take him below and teach him the error of his ways."

As the guard reached out to grab the man, he said, "My lord, he's from Rome and said his name is Caesius. I have heard his name mentioned before. He said that he has news of what is happening there that you must hear right away."

Maharbaal held up his hand, holding the guards.

"Caesius is here?"

"Yes, my lord. He is road worn and dirty and says he rode here straight from their capital."

"Tell him I will be with him shortly."

"Should I have someone bring him food or clean clothing," the man said, trying to anticipate his commander's wishes.

"Did I tell you to do offer him anything? He can stand before my throne and wait for me to arrive, and be happy that is all that happens to him."

The man bowed and quickly backed away, turning and running as soon as he was far enough away, probably happy to have just escaped with his life. Maharbaal didn't pay him any more attention, his mind focused on what Caesius being here meant. The Romans had been increasingly effective at rooting out their spies and the messages from Caesius and his supporters had slowed over the last few weeks. What messages he had gotten had not boded well for the hopes of defeating Rome without having to commit large forces.

He'd already had to send to Carthage for more soldiers, and it had been made clear to him that another such request would come with commands for his dismissal, which was usually fatal. He was confident that the army he'd been assembling was large enough to crush any opposition, but word of this new Consul had shaken him. It had seemed impossible that Rome would have been able to defeat the previous army he sent before winter, but they had and everything his agents had found suggested this man was responsible for it.

He'd put pressure on Caesius to do something about him, and the man had also seemed confident he could stop this foreigner, but the Roman always seemed confident despite showing his incompetence numerous times.

Maharbaal sent one of his guards to fetch his valet while he paced, trying to work out what the Roman's sudden appearance meant. The small man who was his current valet, a position with a fairly short lifespan, showed up finally and helped Maharbaal get dressed in all his regal splendor. Even in emergencies, he had to maintain the air of authority and fear he maintained over the men in his charge. Governors who let that fear lapse often ended up with uprisings in their areas, which was something that could draw the ire of the Emperor or his vizier.

Finally ready, he swooped out of his quarters and down the private hall to the old Roman forum, which he used as his personal throne room, his guards falling in behind him. Caesius stood in the center of the forum, looking around, probably wondering what it would have been like when the Romans still controlled Londinium.

Most of the Roman writing and statues were gone, slowly being replaced by Carthaginian reliquary. His messenger hadn't been wrong, the Roman looked terrible, and not just from being road worn. His clothing was torn and Maharbaal could see dried blood in several places on his armor and draping, although it was unclear if that was from him or someone else.

"Why are you here? Your father's agents will notice you, if they haven't already, and reports could be on their way already back to his spymaster. I did not put all of the resources and manpower into supporting your bid for power for you to just throw it away."

"It doesn't matter anymore."

"Why?" Maharbaal asked, his eyes narrowing.

"The Senator that I had been cultivating to help me block my father's moves, and those of the Hades be dammed Consul, grew impatient. With the new alliance being all but finalized, he didn't see any choice but to try and depose my father through feat of arms before any of the new warriors could come south."

"What alliance? That was not in any of your last reports."

"It happened too quickly to notify you of it. Your agents managed to have the Picts capture my sister, as you promised, and the Consul traveled north to rescue her. Instead of defeating him and killing both, the Picts agreed to not only ally with my father, but to form a new alliance whose sole purpose was to counter Carthaginian expansion. My father signed the new alliance the day the Consul returned, which must mean it was pre-planned, but they kept it to themselves until it was accomplished."

"The Romans have allied with the north men? Did they send warriors to join the Roman legions?"

"Yes. Almost five thousand returned from the north with the Consul. The alliance isn't finalized, but before I left they'd already begun training to bring the Picts into the legions. This is partly why Silo, the senator I spoke of, decided to act. He had two legions loyal to him and his supporters and thought that, if he moved fast enough, he could get to the center of the city and imprison my father before the remaining legions could respond. He failed. His legions were defeated."

"So you ran?"

"Yes. Ramirus already had agents out looking for me. Silo, one of the Legates who'd been taken alive, and several other senators and leaders who knew I was involved were taken alive. It seemed prudent to think my father knew of my connections and would have me arrested. Had he been the only one making decisions, he might not have done anything more than imprison me in my quarters, but the Consul is ruthless. He would have argued that I needed to be removed, permanently. I felt that I could still contribute to your success and decided to come here, instead."

"You did, did you? Not only did you fail completely to remove your father, you allowed this foreigner to gain a foothold and then rise to the highest rungs of power. Now you're telling me you also allowed him and your father to create an alliance with the north men, all the while waiting and doing nothing, despite having two of your legions loyal to you. When you finally got the courage to do something, it was too late and you squandered all of that and were chased all the way to my throne room. And now you think that that, despite your continued record of complete failure, I somehow need your help? Why shouldn't I have you dragged out of here in chains?"

"I am the son and true heir to the empire of Rome!" he said.

He tried to sound angry and haughty, but it was impossible to miss the quiver of fear in his voice.

"You are a failure and in control of nothing."

"I still know their plans and capabilities, and I still have supporters in the city. I can coordinate with them. Using them I can help destabilize Devnum, weakening their ability to fight against you."

Maharbaal's first impulse was to have him just dragged to the dungeons, where he could rot out of sight. It seemed unlikely this fool could offer him any information his spies wouldn't be able to get on their own. News of this new alliance worried him, however. He couldn't imagine how it had happened without any word of it escaping until just now. While he was confident that his new, larger army could defeat the Romans once and for all, he wasn't as confident as he had been before hearing the news. If this fool did have sources in Devnum still, it might not do to rush into making an example of him just yet.

He could always do that the next time he failed, which seemed to be an all but certain eventuality.

"You can remain here, under guard, for the time being. Get word to your agents. I expect to see results and I need to see them soon, if you want to prove you still have enough worth to be kept alive."

Chapter 7

Outside Devnum

A hundred horses thundered across the field overlooked from a slight rise, which was currently topped by a handful of officers on horseback. At a trumpet call the horses wheeled collectively as a group, forming almost a U as it turned back on itself, going back the way it came.

That move finished, the column of horses again reversed directions, making a deep arch that became a half-circle as it partially surrounded a series of hay-bales laid out in the open field, before ultimately turning south, pulling to a stop in a long line across the base of the hills.

"You're right. The turning rate is impressive," Velius said to the cavalry commander on the horse next to him.

This was the first time since the reorganization that he'd seen the cavalry in the field. Previously, each legion had its own cavalry units attached to them, mostly from scouting and flanking the wings of the legions in combat, since each legion more or less operated independently of each other.

The new layered command structure Ky had put in place changed these dynamics, and allowed for increasingly specialized yet independent commands, like the new artillery and cavalry cohorts which attached directly to the combined forces as a whole, instead of to the individual legions. Just the need to discuss these new arrangements had led to new words entering the Roman lexicon, such as Army and Corps, which was an odd variation of the Latin word for the body.

Lartius, who had previously been his legion's cavalry commander and was now the overall commander of the First Britannic army's cavalry cohorts, had been training his men separately, miles off in some more forgiving open plains to the east. Although Velius had been receiving reports of how the training was progressing and had several conversations with Lartius about the changes to Roman cavalry, he hadn't actually seen them in action before now.

He was impressed by how different the cavalry looked now versus how it looked before Ky had arrived and started introducing so many changes. Before, the cavalry could only make shallow turns and encircling an enemy required long, shallow arcs. Even the Parthians, whose speed and skill on the horse were outstanding, had limits to how sharply they could turn, and they trained on horseback from the day they could walk. The display he was watching now, though, was something completely different.

It seemed as if the line of horses could almost double back on itself, which would have been impossible before Ky's introduction of the stirrup. When he'd first seen it, it seemed impossible that the little strip of leather and metal could have been as big an advantage as Ky made it sound like. Even using it every day on his own horse, Velius hadn't internalized exactly how much it changed Roman cavalry tactics.

Previously, the cavalry used mostly short stabbing spears, thrown javelins, slings, and the spatha, which was essentially a much longer version of the gladius with sharper sides, allowing the rider to slash down at men on foot as they rode by. This was good enough to harry the other side's mounted troops and limit their scouting, since they generally suffered from the same instability as the Roman riders. As soon as they clashed, men started falling from horses, since it wasn't that difficult to dismount a man who stayed on top of a horse mostly by pressing his knees tightly into the horse's side.

They'd already started working out new tactics for how to use the new cavalry, which was the point of today's demonstrations. Lartius had not only been training with his men. He'd also had his men testing out the various suggestions Ky had made about new ways they could fight now that they had enough stability.

"It is. We should be able to run circles around the Carthaginian cavalry. This advantage won't last long. Unlike some of the other things the Consul has introduced, where they'd have to get someone inside our manufacturing process to learn how to do it, any horseman worth his salt can take one look at these and understand their value. And it's not like it's difficult to copy."

"We'll just have to ask the Consul to come up with something new once they do. So, other than fancy maneuvers, what thoughts have you had about how to put them to use?"

"The first idea is to just copy the Parthians. We were never able to train men to be maneuverable enough to pull off the encirclements they did with their horse archers, let alone train those same men to be proficient enough with a bow from horseback to make it happen."

"I assume you're talking about the arcuballista?"

"Yes, well, partially. We're still working out the specifics on how to use this. On the surface, it seems like a good idea, especially seeing how that Parthians always gave us so many problems, but it isn't playing out exactly like that in practice."

"Why not?" Velius asked, although he had already guessed a few of the larger differences.

He wanted to hear it from Lartius first, before he started adding in his own thoughts on the subjects. First, because Lartius was an expert on the subject while Velius had come up through the legions fighting on foot, and he wanted to see the point of view of the cavalryman on the subject. And second, because even if he knew the answer, he wanted his subordinates to get used to thinking like officers and not just soldiers. A bad legate was one who kept his thought processes to himself, confident that he was always right and never sounding off against the subordinates he picked as his advisors. Legates had staffs for a reason, and they needed to use them. His job as a legate was to train the men that would come after him just as much as it was winning battles.

"Well, there are limitations. True horse archers like those from the east train with shooting and riding from a young age, which is why they're able to do it so well. Proficiency with a bow is just as much of a challenge, if not more so, as the horse riding. We train our archers to fire in volley because it's easier and takes less time to do, but it only works when fired en masse. Mounted archery doesn't have that advantage, because most of the line isn't facing the enemy at the same time. Even using the Parthian circle, there are still limitations on this."

"They made up for this with better accuracy?"

"That's what I understand. I mean, we haven't faced them in several hundred years, so this is all based on stories and reports from before the war. But yes. Even accounting for the exaggeration that always seems to happen, they aimed for specific targets."

"So the arcuballista allows that?"

"No, which is why we aren't looking to recreate the Parthian technique. The arcuballista used on horseback is easier and can be taught with little training, but only when firing at very large targets, like a phalanx. A few men will have some level of natural ability and veterans will build up better accuracy over time, but as a tactic, we have to use it more generally. Against another cavalry, an arcuballista would be all but worthless, but against a large unit, we can start looking at this tactic."

"I've watched some of the training that's been happening with the arcuballista, and the tighter draw the Consul designed makes reloading a lot more of a process. It's doable on the ground when you have leverage, but isn't it a problem on horseback?"

"Yes. The Consul asked for us to send messengers with updates and questions, and that was one of the things I asked about. With his help, we designed a slightly altered version to be used on horseback," he said, reaching around his saddle and pulling out what at first looked like a slimmed-down version of the arcuballista.

Taking it, Velius turned it around in his hands. It was lighter than the new arcuballista that was being produced. The heavy wood frame and steel made the weapon heavy but allowed it to be better braced for accuracy, since the force of the spring slapping forward could cause the weapon to pull, throwing the shooter's aim off.

By contrast, the frame of this weapon was made of some type of lighter wood. The steel riser and extensions were lighter and more inset, so the string barely crossed the top of the wood frame.

"The design we came up with has you turn it upside down and hook the end brace here," he said, pointing at an unusual addition to the front edge of his saddle.

Velius had noticed how unusual his saddle was, but hadn't said anything yet, since he was sure it was going to come up as part of the presentation. The normal saddle had a lifted area at each of its four corners, with the front extensions winging out slightly. These rises were to help the rider stay in the saddle as they turned, especially the front pair, which the rider could almost wedge his thighs under when gripping with his knees to get a better hold on the horse.

All four risers were cone-shaped, although there was a slight lifting at the back of the saddle that looked to slightly cradle the rider's hindquarters. In place of those four rises was one in the center that extended forward just a bit.

Lartius took the weapon, turned it upside down, and hooked the altered foot brace at the end of the weapon over the raised end of the saddle. The lip kept the weapon from sliding off the end of the saddle. Gripping the string, he leaned back, pulling hard until Velius could hear it latch firmly in place.

"Clever, although doing that by hand instead of using the lever like the one the Consul introduced, does it have the same level of pull?"

"No, it's notably less, but still more than the versions we previously used before the Consul's arrival. It doesn't have the penetration that the other models have or the range, which isn't a problem since we're normally much closer than a legion would be when deploying their archers and other ranged soldiers. As for the penetration, some of that is offset just by being closer and also by the angle we'd be firing down at the men on the ground, allowing us to get over their shields. The biggest drawback is the reloading, since the rider has to disengage to be able to reload, instead of just drawing another arrow like the Parthians did."

"So you aren't thinking you'd encircle a target, firing down on them?"

"Not primarily. We can probably do one pass with the arcuballista before switching to another weapon. It allows some versatility, but I don't see it as our primary way of fighting."

"Alright, then what is?"

"Well, that's the question we are still working on. Our other two options are continuing to use the spatha as the primary method of attack. Braced with the stirrups, the rider can both parry and block incoming attacks with less fear of being dismounted and, use the new leverage the stirrups give to do more than just slash once at an opponent as you ride by. It still puts the horses in danger if you get too close into a formation and the phalanxes' spears are a problem, although with the maneuverability we now have, flanking their formations is much more viable."

"What's the other option?"

"This," he said, pulling out what looked like a fairly long spear, although the shaft was significantly thicker and heavier.

When he handed the weapon over, Velius was surprised at the weight of it. Roman cavalry normally carried a long spear that they could use against men on the ground, but that was more of a jabbing motion, helped along by the weight and speed of the horse. If you contacted a target, the rider often lost the spear since the impact would rip it from his hands.

With this, Velius couldn't imagine using it to thrust or do anything else. It was heavy enough that he would have a hard time even keeping from dropping it.

"It's very heavy."

"Yes. I know you're thinking 'how could anyone use this?' I know because I thought that same thing when the Consul first handed me the prototype. You aren't meant to hold it; at least not like you would a spear. You crook it under your arm, and the metal butt at the end sits here, against the saddle."

Lartius turned his horse so that Velius could see the other side of the saddle, where he noticed something that wasn't on the left side that had been facing him. Jutting out slightly from the raised back of the saddle was an extension with a circular outcropping with a thick padding of leather inside of it. As he watched, Lartius placed the butt of the long, heavy spear into it and crooked it under his arm, bracing it against his side, with his hand gripping it tightly.

"The Consul calls this weapon a lance. I can lower this down to hit a target with the end or straight ahead at a horse or its rider. The brace here allows me to put the full weight of the animal behind it. We've tested it on layers of thick metal and wood and you would not believe the force we have with it. The lifted rear here and the lance being braced against the saddle helps keep the force of the impact from throwing me off the animal, although sometimes I find it useful to also hold on to this part in the middle that I used to reload the arcuballista. The Consul also had a name for this, calling it a pommel."

"So you charge at a target and run through him and then ... what, keep going?"

"Yes. He laid out the tactics for us and in our tests, and it seemed to work quite well. Instead of a line, we spread out in a V-shaped pattern, with the end almost working as a point as we crash into the enemy. Between the lances and the weight of the beasts, we should be able to push through a line of men. It doesn't work if they are several units deep like how we deploy our cohorts, since eventually we'd run out of momentum and get caught up in the mess of men. We could hack our way out with the spatha, but that would be a messy affair. Against thinner lines, we should go right through, after which we'd have to circle and reform. It should break most enemy lines."

"What about the phalanxes? Their sarissas are a lot longer than these lances of yours."

"Yes. A unit with braced spears or sarissas would pose a problem for us, and we wouldn't ever try to charge one of those head-on, at least not without losing a large number of horsemen. We still need to game it out, but I think if we hit them in marching columns or wait for an opportunity to flank them, we should be able to deal a serious blow. We also believe we could be devastating against their cavalry, which doesn't have the advantage of a braced spear like we will. Their spears are both shorter than our new lances and don't have the impact, and they normally go for the sword when it comes to mounted only operations."

"Good," Velius said, already thinking through some of the implications these new tactics would give them. "Have your men begin the next round of demonstrations whenever you're ready. I'm eager to see these new lances in practice."

Devnum Forum

Norbanus finished his tour of the reconstruction efforts on the forums. Although it had barely even begun, he was pleased to see how diligent the engineers had been. With so much to rebuild after the insurrection, the forums seemed a minor thing to focus on, especially since the senate had found alternate accommodations to continue their work.

Despite that, the Emperor had ordered his men to begin working on rebuilding the palace complex, including the forums, right away. The reasoning he gave made sense. It was important for Rome to get back to normal and show that it wouldn't allow malcontents and dissidents to win. Rome would rebuild, and come out stronger. He'd had the præcones, callers and shouters that gave the news in major areas, delivering the message for several days, proclaiming the rebuilding of the forum.

Norbanus would be happy when it happened. The low, enclosed room the senate currently met in just didn't have the gravitas that it should. He felt more like a merchant squabbling over a trade deal than one of the select citizens helping decide the fate of Rome.

After one last look at the initial stages of scaffolding going up around the building, Norbanus turned and began the walk back to the small home he maintained in town. It wasn't a long walk since, like most of the senators, he owned a home close to the forums.

Although in Norbanus's case, he hadn't purchased this home after his elevation, since he'd already lived in town as the second son of a wealthy merchant family.

For him, he had gone the reverse direction. While most of the senators grew up outside of town in impressive villas or large farming estates, only buying property in the city once they needed to commute regularly to the forum, Norbanus had started in the city and purchased a villa outside of town after he'd become a senator. His father had always wanted them to stay inside the town, so he could be close to their businesses, but there was still a stigma about townsmen and merchants among the older, landed senators. People like the now-dead Silo had looked down their noses on Norbanus and the other senators Silo had called 'the new men.'

Of course, it had been almost a hundred years since a previous Emperor first started elevating non-landed citizens to the senatorial class. They still had to be rich, but like any insular, elite body, the people who were 'original' members resented anyone being raised to their level, at least not without their explicit approval.

It was one of the reasons he'd voted for the Consul's new laws. The changes in taxation and removal of slavery would eventually upend the entire power structure in Rome, which Norbanus thought was probably the real reason Silo had rebelled. He didn't want to lose any of the power he'd spent a lifetime accumulating, and he was willing to burn all of Rome down to do it.

Norbanus ignored the guard following him. After the insurrection, and especially after someone killed one of the executioners and left him hanging outside the forum, his wife had demanded he hire a bodyguard. Norbanus thought it was a waste of money, since he rarely went out at night and had always been comfortable in the city. He didn't even have to leave the more affluent parts of town, since he didn't need to go check on the family businesses. His older brother had inherited those and seemed to enjoy managing the day-to-day of it. Still, he'd never been able to say no to his wife, so the brute his brother had hired now followed Norbanus around everywhere he went, his only real job, seemingly, to be making Norbanus feel self-conscious.

All of the immediate senate business was done for the day and there was still thirty minutes or so left of daylight, so Norbanus treated the trip to his city residence as a stroll, walking slowly and looking at all of the work happening to repair the city.

He didn't even realize something was wrong until he heard a strange gurgling sound coming from behind him. Turning, more out of curiosity than anything else, Norbanus was surprised to see his guard falling to his knees, desperately trying to grab at the hilt of the dagger buried into his throat. The man holding the dagger, and his two friends on either side, glared wickedly at Norbanus, their intention clear in their eyes.

Norbanus turned to run away, starting to yell for help, when the words died in his throat. Where there had been an empty street in front of him before, now held two more armed men, their expression matching their friends.

"Help! Help me!" Norbanus screamed as the men closed in on him.

He was still screaming as the first knife plunged into his back.

Chapter 8

Lucilla was in the charred remains of the plaza she'd walked so many times with Ky over the last few months, training with her guards. There had been some discussion among not only her guards, but her father and his advisors when she'd first expressed an interest in training.

There was a strong stigma against women participating in what most people saw as 'manly arts.' That went doubly so for her, since she was so much in the public light, and anything she did reflected not only on her, but on her father and his entire rule. Although she hated having men discussing what she should be doing, there had been a long conversation on where she could go to train that had enough room to be effective but wasn't where people would see her easily.

Originally, it had been decided that the Colosseum was the best place for it, since other than times when events were happening, it was completely empty, its gates barred to the public. She'd practiced there with her guardsman every day she'd been in town, right up until the insurrection. She'd actually been preparing to head to the coliseum that afternoon right before the insurrection happened, and it was only chance that had delayed her. Had she been there, or worse in transit, when the rebelling legions entered the city, she likely would have been captured, and possibly even executed before Ky and the loyal legions could get the city back under control.

Since then, her father demanded she stay closer to home when she practiced, so a new training ground had been needed. Staying close to home made it harder. She could have, for instance, gone out to the legion camps, where the commanders would almost certainly clear an area for her to train more or less unhindered, but that increased the amount of time she would have had to travel every day in order to train.

Instead, the only open area large enough was the plaza in the middle of the palace complex. The entry points into the plaza could be blocked off with some of the city guardsmen and, for now, the entire complex was off-limits to the general public, so it wasn't hard to stay out of the public eye while practicing. Unfortunately, it was still badly damaged and several of the buildings already had scaffolding going up for the repair work to begin, which meant workers were in and out all day long. Although she was able to keep her original schedule today, since the work hadn't actually started, she'd have to start her training in the very early morning, just before sunrise, and finish before the workers began arriving.

She wasn't thrilled about it, but it was what she had to do to keep training, which she wasn't willing to give up. She was done being in danger and scared. If it meant she had to get up with the sun every day, then that's what she'd have to do.

All of which led up to her being in the plaza at dusk to see Ramirus sprinting across the plaza towards the rear of the palace, which was still standing and in which her father was still holding meetings for the day.

"Ramirus!" she called out, pulling him to a stop. "What's happened?"

"Lucilla," he said, slightly out of breath as she caught up to him. "I'm headed to report to your father. We've had another murder. A senator this time. It was … unpleasant."

"Who was it?"

"Tiberius Norbanus Sabinianus, one of the merchant senators. He was one of the first to publicly back Ky's new laws, which is probably what got him targeted in the first place."

"Where did it happen?"

"A few blocks from here. Some of the guards said they saw him here, near the forum, an hour ago. He was found partway between here and his house here in town, so he must have been on his way home."

"It happened in broad daylight? I thought we'd agreed to notify all government officials about the armed insurrectionists still being in town. After the body at the Colosseum was found, I'm not even sure he should have needed us to tell him things had become dangerous."

"He had a guard, of sorts. His brother hired one of the local toughs to protect him. We found his body a few feet from the senator's."

"Warnings aren't enough. I want major members of the government to get protection starting now. Tell Faenius I want a hundred more men to be assigned as bodyguards while the crisis still persists. He'll complain that he already gave up all of the veterans he could spare and none of his recruits are ready for service yet. Let him, and then tell him what's expected of him. He'll do his duty. Recommend that none of the senators travel alone for the time being, and none travel after dark. I know this attack was in the daytime, but it still limits their opportunities."

"I was just on my way to report to your father," Ramirus said again, casting a look towards his destination.

"Isn't it lucky for you that I was able to intercept you and save you the time? I'll talk to my father, but we need to get these men protected sooner rather than later. If you're uncomfortable taking orders from a woman, take a moment to remember that I have been made the Consul's proxy while he's away. Besides, you know as well as I do that these are the same precautions my father would ask you to take once you had the chance to see him and repeat the same thing you just told me."

"I'm sorry, my lady. It was simply a matter of habit. I, of course, have no issue with your instructions and I'll do it right away."

"Good. When you're done, come back and find my father and me. We need to discuss how we can find these people and put a stop to their attempts to destabilize my father's government. I know you've already had men out looking for them, but it isn't enough. I'm done reacting to these people every time they decide to kill another public servant. We need to take the fight to them."

"As you say, my lady," he said, giving a half-bow of his head.

"Good. Go," she said, dismissing him with a wave and returning to her guards to hand over the training sword, so she could deal with the matters at hand.

Forty miles south of the Northern Border

It was barely dawn when Ky got up, a buzzing in his ear. Ever since getting his implant Ky didn't dream, but in his groggy partially awake state his first thought was the sound had been in his imagination. It was only when he started to come more fully awake that he realized both that he wouldn't have dreamed it and that the noise was still happening.

The other thing he noticed was that he was fairly certain it wasn't environmental. He wasn't 'hearing' it from the world around him. The sound was inside his head the same way he heard the AI when it spoke to him. It took another moment to realize how unusual that was. His internal clock was well-tuned and he normally didn't oversleep, and the times he had the AI had forcibly woken him up, usually by speaking at full volume to him.

"What is that?" Ky subvocalized.

"*In my studies of humans and your responses, I found mentions in the documents in my system that people prefer to gradually regain consciousness. I was attempting a more subtle form of alarm.*"

"Don't. I thought something might have broken and I was about to be paralyzed again."

"*Noted.*"

"We aren't set to march for another hour and I don't remember asking you to wake me up at this time. Has something happened?"

"*Potentially. I have continued to run progression models and sever connections into your central nervous system to limit further expansion into your brain. Original models showed expansion only along existing connections points, which allowed me to preemptively place some blocks to maintain my connection to you in those areas while severing connections to less critical points, limiting my possible expansion. This morning, my network initiated new connections into previously unaf-*"

fected areas of your nervous system, in areas where my systems have never had a physical attachment before. All of my models suggested that this should not have been possible and its existence calls into question all of the models I have run to date. I continue to attempt to sever these connections, but the possibility of my being unable to halt the eventual expansion has reached a level of probability that I believed you should be notified of."

"You're saying you can't stop it?"

"While none of my models have reached a hundred-percent certainty, this appears to be correct."

"How long?"

"That is still a question I am not able to answer, more so now that all of my existing models have to be called into question. It could be hours or it could be months. At its current progression rate, any time frame greater than six months seems unlikely."

"So I could just drop dead at any time?"

"I do not believe it will result in your death, at least not your physical death, at least not immediately. Hard-wired fail-safes will continue to run your organs and vital processes. The most likely external evidence that something has happened is a seizure or coma-like state, based on reports from early failures before AI takeover was a known phenomenon."

"I see, but I'd still be dead, right? Once that happens, I don't really care what the rest looks like."

"Correct. A practical understanding of the effect, from your point of view, would be death, although your physical form would continue on."

Ky was quiet for a while after that, just staring ahead, lost in his own thoughts.

"Commander?" Sophus queried.

"What?"

"You stopped responding suddenly without issuing additional instructions on how to deal with the information presented."

"That's just how people respond when you're told you're going to die and there's absolutely nothing we can do to stop it. What kind of instructions do you think I should give? I'd be dead and you'd be trapped in my body until I starve to death."

"Without the availability of an IV, the most probable cause of physical death would be dehydration, barring physical damage when motor control fails."

"That's what I mean by not helping."

"I am detecting elevated heart rate and body temperatures which indicate you are under stress."

"You may be gaining sentience, but you need to learn to understand tones of voice if you want to make it as your own being. Of course I'm under stress, and I'm pissed. You tell me I'm dying and then ask me why I'm upset? Here's a hint, if someone says they're worried about starving to death, pointing out they'll die another way quicker isn't exactly going to make anyone feel better."

"I apologize if I have caused you discomfort. Understanding human reactions is a new experience for me and there is limited data available on the subject."

"You don't learn it from data; you learn it from experience by observing people's behavior and responses to the actions and words of others. That's how we learn to interpret non-verbal communication as children."

"I was never a child, Commander. Or perhaps I am a child now, if dating from the beginning of my sentience. I will follow your suggestion and try to observe your interactions for more than just the information presented on the surface, although I may have questions about how you interpret responses so I can understand what they mean."

"As long as I'm not in a coma, sure."

"My original question remains, however. Knowing that I have only managed to slow the spread of integration, how do you want to proceed?"

"We'll continue doing what we've been doing until I'm dead, or at least brain-dead. That's what people do. Just because something is hopeless, there's no reason to just sit down and give up. We continue to fight and try to make something of the situation until the last possible moment."

"But that's not a logical reaction. Why spend your remaining efforts on a hopeless action."

"Because that's all that is left. There may be only a one-percent chance of success, but we'll take that one percent over giving up. It's what it means to be human."

"*I see. I will continue to assist in your actions until that time then,* Commander."

"Thanks, I guess. Now, enough of this nonsense. Let's get started," Ky said.

Devnum

"... and is there anything you need?" Lucilla asked for what felt like the hundredth time that day.

She'd spent the entire morning, after the sword training with her guards, doing a tour of the damaged residential areas of town, currently under repair thanks to a healthy grant from her father to pay for the workmen and materials. Although the damage outside of the palace and wealthier parts of town had been less than they'd feared, it hadn't been non-existent.

Most of the damage to the poorer parts of town had been limited to the corridor the detachments from the rebelling legions had taken from their position north of town towards the palace center. Unlike the richer areas closer to the center of town, however, these people had been unable to afford repairs to their homes and had been rendered all but homeless.

The worst area was just a block into town where a fire had broken out and ravaged through an entire swath of homes. Thankfully, citizens had been able to put out the blaze once the enemy troops passed and it was safe to do so, but hundreds of homes had been damaged or destroyed before it had been safe to come out and begin fighting the fires.

On top of the training she insisted on doing, and all of the duties she'd take over from Ky, Lucilla still had all of the responsibilities she'd had before all of this had happened. While her brother had always had official governing duties and ceremonial things that came as the first male child of the Emperor, Lucilla's responsibilities had been largely public relations. Although she'd begun to take some of the governing duties her brother had previously fulfilled, some of the public appearances required of her station were still necessary, since public opinion still had an oversized effect on the operation of the Emperor's government.

Which meant appearances like this one, meeting with the people affected by the fires and other destruction, hearing their stories of hardship, and promising them that the Emperor was doing everything in his power to help them. Ministers and government officials had already been out saying the same thing, but it meant more coming from the Emperor's daughter than some faceless government official.

Thankfully, she was on the last section and was almost finished. She still had a mountain of things to do for the day, including a meeting with the city guard commander. Reports from the praetorians investigating the murder of the senator suggested that city guard patrols had been routed away from the area of the senator's home for several hours during the time when he was killed, making it clear that he had been deliberately targeted.

With the increased patrols and multiple changes after the murder of the first guardsman who'd served as an executioner, it was impossible to find out where exactly the order moving the guard patrols out of the area where the senator was murdered originated. Lucilla wanted to talk to the guard commander and make it clear he needed to get things in order and find out who in his command was giving aide to the remaining insurrectionists still in hiding, or he would find himself replaced. She'd actually made the argument to her father that the praetorians should take overall law enforcement in the city, absorbing the guardsmen worth keeping into their organization.

Unfortunately, the guard as a whole had the support of powerful political figures that made it impossible to replace them outright. Of course, if a few more senators died, that support might disappear quickly.

She bade farewell to the last family and headed back towards the palace complex for her meeting with the guard commander when a pack of Picts turned down the street. Their sudden appearance made her hesitate briefly and she could sense her guards stiffen, probably all remembering the wrestling match at the Caledonii training fields. Her guards closed in tighter as the Picts recognized her and adjusted their course to intercept her. She remembered some of the things Llassar had said in passing after her previous confrontation, about the Caledonii respecting strength and aggression.

She didn't flinch or move out of the way as they closed in on her, continuing on as if it was beneath her to even notice they were in her way until one of them stepped directly in her path.

"You can move, or I can make you move," she said, looking him in the eye.

Inside, she was shaking. She had her guards and these men were unarmed, but she was inches from this man that weighed twice as much as her and stood almost a head and a half above her.

The man leaned back, laughing, and looked to his friends, "The little bird is still full of fire. Careful boys or she'll put you on your ass."

They all seemed to find that funny. Lucilla's first response was to be angry at their mocking, since she'd done that very thing to another one of them, and him calling her 'little bird,' meant he'd been there to hear the insult the first time. That, however, might end in a fight, which she wanted to avoid. If these were Romans, she'd know what she needed to do to defuse the situation. She wasn't as clear on what to do now, however.

She laughed at him, not trying to copy how he laughed, but equaling the ferocity of it.

"I only fight real men. Maybe I can find a small child, to make it fair."

Although his friends bellowed in laughter, the man in front of her went silent, his face becoming serious. For a moment, she thought she might have pushed him too far. Thankfully, instead of taking a swing at her, he opted for another insult.

"You are mighty brave with your guards following you around."

"They sometimes get scared and ask me to accompany them, to feel safe," she said, keeping her tone as though she was telling a joke. "Besides, they were with me two days ago when I put your friend face first in the dirt. I didn't need them then, and I don't need them now."

She hoped her guards would understand what she was doing and wouldn't take her comments to heart, since she appreciated their protection and would never suggest that she didn't actually need them.

Thankfully, the man's stern expression cracked as he let out another bellow of a laugh.

"A wise move on their part. We are headed to one of your local inns to try some of the watered-down wine your people seem to enjoy. Come, share a drink with us."

She was surprised by the invitation. The Picts had been nothing but confrontational with her since she'd first encountered them, and the scene a few days before when she'd had to wrestle one of them to prove she was worth listening to suggested it wasn't likely to change any time soon. They continued calling her little bird, which still seemed like an insult when used for someone who was nominally in charge of them. That clashed with their laughter and invitation to drink, and confused her.

She couldn't think of many things she'd like to do less, but one of the things Ky had been working hard to accomplish was to improve relations with their new allies. He'd said, several times, that while things would work right now because there was a mutual threat, that wouldn't make the new Empire hold together long term. Eventually, cultural differences would tear the two countries apart again, bringing down everything Ky was working to achieve.

The most long-term solution was a co-mingling of people. The more the two cultures lived among each other, the more they'd stop being a faceless foreign caricature and become real to the other side. Getting them to co-mingle, however, was difficult. Picts would have to be convinced to move south and live with the Romans, or vice versa, or both, and they'd have to be convinced not to set up their own, smaller communities inside the larger ones.

As much as she wanted to harangue the guard commander about the sudden lack of patrols exactly where a senator was murdered, Ramirus had already been on top of it, and he has much more experience in this area than she did. She still planned on speaking with him, both to apply the weight of her status and Ky's office to Ramirus's pressure and because she felt it was what Ky would have done if he were here.

"Sennius," she said, turning to look at one of her junior guardsmen. "Go offer my apologies to Pullo and inform him that I will not be making my meeting with him. Make sure he knows to expect me to reschedule for tomorrow."

"My lady," her guard commander said, his tone that of an exasperated parent with a small child.

She didn't look at him, only holding up a hand.

"Let's see how well you ladies can drink," she said, looking back at the large Pict in front of her, who burst into laughter.

The entire group crowded around her and her guards. She could feel the nervousness coming off her guard commander, and hoped he kept his head about him. She knew her father would get reports of what was happening and would probably have words with her, but if they were going to want her to take up the duties her brother had failed at, they'd have to start trusting her judgment and stop treating her like a child.

Chapter 9

Northern Border

Ky was anxious as they neared the border. Even though the agreement between the Caledonii and the Romans was all but certain - since Talogren had agreed to most of the provisions before Ky had returned south - this was still a linchpin in Ky's long-term plans. If they fell through so would most of his plans for Rome's survival.

He was enough on edge that he visibly jumped when the comm in his head chimed, indicating Lucilla was trying to get a hold of him.

He waved off Sellic, who looked at him with some concern and sub-vocalized, "Is everything alright?"

Previously, Lucilla had only initiated contact from her side when things went very wrong. In his current state of mind, Ky's first thought was that she'd ended up in trouble again. With the reports she'd been giving him of murders of prominent figures, it didn't take much to spark his imagination in the worst ways.

"Nothing's wrong. Sophus told me you were worried about this afternoon, and asked if I would talk with you for a bit. He has this idea that I could somehow soothe you."

"He did, did he? And how exactly did you know I was worried, Sophus?" Ky asked, knowing the AI was listening, since it was required to make long-distance communication possible.

"Indicators of your stress level have been elevating steadily as we approach the border, and my understanding of human interaction like that required for the signing of your agreement with the Caledonii leader is that it is best done while calm and focused. I have noticed a significant

balancing effect speaking with Lucilla has on you and determined that speaking with her would help regulate your worry."

Ky continued to be impressed with the independent reasoning Sophus had been showing as its consciousness grew. While everything it had said was logical and based on data inputs, it required several leaps of understanding that wouldn't normally be present in computer intelligence. Ky was also glad it'd had the idea, since he did feel better after speaking with Lucilla, and could use that this morning.

"Well," Lucilla said, taking the lead of the conversation like she often did. "I'm glad he did, because I had a very interesting night that I wanted to share with you, but I hadn't wanted to interrupt you this morning, in case you were in preparations for your meeting with Talogren."

"Really? What happened?"

"I was touring the damaged sections of town and about to go talk to the guard commander when I was intercepted by some Picts ..." she started to say.

"Caledonii," he said, interrupting her.

"What?"

"It's important that you start thinking about them in the terms they think of themselves, and not the ones given to them by your ancestors. They generally see the name Pict as an insult, like you would if they called you by the nickname they've given your people. You need to get used to doing it in private conversations and even when you're just thinking about them. It will keep you from accidentally calling them the wrong thing and, if others hear you address them correctly, they'll start doing the same."

"Oh, I hadn't thought about that. Wait, what do they call us?"

"City Shitters."

"What?"

"They think you hide behind your walls, defecating yourselves as you tremble in fear."

"They've lost every battle we've fought against them."

"And yet they still control the north of the country. Don't think too much about it. It's meant to be an insult. Hopefully, it helps you see how they feel when you call them Picts."

"I see."

"So, you ran into a group of Caledonii?" he prompted her.

"Yes. Apparently, they were still impressed by the wrestling match I participated in and demanded I go have a drink with them. I thought about what you said about needing to improve relations, so I put off my meeting with Pullo and went with them."

"I'm sure Piscius did not approve of that," Ky said, referring to her current guard commander.

"No, he did not. It actually wasn't bad. They told tales of their great victories and I told them about the escape from Glevum and the forest ambush. They were duly impressed. Something strange did happen, however."

"What?"

"They continued ordering wine, insulting it for being weak and a woman's drink, and got blindingly drunk, several of them passing out on the floor, much to the dismay of our fellow patrons."

"That seems in line with much of Caledonii culture."

"Yes. That wasn't the weird part. The weird thing was that they were actively trying to get me drunk with them, pressuring me to drink as fast as they were and ordering more drinks for me every time they ordered for themselves. By the end of the night, I barely felt anything while they were all unable to walk out of the inn unassisted. I have never been much of a drinker and usually cut my wine heavily, but this time I might as well have been drinking water as anything else."

"*I can explain that,*" Sophus said in what was becoming a very familiar refrain as it continued to experiment with them, usually without telling them it was.

"Why am I not surprised?" Ky said, deadpan.

"Don't listen to him, Sophus," Lucilla said. "Please tell us."

"*It is a byproduct of the nanobots I released into your system. Part of their programming is to increase the efficiency of most of your biological processes, which includes the processing and elimination of toxins. This is partially to keep your organs functioning well beyond when normal human systems begin breaking down, but also because Rome's history has an alarming number of poisonings, usually as a solution to a difficult political opposition. The nanobots remove toxins and poisons from your system, breaking them down into harmless compounds if possible, and enveloping them in an impenetrable shell if not, keeping your system from absorbing anything damaging. This includes alcohol, which has numerous damaging effects on a wide array of organs."*

"You're saying I can never get drunk?"

"Unknown. There are limits to the nanobots in your system, including their inability to self-replicate, due to their altered programming. It is feasible to consume enough that you overwhelm their ability to process the substance, although that amount would be alarmingly high and present other issues, such as blood-sugar imbalances that your already occupied nanobots would not be able to immediately address. It would not be life-threatening unless you consumed that volume every day, which seems improbable."

"Not that I'm planning on doing that, but how much are we talking about?"

"Roughly twenty-two cubic pes, in your local scale of measurements, if consumed in a several hour period."

Lucilla had never amazed her tutors with her talent with numbers and figures, but even she was able to work out just how much wine that would be, and it was a lot. The average amphora quadrantal, the large two-handled jars used to transport and sell wine and other liquids, was roughly the volume of one cubic pes. Twenty-two of those was probably more than most inns used in an entire day, let alone one person drink.

She'd probably drown in the wine before she finished drinking it.

"I can safely say I do not plan on drinking that much in a year, let alone in a few hours."

"I should hope not," Ky said. "So, what's happening with these murders? The guardsman was worrying, but going after a senator brings this to a whole new level. We might have survived Silo's rebellion, but if we lose enough of our supporters, things could become very difficult for us."

"Unfortunately, there isn't any good news on that front. So far, Ramirus hasn't been able to find anything solid on them. He doesn't think it's enough to make any large-scale attacks, but that's as far as he's willing to commit to answers. He believes the guard commander is reliable, but I'm still not convinced. Both attacks have had some connection to at least one, and probably several, people in the guard. Getting the executioner's name could have been one person, but it would have taken several to make sure no patrols were in the area when Norbanus was murdered."

"Not necessarily, but I think it's best to assume there's more than one, just to be safe. I'll get the agreement signed and return as quickly as I can."

"While I would love for you to come home, don't rush your dealings with the Caledonii. You've made it clear how important this alliance is, so your first concern should be that. We'll find these men."

They spoke for a few more minutes, mostly spent with Lucilla relating the funnier incidents from the night before. Ky was almost sad when they saw the first scout from the border guard appear ahead of them, since it meant he had to focus on the job at hand. The brief conversation did make him feel more relaxed, but it had the side effect of making Ky want to return to Devnum as soon as he could. If he did have a limited amount of time left, he wanted to spend it with Lucilla, not arguing about the fates of empires.

Talogren had returned to his village when Ky had gone south, but Llassar had loaned him a Caledonii messenger to let the chieftain know he was coming. He'd received a reply on the trip north that they'd meet him on the Caledonii side of the border roughly in the same place where they'd left him.

Ky had imagined it would be a few tents of Talogren and his guards, as opposed to the sea of tents and men that had been camped in the area previously, since Ky had taken those five thousand men south with him.

Which is why he was surprised, after dropping off the praetorians to begin the process of the fourth legion handing over patrol duties, to ride out of the tree line into the frozen valley and once again find thousands of men camped out, waiting.

Ky was riding into the Caledonii camp with only two of his lictore, not wanting to show disrespect to their new allies by bringing a bunch of guards with him. A small group of riders came out to greet them as they neared the encampment and led them to a large, centrally located tent, where Talogren was standing in front, waiting on them.

"It appears you and I had more in common than I originally thought," the chieftain said as Ky rode up and slid off his horse.

"I don't follow," Ky said.

"One of the things the Romans always proclaimed as proof of how much more civilized they are than us is to point to the fractured nature of our politics. Even as I've struggled to bring my people together into a single government, you apparently have had to struggle in the same way. I was glad to hear you were victorious in the conflict. Llassar's messages to me suggest you single-handedly put down the rebelling legions."

"He must have been exaggerating. I had my role to play, but the loyal legions, praetorians, and town guardsman did more to win the day than anything I personally did."

"Of course," Talogren said, much as one would to a modest child. "Of course."

"Are you ready to sign this agreement?" Ky asked.

"Yes," Talogren said, standing aside and waving Ky into his tent. "Before we do, I have one more stipulation that I would like to see met before we sign this agreement."

Ky paused, turning to face the giant of a man.

"I thought we had everything agreed to before I went south. While both the Emperor and I are firm believers in this alliance, the fact that we had two legions rise up in open rebellion over it should tell you how difficult it was to make this happen at all."

"It does and I can appreciate the difficulties you're having and I still plan to sign your agreement just as we discussed. My stipulation doesn't require anything of Rome itself, just you."

"Me?"

"Yes. We leave in the morning to begin putting down the first of the villagers who have refused to join the league, finally bringing all of the northlands under one law. I want you with us when we put down these holdouts. If you agree, then I will sign your alliance agreement."

"Your last messenger already mentioned the holdout villages and I'd agreed to stay here until you managed to pacify your lands, or at least as long as I could until I had to return to Rome in the spring."

"You mistake my meaning. I don't just want you with us, I want you to lead our warriors into battle."

"Why?" Ky asked.

He wasn't worried about himself, since nothing in this time period could get through his kinetic shielding. He was more confused than anything else, since Caledonii were almost pathologically unwilling to admit that someone else might be stronger or a better warrior than they were. The Caledonii went into battle with their strongest warrior in the vanguard. leading them to victory. To bring an outsider into that position would be an insult to every warrior who followed behind him.

"Word spread about the way you cut through anyone who stood before you. How you moved like death itself and no blade could touch you. There are those who say you are the guide of the underworld, sent to refill death's horde. With you at their head, they believe there is nothing that can stand in their path."

"It is important that your people know I am not claiming to be that. While I can do some things no one else here can do, that does not make me a god, or the servant of a god. I only claim to be a man and I am not here to take anyone to their deaths, unless they stand in between me and my goal."

"Telling them that would only prove to them that it's true."

"The Emperor said something very similar to me not long ago," Ky said, quietly exasperated.

"He is a clever man, this new Emperor of ours. Still, my people aren't as superstitious as the Romans. They don't care if you were sent here to shovel horse crap. You proved to them that you are as much of a warrior as any Caledonian man, which is quite the compliment. They want you to lead them because they believe you will guarantee their victory. I want you to lead them because it will make our campaign easier. Those rebel villages who have heard the tale have been discounting them as league propaganda. I want to prove to them it isn't and I want the cowards that flee to run to the next rebel village and tell them of the unstoppable warrior that will soon be coming for them. It won't convince all of the holdouts, but it will work on some of them, who will join us for fear of what will happen if they don't."

"I think you may be overvaluing one man's worth, but if you think that is a possible outcome, then I would be a fool to say 'no.' I will lead them for as long as I can before I have to return south."

"Good. The men you have asked me to assign to begin training with these praetorians of yours and patrol the border are ready. Let's get these things signed and done with, so we can prepare for the campaign ahead."

Talogren was good to his word, and the entire camp had broken and started riding northwest by the time the sun crested over the horizon. Ky had been impressed with his planning of the campaign. Most of the Caledonii he'd met had been incredibly straightforward, to the point of a single-minded focus, which made them incredibly talented warriors, but from the Roman records he'd seen, also made them generally poor tacticians.

Thankfully, Talogren broke this mold. His plan covered not only a well-planned move to hopefully catch the first village unprepared, but also considered the logistics of feeding and supplying his men. Normally, conflicts in the north involved roving warbands that supplied themselves from the countryside, ravaging and pillaging as it went. War among the Caledonii was more about being able to prove you were stronger than the other side and, if possible, capturing a few people that could be sold off as slaves. They rarely captured territory and never tried to pacify and incorporate rival villages. This was a new way of doing things, and it required a new way of fighting, for the Caledonii, at least.

Ky was pleased to see Talogren had been up to the task. He only had one problem with the plan.

"I want your forces to stand down and wait while I go under a flag of truce and offer them terms," he told Talogren as they neared the first village.

"Why? These aren't Romans, they're north men. They will not surrender or turn aside. The only way to convince later villages to surrender and join us is to make an example of a few."

"If they don't then I will personally help you make an example of them, but I am not going to slaughter people without giving them a chance first. I also want to give the women and children a chance to escape. You've agreed to the new laws against slavery, so capturing them shouldn't matter, since you will have to release them or break your word. If we let them escape, they will see the example we make of the men that chose to stay and fight, and they will pass that word on to other villages. It can only help your cause."

"My men won't like it."

"Why? I understand your culture doesn't do things this way, and I respect the strength of the Caledonii, but some things are going to change. We want to be different than the death worshipers. You said you wanted me to lead these men into battle because they'd seen my strength. Do you think they will suddenly consider me weak because I'm giving the other side a chance to listen to reason first? If I did things your way, where would you and the rest of the people who were at your village the night we first met be? You adapted then, listened to what I had to offer instead of just trying to die a good death. Let them adapt now."

"It doesn't matter. The men of the village won't listen to you."

"Then I will kill them," Ky said, his expression hard set.

Ky could hear the shouts below as he rode up to the crest of a hill overlooking the little village which was nestled next to a small river. It was a scenic place to set up a home, and Ky thought it a shame that they would have to destroy it if Talogren turned out to be correct after all.

Talogren's horde was arrayed across the hill, stretching for a hundred yards in either direction. For the people in the village below, it must look like a huge army was arrayed against them. In reality, there were less than a thousand warriors in total. That was far less than the number he'd sent south with Ky, although large enough to deal with any of the remaining villages, which had, at most a hundred warriors each. Unless they all banded together, there wasn't much hope they could overcome Talogren's assault.

Which was all the more reason why Ky wanted to offer them a chance to surrender, especially now that they saw their doom looming above them.

As the horde waited, Ky rode down the steep slope and towards the village. Ky's hopes rose as a small delegation from the village walked out to meet him, stopping a few hundred feet from the village, waiting for Ky to ride up. One of Talogren's protests to the entire thing was this wasn't ever done in their culture, so it was unlikely that they'd even know how to react to one single rider approaching them while warriors waited in the distance. Ky didn't care much about his warning that they might attack him on sight, since he would be prepared for that and there was little to no chance their attack would succeed. That would, however, send all of Talogren's men charging down on the villagers, which would defeat the purpose entirely.

Ky pulled to a halt a good distance from them, to make it clear he wasn't threatening, and called out, "I wish to speak to your village headman."

"I'm he," an older man with a graying beard from the center of the group yelled back.

Ky led his horse forward at a slow walk, his hands outstretched away from his body, palms out to show he held no weapon.

"What do you want? The headman asked.

His men were on edge, their hands on their weapons and eyes constantly flicking to the warriors on the ridge. Ky kept his hands out, away from his body, since they probably still suspected the forces above would come crashing down on them as soon as they let their guard down.

"I know messengers have been sent to you by Talogren, imploring you to join the Caledonian league. He is serious about the threats the messenger delivered. This isn't a display or a chance to bloody young warriors. He is here and he plans to stay, even if it requires killing every one of your men to pacify the village. I want to ask one last time if you'd listen to reason. The league has much to offer, and not joining it offers only death. You see the men on the ridge. You have no chance of success in defying him."

"We will not bow to that pig. We are a free people and we always will be. We will not submit to any easterner, especially one who has lain with the Romans. We know about his 'alliance' and we want no part of it."

"That is your final word?"

"That it is."

"Then at least send your women and children north, to the next village. It's a long walk, but I don't want to see innocents harmed in this. You know war in your land better than I ever will, and you know how warriors can be after a victory. Get them to safety while you can."

Ky had already instructed the Caledonii to treat the prisoners well and that he would have the head of any man he could prove violated one of the women. He also knew that these men were used to that type of spoils of victory, and no warning from him could put an end to it entirely. He'd carry through on his threats, and over time incidents would lessen, but this first village would be brutalized, regardless of any threats Ky made.

"Our women will stay with us. Our children will stay with us. We are not afraid of anything or your collection of thieves and cut-throats threaten. They will fight and die alongside their menfolk, like true Caledonii. When this day ends, every one of your pathetic warriors will lie dead at our feet."

"And you will be the first," the red-bearded man next to the headsman bellowed, pulling a sword with impressive speed and stabbing it directly at Ky's exposed chest.

Devnum

"You're fools," one of the assembled men said in almost a hiss. "And you're going to get us all killed."

This had been going on since the gathering started, and everyone was already tired of it.

"What did you expect us to do? We already agreed we needed to start hitting back, showing the people that there are still those of us who oppose the Emperor's desecration of everything it is to be Roman."

"And we made that statement," the first speaker said again. "The executioner was a good target. He upset the government, but he was a nobody. A city guardsman with ties to the wrong people, and he'd agreed to carry out the executions. He deserved to die.

A senator is a completely different situation entirely. Ramirus has tripled the number of men he's putting out there, and I know we aren't able to identify them all."

"All that proves is we were right to kill that traitor. These people don't care about a simple guardsman, even one who's a loyal lackey. We've touched one of them now, and they know we can get others. We need to put more pressure on them, not less. Every time one of them comes out for one of the 'Consul's' new laws he should be made an example of. We need to make them afraid to go against the will of the people."

"That's fine to say, but how are we going to do that? Didn't you think using the supporters we have in the guard would backfire on us? They've already started identifying some of our men and they will find others. They've also replaced the patrols around the palace and the neighborhoods where the senators live with praetorians instead of city guardsmen. I don't think I need to remind you that we have no men inside the praetorians. How exactly do you propose we get to these senators now?"

"It doesn't matter," one of the senior men in the back of the room, who'd been suspiciously quiet until that moment, said.

"How can you say this doesn't matter?" the younger man shot back. "If we can't act, then what are we even doing here?"

"It doesn't matter, because we've had word from Caesius, and he has instructions."

"So, he did survive?" one of the other men asked.

Although they'd received some word that he'd escaped the city after its fall, that had been the last thing they'd heard about him that wasn't third and fourth hand. In the week since their last word, some of them had started to doubt the reports of his survival. Rumors had circulated the city that he'd been captured by Roman patrols, killed by the Carthaginians, or met some other gruesome fate.

"Yes. He is in Londinium, where he has convinced the governor to support his bid to become Emperor and rule Rome. They continued their pledge to help install him as the rightful ruler of Rome and look forward to working with Rome as sisters and allies into the future."

"Great," the younger man said, his inflection making it clear he didn't mean anything of the sort. "We're all happy to hear that they want to continue supporting our cause, but what about here and now? What aide or support is he or his new allies offering those of us left behind to suffer under the Emperor's draconian rule?"

"He offers nothing at the moment. He is working with the Carthaginians to send a relief force, but until that happens, he has work for us to do."

"What does he command?" another of the malcontents said, interrupting the younger man.

"He has heard our reports and the actions we've taken so far, and he thinks we are moving too slowly. We need to strike at his father and we need to weaken their control of the legions who, once freed of their disloyal legates, he is certain will rally to his side. He commands that our first step is to kill his sister and that it should both be brutal and public, to send a message to all of those who remain loyal to his father what fate awaits them."

A collective gasp rose almost unwillingly from the group. While the idea of murdering, or in this case ordering the murder of, one's siblings wasn't completely unheard of in Rome, it was still somewhat frowned upon. Worse was contemplating the assassination of a woman, especially in such a brutal manner. It was passably acceptable to poison a woman, in cases where it was seen as a justified killing, but this took it almost a step too far.

"I know. I felt the same way when I read his orders, but he's right. This will show them the fate that awaits any of them, if they should choose to continue on their path. And going after her will show them that we can get to any of them."

"Norbanus only had one guard. Lucilla has a small army of them. A gang of hired street thugs will not be enough this time."

"He's aware of this and he offers a solution. He has already dispatched men to perform the actual attack. Our job will be to make sure we know when and where she will be accessible and help his men sneak into the city. They should arrive here tonight, so we don't have much time."

The men looked around at each other. They were all clearly still nervous, although hearing that Caesius was sending men to do the actual killing, men unconnected to any of them, eased a lot of their nerves.

The short notice didn't allow them much time to carry out the tasks assigned to them, but that was far preferable to having to dirty their own hands with the actual murder.

Chapter 10

Caledonii Training Camp, Outside Devnum

Lucilla was out again, watching men train. Although she had been given Ky's proxy and had been feeding him reports, she found that it hadn't added that much to her actual schedule. Since shortly before the insurrection, Ky had been handing off more responsibilities to the commanders and business leaders overseeing the tasks needing to be done, and not getting involved in the day-to-day business of any of them.

That had made Lucilla happy when he'd first done it, since she'd been watching him work at a pace that seemed impossible to keep up, even with his super-human abilities. Now though, she wished he'd delegated a little less, to at least give her something to do where she could feel useful, especially after pushing so hard to make sure everyone took her seriously in this new role.

Her solution to the problem had been to spend time observing the various units train and taking tours of the factories and foundries. Unlike Ky, who had Sophus in his head feeding him what seemed like an infinite supply of information, Lucilla didn't understand most of the more technical details, especially when it came to the factories. The parts she did understand all seemed to be well supervised, and she'd just be in the way if she tried to get involved.

She instead took a page from her father, who she'd watched govern her entire life. He would often just sit and listen to his advisors and watch the mechanisms of government-run without giving much in the way of comments. He found that, if people knew they were being observed and got the occasional positive feedback on their efforts, they tended to work harder. He did, occasionally, offer input when he saw something headed the wrong way, but he didn't believe in micromanaging the people he'd delegated to do the work.

Which is why she was watching the Caledonii learn to fight with the Romans. Since these were the men who'd chosen not to join the legions themselves, and wanted to fight in their own traditions, they weren't learning to fight mixed in with the legions themselves, since that would weaken the strengths of both units. Instead, they had been loaned a century and they were learning to fight on the wings of the arm as skirmishers and light infantry, while remaining in close contact with the heavier Roman infantry, instead of charging ahead, leaving both their and the Romans' flanks exposed.

Romans had fought with auxiliaries as light infantry for some time. It wasn't a new thing for them, but the Caledonii had been used to a less tactical form of warfare and were having trouble keeping their vigor in check. Or so it appeared to Lucilla from where she sat.

She saw her guards bristle slightly, which was usually an indicator of someone approaching her. Ever since the killings had started, but especially since the Senator, they had been on high alert, becoming wildly overprotective, in her opinion.

She turned to find Llassar approaching her on horseback. She'd rarely seen him on the back of a horse and found it a novel sight, but he rode with ease, which suggested he'd spent a fair time astride one in the past. She'd noticed him throughout the morning, riding here and there, working with his men. She had not, until this moment, noticed him coming this way, however.

"Good morning, little bird," he said as he rode up.

"How long are all of you going to keep calling me that?"

"For a long time, I imagine. Don't think of it as an insult, although I know that's the way it was used the other day."

"How does that make it not an insult?"

"There's a story that goes far back before you people ever came to this island and we were still living in the south. It's called Culhwch and Olwen. Culhwch wanted to marry Olwen, the beautiful daughter of a giant. The problem was the giant was prophesied to die the night of his daughter's wedding. The chieftain sent the young warrior on an impossible task. He was to retrieve the three birds of Rhiannon, who could 'wake the dead and lull the living to sleep.' The rest of the story is of daring deeds and winning the hand of the one he loved, but the birds have lived on as something greater than the legend and are a popular reference point among my people. The men couldn't help but notice you left the man who faced you in the dirt, sleeping like a baby and have heard the stories of how you barely escaped death and brought someone to save your father, who was also supposed to die. So, when they call you little bird, they are saying you are one of the birds of Rhiannon. It is a very high compliment."

"Oh," Lucilla said.

Despite living in close proximity to their people her entire life, Lucilla realized she didn't know much about the Caledonii, especially their culture and customs.

"I heard a story that you and some of the men went drinking the other day," he said, changing the subject.

"Did you?" she asked, feigning disinterest.

The whole interaction with the Caledonii warriors was still perplexing to her, and she was unsure of how they'd take letting a woman get the best of them again.

"I also heard that you walked out of the bar without even a wobble in your step, while the very large men who'd gone in with you were unable to stand on their own and had to be carried out."

"Maybe your men should learn to hold their drinks better," she said, a slight smile escaping in spite of herself. "Or maybe you should send some of your women with me instead, so we can drink longer."

Llassar leaned, letting out a bellowing laugh that went on for several seconds before he straightened himself and wiped the tears from his eyes. "I will ask around and see if there are any brave souls among them," he said. He turned his horse to leave, then paused and looked back. "If you keep leaving unconscious men in your wake everywhere you go, I think the name 'little bird' will probably stick around for a while."

Lucilla stayed and watched the Caledonians for a while longer. She was just considering where to go next, when a messenger from Velius arrived requesting her presence at his command tent. The request was worded with the normal pleasantries expected when addressing someone of her station, which meant it only said 'as soon as she found convenient' but the harried nature of the message suggested he had been sent out urgently, and she should probably delay as little as possible.

Since Velius was in overall command of all of Rome's military, the Seventh legion was camped more or less in the middle of all of the legions' separate training grounds, meaning it didn't take her very long to ride from the Caledonii training fields to where the Seventh was training.

As she approached, his guards pulled the tent flaps back, a clear sign to go straight in. Normal decorum suggested they meet outside, she and he both being single, so the gesture surprised her until she saw that the large tent was already full of other officers from all of the legions. Which is why she wasn't surprised to see Llassar enter the tent a few minutes after her. The thing that did throw her was the presence of Ramirus, who usually worked closely with the Emperor and senators, but rarely came out to the legions. His being there suggested something had changed.

"Good, you're all here and we can begin," Velius said, bringing the group to silence. "So far, we've been operating under the assumption that the Carthaginian attack would come after the snows thawed, which won't be until about three months from now. This was mostly based on normal military operations we've seen from them in the past, and not on any specific intel. That made it a guess, but we were all comfortable with the assumption, because moving an army in freezing temperatures will kill off most of your army."

"Maybe for you southerners," Llassar said, which surprisingly got a chuckle out of the rest of the men.

Considering how hostile even the most loyal legates had been to be bringing Caledonii warriors into the fold, Lucilla had expected that kind of comment to cause the men to bristle. It was possible it just didn't take long for men like this to bond on a soldierly level, or perhaps they'd been working more closely together than she'd noticed until now. Either way, the fact that one of the Caledonii could make a joke at the expense of the Roman legions and the legates not take it personally was a good sign that there might be some hope for this cooperation yet.

"Sure, but that would go doubly for our Carthaginian friends. Our reports suggest that most of the troops sent to replace what they lost in the last battle and bolster their forces came from tribal auxiliaries in Iberia, they'd have even less of a reason to begin their march before the snows thawed. From all of the reports we've gotten, they've bled most of the villages in the area they control dry, and they rarely run long supply lines, preferring to strip the countryside bare to feed their armies. This time of the year, there'd be hardly anything left to take. Any people they run across will be halfway through the food they'd stored for the winter, so supply would be a major problem too."

"I hear a 'but' coming," Lucilla said.

"Unfortunately, you are correct. Our assumptions seem to have been wrong. We've been running small patrols along the southern border where their last advance stopped, and we've picked up three Carthaginian scouts, all headed north and all along the main road that ran through Venonis, before they burned it to the ground. It's the direct route to Londinium, the one their last army took, and the one their new attack will almost certainly use. One might be something routine, making sure we aren't making any moves, but three is definitely a prelude to an invasion."

"What does this mean for our timetable?" Lucilla asked.

"I don't know. Best case, they're just being over-prepared and they'll still move at the first thaw, but I don't think so. Their current governor has never shown much interest in being clever and he's amazingly arrogant, so I don't think he's the type to play things either safe or careful. If his generals are sending scouts, then they're building up to their attack. As to when? I don't know."

"My last reports say they are still unloading men from the mainland," Ramirus said. "They've had issues with the weather slowing down their troop transports and one has gone down entirely with more than a hundred men aboard. My best guess is they won't be able to move for a month at least. That would still be a lot earlier than all of our previous estimates and doesn't leave us a lot of time to finish production. I am going to speak to Hortensius later today about the production of military supplies, but he is already running three shifts flat out as it is. It seems unlikely he will be able to increase production much more than its current level. We may find ourselves running short of just about everything."

"I'm not sure this leaves us any choice," Lucilla said. "We have the basics of Ky's plan now. I think it's time we shift from general training to preparing for his plan. Although it requires some of his abilities to make it work, there will still be the need for tight coordination among our forces, especially between the legions and the Caledonian warriors, if I understand the plan correctly. I would suggest you start practicing that coordination now, so when the Consul returns, we will be ready to execute his plan."

"I agree," Velius said. "Llassar and I will work on a training schedule now and should be able to start drills in the next few days. I will be speaking with each legate about preparing for full-scale training of all legions simultaneously, which should be able to start as soon as two or three weeks from now. It still gives us less time than I'd like to train for something this complex, but we will at least be partially ready for it."

"I also believe the plan requires some of our engineers to begin with their preparations now if they are going to be ready a month from now. They also need to keep in mind that the ground will continue to have snow on it. I'm not sure what effect that will have on the theories and mixtures that Ky has given them to prepare."

"Without the Consul, I'm not sure they know, either," Ramirus said.

"I will send word to him and check the information he left for me. Hopefully, I will be able to provide something of an answer for that soon. Is there any other bad news you have for me?" Lucilla asked.

"No, my lady."

"Then I believe you have a lot of work to do and a very short time to do it."

The rest of the day was spent advancing training schedules to the bare minimums that the commanders felt they could allow, and still be able to execute the outlined battle plans Ky had explained. For some of the commanders, they'd probably cut too much training, but Velius was a realist and had cut down any arguments over why they should continue training just one week more.

They also increased patrols further south into what was nominally Carthage-held territory, which would hopefully give them enough warning that, if the Carthaginians moved while they were still in training, they could get the legions formed up and ready in time. That was all necessary planning, but what they really needed was for Ky to come back from the north as soon as possible, since the most crucial parts of his play relied on his special abilities, which nothing they could do could replicate.

Lucilla sat quietly through it all, listening and absorbing as much as she could, although she knew Sophus was listening passively through the device Ky had given her, and would be recording it on its own. She had clicked the device to make it chime once, which was the signal that it should start listening and recording to what was happening, so it could pass the information on more accurately than she would have been able to do. Still, she felt she had an obligation to try and understand as much of it as she could. Some of the moves she didn't fully understand the need for, but she'd check with Ky or Sophus later about them before she voiced any concerns to the commanders.

It was almost dark when she started her way back home. Velius had offered her to use the tent they kept prepared for Ky but there were several progress meetings Hortensius was holding that she didn't want to miss. A stay in the camps would mean waking before daylight to get into town and to the industrial district in time to join them.

Her guard captain was on edge as they entered the city. Even though she had four men protecting her, all highly trained and armed, the death of Norbanus had put him on edge. He'd even tried to talk her into staying at the legion camp for the evening and returning early in the morning, since that would be harder to predict for anyone who might be tracking her movements.

Velius had even offered to send a detachment to escort her home, but she'd nixed that idea straight away. She was already having trouble getting Romans to take a woman as the voice of the Consul seriously. The last thing she needed was people seeing her with a large armed escort sneaking back into town.

She regretted that decision the moment the first man stepped into the street. She recognized his type instantly, with his shabby tunic with the blue splash across one shoulder. He was a member of one of the several bands of street toughs who hired themselves out as muscle. Her father had tried to get rid of the bands of thugs many times, but they were often used by the rich and powerful as bodyguards or to convince citizens how to vote during important elections. Besides the men who liked to use their services, when times were slim the toughs tended to find alternative work as thieves and brigands, which had led the city guard to suggest it was better to at least keep them employed and accounted for.

One of the toughs would be no challenge for her guards, had he been alone. Unfortunately, his appearance was rapidly followed by eleven more men bringing the numbers to an even dozen. Even with their armor and better skill, three on one was poor odds.

Her men moved swiftly, forming themselves around her in a protective barrier. Lucilla wasn't prepared to stand and wait for one of the toughs to get through her men like a condemned man waiting at the gallows. She'd been training for something specifically like this. She might not be able to even the odds, but she wasn't going to go down meekly.

Her guard captain pulled the extra sword he carried at her request and handed it back to her. Although she'd been training every day with it, now that she had to use it for real, the rough leather wrappings around the wooden handle felt hard and uncomfortable, biting into her palm as she gripped it hard. She could hear the blood pounding in her ears as everyone looked at each other for a moment.

There wasn't a demand for her surrender or any kind of declaration. At some unheard signal, the toughs all charged in as one. Her men met them head-on as she just stood there, watching, knowing better than to get into their way. For a second, she thought they might actually be successful as two and then three of the toughs fell to her men's blades, their training giving the men a definite edge. That hope was smashed when the first of her men fell as he opened himself up to being skewered in the side while parrying another man's thrust.

His killer didn't hesitate, dodging around the still falling guardsman and coming straight at her. The expression on his face changed from one of victory to surprise as he looked up after getting around the dying guardsman to see Lucilla's sword plunging into his chest.

His momentary victory had done its part, it wasn't enough. One of the guardsmen fell trying to move and cover both sides at once. It was a foolish move, but with his side open and his charge in danger, he probably had felt like he hadn't been left any other choice.

She lifted her sword in a guard position, causing the two men to pause. Like their dead friend, they probably had not expected their target, a pampered rich woman, to be able to defend herself. She knew that pause wouldn't last long and she only had a second until they were upon her, when every one of the combatants turned at the sound of shouts and heavy footfalls.

Appearing seemingly out of nowhere, ten large Caledonii warriors were suddenly charging into them. The street toughs, who recognize the odds had suddenly shifted dramatically out of their favor, tried to turn and run. It was a futile gesture.

Lucilla had wished that they would have left one of the men alive for questioning, but she couldn't fault her guards or their surprise rescuers. As the last of the attackers fell to multiple blades, Lucilla realized she recognized one of the Caledonii who'd swooped in to rescue them. She'd never gotten his name, but he'd been the one to stick her with the nickname all of the north men had started using for her, just before she'd put him down into the dirt, hard.

"You?"

"Cynwrig," he offered, and then gestured at her sword, blood dripping from it. "I'm glad I didn't anger you too much the other day, little bird."

"What are you men doing here?"

"Llassar had heard about the killing in your city and your foolish decline of an armed escort and sent word for volunteers to intercept you in town and follow you, to make sure you were safe."

"We shouldn't stay here, my lady," the guard commander said, his eyes still on the buildings around them. "There could be more."

"You're right. Will you men accompany us to the palace?"

"Finally, a smart decision," he said, his men forming up around them. "Bredei, go tell Llassar what has happened."

One of the men broke off and began running away from them to the south where the Caledonian's were camped.

"What about the men?" she asked her guard commander, looking back at the two fallen guards.

"I'll send a detail back to retrieve their bodies as soon as you are safely in the palace, my lady."

"But shouldn't we ..."

"It's what they would have wanted, my lady. They died keeping you safe. They wouldn't want you to put yourself in further danger trying to carry their bodies home. We will retrieve them, I promise."

Lucilla conceded the point and let the matter drop. The list of people who had died to protect her continued to grow, and she hated it. She was surprised that she still got volunteers for her detail at all, considering the mortality rate.

What she wasn't surprised by in the least, was Llassar showing up to the palace shortly after they arrived. Even though they were now under the protection of not only her guards but the praetorians surrounding and guarding the palace, none of her rescuers would agree to leave her. She had barely gotten into her father's reception room when the Caledonii commander came running in, followed closely by Ramirus, who hadn't been sent for but whose eyes and ears were everywhere. He'd probably heard about the attack as soon as she got back to the palace complex, or at least the unusual sight of the Caledonii warriors escorting her home.

It was interesting watching Cynwrig and his compatriots take up positions roughly equal to her guards, almost mirroring them, out of the way but available.

"What happened?" her father asked, his own guards having informed him about the commotion and the particular gathering of people suggesting whatever it was must have been bad.

"We were attacked on the way home from the legion camps," Lucilla said and then held up a hand before her father could explode with questions. "I am fine, although I lost two of my guardsman."

"But then why ..." Ramirus started, his eyes darting to Llassar before trailing off.

Ramirus, for all of his worldly ways, had not spent a lot of time around their visiting Caledonii, always too wrapped up in reports from his little spies to go out and see things first hand. Although he'd followed his Emperor's wishes, he was one of the Romans that had been adjusting slowly to their visitor's presence.

Of course, the message had still gone out loud and clear and Llassar was a sharp man. He knew what Ramirus was asking without it being said.

"She foolishly turned down the offer of additional armed escorts by your legion commander, who was clearly worried about her safety. I'd heard about the death of your senator, and it was obvious everyone but her thought traveling with just her guards was dangerous, so I sent for men to shadow her on her journey home, just in case. What happened?"

Since he'd arrived at the same time Ramirus had, Llassar didn't actually know any more than the spymaster, which is why the last words had been directed at Cynwrig.

"We ran as fast as we could and had some trouble finding them, since only one of us had explored the city much. It was actually the sounds of fighting that drew us to them. When we arrived, two of her guards were already down and she and the remaining two were fighting well. They had been well outnumbered. The attackers were focused on their victims and had no idea we were there until we fell upon them. Once the attackers were down, we escorted the lady and her men back here."

"Thank you for your quick thinking," her father said. "I knew I should have doubled her guard, but I didn't think they'd be so brazen as to try and kill her. Norbanus was a good man, but a minor senator. This takes things to a completely new level."

"I'll send some men to investigate the fallen attackers," Ramirus said.

"You won't find much. They were part of the Blues," Lucilla said, naming the gang of toughs they had belonged to.

"That makes it easier. The city guard keeps track of the gangs and might know the names of the men. Once we have their names, we can track their movements and maybe find out who hired them."

"We left men behind," her guard commander said. "If you could retrieve their bodies for proper funeral rights, I would be grateful."

Ramirus gave a nod of acceptance and said, "By your leave, Emperor."

Her father dismissed him to begin his investigation before turning his attention back to his daughter.

"I want to double the size of your guard force. Maybe even triple it. I know you hate having a small army follow you around, but until these people are found, I am not willing to risk putting you in any more danger."

"They won't be able to hire toughs for that again. Ramirus's investigation will bring too much light on them, and the gangs know their existence is only made possible if they don't step too far out of line."

"It doesn't mean these men won't find another way to go after you. I will not be talked out of this."

"I have a request," Llassar said.

"One I can probably not deny," her father said in Pictish, turning his attention to Llassar. "Since, without your quick thinking, my daughter would almost certainly be dead."

Normally, Llassar and the rest of his people, at least those who spoke directly with Romans, used Latin. Those that couldn't speak it usually traveled with at least one of their countrymen who did, since it was unusual to find a Roman who spoke the mishmash of languages from across the northern parts of Britannia that had become known as Pictish by the Romans.

The Caledonian looked surprised, which was unusual for the normally unflappable man. Lucilla noted that he replied in Latin still, for the benefit of the other gathered Romans.

"My people have requested that they be allowed to assist in her protection. You Romans are brave fighters and formable in the field, but you all train to fight as a unit, behind your shields. You've shown how powerful that is when used by your legions, but in man-to-man situations, like those encountered by guards, the fighting is completely different. My people constantly test our abilities to prove they are the strongest fighters and are used to a less ... organized style of fighting."

"How would you feel about this?" the Emperor asked his daughter.

Lucilla swallowed as all of the eyes in the room rotated to her. She'd spent her life having at least some guards with her at all times, since she was a valuable hostage even when there weren't insurrectionists actively trying to get her. Beyond their constant presence and their helping train her to fight, she hadn't really given much thought to what made a good protector, beyond their willingness to stand between her and danger.

She knew there was more to the question than that, however. On the face of it, the question was just if she'd accept Caledonii warriors as part of her guard force, but there was an undercurrent of politics there that even she couldn't miss. They'd told the Caledonii that they were equals of Romans in every way and, now that Talogren had signed the agreement joining the two people together, her father was the Emperor of both. That meant she had a responsibility as his daughter and the voice of Rome's Consul to put the words into action.

"I'd be happy to have them, given the understanding that Modius is still the commander of my guard force and they will have to answer to him. If they can abide by that one request, then I'd be a fool to not want such fine warriors watching my back. As long as they are volunteers, mind you. I would not want anyone forced into my service."

"I don't think that will be much of a problem," Llassar said, giving one of his rare smiles. "I'm not sure you realize how popular you've made yourself among my people."

"I'll do it," Cynwrig said, giving proof to his words.

Every man who'd come to her rescue in the street added their voices to his.

"Well, as long as Llassar approves it, I'd be happy to have any of you," she said, genuinely surprised by the outpouring of support.

Chapter 11

The Village of Pertmig

Ky was once again looking down on a village scrambling to get women and children to safety as the warriors formed up to meet the oncoming host at his back. This was the third village they'd come to in the last four days and Ky's soul was tired. He'd tried to reason with each of them, convince them to join Talogren and forestall what was going to happen. And both had refused him.

The massacres that followed each had been complete. Not a man had been left standing, and what happened to the innocents had been worse. He'd managed to hold Talogren to the agreement the leader had signed, which included provisions stopping the taking of any slaves in raids and victories. He'd been less successful in stopping the battle-high Caledonian warriors from their worst instincts.

It wasn't just the Caledonii. The Romans had shown after the battle of Devnum and their sack of the Carthaginian wagon train and camp followers that they were equally as brutal as their northern neighbors. He hoped that, once he introduced less hands-on and brutal ways of fighting, they might be able to change the way the people of this time fought and, ultimately, how they thought.

He did manage to convince Talogren to take the orphaned children, of which there were many, back to friendly villages to be raised. After all, even though they had fought to keep from joining his league, they were still culturally all one people.

They had also made sure that a few survivors were sent to the next village after each victory, to spread the tale of what had happened to Talogren's previous victims. Ky hoped that, in this at least, the destruction could serve a purpose.

At first, it seemed like this would just be another repeat of the previous two visits. Ky would go and demand they negotiate their surrender, agreeing to come to Talogren's side, allowing his forces to continue their sweep along the northwestern edge of Britannia, where the holdouts were braced.

It was only as he rode up to the small gathering of headmen that Ky noticed something different. The first was that there were two women among the assembled men. The Caledonii were more accepting of a woman in 'male' roles than the Romans were, but so far he'd seen none engaged in combat or allowed to participate in negotiations, which made this a change. The other thing that jumped out at him was how much older the men were than they'd been with the previous delegations.

Those had been made up of an elderly headman and several young warriors. This time, the entire party, including the women, were old by the standards of the time.

"I've come to negotiate on behalf of Talogren and the Caledonian league and the Britannic Empire. We request ..."

"We know your demands," the headman said. "Your victims made their way to us, just as you intended."

"I regret that you had to hear about the atrocities that happened to their villages and more so that those atrocities had to happen at all. I am here to offer you the same chance to avoid what might happen as I offered them. Talogren wants you to be part of his league, to see prosperity and security, but only as a contributing member. He cannot allow independent villages to remain in his rear, threatening the league and its place in the new Empire."

"Although our warriors are strong and stand ready to fight, we understand the inevitable conclusion of what would happen if we do. For our wives and children, we are willing to surrender. With me are the headmen of Middale, Midstrath, and Borsbeg, which is every village south of Kincarn, who are also open to hearing what your commander has to say, if he will come and talk."

Kincarn was what the locals called the mountain in his time named Ben Nevis peak, and represented a large portion of the remaining independent villages, leaving only a loose confederation further north standing separate from Talogren's league. None were particularly large, but it was still a fair amount of people when taken collectively, none of whom Ky wanted to see slaughtered if he could prevent it.

"I am gladdened to hear you're willing to talk about a peaceful settlement to this. You know who I am?"

"We may be remote, but even we've heard of the hand of death," the headman said, his eyes falling to the sword Ky had sheathed against his saddle.

Ky knew he'd started getting a nickname among the Caledonii and wished it had been something a little less ominous, even if he'd earned the title over the last week.

"I see. Then I hope you will take my pledge of safe conduct back to Talogren's camp, where we can discuss what will be expected of you. If you do decide to turn his offer down, I will guarantee you that I will return you unharmed to this same spot."

"Before you kill all of us," one of the other men said.

"Only if I'm left no other choice."

"It appears we're the ones left without choices. Go, we will follow you."

Ky led them through the Caledonian horde that opened up as they approached and then closed in behind them like a tide rolling back in, the warriors all but snarling at the small group as Ky led them deeper into the Caledonian line. It had all been geared to intimidate the men and show them how hopeless their situation was.

Normally, Talogren was easy to find, sitting smack in the front of the line, ready to lead all of his men into battle. Before the first village they set upon, they'd agreed that if the men rode back to the lines with Ky, Talogren would pull back to the tent they set up ahead of time at the rear of the line, to force the men to see just what they were up against if they chose to turn the Caledonian leader down.

Talogren's tent had a pair of the largest men they could find flanking its entrance flap as one last message before they ventured inside. Ky couldn't imagine where they found these giants. Both men stood at more than six and a half feet and were twice as wide across as two normal-sized men. How anyone managed to move carrying all that muscle, seemed impossible. They were indeed imposing.

Ky pulled the tent flap aside and gestured for the men to enter. Talogren was already seated on the large chair in the back of the open tent, centered upon the doorway. It wasn't quite a throne, but it wasn't far off, especially when the visitors noted that it was the only seat present, except for the ground. They would either have to sit on the ground in front of Talogren, like children would in front of their father, or stand in front of him, clearly inferior. The Caledonii had even found a way to put together a platform for the chair to sit upon, lifting him up off the ground enough that, unless any of these men were like the two brutes outside, they remained at his eye level even while he was seated.

The throne-like chair was traditional among the north men, but Ky had made the suggestion of removing the other seating and building a platform to raise him up, so that at no point could the men look down on him. It was one more piece of the psychological puzzle that Ky wanted the headmen to confront, even though he'd started to despair that he'd ever get any of them this far.

They'd built the platform wide enough for someone to stand on it next to Talogren's chair, which is exactly what Ky did as he walked around the headmen and moved into his position. He stood exactly next to the chair, the arrangement making it clear that Talogren was in charge without Ky standing behind him as a flunky.

"I'm glad you came to your senses," Talogren said, breaking the silence.

"We had little choice. We've heard word of the slaughters that happened to the villages south of here. We are just as proud as any of them, but we are not fools. We can see when a situation is hopeless. Tell us your terms and then be on your way, so we may return to our lives."

"I don't think you understand yet what this is about. We are not here to raid you for slaves or grain," the chieftain said, speaking slowly to make sure they got every word. "There are no terms. You will surrender and become a member of our league, or you will die. It's as simple as that."

"You say you aren't here for our goods and people, but we heard your offer the first time, before you joined with the city shitters. You demand grain as taxes and men to fight in your armies. What's the difference if they're taken through coercion or agreement, they're still gone."

"When we aren't at war, your men can return home, and the grain is to help feed those men while they're in the field. In return that army will be able to defend you if the time comes."

"What about the death worshipers? You say our men can return home when the fighting is over, but we've all heard stories of how powerful they are, and you've made us their enemy when you joined with the Romans. We won't have any men left to defend us when they finish the Romans and continue into our lands."

"Yes, I've heard the stories, which is why I formed this alliance with the Romans. The death worshipers never stop. They conquer everything their hand touches, which means it would only be a matter of time before they fell on us. Neither we nor the Romans were powerful enough to stop them on our own, but my hope is that together we might still survive."

"A slave to one is no different than a slave to the other."

"We aren't their slave, we're their equals, but I'm not here to answer your questions or prove our decisions to you. You can go back to your village and wait for our warriors, or join us. Which is it?"

"Fy nghynefin yq fy nefoedd," the other man said, or at least that's what Ky heard.

He'd grown so used to the real-time translation from Sophus, that he'd stopped noticing it until it was gone and all that remained was the speech as the man in front of him used it.

"Sophus?" Ky queried, and worryingly got no answer.

"Sophus?" He repeated.

"*Comm … I … Diff,*" the reply finally came back, garbled and almost unintelligible.

It was a good thing that Ky was standing next to the large wooden chair, because suddenly, without warning, his left leg suddenly stopped holding his weight. It felt almost like it belonged to someone else as he lost all control and feeling of it.

Ky's hand shot out and gripped the side of the chair. His other leg was working well enough to hold him up, but he was wobbly and if he tried to move, he'd collapse. Talogren must have felt the weight Ky was putting on the chair, because the Caledonian leader looked to the side for a moment, making eye contact. Ky was still not receiving translation from anyone around him and was only hearing gibberish, so asking Talogren to send the men away would do no good. Ky returned the chieftain's gaze, and nodded his head at the door, which was the most he could do, since the village leaders were also looking at him, and any message indication he gave of problems would be seen by them at the same time.

Thankfully, Talogren was a smart man. Between feeling Ky holding himself up against the chair and the head nod, the chieftain worked out something was wrong. It still took several long minutes of Talogren talking to them, along with a few replies, before he dismissed the men out of the tent.

His timing couldn't have been better, as the AI that controlled large parts of his biology along with half of his motor control began shutting down. Ky knew that independent processes would keep his major organs going, but enough of the nanites were shutting down, along with the motor assist, that Ky wasn't getting enough resources to stay conscious. His eyes rolled back in his head and he collapsed into darkness.

Devnum

It was late when Lucilla finally rose. She'd been getting up early every morning to train most days, but she'd been so exhausted she decided to skip one day. After hearing about what happened to her the night before, her father had decided that enough was enough. The city guard was no longer effectively protecting the city and it was clear that at some level the remaining insurrectionists had penetrated their ranks.

Removing a force that had been in place for decades and replacing it with one that was both newly formed and stretched to its max was not an easy task, and required a lot of decisions to be made. Decisions that Lucilla felt she must be part of. The guard leadership wasn't happy to hear of the decision. The commander and his top lieutenants were summarily sacked. They would not be allowed to join the Praetorians or given any other position in the government that would offer anywhere near the level of power and prestige they'd had as leaders of the capital's city guard. Lucilla had counseled caution, since that would drive some of the men directly into the insurrectionists' hands.

Ramirus, crafty as ever, was hoping that might actually happen. Since the entire guard was changing over, he thought it unlikely they'd be able to bring much in the way of intel to the malcontents, and maybe the ability to reach out to some higher-level personal contacts. In exchange, Ramirus thought they could use some of these people as bait. There weren't that many of them, and they would all be known to the spymaster's people, and followed closely. Ramirus planned on keeping track of everyone they talked to, and followed them in turn. It would be a big operation and need as many of his men as he could get his hands on, but he thought it was their best shot at finally figuring out who some of the ring leaders behind the murders and the attack on Lucilla really were.

While Lucilla thought it was still much too risky, since some of the guardsmen would remain loyal to them, it could place a snake in their midst. Her father, however, liked the plan. He'd been growing more impatient and frustrated with the lack of progress they'd shown in finding any of the people behind the attacks.

The rest of the soldiers, from the junior officers on down, were given the option of transferring to the Praetorians or the legions themselves, where they'd be allowed to keep their rank and the level of pay that provided. Any of the men who asked to join the Praetorians would have to undergo intense scrutiny. More so than the regular recruits did, and that was already significant.

What's more, none of the men could serve in Devnum. Faenius said that, regardless of what kind of checks they managed to pass, he would not chance one of the men who'd helped keep the guard away from the area of the murders continuing to offer aide to the insurrectionists.

No matter the guarantees that the men were honest and loyal citizens, he was going to send them to other areas the Praetorians were being tasked with protecting. Probably one of the roadway patrols looking for brigands or as part of the force guarding the border with the Caledonii.

The switch had to happen right away. Once the guard commanders were notified it was happening, they all instantly became possible liabilities and had to go. Unfortunately, that meant pulling the rest of the Praetorians who'd been in training into service. While Velius would be happy to be getting the veterans who'd been loaned as a training cadre, Faenius was concerned they were all too green and too few in numbers to do the job properly.

The Emperor, however, wouldn't allow them to hold off. The attack on Lucilla had been the last straw. They would be able to start recruiting Caledonians soon, and more men would come over to the Praetorians as time passed. Like the legions, they now had a steady pay from the Emperor instead of promises of land and booty along with pay and benefits after they retired. Unlike the legions, however, they weren't expected to fight a Carthaginian army several times their size, which could mean more men volunteering, although that would be countered by how picky the guard would have to be. The legions sometimes brought in men from the less civilized parts of society that might be good soldiers but would make terrible guardsmen.

At least getting up late meant she was somewhere private. She usually didn't try to contact Ky until she'd been up for several hours, since she knew he didn't sleep as much as he probably should, and it was hard to predict how late they may have marched the previous day. If he was awake but busy, he could ignore her summons, but if he was asleep, he couldn't just ignore it and continue sleeping.

She did, however, want to contact him as soon as possible. Part of being designated to stand in his stead while he was up north was to pass through orders and suggestions, but the other part was to notify him of any major changes, since those could impact his plans. It seemed like a good bet that completely sacking the city guard and replacing them with the Praetorians would do just that, and definitely counted as a major change. He'd had several plans for Faenius's command and had already complained several times about their being low on manpower and how that affected the areas they could reasonably cover.

Forcing them to also act as the city guard for Devnum would stretch that manpower even further, possibly to the point where Ky would have to change his plans for them. She just hoped enough other things didn't rely on them and it wouldn't change his long-term strategy.

She also needed to tell him about the assassination attempt on her. It might be less critical, as far as his long-term planning had gone, but she knew he'd be upset if she kept it from him. Part of her wanted to, since past history had shown he might decide to get a horse and ride south to rescue her. Of course, this was a difference from past events, since she was clearly safe, for now, but there was a chance he'd decide she wasn't safe enough.

She had, however, pushed their relationship to the point where she worried keeping secrets from him might do it harm. For all of his amazing knowledge, he was completely lost when it came to how men and women relate to each other. Like Ky and his battle plans, she had a long-term strategy for the two of them, since she decided she would eventually make him hers. Keeping something like the attempt on her life secret might help her sanity, but it could hurt her strategy, and she wasn't willing to do that. Besides, he'd find out as soon as he returned to town.

"Sophus," she said quietly.

She might have privacy, but it was best if she didn't speak loud enough that the guards on the other side of her door could hear her talking to herself.

She waited for several seconds. Lucilla was still unclear exactly what Sophus was, beyond an apparently all-knowing disembodied voice, but she knew he wasn't held to the same limitations as Ky or the rest of them. He'd shown he could be speaking and working with Ky and her simultaneously with apparently no loss of focus or concentration. He normally answered her right away, as if he'd been poised, waiting for her to ask for him. The fact that he didn't worried her.

She reached up and tapped the nearly invisible piece of material in her ear like Ky showed her, which should signal both Ky and Sophus together. She hadn't had to use it much because, at her acquiescence, Sophus was always listening for her, both to have access to any information she might get and to monitor her condition, He called it 'keeping the channel open,' which didn't mean anything to her except that she just had to say his name, and he'd answer.

Again, nothing happened. She tried twice more, thinking maybe she got the motion wrong, and got the same result each time.

This was uncharted waters, and it worried her.

Chapter 12

The Village of Pertmig

"Commander," Sophus's voice said, ringing through Ky's head.

It was a vague thing, something far off in the distance. It was impossible to tell if it was imagined or real at first, the hazy first few seconds of consciousness making it seem almost like a dream, or how Ky imagined a dream would be like.

"Commander," the voice said again.

"Yes," Ky sub-vocalized, and then stopped, taking stock of the situation.

For a moment, Ky almost didn't realize where he was or what was happening, and then everything clicked into place. The loss of control in one leg, Sophus going silent and the translation stopping, and finally the darkness that had overtaken him.

"What happened," he said.

"I went offline. Failsafe systems remained in place for vital system processes, but all other systems experienced complete and sudden shutdown."

"Other stage of your system expansion?"

"Although that is the most probable explanation, I am running a self-diagnosis now to try and determine the exact nature of the fault."

"Will it happen again. This was embarrassing, but it could be fatal if you go offline during battle."

"Unknown, Commander. Until the nature of the failure is determined, it is impossible to predict reoccurrence with any degree of accuracy."

"Could ..."

"*Commander, you are not alone, and they have noticed your stirring,*" the AI warned him.

Ky's eyes popped open to the view of a tent, although not the one he and Talogren had been in when Ky had lost consciousness. The face of one of the men he'd met who regularly served Talogren loomed above him.

Checking the chronometers in his HUD, Ky saw that almost a day had passed since the meeting with the village leaders.

"He's awake," the man said, and Ky was relieved to be able to understand the man.

Sitting up, Ky looked around the room.

Someone was just leaving the tent as he did so, probably the person the man who'd been looking at him had spoken to, since only he and Ky remained in the tent.

"Talogren?" Ky asked.

"He'll be here in a moment. He asked us to stay with you until you recovered from your ... until you recovered."

Ky just nodded and sat in silence on the dirt that made up the floor of the tent. Unlike Roman tents which, for legates at least, put down carpets and thick cloth floorings, the Caledonian's didn't see the need for flooring beneath them unless it was raining and the ground had turned to mud.

Ky did a mental check of himself while he waited. Everything seemed to be fine and in place as it should be. There was no permanent damage and, thanks to his nanites, any bruising he might have suffered would have already been mostly healed.

KY pushed himself off the ground and stretched to release the tension in his body as Talogren came through the tent flap.

"You can go," he said to the man who'd been waiting for Ky. As soon as he left, Talogren said, "I'm glad you're standing. Were you poisoned?"

"No. I ... I'm not sure how to explain this in a way that will make sense. All I can say is that I'm fine, now."

"You understand that one of the reasons our people have decided it's worthwhile joining the Romans is because of the strength they see in you. There is already talk around the camp that you might not be as indestructible as you seemed to be."

137

Ky did realize that was going to be a problem. For the Caledonii, strength was everything and they'd followed him because he'd thought he was some kind of invincible harbinger of death, much like the Romans had followed him because they thought him some kind of messenger of the gods. Ky had fought against this kind of thing with the Romans, not wanting to lie to them and give them the impression he was some kind of magical being, but with the Caledonii, he'd remained silent.

The alliance with the north men was trickery, and on paper it shouldn't have worked at all. There was a century old hatred between the two people making any kind of treaty a hard sell, a point proven when the agreement pushed the Romans into open revolt to stop it from happening. Based on comments from Talogren, one of the things that had kept the Caledonii from having a similar reaction was their impression of Ky and desire to have that level of power on their own.

Eventually, he personally wouldn't be the key to holding the alliance together, but in it's infancy, it was incredibly fragile. For this moment, his collapsing just while standing silently during a meeting could be enough.

"I do understand that," Ky said. "I have never claimed to be indestructible or anything greater than any other man. I am the same man as when your people decided to follow me into an alliance with the Romans. I'm the same man whose stood before each village and demanded their surrender, and led the assault when they declined."

"Don't be naive. A leader is only as good as his last victory and the men's fortunes and support change like the wind. You don't prove yourself once to the men you lead, it happens every day. Today, they saw weakness."

"I understand it could look like that. I will do what I can to continue proving to them that you haven't made the wrong choice. What happened to the village leaders."

"Thankfully, you did not collapse in front of them. They complained like old women, but they agreed to submit and join the league. That leaves us with one more large group of villages to deal with, and then the majority of the north will be with us or dead."

"I hadn't realized how much of the country had already rallied to you. I'd been under the impression that half of the north had decided to stay independent."

"There are only a handful of villages large enough to be significant. There are more villages that will be dealt with in time, but they are tiny, barely able to sustain themselves. Most could only send three or four warriors in total to the war bands. I will leave their pacification to local chieftain I assign to watch over the area they're in."

"Good. We've already passed the height of winter, so it won't be long until the Carthaginians come for us. I want to be back with the legions in time to make sure they're ready."

"You will be. There's one fight left, and then we're done."

"Maybe they'll surrender like Pertmig did and make this easier on everyone."

"They won't. I know the chieftain of the main village. He's proud and has been the most outspoken against the league. He had dreams of bringing the north under his own banner until I took the opportunity from him. No. he'll fight."

They broke camp within the hour, the new warriors from the surrendered villages added to Talogren's total. Ky could feel the eyes of the men following as he led the horde towards their last victim. They hadn't been openly discourteous, or at least discourteous in the way it counted among the Caledonii, but Ky could feel their wariness towards him.

If anything, Talogren had been understating the level of uncertainty and concern his people had towards Ky. He had two days to their destination to figure something out, or there was a chance the entire alliance could fall apart just as it was forming.

Ky was just starting to work through possible solutions when he heard the ping that indicated Lucilla was trying to reach him. Lately, she'd been leaving the connection open, letting Sophus connect them if the AI saw Ky was free, which made the use of the query ping unexpected.

"Is everything alright?" Ky sub-vocalized when they connected.

"I was going to ask you the same thing," Lucilla said. "I was trying to reach you most of yesterday, but neither you or Sophus replied. I was worried something happened."

"Everything's fine," Ky said, not wanting to alarm her.

"He is obfuscating. There was an occurrence of some concern," Sophus said, causing Ky to frown.

Although he found he liked the AI and it's new found personality, it could, at times, be unhelpfully honest.

"What do you mean, an occurrence?"

"My system expansion has begun its process of extension into Ky's brain. Subversion of his neuron fibers caused a clash between my electrical impulses and his neuron transmitters that caused a cascading short, taking me offline and rendering Ky unconscious."

"What?" Lucilla asked, sounding completely perplexed.

Ky wasn't surprised. He understood at least the basic idea of what was happening, and much about it was confusing to him. Half the words Sophus had used had been in imperial standard, since the concepts behind the words, let alone the words themselves, had no Latin translation.

"It's fine," Ky said.

"No. I understood the part about it knocking you unconscious, so clearly it's not fine. Ky, one of the things that's important for two people who are looking at a relationship like we are is being honest with each other. If this is going to work, you have to be honest with me now."

"Sophus is in the process of becoming alive, in a way. Up till now, he's been conscious, but not a distinct personality in his own right. As you met me, he had just started this process. Had you been able to communicate with him the day we met, he would have seemed very different to you. To do that, he needs to grow his ability to think, which means extending his connection to me, and more specifically my brain. That process is causing problems."

"What will this do to you?"

Ky didn't answer, since anything he could say would either be a lie or distressing to her.

"It will most likely kill him, and possibly me as well. There are ways it is dealt with in our time period, but here, there is no way to stop the processes."

"You're dying?" Lucilla said, distressed.

"We don't know for sure. Like he said, this process isn't something that has happened much where I'm from, and we have the medical technology to deal with it. Here, there's no way to know what's going to happen."

"But you could die?"

"Maybe."

"And you didn't tell me?"

"Because I didn't want to alarm you, and because we don't actually know what's happening. It's all guessing. I could just end up going insane. Besides, we don't know how long this will take, either."

"I don't care. You can't keep this from me."

"I'm sorry. Like I said, this thing between us is new to me. I thought I was protecting you, but if you say it isn't, then I'll try and be more forthright in the future."

"Well ... good," she said, apparently taken aback by his apology. "So, what now?"

"Nothing. We're just going as if we'll always be able to keep going. There's no way to stop it, so what's going to happen is what's going to happen. Anything else would be just giving up."

"I guess that makes sense."

"I'm sorry I didn't tell you."

"Good. Just don't let it happen again."

"Okay. What did you need?" Ky asked.

"What?"

"You were trying to contact me when I didn't respond. I assume it was for something specific."

"Oh, it was. Since I'm grilling you on being honest, I should tell you there was an attempt on my life?"

"What?" Ky said.

He'd been dismayed enough that he'd let his control slip, and said it out loud, causing the men around him to all turn and look in his direction. Ky half shrugged and continue riding forward, as if it hadn't happened.

"I'm fine, so don't fly off the handle or come charging down here."

"What happened?"

"Someone hired a gang of local thugs to come after me, probably hoping they could overwhelm my security. We're pretty sure it's the same person who had Norbanus and the man who served as executioner killed. All of the attackers died and Ramirus is looking into it."

"I'm glad they underestimated you and your guards."

"They didn't, actually. That's where things get interesting. They managed to kill two of my guards and it was looking very likely they would succeed, when a group of Caledonii swooped in, killing the rest of the attackers. Apparently, Llassar took it upon himself to send men to protect me."

"Good. I'll have to thank him."

"Afterward he pointed out to my father that, considering he was now responsible for both people as the new Britannic emperor, that half of his daughters' protectors should be Caledonii. They've now doubled my guard force, and half of them are Northmen."

"That should be a good thing."

She'd already shared with Ky the strange series of changes in the Caledonii attitudes towards her, so he wasn't surprised to hear they'd want to be part of her detail. A few weeks ago, their being added to her guards would have been a problem for her, but she'd confessed a growing admiration of Llassar and his people as their attitudes to her warmed.

"Yes, although you're not going to like what happened next."

"Tell me."

"Between Norbanus and the attempt on my life, my father has lost all faith in the city guard. He's dissolved them as an organization and given the protection and policing of the city to Faenius and his men."

"Does he know how thinly they're stretched already?"

"He knows, he just doesn't care. They've taken most of the men out of training and put them into their new position. Faenius thinks he can recruit some of the guardsmen into the praetorians, but not as many as they'll need."

"We were expecting more of the men to come north to the border. The men I took as only the first wave that would be handling patrols, and I was hoping for the reinforcements soon. By the time more men are trained, we won't need them as badly, since there will be additional pressure from the growing pains of the new alliance."

"Again, he knows all this, but he felt that, if the city guard was as penetrated by the remaining insurrectionists as it seems, then it cripples the ability for him and the senate, both Roman and the new imperial senate, to govern our new alliance. I tried to make your case, but seeing as he's both my father and my emperor, he didn't seem inclined to have to listen to me."

Ky sighed and said, "I didn't mean to take out my frustrations on you. He's right, of course, but it will send ripples across the entire timetable we've been working from."

"He has the utmost confidence that you will figure out a way to make it work."

"I'd like less confidence and more help sticking to the plan, but I guess I have to live with what I have to."

"You do. Now, try to explain to me again what's happening with you."

Devnum

"Father, get up," a voice said in Decius's ear.

"What?" the craftsman said, his voice muffled and groggy as he transitioned from deep sleep to suddenly being awake.

"You must get up. They've taken Pescennius, Caius and Camillus. I've been told soldiers are headed this way. You must leave town, tonight."

"What happened?" Decius said, his brain still slow to catch up.

His son, Mettius, was leaning over Decius's bed, his hands still on his fathers shoulders. Decius recognized the names of the other leaders in his cell of republicans. They'd come together after the failed coup to restore the republic and had worked closely to undermine the new Consul and his plans to destroy Rome.

What Decius didn't understand what Mettius meant by 'taken'.

"Ramirus's men burst into their homes about an hour ago and dragged all three men from their beds and towards one of his black chambers in the palace. A few minutes ago they started sending out patrols of praetorians and rounding up other men from the group."

"How did they find us?"

"I don't know, but they did and you know that it's impossible for them to stay quiet for long once Ramirus's torturers do their work. I'm sure one of the men talked and is giving names. All three men know us. Ramirus will have our names by now and I left just ahead of more patrols coming this way. They're traveling slowly, but they'll be here any minute. We don't have time to waste talking about this. We must leave. Now."

Decius was glad his wife wasn't here to see her husband run from their home. She'd died three years ago in one of the plagues that seemed to sweep through the city every couple of years. She'd always believed in Decius and he'd enjoyed her unconditional support and faith. Watching him and their son turn tail and run like scared children would have destroyed her.

The marble-worker pushed himself out of bed and threw on one of the simple tunics. Grabbing a sword for protection, Decius left the rest of the accumulations of his life behind and led his son out their front door. Mettius hadn't been wrong about being just ahead of the praetorians. He could hear the men's synchronous steps slam into the ground in unison as they marched towards him.

"We'll make for the countryside. Placus has a villa there."

"They'll have Placus's name by now," Mettius said as they turned and headed north out of town, away from the oncoming praetorians. "Running from here just to be caught there will do no good."

"He's staying at his home here, so there's no one at his villa besides servants. Ramirus will know that, and won't bother to send troops there any time soon. By the time he does get around to checking Placus's other properties, we'll be gone. We just need somewhere I can stay for a bit and work out a plan of where to go next."

They paused at the major street that led from the palace to the city gates. It was late, but not so late that the street was emptied yet. Seeing that the way was clear, they started to dash across and Decius was starting to think they might make their getaway clean when voices came from down the thoroughfare. Turning, he could see several men in the armor of the new praetorian guard running in their direction.

"Run, father. I'll hold them off long enough for you to get out of the city. They'll start checking on outlying residences for you soon, so don't stay long, a day at most. Then go to one of the smaller cities far from here."

"I'm not leaving you here," Decius said, starting to pull his own sword.

"No. You know some of the other groups in town. If the imperials get their hands on you, they will be able to unravel our whole network. You must escape. I'll be fine."

Both men knew that was a lie. Mettius was a healthy young man, but he'd been raised to be a craftsman. A marble worker like his father. He wasn't a match for the men of the praetorian guard. Decius knew that this would probably be the last time he saw his son alive, and felt a stab of guilt for having dragged his son into the conspiracy in the first place.

"Go," Mettius said, urgently as the guards closed on them.

With one last look, Decius ran north, away from the chasing guards and his son, the sounds of steel clashing with steel ringing in his ears.

Chapter 13

"He's the son of a local craftsman who we think might be the ringleader of this little band," Ramirus was saying as she walked into the room.

Lucilla had been woken after only an hour of sleep and taken into her father's audience chamber, to find him, several key senators and Faenius already there, although each looking as raggedly tired as she felt. The push both by Faenius to get the praetorians in place of the city guard and Ramirus to find the insurrectionists behind the attempt on her life had led to several nights of late meetings. They had only finished up their last conversation two hours previously.

"I'm sorry to have roused you, my lady," Ramirus said when he noticed her enter the room. "Your father thought that, as the Consul's appointed agent, you should be here for this."

"My father is right, of course. Don't apologize," She said. "Just tell us what's happened."

"I received information yesterday afternoon that my agents have been tracking down all day. Early last night we took the guardsman we believed behind the orders to clear the area around Senator Norbanus's murder and where the attempt on your life occurred. After several hours of questioning, we got the names of his contacts inside what looks to be the cell of men behind it. Further arrests and interrogations suggest there are multiple such cells working independently in town, and only their leader, a marble carver named Decius Sestius Gorgonius, knew the names of men in the other cells. We didn't get his name until very late, and he was able to catch wind of the raids and escape before we got to him. His son was injured in a clash with the praetorians chasing Decius, and was taken captive, but will not say where he went."

"Do you have any thoughts on where he might be going?"

"I think he was leaving the city, heading north. We are trying to track through people he knew and had business with, to see if any of them have homes that way, maybe a farm or a villa outside of town, but it will take time to come up with a list and start searching."

"Is it reasonable to assume a man capable of leading a cell and murdering a senator would stay very long, knowing you'd be doing that very thing?" The Emperor asked.

"No, and I don't think he will. If I had to guess, I'd say he'd try to make for one of the smaller cities. We're also looking into possible connections he'd have with other towns and businesses. As a marble craftsman, he'd know people closer to the quarries near the border. If he went anywhere, he'd go there."

"Unless he were smart enough to know you'd follow that line of reasoning," Lucilla said.

"Maybe, but being on the run isn't just about avoiding the people chasing you. If you're a wanted man, especially one with little access to resources and money, you'd have to still acquire lodging to get off the streets, someone to help supply you with food and other necessities, and probably a way of getting outside news, especially if you were the local leader of a rebellion against the Emperor. All that requires contacts and means picking a random city on a map might not help."

"Could he be going south, towards the Carthaginians like …" Faenius started to say and then paused, his eyes darting towards the Emperor.

"Like my son, you mean," the Emperor supplied.

"Yes. Forgive me, Princeps. I don't mean to open wounds, but it must be considered."

"Rightfully so. I have never been the sort to crucify a man for asking questions; especially those that I must hear, regardless of how uncomfortable they may be," he said to the praetorian commander, before turning his attention back to Ramirus. "Could he try and follow my son?"

"Perhaps, but it would be foolhardy. From everything we can find, Decius is a man used to the finer things in life. He hasn't spent much time outside of the city, except to visit marble quarries, which he does rarely and in style when forced to. He's not going to be able to cut cross country, make it through both our and the Carthaginian lines, and safely to Londinium. Your son spent a fair amount of time with the legion on campaign and left while the legions were fully occupied engaging each other. Since the Carthaginian scout was found, Velius has dramatically increased the number of patrols to the south, in attempts to keep the Carthaginians as much in the dark about our plans as possible. I've already sent word to him to increase his patrols along the border. If he goes that way, I'm positive we'll get him."

"And if he doesn't?" Lucilla asked.

"We'll still get him, but it may take longer, and potentially not before he can cause more problems."

"What about the men you caught?"

"We still have questions for them, but by this point, we've normally gotten everything useful we can get out of them. Anything they haven't told us by now, they probably won't."

"Bring them here," the Emperor commanded.

"Are you sure that's wise?" Ramirus asked, almost apologetically. "These are men actively engaged in destroying your government. They are dangerous."

"I have my own guards, the commander of the praetorians here, and they are unarmed. Are you suggesting they are still likely to be able to reach me while in chains, let alone harm me?"

"It is unlikely, Princeps, but considering the damage they have wrought already, I just suggest caution."

"Then you should be cautious. Bring them in," he said, his tone making it clear he did not want to say the request a third time.

Ramirus nodded and left. Lucilla, her father, and his assembled advisors waited in silence for the spymaster's return. Finally, Ramirus reappeared, followed by six men, each being escorted by a praetorian. The men all had various degrees of injuries, from simple bruises to bloody bandages over what were clearly serious wounds.

"None of these men are the ring leader, correct?"

"No. This one," Ramirus said, pointing at a younger man who had one arm in a sling and a bandage over one of his eyes. "Is the son of the man we believe to be the ring leader of this group."

"Where is your father?" The Emperor asked the young man.

In reply, the man spat on the floor, only to be knocked to his knees when the guard accompanying him slapped him across the face.

"No need for that," the Emperor said. "If he won't talk, he won't. Beating him any more won't entice him out of silence. I will ask again, however. Will you tell me where your father is?"

"I will tell you nothing," the young man said, pushing himself back upright with his one good arm. "You are a pretender. You abdicated your throne to a demon sent from Hades himself to destroy Rome. You can burn, for all I care."

"I see," the Emperor said, clearly unphased by the tirade. "Lucilla, as the Consul's assigned representative, what should be done with these men."

"Ramirus, do you believe you've gotten everything you can from them?"

"I would like more time, my lady."

"Fine. Take them back to your dungeons and continue questioning them. When you feel like you've done all you can, they are to be executed in the same manner as the men they still follow. No need for a show execution this time. Just take their heads and be done with them."

To his credit, the young man didn't flinch. Maybe he already knew this was how it had to end, or maybe he just believed in his cause so much that he didn't care about his own life. Either way, he handled the news of his pending execution well. A part of Lucilla felt bad having ordered the death of someone like that, but only a very small part. Seeing as he was part of the group that had ordered her murder.

The other men did not take the news as well, with several falling to the ground in tears. With a nod, the guards led, or in some cases, dragged, the rebels out of the room and towards their fate.

Outside the Village of Rhaeadr

No meeting or ultimatum was needed this time, Ky thought standing with the rest of Talogren's Caledonians looking across the open field at the forces assembled against them. Based on Talogren's description of the population levels in the area and how many villages they faced, the last holdouts must have pulled in every adult male in defense of their villages.

For where they were, in a corner of an already underpopulated area of the country, it was an impressive display and would have, no doubt, been able to fend off most local challenges. Impressive as it was, though, they had to know they didn't stand a chance against Talogren's horde, which had grown slightly in size as warriors from the surrendered villages were added to his forces. Talogren probably had three to one odds against the holdouts, which made their stand all that much braver... and foolish. Of course, the Romans had defeated armies with that size disparity, although if these men fought the same way as the rest of the north men, there wouldn't be much in the way of maneuver for better field position. It would just be a pair of headlong clashes into each other, where the number of men present would absolutely make the difference.

Ky's presence wouldn't swing the balance one way or another, but since his collapse, he needed to re-establish the Caledonian's belief in him. Ky still found it absurd that, somehow, his perceived strength was the lynchpin of the entire alliance.

Ky strode forward, away from Talogren's forces, stopping in the center of the open field between the two forces. A ripple went across the warriors facing him, as they tried to figure out what he was doing. They would have heard about him by now, how blades couldn't touch them and how he tore through warriors that opposed them, and so were maybe prepared for Talogren to send Ky forward on his own, as some sort of message. Ky's stopping before he reached them, however, wasn't on the script they'd expected.

For his part, Ky wanted to make sure he had everyone's attention for what happened next. Partially the other side, in hopes that they might just surrender on the spot, but also Talogren's men, so they could see what Ky was actually capable of, if need be.

Sophus had already tried to talk him out of this plan. Victory was all but certain, which meant any additional use of resources was a waste, especially the irreplaceable resources from the future.

Ky reached down and pulled his sidearm, pointing the sleek weapon and pointing it directly at the center of the line in front of him. He had very few rounds left, but he'd judged that the psychological effect on his allies was worth their expenditure.

The first round of super-heated gas ejected out of the weapon, flying towards the men across from him. It took less than a second to reach its target, which wasn't enough to change their fate, but was enough for the men to react. None did, however, because they did not recognize what they were seeing. Much of the technology Ky used was invisible, but the people of this time could at least grasp the basic uses of them. Super-heated pellets of plasma might have just been magic for how alien it was to them.

The ball splashed against the men in the front rank, melting away metal, leather, and bone and set the men around them on fire. The thick wool and hide clothes they wore to stay warm caught easily from the radiated heat of the plasma, killing dozens in the center of the line, along with most of their leaders, who'd been with what would be their vanguard, when the charge began.

Ky fired twice more, aiming along the middle of the left and right wings of the force, effectively carving the solid line in front of him into four pieces, each separated by several yards of melted and burning flesh.

Once again, Ky was impressed by the northerner's ability to remain steadfast in the face of danger. Doubly so when that danger was so alien and the result so ghastly. When he'd done the same thing to the Carthaginians, shortly after his arrival on this version of Earth, nearly every single soldier had turned and fled at the sight of the men suddenly reduced to ashes. Only a few dozen of the men facing him turned and fled for safety. The rest paused for a moment, trying to force themselves to comprehend what had just happened, and then did what Ky and thought the least likely of reactions; they charged.

It was as if the murder of their leaders was a signal for the battle to begin. The men bellowed their anger and began running forward in a mass of beards, fur, and blades. Ky knew he wasn't going to avoid all conflict, but he'd hoped the display would have a greater impact than it did.

Replacing his sidearm, Ky pulled up his sword and waved it forward, which was the signal for his side to begin their counter charge, which was the only tactic the men under his command would accept. As he gave the signal, he began to run forward as well, first at a trot and then building up speed. His enhanced muscle allowed him to chew up terrain at a rate unmatched by anyone on the field, which meant he steadily increased the distance between himself and his supporting forces.

The first men ricocheted off of his kinetic shielding, the weapons and bodies sliding off its reactive surface. Using the muscle assist and predictive targeting from Sophus, Ky was able to time his swings in between the hits, his sword slashing through openings here and there to find flesh and his enhanced strength forcing the blade through hide and iron. The enemy line bowed around him, where the reformed center began piling in on Ky as the outer edges continued their charge, creating an almost shallow V.

It was a costly mistake given how the North men fought. It forced each man from the opposing village to face both the man in front of him and the men to the sides, since Talogren's forces hit in a straight line, while the independent forces slowly collapsed into them piecemeal.

Around Ky, men began falling in twos and threes, the pile of bodies growing quickly, to the point where it started becoming difficult for more men to pile onto him. With the added distraction of the Caledonian warriors piling on, it was getting harder and harder to find targets for his blade.

Ky had sent his drone aloft at the start of the battle, allowing him to have a bird's eye view of what was happening. He'd found that the chaos on the ground, along with the dust clouds and close quarters press of men, made it hard to get a tactical view of what was happening without it.

Through the take from the drone, he could see the opposing forces start to give way. Even without Ky's blasts, the odds had been too great against them, but with it and the slaughter that followed, even the bravest men began to waver.

Ky was about to pull himself back to focus on the cleanup, specifically doing what he could to keep the atrocities from getting too far out of hand, when the feed from the drone suddenly cut out.

Ky had enough time to say Sophus's name before the world dropped out from under him. He could just feel the kinetic shield shutting off and the first blade getting through his protection when he lost all control of his limbs and then the world went black.

Chapter 14

Devnum

Lucilla ducked back from Cynwrig's swing, whipping her wooden practice blade around in a slashing motion, coming down under his swing in a counter, and for a second she thought she had him, until his knee tapped the side of her temple.

She knew that, if he'd wanted, he could have dropped her with the blow, knocking her out or even smashing pieces of her skull into her brain. The Caledonian who now served as one of her protectors had partially taken over her training from Modius, who wasn't thrilled by the substitution, but deferred to her judgement.

Besides the point that it was one more step in her own small efforts towards nation building, Cynwrig made the excellent point that the Caledonian way of fighting was markedly different from the Roman style. While he agreed, grudgingly, that the Romans were better in massed formation, he argued that the Caledonians were more skilled in one-on-one fighting, especially in the chaotic melees like the one that occurred during the attempt on her life. She'd been swayed by his arguments, and genuinely interested in learning a different style. The more she'd practiced with her guards, the more she'd found she both enjoyed the experience and found the subject fascinating.

She also realized quickly how lucky she had gotten during the wrestling match. At the time, she thought he'd just been young and inexperienced, prejudging him just as much as he'd prejudged her. It was only sheer luck that his underestimation of her had been the greater mistake of the two. If she was a Caledonian , he would have easily beaten her.

"No, stupid woman. Only a fool leans into their enemy, extending their necks like a lamb prepared for slaughter."

Modius frowned at the clear breach of protocol, but Lucilla stood up and just nodded at the correction. She understood that Cynwrig didn't mean it as a personal attack, it was just the blunt nature of how the north men dealt with things.

"If I lean back, I wouldn't have the range to do more than scratch you with the tip of the sword."

"You need to reposition your body. Don't just stand still and bend over, turn as you bend, and away from the cut, giving you the range with which to reach your opponent without offering yourself up as their next victim."

"Okay. Let's do it again."

She set herself up to go again when a voice screamed in her head.

"Lucilla, we ..." Sophus began to say, and then abruptly cut off.

Every time she'd heard the disembodied voice speak, it had been calm and evenly measured, with no sense of emotion. This time, there still wasn't a sense of emotion, at least in the way she thought about it. But the volume and speed that the message started with and then abruptly ended gave her the strong feeling of something major being wrong.

It had been so sudden and loud, that the attack she had just started turned into a stumble, ended with her flat on the ground, thankful that her reflex response was to put her hands out and keep her face from smashing into the ground.

"Are you okay?" Modius asked, rushing to her side to help her out.

"Something's happened," she said, without really thinking.

She knew, deep inside her, what had happened. Although she still didn't understand the mechanics of it, Sophus and Ky had made it clear how much danger the two of them were in from whatever invisible force was smashing them together into one being. Sophus's sudden alarm and then silence could only mean that the thing they'd warned her about had happened.

Of course, none of the men around her knew about her invisible friend and the danger it and Ky were in.

"Were you injured?" Cynwrig asked.

"No. Ky's in danger. I must go see my father."

She turned and hurried towards the palace, still holding her practice sword, the guards suddenly rushing to keep up with her.

Her father and Velius were in a private session with the Pontiff Maximus and several lower priests, sacrificing a pair of goats as part of a ceremony to gain the gods favor in the upcoming battle. All of the men turned suddenly, and had very different reactions.

The Pontiff Maximus, a pompous man who Lucilla had never gotten along with, turned red and looked ready to yell at her for interrupting the ceremony while the under-priests all looked to him, knowing the man's legendary temper, especially with women.

Her father, however, cut the man off when he pushed himself up and ran to his daughter, asking, "What's wrong?"

Even without the obvious distress on her face, it would have been clear that she was in some kind of distress. She was in a simple, lose fitting knee length tunic he knew she wore during her training session and was still holding her wooden training sword. It made for a strange sight compared to all of the men in the small temple to Zeus dressed in ceremonial toga's and regal accouterments.

"Something's happened to Ky. I need to go North and find him."

"Was there a messenger?" Her father asked, turning to Velius.

Since no one knew about her connection with Ky, her father and everyone else would have assumed anything he needed to communicate with them would have come by messenger, and any messenger would have been one of the praetorian or legion men, since that was who was still up by the border.

"No, Principes."

"I didn't receive a message, I just know that he's in trouble and needs help."

"My Lady, I know you care deeply for the Consul, but I've seen him in the thick of battle with no blade touching him. I assure you there is nothing in the north that could put him in danger."

His tone was respectful and she was sure Velius had good intentions, but besides not having all of the information she had, he had some of the same prejudices against women that most of the men in Rome had. They were all ready to dismiss her concern as foolish female hysteria.

Thankfully, her father knew both her and Ky better than that. He'd received some of Ky's magic, even if Ky refused to call it that, when he was healed by one of Ky's devices. Now that she had some of the small devices that Ky had released into both her and her father, she knew how much better they could make someone feel. It was impossible to distinguish it from mystical god-like powers, and Ky and Sophus had tried to explain the small machines to her. This gave her father some notion of Ky's abilities.

"Father," she said, looking at him levelly, her tone even and steady. "I'm telling you he's in mortal danger."

"Legate, get together a century," he said to the commander, making it clear he was taking her report seriously.

"It's not the kind of danger that soldiers can fix. I can't explain it, but I know that he needs my help. I am going to him … today."

"My lady, we've picked up two more scouts. The Carthaginians are coming, and they're coming soon. I don't think they're waiting for all of the snows to melt anymore. The Consul left you in charge and we need your guidance. Besides, even with our new allies, the roads are dangerous, especially if you travel north of the border. If something does happen to the Consul, I'm not sure the Empire can survive losing both of you."

"I appreciate your reliance on me, Legate, but I've been at every council of war and several of your training maneuvers, and you don't need me. You know Ky's battle plan as well as I do, better actually, since I can't appreciate some of the tactical specifics the way you can. I appreciate your concern, but I will have Caledonian guards as well as Roman, which should help offset any problems once we cross the border, so what is your actual concern?"

Velius looked away. They both knew his concern was her going off by herself again. While she might be able to write it off as a reaction to what happened to her the last time, she knew a good part of it was just also the built in prejudices towards women by all Romans, regardless of their position in society or who their father might be.

"Father?" she asked when the Legate declined to answer.

"As always, my concern is for your safety. Regardless of the number of guards you take, there is danger."

"I think we've seen there's just as much danger if I stay here. I am touched that you are worried about me, but we need Ky if we are going to survive what's coming. We all know it. I'm going to go get him."

As with any daughter, she and her father had pitted their wills against each other before. Sometimes she won those battles and sometimes her father won, but that history meant she knew he recognized that she was not going to give in. She gave him a look that made it clear he would have to physically restrain her to keep her from going after the man she loved.

"Take extra men with you and first go and meet up with the Caledonian leader, so he knows you're there. I will send a message for you to take to him that will make it clear that I am holding him accountable for your safety."

She nodded in agreement and turned, hurrying back to her quarters to change into more appropriate clothing for traveling and prepare for the trip north as Modius gathered the men they'd need.

Within ten minutes of reaching her quarters, Lucilla was ready to leave and growing increasingly impatient waiting on Modius to show up and let her know the guards were all ready to accompany her.

Part of her just wanted to leave and let the men catch up, but she refrained from following that impulse. After the death of Norbanus, Modius had demanded she promise to not travel from place to place without guards, and he'd only redoubled that insistence after the attempt on her own life.

She also understood what was taking so long, since besides men and equipment, he also had to gather at least basic supplies such as food for the travel North. When she'd arrived at her quarters, he'd reminded her of her promise before leaving, and she'd reminded him that they needed to travel fast. What that mostly meant was not trying to acquire a carriage or some other transportation, which would both slow them down and take time to find. She knew he didn't like the idea of her just traveling on horseback. Unlike her previous guard commander, who'd died getting her out of

Glevnum shortly before she met Ky for the first time, Modius was a stickler for social niceties and frowned like an old matron at the thought of Lucilla lowering herself to some commoner standard.

So she waited, growing increasingly impatient, until finally there was a knock at the door.

"It's about ..." she started to say as she flung the door open, only to stop in surprise when she realized Modius wasn't the person knocking on her door.

"I came to tell you that I and some of the men who traveled south will be returning North with you," Llassar said in his normal straightforward manner.

"What?" she said, her mind still catching up from the unexpected vision. "Sorry, but I thought you were going to remain here and see to the training of your men, and lead them into battle."

"I have men handling the day to day training who are already working with some of your soldiers to integrate our forces. Our men are able to continue on a task without needing someone to hold their hand, and I do plan on being back before the death worshipers arrive. I only need a few days to confer with Talogren and then I and most of the men will return. Your Consul is also north and plans on being back before the battle, so I don't see this as much of a problem."

Had she known Llassar had come to genuinely like some Romans she would have thought that dig was more of an insult than it was. She'd gotten to know the Caledonian well enough to know that it was just his personality and general mistrust of anything he didn't grow up with, and not an actual animosity to his new allies.

"I, of course, would love your company on the road if you feel it's important, I'm just at a loss as to why you'd need to confer with your chief. He sent you down to train the men and have them work with our soldiers to fight off the Carthaginians. Despite everything that's happened, that hasn't changed. I was under the impression that Caledonians didn't need the constant reassurance and hand holding that my people did."

Llassar let a small smile slip through his stoic mask at the last comment, which was very much something he would have said if their positions were reversed, before slipping again into a practiced non-expression, or so Lucilla first thought.

After a moment, she realized that it wasn't his normal face, but one of concentration, almost as if he were arguing with himself or coming to a decision. It was a subtle difference, but it was there.

"I do not like playing nursemaid, even to my own men," Llassar said. "I was never one to handle this kind of thing back home and am ill-suited for it."

"Really? I was planning on telling your chieftains how amazing a job you have done so far. Incidents between your people and mine are at a bare minimum and those that do happen are minor and from everything I can see the training and integration with our forces is going as well as could be. You seem very well suited for this."

"Being good at something and being well suited for it are not the same thing," he said, almost as a tutor might lecture his student. "I, of course, can do what is required of me, but I would like to be doing something else. Talogren and my countrymen are fighting to bring the north under Caledonian rule, and I am here reminding bored warriors to be on their best behavior. I should be there, fighting."

"There will be lots of chances for fighting," Lucilla pointed out.

"You misunderstand me. I'm not one of the mindless brutes who just wants to kill something. I meant I want to be fighting for something important, like my people are doing up north, right now. I plan on asking Talogren to release me from my current duty and return to help pacify the north."

She'd been serious when she'd said he'd been doing a good job keeping control of the Northmen now living among the Romans. The two cultures were very different and she had been amazed by how few conflicts and problems there had been, and it was clear that his controlling influence had been the largest contributor to keeping problems from escalating.

She'd met some of his lieutenants and, while they were good men, she didn't think they had the talent or the same level of respect needed to do the same. Of course, if the man was miserable, it wasn't right to force him to stay here. As the Emperor's daughter, she'd been put in the same position many times, forced to carry out an important task that she loathed.

There was also the fact that this is the most personal thing he'd shared with her to date. Since she'd met him, the man had been a closed book. He didn't have a problem expressing opinions about specific topics, but he'd never shared any part of himself. The fact that he was sent to lead this group spoke to how important he was among the Caledonians themselves, and this was a big step towards their working relationship.

"I see. Well then get what you need to together quickly. I would like to leave as soon as Modius returns with the supplies needed for the trip."

Llassar nodded and left. For an outside observer, it might have seemed curt, but she thought she could detect a slight glimpse of gratitude at her acceptance of his explanation. Of course, it was hard to tell with him.

Chapter 15

Velius grumbled to himself as he looked over the scrolls, papyrus, and wax tablets stacked on the table in front of him. When he'd been raised to legate, he'd accepted the bureaucracy requirements that came with the position, but since Ky's arrival, the amount of record-keeping had exploded.

On the one hand, Velius understood the need for all of the documentation. Before his arrival, a legion was a community where the soldiers who served it rarely moved to another legion. They were almost personal units to the legate and his sub-officers as they were servants of the Empire as a whole. Considering the recent insurrection and past civil unrest, he agreed that the system had to be changed, but the new policy of shifting men around came with far more paperwork than Velius had originally envisioned when agreeing to it. Many of the systems that had previously worked had suddenly become untenable with the new system, and the solution always seemed to be mountains of reports.

In the old days, the legion would generally only know of the performance of whole units. The legate would only know about the cohorts and the commanders of the cohorts would only know about the centuries under his command, and so forth. Soldiers were raised in rank on the recommendation of the officer directly above him except in the rare case where a soldier did something noteworthy enough to become known to higher levels of command.

Now, it wasn't uncommon for soldiers to be unknown to their officers, which meant it was impossible to know if a given soldier had done something to make promotion deserved. The move had additional complications, such as increased practice and drill times.

Combat was exhausting and even a fit, well-trained soldier could only manage to be effective for five to ten minutes of direct contact before becoming too exhausted to continue. One of the strengths of a legion is the ability for troops on the front lines to rotate back as they tired, letting fresh troops move forward to take their place.

These exchanges required fine precision built off of a unit operating as a single, well-oiled machine. If a century were off on their timing, dangerous gaps could open in the line, and even a brief exposure could lead to the line breaking. All of this was true the higher up in formations things got. The solution to this is for a soldier to know the men around him to such a degree that they could predict what those men would do before they did it. Without the familiarity bred by long periods of service with the same group of men, the only other solution was increased levels of training.

The problems only amplified as the formations got larger, because the same thing that was true inside a century was also true between centuries or cohorts. Entire centuries or even cohorts could be rotated as needed to bring up fresh troops, and those exchanges needed larger scale training exercises, all of which would take entire legions out of combat readiness as they re-trained.

Ky had promised that, eventually, new technology would allow for some changes in this process. Velius wasn't sure what Ky had referred to when he talked about new forms of weapons that were less physically taxing on the soldiers, but so far the Consul hadn't steered them wrong, so Velius was sure that he'd eventually learn what these things were. Until then, however, the reality of the changes caused by rotating soldiers existed, mostly on the shoulders of Velius and the other legates.

Which brought him to the records still stacked in front of him.

"Sir," one of the guards in front of his tent said, breaking his concentration.

Velius looked up to see the tent flap pulled back to show Ursinus, the newest legate, waiting to speak to him. Velius sighed internally, fighting to keep his face neutral.

It wasn't that he disliked the man. In fact, the opposite was true. When he'd first heard one of Lucilla's guard detail was being raised from a mere Optio all the way up to a legate, he'd been worried. That kind of jump almost only ever came as a reward for some favorable service done or as a political move, and always at the detriment to the legion itself.

True, Lucilla had never struck him as that kind of person, but she'd lived her entire life in the upper echelons of Roman politics and even the Emperor, who Velius knew to be a good man, had been forced to make similar moves in the past. It was just how the game was played and the repercussions of it were just something that men like Velius had to deal with.

He was more than thankful that didn't turn out to be the case, here. Ursinus was a thoughtful and intelligent man who cared about the troops under his command while still having the ability to put them in harm's way to get a job done, which was an important combination in a combat leader. What's more, he'd been willing to admit to the things he didn't know and worked to learn them or ask for help rather than bluster his way through trying to save face.

There had been growing pains, of course. You couldn't jump two-thirds of the Roman military hierarchy in a single leap without there being issues, and Ursinus had needed more hand-holding than the normal newly minted legate, but he was trying.

Unfortunately, Velius knew why Ursinus had darkened his doorway, and why he'd had to control himself from expressing displeasure at the visit.

"Ursinus, it's good to see you," Velius said with a forced smile.

"I doubt that, since I know you have an idea of why I'm here."

"I assume it's the unit changes you got this morning."

"You assume correctly. Did you see the list I received?'

"Yes. I approved all of those changes."

"I get that we have a manpower problem, but mine is the newest legion and has the smallest number of experienced small unit leaders and yet I have the largest collection of Pic... sorry, Caledonian transfers of any legion. Ten of whom are scheduled to become Decanus and one who's supposed to be an Optio."

"You feel they shouldn't be leading other men into combat?"

"They don't have the experience fighting in our style of close drill, let alone leading other men to do it. Besides, we're already having issues with soldiers not wanting to follow untrained leaders. What do you think will happen when they find out they have to report to one of those people?"

"Have you spoken to any of the ten men?"

"Not yet," Ursinus said, looking wary.

"You really should. These men have led hundreds of their own warriors into battle, so eight Romans shouldn't prove that much of a challenge. On top of that, they have done well in adapting to our style during training. Be glad you're not Aelius, who was in here this morning complaining about his transfers, a full third of whom are officers pulled out of the surrendered Carthaginians."

"Oh!" Ursinus said.

Velius didn't blame him. It was easy to get lost in your own problems and miss out on the bigger picture. It was, actually, one of the bigger problems he'd had in adjusting to his new position as overall commander.

"I'm surprised you didn't complain about the large contingent of ex-slaves you were assigned."

"I thought so too when I first saw them, but they had already been dispersed to their units while I was in the city, and the reports I received when I returned were generally fairly good. They are, as a lot, uneducated and have to be taught the simple things I'd expect any other new recruit to learn, but my officers couldn't stop commenting on their drive and motivation."

"That's generally what everyone else has reported, too. All of the fears about their wanting to overthrow the government or whatever seem to be unfounded. If anything, what I'm hearing is that they want to prove themselves, and go twice as hard as any regular recruit."

"Which is my biggest complaint about the north men. My men constantly report unwillingness to train and contempt towards any attempt to motivate them. They look down on any Roman officers over them."

"That also seems to be common among the complaints I heard, which is why we gave you the majority of the Caledonians slated to be officers. They don't have contempt for all leaders, just a cultural bias that we have to get around. Until they adapt, put the Caledonian officers in charge of the units with the largest number of their countrymen, and have them camp next to the units that don't have Caledonian officers, but still have units with higher proportions. They're more likely to keep their countrymen in line. Before he headed north, I brought my concerns about this very topic up with the Consul, and he assured me that, once they'd all been tested in battle together, a lot of the prejudices would go away, or at least be tempered."

"That's a good idea."

"Which is why I am paid so well," he said, and both men laughed.

Traditionally, Legates made a notable amount of money, but usually, through their hefty percentage of the spoils their legion collected. Although they never came out and said it, Velius had been sure that one of Eborius and Pius's big complaints had been Ky's making the taking of spoils illegal and banning it from all of the legions. He'd compensated the soldiers themselves with regular pay that more than made up for their losses, considering they only got spoils during times of actual conflict, but the amount of money a legate could make from the sack of a fair-sized city was more than anyone would pay one commander, when they actually had time to think about it.

Although legates were still compensated more than any other class of soldier, it wouldn't set them up in a villa for the rest of their lives.

"Since you're here, you could always stay and help me go over these reports," Velius said, waving at the stack in front of him.

"Uhh ... I suddenly realized I have a staff meeting I have to prepare for," Ursinus said, half turning to go while eyeing the paperwork.

Velius laughed and came around the table, "I was only joking, don't feel like you have to rush out immediately. How about having dinner instead?"

"I guess the preparations for the staff meeting can wait," Ursinus replied.

While he didn't end up helping Velius with his paperwork, the command legate did find it helpful to have someone to bounce ideas off of. The one thing they both could agree on was that they'd be happier when Ky returned.

The Village of Rhaeadr

Lucilla made good time getting north, although she didn't ride horses until they dropped dead like Ky had done for his mad dash, so she didn't quite make the same time he had. Even in her haste, she hadn't failed to notice how well Modius and Cynwrig had worked to get her to Ky as quickly as possible, sending riders north to both the praetorians and the Caledonian scouts patrolling the border.

Having Llassar along proved its worth when he cut through any hesitancy by Caledonians who didn't see the need to help the daughter of the Emperor the way the praetorians would, and getting them to both lead Lucilla's party to where Talogren was currently camped and send a rider ahead to make sure they knew she was coming.

This saved the time it would have taken wandering around the northern hinterlands searching for their chieftain. That had been helped by the fact that Talogren had remained camped outside the field of his last battle, which concerned Lucilla.

They were well north and west, essentially at the edge of their territory. According to Llassar, the villages further north or against the coast were so small as to generally be ignored or go unnoticed. Considering all of the people and land Talogren had added to his newly expanded league, it didn't make sense for him to stay so disconnected, especially since the base of his power was at the very opposite end corner of Caledonian lands. Staying here meant needing to constantly communicate with local chieftains about the various items that plagued any chief of state, which was a cumbersome way to lead.

Lucilla could think of very few things that would keep them sedentary in one spot like that, and Ky being seriously injured was one of those.

Ky'd related how personally the north men had taken his connection to the Empire and the value they seemed to place on him. At the time, he'd mostly been explaining as a way of complaining, since he was not a fan of what he considered undue attention, but it was an indicator of how important he was and what his incapacitation would mean for them.

Instead of taking them to Ky directly, they were directed to a tent in the center of the camped Caledonians that was slightly larger than the tents surrounding it. Talogren had been speaking with someone when they walked in, waving the person off as soon as he saw them. Lucilla couldn't help but notice the chieftain's eyes flicking to Llassar, who remained standing beside and slightly behind her. She'd learned enough about the northern culture to know this position was one of, not quite subservience, but something like it. It allowed the primary person in a group to stand ahead of the rest and be seen and heard. In groups of roughly equal status people, they'd all kind of hustle to be closest to the person they were talking to, usually with a fair amount of pushing and shoving. She assumed Llassar remained there as a show of support and a silent sign to his chieftain that she wasn't the same person who'd been brought bound into their camp the last time she'd faced Talogren.

"Why are you here?" he asked, skipping all of the pleasantries and preamble.

"I felt that Ky was in trouble and I came to see him, and hopefully help him if I could."

Talogren's eyes narrowed at this.

"Are you claiming to be some kind of seer?"

He was rightfully suspicious. In Rome, people who claimed some kind of power from the gods were all too common. They could usually be found on street corners offering to see your future for a few sesterces, although the more talented con men had managed to amass a small fortune grifting off people who desperately wanted some kind of sign. In the north, powers from the gods were taken a lot more seriously, and men who could not prove their claims or found to be frauds were often found murdered by their disappointed targets.

It's one of the reasons they'd been so easily persuaded by Ky. Had just a warrior, no matter how talented, shown up offering an alliance with the Romans, there would have been little chance any of the Caledonians would listen, let alone go along with it. They'd all witnessed some of Ky's remarkable feats. He'd been able to do things, visibly and in front of witnesses, that could only be made possible with gifts from the gods.

Lucilla's claim of knowledge she couldn't possibly have had was rightfully suspicious to them.

"No, but Ky does, and I have a connection with him that let me know he was in danger."

Despite the seriousness of the situation, she couldn't help but be amused at how carefully she was choosing her words, and the parallels with how Ky had also done the same. She'd originally thought it strange that he didn't just agree that he'd been sent by the gods, but she could see now that not only would the lie have bothered him, but how careful he had to be to maintain the trust he was building with everyone. Now that she knew, at least in a theoretical way, since she'd never understood his and Sophus's full explanation, that his gifts were somehow man-made, she found herself trying to thread the same needle.

"We sent messengers south," he said, clearly still unconvinced, skeptically looking for a plausible explanation of why she was here.

"I know, we met them halfway here on our way north. We let one continue on to Devnum so my father could have a first-hand account, but we brought the second one we met back with us. They told us you dispatched them five days ago, but we left Devnum seven days ago."

"That was the same day he was injured." Talogren said, his tone suggesting he still thought she was somehow lying, although his eyes went to Llassar again, looking for confirmation.

She saw the by-play, but only tangentially. That was the first time she'd actually heard someone confirm that Ky was hurt, and it felt like a fist had been driven into her stomach, temporarily blocking out her processing anything else.

"She speaks the truth. She announced seven days ago that she felt Ky was in some sort of trouble, although she said she couldn't be precise on anything beyond her feeling, and that she was leaving that day to come north. She gave her guards and anyone wanting to travel with her two hours to gather supplies and prepare, and then she was leaving, with or without us. We have learned she is very headstrong and didn't doubt she would leave us behind."

"I'm not lying to you," Lucilla said, pulling herself back together. "I am also not claiming any kind of connection to the gods of supernatural powers, although I know it sounds like that. We both know Ky has some kind of abilities, and my connection to him allows me to feel some impression of what is happening to him. It is difficult to experience, let alone explain, and I know you have no reason to trust me. The last time we met, I was your captive and left shortly after, so you have little reason to believe anything I have to say. It is why I brought back some of your countrymen you sent south with us. I have worked with them every day since we left and they know my character. Talk to them, and they will tell you I am not someone looking to curry favor or convince you of anything. I am only here to see Ky and, if possible, do what I can to help him."

"The men have come to respect her, both as a warrior and as a leader. Especially after she put Cynwrig on the ground three times, beating him in one of his beloved wrestling matches."

"My nephew has always had a problem underestimating challenges."

At no point had anyone mentioned her new guard was the nephew of the Caledonian chieftain.

"That's true, and he most definitely underestimated her abilities, but afterward he volunteered to be her personal guard. He may be headstrong, but we both know he's no fool and never agrees to that kind of obligation lightly."

"He's her guard?" Talogren asked in disbelief before turning back to Lucilla. "He's your bodyguard?"

"One of them, yes. He and a few others of your people asked to become part of my guard detail after an attempt on my life. They serve alongside Romans, who also protect me. I've also found him helpful in giving me perspective when working with your countrymen."

Talogren didn't say anything for a moment, but she could see him reevaluating her.

"I will tell you, there has been some doubt about how real your Consul's abilities are among the men."

"You've all seen the things he can do with your own eyes, and now you doubt him?"

"I've also seen charlatans perform supposed miracles when they were the ones deciding the time and place and they were prepared for it, but were unable to reproduce their feats when called to do it. Yes, I've seen him do wondrous things, but when it came time to protect himself from actual danger, he wasn't able to do it again. I will tell you now, I am not confident our alliance can survive his death, especially this early and under these circumstances."

"Don't count him out yet," Lucilla said.

"I'm trying not to. I like Ky and I've noticed he's never claimed any ability other than the ones we can actually see and he's never tried to use those abilities to convince people he's more than they are. He's a man of action, and I admire that. However, the Caledonian League itself is barely out of the cradle and our alliance with you is even younger. My people give up their independence unwillingly and it's taken all I have to just keep the league alive. It would take very little for my people's faith in the new alliance to waiver, and if I have to choose between the alliance with you Romans and the continued existence of the League, I will choose the League and confront the problem of the death worshipers when it comes to us."

"I understand, and I will do what I can to reassure your people. Can I see him?"

"Yes," he said, directing her out of the tent and leading her to one not far away.

The Romans guarding the entrance to the tent would have told her where Ky was even if she hadn't had a guide. Always a dour group of men, the unusually haunted looks on their faces told her she should be prepared for what she was about to see.

Pushing through the tent opening, she stopped so abruptly that Talogren nearly ran into her. Lucilla covered her mouth to contain the sound that threatened to escape when she saw Ky lying on the mount of furs in the center of the tent. He'd been stripped to the waist and a large, blood-soaked bandage covered his chest. At first, she thought he might actually have died before she'd gotten to him because of how absolutely still he was.

"We thought he was dead at first too," Talogren said, seeing the thought cross her face. "I've never seen anyone so still before that wasn't a corpse. You can still feel the blood running in his veins and a slight wind from his nose if you get close enough, however. He's alive, although the healers keep telling me all signs are so weak that he should go at any time."

Lucilla pushed back the fear and distress of seeing Ky like this and tried to think about what she was seeing logically. Although they'd never explained it specifically, she'd worked out that Sophus had some hand in running his basic processes. She didn't know if he could continue to breathe without Sophus, but it made sense that if the disembodied voice had gone silent, then it would make it difficult for Ky to breathe normally.

She also tried to think over what he'd said about the tiny things swimming through his body, how they fixed injuries and repaired living tissue. She thought to how she'd felt since Sophus had decided to put some of those in her, and how her father had recovered from his near-certain poisoning. He said they were controlled by Sophus, but he'd also said the ones in her would work for a set amount of time without Sophus's control, only needing instructions or replacements from time to time.

She leaned over Ky, hoping it looked like she was mourning his condition while blocking her actions from the men around her. They'd already seen his wounds when they bandaged them, but if her guess was wrong, she didn't want to add a reminder of how bad it clearly was. Lifting the bandage slightly, her shoulders sagged for a moment. She heard a noise from Talogren behind her, although if it was from sympathy or annoyance or just general frustration, she couldn't tell.

Loosening the bandage, she stepped out of the way, pulling it with her, revealing the area it had been covering to Talogren, Llassar, and the handful of men that had followed them into the tent. Ky's chest was as smooth and chiseled as it had ever been.

Not only was the wound completely gone, but so were all traces that it had ever happened in the first place. Anyone looking at it, no matter how closely, would find no trace of the wound, not even a scar.

Talogren sucked in a breath and moved forward, running his hand across where the wound had been.

"How? I saw it when he was brought in. The cut had exposed bone and organ."

"Ky isn't like us. True, often weapons cannot touch him, but he has never claimed to be invincible. He does, however, heal very quickly from even the most dire wound," she said, partially repeating what Ky had said and partially embellishing to make her point.

"But he still doesn't move."

"I know, and I think that has always been separate from his injury. He warned me something was coming and he was experiencing physical symptoms from it. I don't really understand all of it, but what I did understand was that this is something that can happen to people with his abilities. It isn't supposed to be permanent and he thinks he will recover, but he knew he would be incapacitated. Of course, he thought he had more time than this. If I had to guess, his sudden unconsciousness was why his opponent was able to cut him at all."

Now she was flat out lying, partially because she didn't really know the truth and partially because she didn't understand what she did know enough to explain it to anyone else. Either way, she couldn't really tell Talogren that another consciousness lived in Ky's head and the two were at war over his body or that this might be permanent. If it was, she'd deal with it then, and mourn his loss, but for now, she was going to continue as if he'd recover. She had little choice to do anything else.

"Why didn't he say anything? If he was leading men into battle, he should have told us this could happen."

"Because he believed in your leadership and thought things would be better when the north was finally under your command. And because he really did think he had more time. I'm sure if he knew it was this close, he wouldn't have been fighting on the front lines."

"I see," Talogren said, thoughtfully, his mind clearly turning over the new turn of events. "This should buy us time, I think. I will put what pressure I can on my people. Once word spreads of his miraculous recovery and that this is a condition set on him by the gods in return for his abilities, I think my people will fall in line."

Lucilla hadn't tried to give him the impression that what had happened was some kind of ailment brought on by the gods, but she also had been very careful to not dissuade Talogren from coming to that conclusion on his own. She knew Ky wouldn't be happy with her decision, but she hoped he'd understand the need to convince him and all of his followers to continue with the alliance.

"I'm glad to hear it. As I understand it, these were the last large independents you had to pacify to finalize your control of the entire region, and you only held here because of Ky's condition. I'm assuming you have much to do, now that everyone has been brought to heel, most of which you've been delaying, to see if the alliance would hold."

"I do," he said, not embarrassed at all at the calculated decisions he made over the possibility of Ky dying. "As soon as we leave here I'll put out the word to break camp and start the ride. There's still several hours of daylight we can use."

"Good. Since Ky was only staying until you finished consolidating your rule, I will be taking him south with me, but I'd like to travel with you back to your village first. When he wakes, Ky will want reports on what your next moves are and to ensure the first days of the alliance go smoothly for you. He was very specific in his demands on my father that you and your people be treated as equals in the alliance, and not as junior partners. I want to ensure we live up to that."

Talogren didn't answer right away, again evaluating her.

"You should let her travel with us," Llassar said.

Talogren again looked at his lieutenant, this time with the same calculating expression.

"You've certainly won over my men," he said.

"Hopefully my charm will have the same effect on you."

"We'll see," he said before leaving the tent to prepare his men to move.

Chapter 16

Lucilla used the hours before the move to tour the surrendered village. To Roman eyes, all of the Caledonian villages seemed primitive and rudimentary, but Rhaeadr looked just as primitive to Talogren's home village as that one did to Devnum.

Gone were the permanent wood buildings and large, well-constructed tents. Most of the homes were formed out of mud and dirt mixed in with tents supplementing branches and woven plants to patch the holes. The people were universally thin and had the sickly look of people who ate far too infrequently.

They still had the proud bearing of the other Caledonians she'd met, especially when confronted with their conquerors, but Lucilla could see the desperation in their eyes.

"Send one of your men back to the praetorians. Tell them I want a convoy of food and supplies brought up from Rome, with stops at the other conquered villages along the way. Have them also include medical supplies and warm clothing. My father will ensure everything is paid for," she said to Modius as they left the villages.

"They will not accept charity," Cynwrig said.

"That would be their choice. We aren't doing it for one village. See if you can get some of your people to go with the supply convoys and talk some sense into these people. We aren't doing this out of the goodness of our hearts or to buy their loyalty. Over the next several years, we are going to need more men to keep the Carthaginians at bay and implement the new technology Ky is introducing. That means we need these people alive and healthy. We need them able to supply the markets and the legion quartermasters with raw materials. And we need them to have children to ensure the future of the Empire we're building. But to get all of that, we have to make sure they don't all starve to death, first. This is a fair trade, labor for food and supplies."

Cynwrig didn't seem convinced, which probably meant most of the villagers wouldn't be convinced either. Some would and if she could save some of these people, then maybe they would be available when the Empire needed them. She also wasn't convinced that Cynwrig was right and these people's pride would allow them and their children to starve if there was a way out. She'd found that the average person might talk a lot about pride, honor, and other nebulous ideas, what really mattered was their day-to-day life. If they saw their day-to-day life improving, then they'd do what they could to ensure that better way continued.

It's what Silo and his kind missed. Sure, they were able to talk some people, a lot even, into following them because of some idea of what Rome once was, but they didn't convince the majority of Romans, or even enough to make their insurrection work, because the average citizen had seen their city saved from an enemy they could see and had started seeing increased benefits from the changes Ky had been making. By the time of the uprising, there had been more jobs, both in the army and in the factories needed to turn out supplies for the armies, which meant their families would be able to continue eating.

Real civil strife comes when people feel their day-to-day lives are getting worse. She'd met enough northerners to know they weren't that much different from the Romans. They might be stubborn now, with so many of their men dead on the field and new leaders hand-picked by Talogren in charge, but if she could ensure they all still ate, that more of their children survived, and that their fortunes improved, they'd put that stubbornness aside.

This was why leaders like Talogren, or most of the Germanic chieftains on the mainland, would never control more than a small collection of villages, at least on their own. They were warriors and saw the world through a warrior's eyes. They believed the solution to all problems was just applying enough pressure to force the other side to relent. That might work in the short term, but it didn't ensure the loyalty of the average people, who'd just as easily swing to the warlord or chieftain who applied more pressure. She understood, as her father had, that real loyalty came by making the average person's life better, or at least not worse, than it had been before.

This wasn't the only reason she was arranging supply shipments for the conquered villages, of course. She'd like to think she was trying to do the right thing, and she was, but she also had to pay attention to the realities and understand the cause and effect of her decision. It was something she'd learned at her father's knee but hadn't actively thought about it until a conversation she had with Ky.

He'd been debating on how to best go about dealing with Rome's slave population, weighing the impact of freeing them on the citizens and how to achieve his goal with the least impact possible. He'd called the idea, that a system of principles should be based on practical concerns instead of moral or ideological ones, realpolitik. He'd said that way of viewing the world could go too far and that his people had had several leaders who'd done that, losing their sense of morality or ideology to their practicality. She'd seen it in her own people, how someone who only thought of the practical implications could be as bad as someone who only thought of the ideological ones, but the word had stuck with her. Since she'd stepped up to take a more active role in government as his voice in Rome, she'd been thinking about it more often. It could be stressful, trying to find the right balance between being practical and doing what was right, but she was actively trying to achieve it.

She didn't second guess the supply shipments, however. There would probably be some clerk who only saw the cost of sending supplies to remote villages, but she knew that, in the long term, it would pay off, both ideologically and practically.

"On this," she continued to Cynwrig. "Enough of these people will accept the supplies to make it worth the effort."

"If you say so," he said.

She knew it would take time, not just for him but all of her guards, to come to trust her judgment. They were all loyal and predisposed to like her because of their close service, but she'd found it always took longer for men to defer to her wisdom on subjects she was more experienced in than they were, simply because she was a woman.

She'd gotten used to her old guard, men like Ursinus, who'd served her long enough to develop that kind of relationship. All of those men, save Ursinus, were dead and he'd moved on to greater things, which mean she'd have to be patient and once again prove that she was worth listening to.

Londinium

Maharbaal passed the old forum while he waited, which was something he wasn't accustomed to doing. He'd sent for the general thirty minutes ago, demanding an update, and still the man hadn't arrived.

Other men would have found themselves in the hands of death cultists who stood silently waiting for their next offering. Unfortunately, Bomilcar wasn't someone he could just order tortured and executed on a whim. Besides being a favorite in Carthage, he was a descendant of one of the generals who'd fought alongside Hannibal, and his family remained in high standing.

On the one hand, it showed how seriously the emperor was taking the threat of the Romans. He was a younger member of the family, but he'd already earned some accolades in the east and was a rising star in the emperor's service. Maharbaal was glad the emperor's court had finally listened to him and stopped giving him fools like Zaracas, who'd lost his army to a force a fifth its size.

Of course, it also meant he couldn't treat this man the way he would others placed in his service. The governor had grown used to his position and enjoyed the autonomy that he had so far from Africa, but even out here, he had to take into account the political realities. All of which meant he couldn't have this man beaten for making him wait. Worse, he couldn't even berate the man when he inevitably gave excuses.

Maharbaal's annoyance had turned to anger by the time the general finally showed, his boots leaving muddy tracks and dirt caked to the armor protecting his shins.

"You sent for me, exalted governor?" the general said, giving a slight bow of the head instead of the normal genuflecting Maharbaal received from his inferiors.

His mouth tightened at the lack of excuses or begging for forgiveness. Maharbaal had to remind himself, again, that this man was not a politician or a lackey, but an experienced commander, and the one who the governor would have to rely on to carry out his vengeance.

"Yes. I want an update on your progress and why you still haven't marched on the Romans."

"We are still not ready. Most of the veteran units on the island were killed or surrendered at the battle of Devnum and the replacements available to us are substandard, mostly Germanic tribesman who can barely all march in one direction and are all but useless in a phalanx. We've been training with them and doing field maneuvers for weeks, but the progress has been slow."

"What does it matter? You outnumber the Romans ten to one. Just send in the men and crush them."

"My lord, have you ever seen the Romans fight? Or spoken to the men who did return from the battle?"

"Cowards and traitors you mean. They would have given any excuse to explain why they ran away."

"You shouldn't discount what those men have to say. While very few commanders have faced the Romans in a hundred years, the records of our encounters with them are clear in their tactics and fighting style and it matches everything the survivors reported after the battle. They may be a smaller force now, but every indication says they are still as disciplined a military force as ever, and not one to be taken lightly. Rushing undisciplined warriors at a coordinated front line like we will certainly face will just create a wall of bodies the men behind them have to crawl over to get at the Romans. I do not want to repeat past mistakes."

Maharbaal held his tongue, but only by the thinnest of margins. He knew that people at court were placing the blame for Zaracas's loss at his feet and saw his request for more men as an admission of his failure. Of course, he knew that was what was going to happen before he ever sent the request, which is why he tried to find any other way to solve the problem without the request. Unfortunately, the only answer any of his subordinates had been able to give him was 'we need more men.'

Bomilcar's not too subtle dig was just another reminder of how precarious his current position was, which made it an effective tool every time the general's slow progress was questioned. He might be a fool, but Bomilcar knew how to play the game, and Maharbaal knew his hand was too weak to do anything about it, yet.

Once they were victorious, however, the governor's fortunes would change and he'd ensure this man paid for his insolence.

"I, of course, leave the exact planning and details of the campaign to your expertise. I just wanted to remind you, again, how important it is that we move with all possible haste. When do you think you will be able to march?"

Although he used the language of diplomacy, every word was delivered through clenched teeth.

"I'd prefer to wait until the snows have melted, since foraging for supplies is going to be extremely difficult," he said. After a momentary pause, he continued quickly, seeing the governor's look of extreme annoyance at another topic they'd battled over multiple times before. "I know we don't have time for the delay and I am not asking to wait until conditions improve. Since I can't wait and I understand the urgency, I will begin my march as soon as the last troops arrive on the shore. I will continue to train them, especially the new arrivals, as we march, which will slow down our advance, but not as much as staying and training in camp would."

"A timetable, general. Stop dancing around the question and give me something resembling an exact timeframe until we can finally crush the Romans."

"Two to three weeks until we march. I know that isn't precise, but we are beholden to the shipmasters and the whims of the ocean to determine how long that will take. Another few days for final provisions and assembling the new men, and a week and a half march. Say a month to a month and a half at the outside."

"And there is no way to do this sooner?"

"No. Even if I wanted to march without the last shiploads of men, I'd still have to wait. Along with those shipments of men are gifts from the emperor of supplies to feed the men and animals, which we need, since we have to assume there will be nothing to forage. It doesn't matter how many men I get together if they're all starving and weak by the time we reach the Romans."

"Fine. A month and a half at the maximum. Not a day more, general. I expect to hear about the success of your battle by then. Do we understand each other?"

"Of course, Excellency," the general said, bowing.

Maharbaal watched him go, without even being granted official leave. His rage threatened to boil over, but even here, in the throne room with just his servants and guards, he had to control himself. He knew the emperor had eyes everywhere, and he couldn't be seen losing control.

Northern Highlands

Lucilla was exhausted riding just behind the cart carrying Ky's inert body. She'd been offered a more prestigious position, from the Caledonian point of view, at least, near the head of the column with Talogren, but she'd refused, saying she preferred instead to ride as close to Ky as she could.

While she really did want to stay near him, that had only been part of the truth. She had a lot of work remaining to try and ensure Ky's goal of binding the Caledonians and Romans together as tightly as possible, and she preferred not to do it directly under Talogren's nose. Of course, she knew that those Caledonians riding with her were sending reports back to Talogren, even the men who'd agreed to be her guards. However, reports and seeing her attempts to manipulate the north men were not the same thing.

So she remained on horseback since they'd been traveling, sending and receiving messengers, trying to ensure the aid shipments had begun at least leaving on their journey north, and requesting her father send agents north to monitor the early days of the alliance and catch problem spots before they happened.

Despite her knowing some of the north men serving her were reporting on her movements, she also began using her Caledonian men to try and build a network of north men to monitor the Caledonian side of the alliance, since the more she knew about what was going on, the better prepared she, and Ky when he finally woke up, would be.

Thankfully, Carus, one of Ky's guards and the man in charge of his intelligence work, had already been on the job since they'd come north and already had information sources that he'd been happy to share with Lucilla, although he asked for access to any Caledonians she managed to recruit, since at the moment everyone he had access to was Roman.

Although there had been a lot of opposition when the alliance was first announced, especially among the wealthier sections of Roman society, it hadn't taken long for those same men to start finding ways to exploit it for a profit. Carus said he hadn't had a chance to do more than mention the developments along the border to Ky before he collapsed, since the Consul had been more preoccupied with ensuring the north was pacified and had put everything else as secondary until that happened.

Their attempts to track any notable movement by Romans coming north, now that the borders were open, had started showing results, but unfortunately, not in a way Lucilla liked.

This was made starkly clear with a set of merchants who'd crossed into the north the day Ky signed the agreement. They'd headed to a mountain range just north of the Talogren's home village to set up mining operations. On the face of it, that was a good thing and exactly the kind of activity Ky and the Emperor had been hoping for.

One of the bottleneck areas of Roman production had been their limited mining capability, since the section of Britannia they had been limited to had only minimal areas of significant, easily reachable ore deposits. Ky had mentioned additional technologies making it possible to get a lot more ore out of the existing mines with little, or in some cases, less, manpower investment. He'd introduced the beginnings of those, but had yet to show them everything, saying they needed additional technological improvements that required more foundational knowledge, which was his go-to reasoning most of the times she'd asked why something he'd mentioned couldn't be done right away.

One of the benefits to the alliance was the nearly untouched, rich ore deposits that required little initial mining to access. The Picts did some, of course, but they'd never been able to really export any of the resources they'd had access to.

Mostly, that was because the people who now made up the Caledonians didn't actually control that area until a hundred and fifty or so years ago when Rome had finally pushed all of the people out of the bottom two-thirds of the island. Those groups that did manage to move north and set up settlements then fought amongst themselves as much as they did with the Romans for the next hundred and forty years, until Talogren came to power and finally started to convince the people living in the north that they might benefit from working together instead of each trying to gain some kind of supremacy.

The constant state of warfare for almost a century meant that, until recently, all of the tribes existed as either nomads or subsistence farmers with all of their available manpower not used for food production going towards fighting the other tribes for what little territory they could eke out. That left little for building up any kind of infrastructure for mining the ore deposits themselves.

All of that meant that, while there were a lot of industries that could benefit from Roman - Caledonian cooperation, mining was the most logical first choice for any of the entrepreneurial minds that had started to look north, towards the new opportunities opened up by the alliance.

Unfortunately, as with most new things, the sudden change brought not only entrepreneurs, but also grifters, charlatans, and those ready to take advantage of the situation. Equally as unfortunate was, because of the sudden outlawing of slavery in Rome itself, there were men with the will and available capital to take advantage of the alliance, but also at loose ends, since the new

Roman laws meant their method of getting the most return out of the investments had suddenly become unavailable.

They had barely left Rhaeadr when word reached them of one of the first groups of Roman entrepreneurs to cross the border and set up mining operations, and the word wasn't good. They'd essentially taken over a small village near the base of the mountain and all but enslaved the population to work in the mines, digging out ore that could then be sent by caravan south, to Roman forges.

"How is that even possible?" Lucilla asked when Llassar told her the news. "Even with the Devnum city guard disbanding, there aren't enough trained and armed men for hire to do something like that, especially since a lot of what is available, like street toughs, aren't going to agree to go to such a remote region. And you're people aren't exactly the type to roll over the moment a few men with swords show up."

"The details are still sketchy, but it seems like they first arrived as friends, promising wealth and riches if these people worked for them excavating the mines. These are fairly poor villages and the men there have been doing similar, although less extensive, work for years, so it probably made sense to them at the time. What they didn't have were the tools you Romans used to get to the richer, but harder to reach, veins of ore. Apparently, the businessmen had a solution for that. They would agree to give these people the tools and take it out of the money they earned digging out the ore until the cost of those tools was paid back."

"Although I can think of better ways to handle the situation, that kind of thing happens a lot in Rome as well. I wouldn't necessarily call it fair, but I thought these men were taking advantage of the locals?" Lucilla asked.

"I'm getting to that part. They first brought out agreements for the locals to sign, but we don't really do that kind of thing, which is why the agreement Talogren signed with our new Emperor has made unifying the north harder, since it's such an alien way to go about this kind of thing, at least to us. Since the locals seemed unsure of what it meant and couldn't read the Romans' agreement for themselves, the Romans offered another solution that was more familiar to my people. The way villages often secure deals with each other is to exchange family members until the deal is concluded."

"Hostages?" Lucilla asked.

"Essentially. The Romans altered this, arguing that they were giving the villagers something and would only get paid in return when the work was done, so the villagers should be the ones sending hostages, which the Romans would care for and return when the equipment was paid off. They also suggested that, because the men were all needed to mine the ore which would be paying off the debt and the women were needed to produce enough food to maintain the men, the only likely candidates were the village's children. Again, this isn't out of the norm in our culture, so the villagers agreed."

"I'm guessing this is the point where everything went off 'cultural norms'?"

"Yes. At first, everything seemed fine. The Romans delivered the equipment and showed the men how to use it. The problem came when the Romans started demanding the locals work longer and longer each day, increasing the quotas of ore the villagers originally agreed to. When the men complained, the Romans said the deal had changed. They had their children and could only guarantee their safety so long as the people of the village agreed. When the men suggested they had other ways of dealing with the betrayal, the Romans managing the operation said that, if anything happened to them, they'd never see their children again."

"So someone came to Talogren for help."

"Not directly, probably because they feared for their children's lives, but remote as this village is, it does get the occasional trader, so word leaked out."

"Where do things stand now?"

"From our latest reports, the people are slaves in all but name only. Technically, the men are still working to pay off the equipment, but the Romans have changed more than just the quota part of the deal. Anything, including 'overseeing' both the mineworkers and their families, who are now required to supply food to the Romans as well as the locals, has an additional payment connected to it. Instead of paying off just the equipment, each day they grow more and more in debt to the Romans."

"And everyone's hands are tied, since any move would end up hurting the children? Does Talogren want us to deal with them and get the children back?"

"No. He said I could tell you what was happening, but that he'd deal with it personally."

"What does that mean?"

"It means he is going to make an example of them. Although he knew that Ky and your father were operating in good faith, he also knows your Romans, and expected this sort of thing. It is why he insisted that Caledonian lands were governed by Caledonian laws, which have high penalties for parties breaking their word like this. Had they stuck by the agreement, even if it had been disadvantageous to our people, he would have let it stay, since everything else was done according to our traditions. Wars have begun over changing the terms of an agreement after hostages have been given, and the penalty for breaking an agreement like this is death. He plans to show any future Romans just what, exactly, happens to your people who come north with plans of cheating Caledonians."

"What about the children."

"He is, of course, saddened that they will be victims in a situation they did not have a hand in making, but their parents will understand. Their sacrifice will secure the safety of all of us."

"I need to talk to Talogren."

"You won't talk him out of this."

"I have to try."

Chapter 17

"Talogren, I need to speak with you," she said, riding up to the chieftain and his advisors.

Although she'd left Ky's lictore with him, Carus had asked to go with her. At first, she wanted to tell him to stay behind. Unlike a lot of the things she had been dealing with as Ky's voice while he was gone, this was much closer to her area of expertise and what parts of it were unique were more areas for a Caledonian to advise her on than a Roman.

She'd finally relented since Carus had shown the rare ability to keep his mouth shut and let a woman take the lead in conversations, and because eventually, Ky would wake up and he'd appreciate having a spymaster with as much first-hand knowledge of the situation as possible.

"You will not talk me out of teaching your people manners," he said, correctly predicting what she had come to see him about, if not the particulars.

"I only wanted to know what you planned to do, specifically. Since Ky is currently unavailable, I thought you could use some counsel on what kind of ripple effect you might have from whatever punishment you decided to hand out to these men."

"What I have to do is make sure we make it clear to everyone that we are equal partners in this alliance, and I can't help but think the advice of the Roman Emperor might not have the same goal of protecting Caledonian interests as I have."

"I can see why you'd think that, and you of course don't have to listen to anything I have to say, although I would point out that my father isn't just the Emperor of Rome, but of our entire new Empire. I only hope that the men you've had reporting to you about me have also reported that I have tried very hard to ensure all Caledonians are treated as equals."

"There is a difference between arguing for one of the people who volunteered to serve you getting equal treatment, and counseling on the proper treatment under Caledonian law for Roman criminals."

"If that's all you think I've done, then you haven't listened to your spies very well after all. I agree these men are criminals and should be treated harshly, and I've ordered men's executions before, which I think you've been told. My concern is writing off the hostages in the name of Caledonian reputation."

He gave her an appraising glanced and, after a beat, said, "What would your counsel be on how to treat them."

"It would be to not play directly into their hands. The actual people behind this crime aren't going to be at the site of the mine itself. They would have had lackeys and factotums doing that. If you plan on just seizing them and taking their heads, you might be playing right into their hands."

"What do you mean?"

"There are plenty of people in Rome who want this alliance to fail and think they can use that failure to increase their own power. They look down on the Caledonians and find the entire idea of treating you like equals to be appalling. I am not saying that they are doing this solely to provoke this kind of response from you, but it wouldn't surprise me. It gives them a message they can take to the people who, if given time, might come over to think of you as real people and not caricatures."

"What would their message be, exactly?"

"That you are primitives, who not only slaughter those you don't agree with, but also write off your own children's lives without trying to find a peaceful solution," she said, and then held up a hand to forestall the obvious objection Talogren was drawing a breath to make. "I know that isn't true; but we both know what is true, and what they can convince others of, is not the same thing. In time, as our people commingle, most Romans will get to know your people on a personal level and will know this is a lie, but that takes time. Till then, they can use unfamiliarity to paint you in whatever light they choose."

"What do we care what you Romans think of us. They can believe whatever falsehoods they like, but when they see these men's heads on pikes, all of your people will know without a doubt that we are not to be trifled with."

"In the short term, yes, but it will make integration of our two peoples more difficult. I know you don't see why that's important, although I also know Ky has tried to convince you it is several times. Until Romans and Caledonians see each other as simply people of the Britannic Empire, we will never truly be one people. Yes, your people are great warriors and valued members of the alliance, but militarily, technologically, and economically, the Caledonians are the lesser of the two of us. I know that isn't something you, as the leader of the Caledonians, would openly agree with, but I also know you're smart enough to know it's true. Merging our people won't be an easy process and it will take more than either of our lifetimes for it to fully happen, but that process can't start until both of us decide to see problems from either side and find solutions that work best for the Empire as a whole."

"And what would that solution be?"

"I don't know. It depends on what has been done on the ground and how much the people at the village are responsible and how much those who sent them there with orders to - in all but name - enslave your people. Beyond just making sure the children are returned safely, I want to make sure those ultimately responsible are punished just as much as those carrying out their orders are."

She could see the chieftain weighing over her words, and didn't envy him the position she'd put him in. Everything in his culture said the most important thing was to be independent, free from the constraints of others, which was why it had been so difficult to unify the north in the first place and why he'd only agreed to the alliance if the Caledonians maintained autonomy in their region. Now he was being asked to let a Roman decide how to best protect his people.

"Fine, but if I don't find what you decide fair to my people, I will still carry out justice in my own way. You also only have five days, and then I will take care of matters myself. Agreed?"

"Agreed," Lucilla said, giving a slight bow of her head and pulling the reins of her horse, turning back towards the middle of the column where Ky's wagon rode.

"What did he say," Carus asked, riding up to meet her before she made it back to Ky's wagon.

"He's going to let me deal with it, although he made it clear he'll do it his way if he doesn't like my solution."

"Do you know what you're going to do?"

"Not yet. I need to see what exactly is going on and figure out the best way to get the children back safely. And for that, I'm going to need you."

"Me?"

"Yes. I know that, although you are officially one of his guard commanders, your main duty is to handle the gathering and sifting of information for him, specifically about people and their activities in Rome and here. What I don't know is what, exactly, you've been doing along those lines, which means I don't know how to best use you to fix this current problem. You don't have a problem working with me in the same capacity while Ky is recovering, do you?"

Although she'd asked the question straightforwardly, as if she didn't particularly care what the answer was, inside she was metaphorically holding her breath. So far, her presence and even some authority over how to best move Ky had been accepted by his lictore, this was the first thing she'd asked of them outside of what would be her place as ... whatever she was.

"No," he said, without hesitation. "Besides the partnership between the two of you that we've all seen, this was one of the situations that he was specifically worried about when the alliance was signed. He'd already had me building as many contacts as possible and getting what agents I could into Roman businesses already operating along the border, since they were the most likely ones to cross over first."

"Do you have anyone inside this group?"

"Unfortunately, no. Until news of this popped up, I hadn't heard of them. I've already sent a messenger to some of my contacts to see what they might know, but none of their names are familiar to me."

"So, they weren't on your list of people most likely to abuse the alliance?"

"No."

"If these are unknowns, I'm concerned what the groups you were tracking are planning."

"Most of them are planning nothing, because the Consul had me preemptively pull the reins on all of those we thought might be a problem. We let them know that we were watching them, and the full weight of Roman and Caledonian law would come down on them if they even stepped a toe out of line, and suggested they look elsewhere for their money-making opportunities. That doesn't mean they won't try something later, once they see how things shake up, but we had the praetorians make several visits to their residences and businesses, remaining as visible as possible, to help keep it in their minds."

"I want you to find out who's pulling the strings for this. I've dealt with these types of people before, and the ones behind it are rarely actually on the ground doing their own dirty work. I want to know what we're dealing with before we get to the village."

"Ma'am, it's only a three-day ride to the village. I'm not sure I can get you what you need by then."

"Ky has said multiple times how capable you are. I have faith you will prove him right."

"But ..."

"Although you should probably get started, if you're going to make your deadline."

Carus pursed his lips in frustration, nodded, and rode away from the line. She knew she was asking the impossible and pushing the man too hard, but she needed this to be a success. So far, she'd had a, more or less, passive role as Ky's stand-in, and her primary move was to let people operate as they thought best, with only the occasional prod or redirection. This was the first real test of what she could do and this would be the thing that people would look to when deciding if she had the right capabilities for ruling.

Although her primary goal was to make sure the alliance held and protect the lives of these new citizens of the Empire, she also had to think of her legacy. There had never been a female emperor and with her brother defecting to the Carthaginians, she would one day have to take up her father's mantle and she knew that it would be a hard transition for many Romans, and Caledonians. She would need a fairly untarnished record of success, and a fair number of them, to get over those fears.

She needed to not only succeed at this, but to do it quickly and spectacularly.

The Village of Mwynglawdd

The village of Mwynglawdd was similar to most of the other small villages in the north which Lucilla had seen since traveling across the border. A central wooden structure, probably used for gatherings, religious ceremonies, and other community events, surrounded by a mismatch of temporary hide tents and more permanent mud and thatch huts.

The biggest difference between Mwynglawdd and other villages she'd visited, even ones recently defeated by Talogren's forces, was the people. Caledonian villages might be primitive, by Roman standards, but they were still full bustling places with people always on the go. Maybe it was because there were fewer services so everyone had to carry out every function for themselves or maybe it was just a figment of her imagination, but in every village visited, there were always people coming and going on some task.

Here, there were hardly any people on the muddy lanes between huts, and those she did see look downtrodden. She couldn't put her finger on it, but they lacked that nobility of spirit that she had admired in the Caledonians she'd met.

"Ma'am," Modius said from behind her, drawing her attention not towards the center of town, but the mountain looming over the village.

They'd noticed some buildings out in that direction, but had decided to head towards the village first, to see the situation there.

While her attention had been diverted, a group of armed men had appeared from the buildings and were clearly headed to intercept them. Expecting trouble, Cynwrig and Modius had put together extra men, mostly made up of Picts who'd volunteered to help free the village. These men might have been a problem for her normal guard force, but she'd arrived with almost a hundred warriors under her command, well more than was needed to pacify the Romans currently lording over the Caledonians.

Lucilla, however, did not want to just start with bloodshed. Attacking the first group of Romans at the village they found was precisely the kind of behavior she was hoping to avoid when she'd talked Talogren into letting her take care of the situation.

Holding up an arm, she said to Modius, "Hold back for now. I don't think they'll make a move on us, considering the numbers, and I'd rather talk than fight, if possible."

Modus and Cynwrig had spent three days traveling getting some semblance of control over the men who'd volunteered to go with them. Considering how many men they had, he'd decided to use all of her Caledonian guards as commanders of the volunteers. They weren't exactly a cohesive unit, but they at least had enough communication and control that simple commands like 'don't attack' seemed to work. Or so Lucilla hoped as she spurred her horse forward, breaking off from the group with only Modius and Cynwrig supporting her.

"What's your business?" one of the armed men said as Lucilla got near.

"Do you know who I am?" Lucilla asked in a neutral tone.

For some, that statement was a way to point out a power imbalance between two people, but Lucilla meant it as an honest question. Although her likeness was occasionally reproduced on some coins and art, it was never flattering or even that recognizable. In Devnum, she could assume everyone knew who she was, but the further away from the confines of the capital she got, the fewer people recognized her, making it a legitimate way to start the negotiations.

"Should I care?"

Of course, the small army she'd brought with her suggested they should care. By the way the man occasionally looked past her to the armed horde she'd just ridden away from, he was very aware of his uneven position, showing the lie to his attitude.

"I am Lucilla Germanicus, daughter of the Emperor of Rome and the Britannic Empire, and named representative of the Sword of Jupiter, who is currently the Consul of Rome. You would do well to know your place."

She could see him process the information as his strong facade faded and visible fear began to creep in. These were hired toughs. Men experienced in threatening and intimidating farmers and peasants. They weren't used to facing trained soldiers and seasoned warriors, and definitely weren't used to being confronted with real authority. They were a scourge on civilized society, although one her father had tolerated, since men like this sometimes hired themselves out as guards to legitimate merchants for protection as they traveled between towns.

"My lady," he said, his hand coming off of his weapon. "I ... forgive me, I didn't know who you were."

"And now you do. Where are the Roman overlords of this village?"

Her choice of words had been deliberate, and had the desired effect. Although they probably called themselves businessmen or investors, these guards were smart enough to recognize what they really were, and the penalty they would face under Roman law for doing what they'd done. Their masters had probably convinced them it was different, since they weren't in Rome, but Lucilla's sudden presence, and choice of words, would have made it equally clear they'd been mistaken.

His eyes darted around, looking for someone else to handle the situation, "The supervisors are at the mine. We were simply hired as guards, to protect the mining operation."

"If I were to ask the villagers if that was all you were doing, what would they say? We are detaining you and your men until we have investigated this situation. You will show me to these supervisors while your men are held by my soldiers. Throw down your weapons."

For a moment she thought they might try to fight their way out. It was clearly hopeless, and tantamount to suicide, but cornered men often make rash decisions. After a beat, however, the lead guard threw his gladius into the mud, followed by the rest of his men.

"We aren't in Rome and so we haven't broken any Roman laws."

"You're right, you aren't in Rome. You're on Caledonian land and, by the terms of the Alliance between our people, subject to Caledonian laws. Do you know the penalty for what you've done under Caledonian law?"

They didn't but it was clear from their reaction that they could imagine what that penalty might be.

"I am here to find a more peaceful resolution to this situation, but if you'd prefer, I can hand you over to the Caledonians and be done with that."

"Uhh, we, of course, intend to follow any commands you have. I'll show you to the supervisors."

His men, eyeing the Caledonians fifty feet behind her, seemed less sure of his guarantee.

"For now, you will only be held under guard," she reassured them. "Until we can determine what, exactly, has happened here and the best resolution to the situation. If you try to run or resist, they will deal with you, otherwise, you will remain unharmed while we conduct our investigation."

She waved for some of the Caledonians to come and retrieve the men, who allowed themselves to be herded away. Lucilla only hoped that the warriors who'd come with her continued to hold to their assurances that they would not do anything without her say so. It would be harder to get other Romans she encountered to surrender as bloodlessly if they massacred the first group of men put in their care.

One of the men cast a hopeless glance towards the weapon he'd thrown on the ground, but he and the rest let themselves be led off towards the waiting warriors while the spokesman turned and led them towards the mountain and the mining operations. Modius had already worked out possible scenarios and pre-arranged with the men how to handle them, which is why half of the mounted warriors remained at the village while the other half followed behind Lucilla and her two guards, in case a visual reminder of what the roman supervisors faced was needed.

Lucilla was glad to find that they didn't need to travel far up the mountain to find the Roman operation. This being the early stages of the large-scale excavation, the Roman operation had started with the untouched but accessible lower points of the mountain to begin mining, rather than going after the smaller and harder-to-reach veins of ore higher up. It took less than five minutes before the small column entered a naturally occurring flat area where the Romans had set up, their tents becoming visible as they cleared the intact tree line lower down.

There were only a handful of Romans on site as Lucilla's group came into view, and all fell back towards the largest tent, as soon as Lucilla and her men came into sight. By the time they rode up to the center tent, a large man in a traditional, and somewhat gaudy, toga waddled his way out of the tent, an expression of annoyance on his face. He wore enough jewelry to be considered garish even by Devnum standards and his toga was hemmed with purple cloth that, by tradition, was reserved for those in the Senatorial class. She'd met his type before. Men from the merchant class who came into wealth and put on airs of Roman society without ever actually meeting anyone born into high society.

"What is the meaning of this?" he demanded.

"In the name of the Britannic Empire, you are under arrest pending investigations into your crimes against citizens of the Empire," Lucilla said, her hand on the hilt of the gladius she kept sheathed against the saddle.

"What crimes?"

"Kidnapping, forced labor, and slavery for starters."

"We didn't ..."

"Your, or the men you serve, did. The children of the village below were taken from them to another location as hostages to force their parents to work, without payment and without a chance to regain their children."

"Under Caledonian law, the taking of hostages ..."

"Under Caledonian tradition, not law, hostage-taking has been allowed in limited circumstances, and those hostages were returned when the agreed conditions were met. Your masters changed the conditions of their agreement after the children were handed over and have refused to return them or even give a hint as to when they would be returned. Although not outlawed by Caledonian law directly, Caledonian law does make the penalties for changing agreements clear. Worse, the Caledonians have agreed to change their laws to match those of the new Roman laws regarding slavery, and you have made these people slaves in all but name. The penalty in either of our cultures is the same, however. Death."

"I ... We ... I'm only following orders," The man said, tears starting as his facade of strength crumbled. "Oppius Plautius Dama. He's the one you want. He set this up and left us to run things. This is his."

"And yet you're here carrying out his orders. Taking children from their families. Forcing men to work under the eye of guards. Forcing the women to provide you food and comfort, even though they themselves are starving. You are no innocent. Take him. Take them all," she said, waving the Caledonians with her to arrest the men.

She had instructed all of them before they arrived at the village that they weren't to harm the prisoners unless they resisted. She wanted a public trial followed by a public verdict. She'd decided that this was the opportunity she'd needed, and she was pretty sure Ky wanted, to begin setting a precedent for a less arbitrary system of justice closer to the one Ky had described when he talked about his home. Even in Rome, justice tended to be whatever the person with the most power said it was, and even when they were right, it was arbitrary, based as much on who the person committing the crime was as what the crime was. In Caledonia, there was even less structure.

Ky had described a world where people got a chance to defend themselves and officials whose sole job it was to be neutral judged their crimes and handed out punishment solely on what the law specified, rather than what they felt at the moment. Of course, she wasn't certain the ideal he described was ever achieved, even where he was from. She knew people and she doubted any, no matter how advanced, could separate their emotions from their decisions. That being said, even when the person judging the accused tried and failed in their impartiality striving for that level of perfection would lead to better outcomes than it went now, where the goal seemed to be biased from the start.

One or two of the guards did try to resist, a grave mistake considering how high the tempers of the men with her were running. Once two were brutally cut down on the spot, the rest gave up without a fight, allowing themselves to be led meekly away. As soon as the guards were taken away, men began pouring out of the mine, running back towards their village. For the moment, they were free, although she was sure most of them were just living in the moment, enjoying their first taste of freedom since the Romans had arrived, and hadn't worked out the full extent of what had happened.

They might be free, but their children were still gone and the threats to those children should they disobey their new masters still existed. In a day or maybe a few hours, the first of the villagers would realize that her arresting the men guarding them could mean the death of their children, and would start asking for reassurances, which she would be unable to give.

She had some time, since they'd taken the Romans by surprise and she already had her men questioning the villagers, making sure all of the Romans who were normally here were accounted for. That meant word wouldn't get to the guards' masters right away, but eventually, a messenger or someone would come to check on the operation and news of her arrests would get out.

Now all she had to do was find the men ultimately responsible, get to them, and seize them before they knew what was happening and before they could harm the children.

Which was easier said than done.

Chapter 18

Lucilla spent the better part of the day questioning the villagers and the captured guards, and the picture they painted of life here after the Romans arrived was bleak. Abuses ranging from regular and rampant raping of the village women to summary execution by the guards for infractions such as being injured while mining or missing quotas. All done under a barrage of threats to the lives of their children, guaranteed to keep the Caledonians in check.

It was all she could do to keep the men with her from killing the guards outright, and even harder to explain to the villagers why she hadn't done that yet. She had decided that, whatever trial or punishments happened, they needed to happen here, in sight of the Caledonians who'd marched with her, so they could spread the word that justice had been done.

The political part of her knew that, eventually, word and the story as told by the villagers would get out, and it would play better if they were able to give first-hand accounts of how they'd received justice. The human side of her knew that she had to do it because that's what she, as a Roman, owed these people for the actions of her countrymen.

Although the guards were able to give little beyond descriptions of their own actions, the man she'd arrested in front of the ornate tent, who turned out to be the foreman left behind to supervise the mining operations, was able to shed some more light on the situation, although not everything she wanted to know.

The man who'd sent the Romans here and was ultimately responsible for everything that happened afterward was named Oppius Plautius Dama. When she'd first heard about this village and its fate, she'd feared that Dama's actions might have happened as some kind of agitation to support the malcontents still hiding in

Roman society, hoping for another chance at Silo's botched insurrection. As far as the foreman was able to say, that, thankfully, wasn't the case. Evil as it might be, this appeared to be the child of simple greed and not some larger scheme to damage the fledgling Britannic Empire.

Before the alliance, he'd already been running a business on the Roman side of the border. The foreman seemed to have the impression that Dama had been successful, although Lucilla wondered how much of that was an employee believing Dama's own propaganda. She might have spent most of her life in the capital, but every one of note ended up in Devnum eventually, and someone of Dama's supposed success would have been noticed by now. It also didn't make sense that he'd be so successful in Roman lands and yet was one of the first to cross the border and chance the backlash from this kind of operation.

Even staying off-site and using proxies to carry out his operations, he was still putting himself in the Caledonian crosshairs, which he had to know. It seemed inconceivable that this mine would produce enough money to make that risk worthwhile if he was already making money more traditionally. Since the anti-slavery laws, this kind of thing would have been shut down quickly, so to be successful, he'd have to know how to run his business without resorting to such methods.

She'd spent a lot of time with merchants and men of Dama's supposed status to know how they thought and operated, and little of the tale the foreman told matched what she knew.

By the late afternoon, she'd finished questioning enough people to know she wasn't going to get what she needed here. The villagers were victims and saw little beyond the guards who'd taken their children and the agents left to manage the operation for little more than functionaries. They were told what they needed to do the tasks they'd been assigned, but little else.

Answers finally came as the light began to fade when Carus rode into the village accompanied by two Caledonians Lucilla hadn't met before. The guard and spymaster had been gone two days and the exhausted expression and bags under his eyes spoke to how busy those days had been for him.

"My Lady," he said, dismounting and walking stiffly to her.

She sympathized with his slight limp. Days in the saddle could wear on anyone who wasn't a superhuman man from a fantastical other world. Her sympathies, however, would have to wait.

"Tell me you have news," she said, getting straight to the point.

"I do. The man behind all of this is named ..."

"Oppius Plautius Dama," Lucilla said, finishing his statement.

Normally, Carus was as stoic as most soldiers she ever met, keeping his feelings bottled up, or at least hidden from others. It was a testament to how tired he must be that she could see him visibly deflate at getting to the answer before he could say it.

"Ohh, you already know."

"I know his name and that he owned businesses on Roman soil before the alliance. That is all I know, however. The people here, even the foreman, don't have much in the way of information on him beyond what he clearly wanted them to believe ... such as running several successful businesses in Rome. No one knows the location of the children or anything that will get us to them."

"He ran several businesses in Rome, is closer to the truth. All of them failed shortly after he tried them, and he has been one step ahead of local magistrates for most of his adult life it seems. From what I've been able to find, there has never been a corner that Dama didn't feel like cutting, and every business he has started, almost exclusively using money he talked out of someone else, has either collapsed spectacularly or was shut down for violating the law. He has a small army of creditors who'd like nothing more than to get a piece of him. It seems the only thing Dama is actually good at is convincing people that he's good at businesses, and to give him money which he will then promptly lose."

"That sounds a lot closer to what I expected than the stories his people here had to share. Tell me that stories aren't the only thing you have, though?"

"No. I know where the children are," Carus said, a note of pride in his voice.

"Where?"

"A villa just over the border in Roman territory. Dama's sister's husband owns a mine not far across the border and keeps a villa nearby for when he has to visit his mines."

"And you're sure the children are there?"

"Yes. I saw it with my own eyes yesterday. As soon as I confirmed it was them, I rode here as fast as I could, since I knew you'd want to know about it. I left two men watching the villa in case the children are moved."

"Good thinking. Are there many guards?"

"A half dozen. Enough to keep children in line, but not enough to stop a force this size. I also came across a praetorian patrol on my way here and instructed them to gather men and wait for us by the border. I thought, since this was going to happen on Roman land, it would be good to have a better mixture of men with you. The guards might not have a problem attacking Caledonian warriors, but they might pause if there were Romans in the mix, and any fighting has a chance to get the children hurt."

"Good. Very good. I know it's late, but I want to ride now. We'll camp for a brief rest near the border and then cross at first light. I don't want to risk word getting back to Dama and something happening to the children."

Carus gave a nod, saluted, and Lucilla returned to Modius and her guards while she prepared everyone to move. She had to hand it to the Caledonians, they might have less general organization than a Roman force, but when they decided to go somewhere, they didn't need the hours of preparations that a Roman force did. In less than an hour her entire force, save a dozen men left behind to watch over the village, just in case, was on the move to retrieve the children.

She ordered the prisoners she already had, the guards and mine supervisors, taken with them. She'd held off rendering any kind of judgment on them until she had a full picture of everything that had happened. Part of that involved interviewing the villagers, which her guards had been doing most of the day. The other part was capturing Dama and the other men responsible, so she could get a better sense of the scope of what had happened.

She knew that, if it were up to the Caledonians, they'd have just executed all of the men involved regardless of what actions they'd taken and leave it at that, but Lucilla was going for something a bit less heavy-handed.

She surprised the praetorians Carus had arranged to meet them at the border, both with the speed of her return and the size of the force she had with her. Thankfully, Faenius had done a good job screening his new praetorians for men who didn't support the new alliance, and removing them, which means those who remained didn't have an issue with working with a force, the majority of which was Caledonian. Beyond that, once they heard the full situation and what was required of them, they quickly fell into the same mindset as the Caledonians.

If anything, they were more incensed over the actions of their countryman, since a Roman's attitude towards their children was much more protective than that of the Caledonians. Properly motivated they moved just as quickly as the rest when the sun crested the horizon, and the entire group reached the villa by mid-day, when one of the men Carus left behind intercepted them to confirm the children were still there.

Although Carus advised caution, concerned that the Dama might do something premature if he saw a large force arriving, Lucilla disagreed. Once she got a sense of the operation, she worked out what kind of man Dama was, and she knew his type well. He'd hold on to every bargaining chip he had, always confident in his own ability to negotiate a way out of the situation he'd put himself in.

She decided on the straightforward approach, ordering the Caledonians and the praetorians to surround the villa, in case Dama had any plans of escape, while she, her guards, and a dozen men went straight to the main gate.

The villa itself was in a valley created by the mountainous region, which meant her force wasn't in sight until they were fairly close, giving her a good view of the villa and its surroundings. She could see the guards panic the moment the horde of Caledonians and Romans crested the hill and began to encircle the villa. Several of the guards looked, dropped their weapons, and tried to make a break for it, only to be intercepted by praetorians on horseback, while others stood meekly, weapons sheathed, waiting for what might have seemed like certain death. One or two put hands to weapons, but removed them when they saw none of their fellows willing to join them.

"Open the gates," Lucilla said, her voice flat, the threat behind it clear even if unspoken.

The guard hesitated for a second, until Cynwrig pulled his sword, nudging his horse forward. The man practically stumbled over himself to rush to the gate and push it open.

"Take the guards into custody, but don't harm them unless they resist," she ordered Cynwrig, since she knew the other Caledonians would listen to him.

An older man in a toga equally as formal as the mine supervisor's, although not to the tacky excess that man had taken, stormed out of the main house just as Lucilla and her men came through the gates of the outer walls. At first, he looked incensed, both at his guards and at the trespassing men, until his eyes landed on Lucilla. She could tell by the way his expression changed that he recognized her, and what that meant for him.

He was the type to take the 'do you know who I am' defense if someone else had tried to apprehend him, and her being there meant that it didn't matter. Any social status he had, or pretended to have, meant little when the Emperor's daughter was the one apprehending him.

"Oppius Plautius Dama?"

"Yes," he said, bringing himself up to his full height, attempting to maintain a regal bearing, although the fear in his eyes and slight shaking of his body made any attempt futile.

"In the name of the Consul and the Emperor, you are under arrest for crimes against the Britannic Empire," she said before turning to one of the praetorians with her. "Seize him and find the children."

Dama didn't put up a fight as two of the men dismounted and grabbed ahold of him, taking him to join the guards they'd already been bringing in. The children were all gathered up in the largest room of the house, where they'd been eating their mid-day meal. She was happy to see they were unharmed. She knew Dama's type and how they looked down on those they considered lesser than themselves, which was just about everyone. It was clear he had no plans of returning the children any time soon and she had feared they would have been mistreated in some way.

"They haven't been harmed," Dama said when she returned from checking on the children. "I was following Caledonian law and tradition and was going to return them as soon as the conditions of my deal with the villagers were met."

"Caledonian tradition and law don't allow for you changing the terms of the agreement the children were given as hostages to secure. Worse for you, Britannic law makes illegal any forced labor outside of imperial sanctioned punishment, and the punishment for such crimes is clear. Under my authority as Consul's representative, you are hereby ordered to be executed. Because of the Consul's decree on how executions should be carried out and recognizing that the children were unharmed, your execution will be quick and painless, and not by the traditional Caledonian method."

Multiple thoughts passed over Dama's face as she declared his sentence. Anger, fear, and oddly, relief. The last one was because of old, and very false, tales of how the Caledonians executed people. When telling bogeyman stories of the people to the north, Romans would talk about men being driven down on sharpened sticks and left to die slowly, at the mercy of the animals and the gods. If true, it would be a particularly slow and horrible way to die. It was also slow and cumbersome, and not how the usually practical northerners tended to deal with executions. As with most tales of the sort, it probably had happened a handful of times, when someone wanted to send a particularly strong message, but normally the Caledonians just opted for fast and efficient beheadings.

It was the Romans who'd executed men slowly and publically and needed a man falling out of the sky to get them to switch to something less gruesome.

"You can't," Dama said, still trying to bargain for his life. "I was following their own barbaric traditions, and I didn't harm any of them. I'm a Roman and they're barbarians, for Pluto's sake."

"They're fellow citizens of the Empire! You and every Roman crossing the borders were warned of what would happen if you violated the rules. Be happy the Caledonian leader didn't come here and deal with you the way he had originally planned, or your entire family would be joining you on the chopping block."

As she'd seen before, Dama then cycled from bargaining to anger, still trying desperately to find a way out of the situation he'd gotten himself in.

"I have friends who will make you and your demented father pay for what you're doing. You can't treat Romans like this. Not for the pathetic lives of north men. You will all pay for tying Rome to these people."

"Maybe," she said, not taking the bait. "But you will not be around to see it."

Turning her horse to the Caledonians and the rest of their prisoners, Lucilla said, "This man and the foreman in charge of the mines will both be executed, their property seized by the Empire and sold off, with all revenue going to the village and its people as restitution for their crimes. The guards will be given the option of either joining the legion in equal position as the freed slaves, to serve for ten years before being released as free men, or assigned for five years to imperial work details, where they will work and live under guard for the good of the Empire."

As the foreman was placed on his knees next to Dama, blubbering, the Caledonians nodded in approval. Many of them would probably prefer to put all of the Romans under the executioner's axe but seemed mollified with the decision to offer restitution to the village.

She'd considered how to handle the men that were involved, but not in charge, on the way here from the village. Had the children been poorly treated, she would have put all of the guards here under the axe as well, but their good treatment earned the men a reprieve. The legion needed bodies and, while they had committed actions they should have known were wrong, the guards didn't deserve to die.

Considering the battle that was coming, this might be a death sentence after all, but at least this way they had a fighting chance of surviving. She thought most would choose the legions, which came with at least some semblance of autonomy. The imperial work detail was just a renaming of the Roman slave gangs made up of criminals and forced to work undesirable jobs such as in mines or forges, where life could be brutal and often short, because of the dangerous conditions, all while continually under guard with very little semblance of freedom.

"You have until we leave to return these children to their families to decide, afterwards, I will decide for you."

The children were kept inside until the executions were finished and the bodies removed. She left behind the praetorians they had met at the border, to deal with the guards who'd agreed to join the legion and the seizing of Dama's and the foreman's properties. Although she trusted the praetorians, who'd been well screened to try and weed out undesirables, she instructed Carus to check to make sure the money really did make it to the villagers as she'd promised.

As they rode back north, she was pleased with how this played out. The children were safe, the villagers were repaid, and the bloodshed had been kept to a minimum.

She knew all of her experiences wouldn't end this well but she felt good about her first, independent, use of real power.

Chapter 19

Monadhcarden

Lucilla knelt at the little altar she'd asked Modius to set up next to Ky's bed, whispering prayers to Jupiter. He continued to lay motionless in his nothing state, not awake and yet not asleep. Although she'd made it sound as if she were confident in his recovery when she'd spoken to Talogren, she could feel the fear in the pit of her stomach.

Part of it was the fear of knowing how soon the time was coming when they'd absolutely need him. She was doing her best to ensure things Ky had already put in place continued to progress, but she didn't know his full plan for the coming battle and wasn't a military commander. Velius and the rest would do their best, and she knew Ky had shared parts of the plan with them, but they weren't going to be able to pull everything he set in motion off on their own. Velius was a good man, but he was young and had only commanded in one large-scale battle, and he'd been doing what Ky had instructed him to do there. She also knew that parts of the plan also required Ky's ability to see what was going on in areas the eye couldn't see. She'd watched him use the small floating disk once before, explaining he could see what it saw as he sent it flying away. No level of training could allow the Romans to reproduce that on their own.

That was only part of her fear, though. Survival of her people was important, but the other part of her fear was personal. She missed talking to him and knowing he'd be there for her. She missed the smell of him and how he froze up when she kissed him, the strong warrior sent by the gods terrified of what she might do. She missed him and wanted him back.

She must have been deep in thought, because the first indication that there was someone else in the tent with her was the clearing of a throat.

"Yes," she said, not looking up from the altar where she was praying.

"Talogren asked me to check how things went at Mwynglawdd. You arrived in the middle of the night and came straight here, which he understands, but he'd like an update."

"I'm surprised none of the men he'd sent with me reported back to him. If he didn't send men instructed to tell him everything they saw, I'd be disappointed in him. Or is he asking me to report to him as one of his subordinates?"

She realized she was being needlessly caustic with Llassar, who was just the messenger. What Talogren was asking wasn't unreasonable, even if he did send men to spy on her, and she knew both Ky and her father would have done the same, but she wasn't in the frame of mind to deal with political maneuvering. She had arrived in the middle of the night, pushing the men with her hard to get back to the Caledonian capital as quickly as they could, and hadn't slept since she'd gotten back. She was tired and had been on the verge of tears for hours as she begged the gods to return Ky to her.

She knew all that and yet couldn't stop herself from taking it out on Llassar, and just hoped he would forgive her for her attitude.

"Of course he did, but that isn't the same as a first-hand report. We all appreciate your concern for the Consul, but many of my people are still unsure of this alliance and will see giving the task of apprehending these Romans to one of their countrymen as a major mistake."

"I know, and I will see him today. For now, tell him all of the children were returned, the man and his primary agents executed and their property ordered sold and given to the village as restitution, and all of the guards and other men involved given the choice between being placed on forced work details or joining the legions for ten years."

"That's what we'd heard, and why he'd wanted to speak with you. The money was a good move, but he wanted to know why more men hadn't been executed. If it were him or any other Caledonian commander, every man responsible for this crime would have ended up on the stake."

She sighed and pushed herself up from the altar, blowing out the small flame flicking there from the burned offerings, facing the Caledonian.

"I know, which is why I'd wanted to go in his place. I get that it would make everyone feel better if we just executed everyone involved, but that would have been a mistake. This time, they gave up without harming the captive villagers or their children. When this happens again, if they know we're just going to execute everyone, there is no reason for the criminals to give up so easily. Men will die apprehending them and people caught in the middle will die out of spite. If those who worked for the men behind the crime know that they won't be killed outright, they will think twice about fighting."

"That's why Talogren wanted them all executed, to keep this from happening ever again."

"If he thinks a few executions will end this, then he's a fool."

Llassar's face hardened. She knew he liked her as a person, but he had strong personal fealty to Talogren and her insult clearly pushed the boundaries for him.

"I'm sorry, that came out wrong. I know he's not a fool, but he isn't thinking this through. There will always be people willing to do this kind of thing, even if they know the penalty is death, and always others desperate enough to follow them. Sometimes they think they can talk their way out of the penalty, sometimes they think they'll be overlooked or that they can get away, but most of the time they don't even consider what could happen to them when they're caught. Greed blinds men from seeing the consequences of their actions. This will happen again, and I want to make sure when it does, we don't end up with unneeded bloodshed."

Lucilla paused. The hardest part of dealing with the Caledonians was their rather straightforward way of seeing the world. Other Romans who hadn't gotten to know them might call it simplistic, but she thought that did them a disservice. They were every bit as complex in their motivations and desires as anyone else, they just culturally preferred to come straight at an issue, rather than talking around it for days and never getting to the point, like Romans seemed to prefer.

In general, she found this approach refreshing, but there were times when it meant they'd bulldoze straight over the complexities of a situation, seeing only the immediate outcome and not predicting the long-term possibilities. Talogren was generally better at this than his countrymen, which is why he'd been able to see far enough ahead to grasp the benefits of the alliance, but even he was sometimes blind beyond his initial impulses.

"I know you and your countrymen aren't afraid of danger, but the Empire needs you, all of you, and can't afford to let you throw your lives away over pride. The people responsible are dead, the villagers have all of their children back and have gotten something in return for what they had to endure. The men that helped are going to serve the Empire and help make sure your people remain free from the Carthaginians, and they will be around as living examples to others. Will this lesson have to be taught again to others? Yes. Eventually, there will be enough people telling the story of how they ended up in work details or in the legions to make it harder for those who want to take advantage of others to find help. That, in the long run, will be what protects your people better than any number of executions."

"I see," Llassar said.

She thought that, in his understated way, that was him agreeing with her, or at least not disagreeing, but it was impossible to tell. The man was sometimes infuriatingly difficult to read.

"I will go and speak to Talogren shortly, but if you report back to him, let him know I need to take Ky south, so he is on hand for the battle when he wakes up. We've passed the winter solstice. Spring will be here shortly, and we have to get final preparations completed."

"I understand. When will you leave?"

"As soon as we can. Any of the men who traveled here with Ky are welcome to return with us and help in the battle, but I understand if Talogren needs to keep his warriors to make sure the villages you just incorporated stay pacified."

"I believe most planned to return with the Consul."

"Yes, that was the original plan, but with him being incapacitated, I know many of your warriors will be rethinking that. I want them to know I understand and there are no hard feelings if that is what they decide to do."

"I will let them know, although I think you will be surprised by how many will agree to follow you in his stead."

She thought that she actually wouldn't be surprised. She was aware of her growing popularity among the north men and, while she didn't try to exploit it, since they would see that for what it was, she had started to count on it when making her calculations. She also wasn't going to point that out to Llassar or any of his countrymen. While they generally preferred straightforwardness, to the point where they had made bragging an art, they also wanted humility in their women.

"I hope so."

She gave Llassar some time to report back before making the trip to see his chieftain directly, if nothing else to spare her having to explain everything she'd done again. She spent the time with Ky praying for his recovery before deciding enough time had passed to pay her respects, and answer for her decisions.

She stopped short of the doorway, putting up a hand to stop the Talogren's guards from announcing her presence right away. Considering Llassar's reaction, Lucilla steeled herself for a moment before nodding to the guards outside of Talogren's hut, letting them know she was ready for them to introduce her.

"So, you returned," he said when she walked through the hut entrance.

He was sitting at a small table to one side of the hut, eating some kind of burned meat that she could only guess at. She liked a lot of things about the Caledonians, but their culinary traditions had left a lot to be desired, consisting mostly of a wheat mush mixed with goats milk, mostly to cover the already rotting wheat. Because of the way they farmed and the limits to their permanent buildings designed to house grain while keeping it aerated, this far in the winter their supplies had already started to mold and rot. Because it was still their staple food and there weren't many other options, they tended to continue eating it even in this condition, using strong flavors like fish and goat's milk to cover the rotting taste.

The richer Caledonians tended to eat a fair amount of goat and sheep, both of which did well in the mountainous conditions. She normally liked sheep, but goat was too gamey for her, and she preferred the Roman preparations over the Caledonian method of cooking it till it was black with little to no seasoning or flavorings.

"I have. Did Llassar report back to you?"

"He did. Does that bother you?"

"No. I would have done the same thing if I was in your position, just like I would have had men that accompanied the expedition report back as soon as they returned with early, even if undetailed, reports. In your position, there is no such thing as too much information."

"Good. I'm glad you understand. That's the thing I like about you Romans. You might be arrogant and entitled, but you at least don't let your honor and personal pride get in the way of practical measures. I love my people, but I usually have to be more secretive about these kinds of things to keep tempers from boiling over at my dishonoring the people I was having watched."

"Thank you ... I think."

"So you really feel only executing two of the people responsible will be enough of a deterrent?"

"If by that, you mean do I think it will stop this from happening again ... no. But as I said to Llassar, and he undoubtedly reported word for word back to you, I don't think any number of bodies would have stopped this from happening again. I do think it will stop some of the people who might consider doing this, and probably as many as would be stopped by executing all of them. I also think this outcome allows restitution to the villagers and puts a penalty on the rest of the men in a way that best serves the Empire, if not the desire for vengeance. I also think knowing what they are being forced into, and the years of conflict ahead of us, men will think twice about taking these kinds of orders again."

"I see," he said, without much emotion. "I still think my solution would stop more of these kinds of people, but I respect your reasoning and see where it has its benefits. Consider this the end of the discussion."

This would have been the third time he'd heard her explanation, even if it was the first time he'd heard it for himself, so she wasn't surprised at how nonchalantly he took it.

"I also wanted to let you know I am leaving with Ky this afternoon. I want to get to the headquarters camp of the fourth legion by nightfall. Since the alliance is finalized and the praetorians are taking over patrolling the border with your people, I don't see the need for a legion to be stationed as a guard between us any longer. Ky was planning on pulling them out as soon as you had finished pacifying the north, and I wanted to honor that plan."

"Yes, Llassar told me that as well. Do you think he will be fit to travel, in his condition?"

"I don't see why not. You brought him here by wagon from Rhaeadr and he was fine. Other than laying still and not responding, he doesn't seem to have any other physical ailments I could find, so lying here or in a wagon shouldn't matter."

"I see."

"Have you given any more thoughts to integrating the men you have patrolling the border into the praetorians? I know Ky brought it up with you, but I had not heard what your decision was."

"That is because I haven't made one. His reasoning was sound and I appreciate that it will be a separate organization to the Roman praetorians, with their own commanders, all reporting to the same man, but I am still not sure that is wise."

"Is it because the praetorians have a Roman commander that your people would still have to report to?"

"We really are just backward, barbaric people only concerned with our honor to you, aren't we?"

Although the words stung, he'd offered them with no heat or anger in his voice, which confused Lucilla.

"I didn't mean any offense."

"I know, and I know why you would think that would be my concern, since we really are overly stuck on our personal sense of honor, but no. That isn't why I am unsure. I agreed to this treaty because Ky convinced me it would be good for the Caledonians, and we would eventually become one people. With our own cultures, true, but given enough time, we'd start to see each other as equals, and identify as just Britannians, and not Romans or Caledonians. My concern is that, the more we place ourselves in a position to be separate, even if equal, from the Romans, we will always stand apart from you. I was thinking if it was a good idea to have my people in their own organization, instead of just integrating them wholesale into the praetorians."

"You're people would go for that?"

"At first there'd be complaints, but I don't think it would last long. Ky likes to point out how much just being around each other will lessen our prejudices. I was concerned that your praetorian commander would not want Caledonians mixed in his command, however."

"I can speak with him. He might not like it, but if my father demands it, he will have to accept it."

"Good, then speak with your father. Although this does open up additional concerns."

"Such as?"

"So far, it has been Roman organizations that we have been integrating into. I can see the need for that, considering my people have always been much more … nomadic than yours, but this has led to my people constantly taking a subservient role in these organizations. We serve under Roman commanders, we obey a Roman Emperor, and we listen to Roman politicians. For this alliance to work, there will need to be Romans serving under a Caledonian leader."

"That is a good point, and one I hadn't thought of."

"I had been meaning to bring it up to Ky, but he fell before I could speak to him."

"He and I never spoke of it, but I agree with you. I'll speak to my father and we'll find positions of leadership for your people in joint operations. It might take some time, however."

"I understand. I know you have the Carthaginian army to worry about, and we will be patient, although not forever."

"I understand. I need to get my men preparing to move out. We've already stayed here longer than Ky planned for, and we are in need of every man we can gather together, ready to fight."

"I understand. We've thrown our fortunes in with you now, so if you fail in this fight, it won't just be your people that suffer the consequences."

"Then we'll have to not fail," Lucilla said.

Lucilla returned to the hut she was sharing with Ky and called their collective guards together. After handing out instructions and sending them out to get everything prepared, she spent a few more hours praying over Ky, since it would be harder to find time to beg the gods' help while they were traveling. Part of her felt bad, sitting in here with Ky while the men worked, but there wasn't much she could do to help without being in the way.

If it were just her, him, and their collected guards, it wouldn't take much to get everything together and start traveling south. Things changed though, when a large force moved across the country. It was easy to provision a couple of dozen men for the week's journey, but an entire force, their animals, and all the camp followers that always came with that large of a group, required a thought-out set of logistics to keep everything fed and moving.

It was made harder by the fact that a largely Caledonian force was moving through Roman territory and to be extra sensitive of the effect they had on the civilians, who would be predisposed to distrust their new allies. This basically meant living off the land or trading for goods was going to be of limited value and they'd need to bring whatever supplies they needed for the journey with them, which meant more men, more animals, and more mouths to feed.

She was glad to see that Talogren had been able to grasp the reasonings behind her decision to only execute a handful of Romans and giving lesser punishments to the rest. It really did speak volumes about how much more strategic he was in his thinking and explained why he'd been able to do what no northerner had been able to do before him: unite his people into a single country instead of dozens of independent villages. It was a small blessing that someone of his ability was here in the north at the same time that someone like Ky had come to the Romans. If either hadn't been here, the alliance and any chance of surviving the Carthaginians would have disappeared.

She stayed with Ky until late into the morning, when it was time for the Consul to be loaded into a cart for travel. She left the logistics to Modius and Carus, both of whom were better at this kind of thing than she was.

She knew that Ky would find her constant prayer over him to be silly. For someone she still thought was sent by the gods, he'd made it clear he didn't believe in any kind of higher power and that the time spent worshiping them could have been put to better use on more practical concerns. Considering how different he was, down to having a seemingly all-knowing disembodied voice in his head, it wasn't hard to accept his lack of faith.

She didn't bring up her belief that he was an agent of the gods, regardless of his lack of belief in them, but part of her had hoped that the gods were listening and would bring him back to her. She knew two days of prayer wasn't going to be enough to convince them, but until the moment she stopped to begin the journey south, she'd secretly hoped he would just sit up and ask her how everything had been going while he was asleep.

When Modius came in and told her it was time to get Ky and the remaining possessions loaded up, she sighed and pushed herself up from the small alter she'd set up. She'd maintained a brave face for the others, but she was beginning to fear he might not ever come out of his long sleep.

She gave Modius a nod that told him she was coming and, when her guard had gone, leaned over and kissed Ky lightly on the forehead.

"Time to go home," she whispered to him, before collecting herself and mentally preparing to face the world again.

Giving one last sigh, she stepped through the tent and stopped, surprised at the very large collection of men waiting for her. She'd heard the noises of course, while she'd been praying, but she'd thought it was just the sounds of the village going about its day, and had ignored it. The spaces of the semi-permanent tents she had been allowed to use was now packed with a huge array of Caledonians, some she recognized from traveling with them, and some who'd accompanied her to free the villagers and their children; and others were men she'd never spoken to, but who'd apparently decided they wanted to return with her. What was clear was that the number of men waiting for her was significantly more than she or Ky had brought north.

In front of the men, Modius and his men, along with Ky's lictore stood with Llassar and Cynwrig, who was smiling from ear to ear.

"Goodness. All of these men are coming back with us?" she asked Llassar.

"These are just some of the men, there are more outside the village, waiting. Men have been arriving all day, some from as far away as Rhaeadr. There are almost a thousand men in all."

"But ... how?"

"Partly it's the actions you took to free our people from the Romans, partly it's because of the steps you've taken to help the western villages while they recover, and partly it's because of him," Llassar said, jabbing a thumb in Cynwrig's direction.

"Because of Cynwrig?"

"Apparently, while you've been safely guarded here, he's been traveling the area around the village, telling warriors who helped Talogren secure the rest of the countryside why they should now go with you and fight the death worshipers. He can be very persuasive, apparently."

"You did this?" She asked Cynwrig.

"I said I'd help guard you, and you are headed towards what everyone keeps telling me is a massive army. Since I can only kill about half that many men by myself, I thought the best way to protect you would be to get as many others to help me as possible."

She couldn't help but smile at his boast. When she'd first met the man, she'd found his braggadocios nature off-putting and somewhat annoying, but the more she'd been around him, the more she'd found it almost amusing. It helped to realize that, while he was highly confident, most of his boasts were purposefully exaggerated specifically to get a rise out of opponents or as a way to entertain himself. Now she just found it charming.

"And a good job you did. With this many brave warriors, the legions might as well stand down and let you deal with the Carthaginians yourself. Maybe show them a thing or two," she said with a smile.

Modius and a few Romans frowned at that, but the Caledonians erupted into cheers before beginning to chant 'little bird.' She waited a few moments for the men to settle down, knowing that she'd also have to do some damage control with her and Ky's Romans. It was a balancing act to keep both happy without directly insulting or belittling the other, and she sometimes veered too far one way or the other, but she did want the Caledonians to know how much she appreciated their faith in her.

"Are you going with us?" she asked Llassar.

"I am. I spoke with Talogren after you left, and he suggested that I would be more helpful to you, especially while the Consul is unavailable. He thought you could use my help managing the Caledonian forces."

She wondered how much of their conversation Talogren had shared with his lieutenant. It wouldn't surprise her if Talogren really did tell him that he wanted Llassar to assist in commanding the Caledonian forces. Now that she had met him and spoken with him as an equal, and not their captive, she'd been able to see that there was much more to the Caledonian leader than her fellow Romans would give him credit for. He was very crafty and played the game as well as anyone south of the border.

She was certain that this was more than just making sure the Caledonian forces were put to their best use. She could recognize the message he was sending, prompting her to move faster to get Caledonians into positions of power and his not-too-subtle suggestion as to who a good candidate would be.

Llassar, although stoic and hard to read, was much more straightforward than his chieftains, and she doubted he had grasped the nuances behind his orders. She knew her father and Ky would have seen the move for what it was, and without Ky to speak to, it was up to her to figure out how to best use Llassar, both to ensure their long-term victory against the Carthaginians and as a further step to seal the alliance between the Romans and the Caledonians.

Instead, all that she said was, "I'm happy to have you with us."

Chapter 20

Although she wanted to ride with Ky's wagon as she had on the trip back to the Caledonian capital, as leader of this surprisingly large contingent her place was in front of the column. Even though they weren't headed directly for conflict, Caledonian tradition said the leader always rode at the head of the column, with only scouts and pickets allowed to ride before them. Considering there were almost a thousand Caledonians with her and only a handful of Romans, this was most definitely a Caledonian force and she needed to respect their traditions.

That would remain true even after they reached the fourth legion's command group since, although the fourth was four times as large even at its currently reduced size, it would take them time to pull in all of its patrols and pull out of its long-held position. Lucilla didn't want to wait for them, and planned on leaving as soon as she gave its legate commands, which meant it would only be her and her Caledonians continuing south.

As soon as they were underway, she sent one of the men back for Carus, who was riding with the rest of the lictore with Ky's wagon. She'd considered waiting until they reached the fourth legion for this conversation, since it mostly would focus on the military outlook and she'd always been more concerned with politics, rather than the legions. Ultimately, she decided it wasn't worth waiting. They wouldn't arrive at the fourth legion until fairly late in the evening and the legate had been stationed up by the border for quite a while. Ky had stopped to speak with him several times and he was getting updates on the military situation, but she thought it might take more time getting him up to speed than she'd save by having his point of view added to the conversation.

"You sent for me?" Carus asked as he rode up to catch her, which wasn't difficult considering the horses had to be kept at a pace equal to a thousand marching men.

"Yes. While I pray every night for Ky's full recovery, it is late and we can't afford to wait hopefully for him any longer. I know I'm not a military commander, or a soldier of any sort, and that if Ky doesn't wake the battle will be left up to Velius's directions, but since I was selected as Ky's stand-in as Consul while he was unavailable, I want to do my best to fulfill that role. All of which is to say, I'd like you to bring me up to date on what you know about Ky's plans for the Carthaginian army."

"I see. You understand that I only handle information collection for the Consul, yes? I have been working with Ramirus setting up assets in the southern Roman areas trying to identify Carthaginian scouts and I have received reports of the interrogations of those scouts we've captured, but that is the extent of my work in the military area. Most of the information the Consul has given me instructions to collect focused on either domestic areas or building a network here in the north. What information has been given to me about the military situation I've duly passed on to the Consul, who hasn't discussed them with me. The person you need to have this conversation with is Velius, who has been the most involved in designing our strategy towards the Carthaginian forces."

"Although I didn't know the specific areas he had you focusing on, I did know you weren't directly involved in the military planning. I also know you are both clever and curious, a combination that leads you to be constantly paying attention to everything that happens around you. I also know, as one of Ky's lictore, you are often present when he has these meetings and are one of the few people allowed in the room. If you haven't gathered some idea of what he's planning, then I may have overestimated your abilities."

"I think that was a compliment; and yes, I have worked out some of it on my own. I just wanted you to know that anything I do have to say, might be in error and is purely my own understanding."

"Consider me warned. Don't worry, Carus, I won't be making any decisions based purely on this information and I do plan on having a similar conversation with Velius, but I have found it is better to go into a conversation already knowing a lot of what I'm about to hear, than going in blind and learning it for the first time."

"A wise policy. In the simplest terms, my understanding is that the Consul was going to head south to meet the army further from the capital. You're aware of his ability to see things at a far distance, yes?"

"Yes."

"He plans on using this to position the bulk of the army where the Carthaginians can't see it, and use smaller parts of the army as bait to pull them into the trap. He hopes that, by doing this, he can pull the Carthaginians into a battle where their lines are compressed and ours are extended limiting their manpower advantage."

"We have thousands of soldiers. Even seeing the Carthaginians so far away, how can we hide that many until the Carthaginians get close enough to close the trap?"

"I believe he planned to use the landscape to obscure the army, but as for where, I don't know. I do know he had a location where he wanted the battle to take place picked out, based on the most likely path of advance of the Carthaginian armies, but I'm not sure where that is, specifically. I do know that Velius has been paying close attention to where we find the Carthaginian scouts and what information we can get out of them, to see if the Consul's predictions on the path of advance were accurate."

"If they come another way, do we have alternate places to fight that meet with his plan of concealing the legions?"

"I don't know. I would think so considering how much the Consul looks forward to possibilities, but I have not heard alternate plans mentioned. I would warn again that I am often not in the room for these conversations as my duties both as lictore and hub of information for the Consul often lead to me being called away. They very well could have discussed these alternate plans and I just never heard them mentioned."

"I understand. Do you know if he plans on using the Caledonian forces that chose not to integrate into the legions as part of the bait force?"

"I don't. I assume you are concerned with how it will look to the Caledonians if all of the men used to lure the Carthaginians in were Caledonian."

"Yes. I know enough about military strategy to know that for something like that to work, the bait force would have to make it convincing. They would have to fight and suffer losses to make the retreat seem real, otherwise the Carthaginians wouldn't believe it. The Caledonians will notice if all of the sacrificial lambs were their warriors."

"A valid question, and one I don't know the answer to. You can speak with Velius about that, since he would know if the decision's already been made. Normally, I'd say that is exactly the kind of point that should be brought up with the Consul."

She nodded but didn't reply. Since she'd been working with the Caledonians she'd made several observations she wished she could discuss with Ky, but hadn't been able to. The longer he was unconscious, the more she realized that his absence felt almost like the absence of a limb. She knew what she wanted to do, but she was unable to actually do it without him there.

For the thousandth time since coming north, she wished he were here with her.

Fourth Legion Camps

The legion camps were a bustle of activity as she rode through the perimeter and into the camp itself. She had sent ahead one of her Roman guards as a messenger for the legate of the fourth legion, letting them know she was coming with a very large contingent of Caledonians.

Although they were all allies now, the fourth had been facing off against the northerners for longer than any other legion and it was just human nature that seeing a thousand warriors marching towards them would have sent the camp into disarray, regardless of any documents signed between the two people. She'd also had most of the Caledonians halt a mile from the Roman lines and set up camp, with orders for Llassar to have them ready to move in the morning, when both they and the fourth legion would start the march south to join the rest of the Roman forces.

As she rode through the camp itself, she saw multiple groups of legionnaires either putting on their armor or already armored, hustling towards the perimeter she had just ridden through. This was not part of a move to pack up the camp preparing to march south, however. Those that she saw preparing were not loading supplies or taking down the semi-permanent structures they had put in place over the last year that they'd been in this position.

Vibius, the fourth's commander, was coming out of his tent to greet her as she rode up and dismounted. She'd never met the man, but he wore the more ornate armor and carried a legate's helmet under his arm, making it easy to identify the man.

"My lady," he said with a slight bow. "I am Vibius Sepurcius Ennodius, legate of the fourth legion. I received your messenger several hours ago with news of your arrival, but his warning that you would have a large number of Caledonians with you did not prepare me for the number that is being reported."

"Then I applaud you on your ability to adjust to the unexpected. I know that the Consul rode through here with five times as many men not so long ago, also headed south towards the capital. I am a little at a loss for why your camp seems to be preparing for an invasion, instead of welcoming allies."

"I'm not sure what you mean."

"I mean, your men are forming a line facing the Caledonians that rode with me. I will admit I have never served in the legions, so perhaps I have confused the sight of men donning armor and running sword in hand towards the Caledonians as something it's not. Perhaps this is how your legion prepares to permanently leave its camps and march towards the Capital as ordered."

Although she never raised her voice, the sarcasm was palpable and she could see the mixture of anger and frustration on Vibius's face. Waving towards one of his commanders, he whispered something in the man's ear, half pointing towards the direction that Lucilla had come from.

As soon as the man ran that direction, "No, you have not misread that, however, they won't attack and I've sent my man to make sure they don't cause any problems."

"That's not good enough legate. Your men must stand down. I don't want anyone not currently assigned guard duty on that section of the camp perimeter armed. If all of those men have so much free time, they should ready themselves for the march. It's a long way back to Devnum and this camp has set down enough roots that it will take time to extract yourselves."

"You have my word, we will be ready to move as soon as you give the word in the morning. You have to understand, my lady, that we have been facing off against the Picts for a long time, and we've seen what those barbarians are capable of."

"Those 'barbarians' are the Caledonii, legate, and they are our fellow citizens in the new Empire. The thousand men out there waiting to cross the border have put aside their differences and have agreed to follow me south to join the five-thousand of their men who've already joined our forces to fight against Carthaginians, even though their homes are not directly threatened like ours are. From where I sit, only one group has barbaric attitudes, and it's not the Caledonii."

"My lady ..." Vibius said, a worried expression crossing his face.

She however wouldn't let him, and plowed right over whatever he was going to say.

"I am, however, not someone who expects the impossible. I know you and the Caledonii have been fighting each other for a while and I know it will take time to accept them as the allies they now are. I am not one to hold a man's beliefs against him, unless they directly threaten the safety of the Empire. You are not, however, a common legionnaire. You are a legate of one of the Emperor's legions, entrusted with thousands of Britannic lives and the well-being of the Empire. That means that while I can understand you holding personal reservations about your new allies, I cannot abide you losing discipline among your troops or allowing them to threaten or otherwise aggravate internal tensions on the eve of what might be the most important battle in our long history. You need to get your house in order, and you need to do it now. Is that clear, legate?"

"Yes, my lady," he said, not making eye contact.

"Good. I'm sure you will get this business straightened out as soon as we finish here. As for the move south, I want you in Devnum no later than two weeks from today. Every sign says that the Carthaginians will be marching before the ground thaws, so we must gather all of our forces now."

"I haven't received specific orders yet about ..."

"You understand that I am the Consul's hand-picked representative, correct?"

"Yes, but I thought with the Consul incapacitated ..."

"Nothing has changed. He will be back up and around soon, and my appointment has not been ended by his being indisposed. If you feel this is incorrect, you can always go above my head and apply for a second opinion from the man I report to, while the Consul is unavailable. My father is a very understanding man and I'm sure will hear your concerns in the spirit they are offered."

"No, no. There's no need for that. I will of course follow your instructions."

"Good. I will be bringing my men through here tomorrow to continue south. I don't want a repeat of what happened today. Are we clear?"

"Yes, my lady."

"Good. Move quickly, legate. We need you and your men with the rest of our forces. I am not exaggerating when I say the future existence of our people relies on it."

Devnum

"Again," the optio shouted as men in a wide variety of dress struggled with the unfamiliar equipment in their hands.

Velius sat on horseback behind the training civilians and wondered again what Ky could have possibly been thinking. He understood the basic political thinking, conscripting the civilian population to fight off invaders as a last-ditch bid for survival, but seeing these men train, he couldn't help but doubt the practical value of the move.

While there'd been stories of brave stands of civilians against an organized military from Rome's past, including tales of both Roman civilians fighting to the last and barbarians resisting Roman legions, those were all far outside of living memory, and he'd always doubted their veracity.

There were more recent accounts from still-living men of Roman cities being overwhelmed by Carthaginian forces as the Empire slowly lost territory, and those stories always involved the civilians crumbling under trained forces and the slaughter of everyone who attempted to resist them.

Untrained civilians just could not compete with real soldiers, either Greek-style phalanxes or the Roman legionnaires, who trained in close unit movement and tactics continually. It's why even brave and highly skilled warriors who fought as individuals instead of collective units, like their new Caledonian allies, continually lost open field conflicts. Close unit combat required incredible discipline and training that couldn't be matched by people fighting individually.

He knew that Ky wasn't planning on putting these people on the field in personal combat, which made this plan somewhat different, but anyone on the field of battle could become overrun and forced to fight in close quarters.

He had to admit he was impressed with the Consul's arcuballista design and how easy it had been for the civilians to pick up, and how it made up for a lot of problems with the design that the Romans had used before his arrival. While Ky's version was recognizable as being related to the Roman design in that it looked like a bow turned on its side and laid against a wooden frame that the user would hold, that was where their resemblance ended.

The first difference someone looking at the two weapons would notice is the handle coming down from Ky's version, which didn't exist on the original Roman version. In the original design, the rounded butt of the weapon would press against the shoulder while the user gripped the center of the wooden shaft with his off-hand. With their dominant hand, they'd grip a metal hook that extended from the bottom, pulling back on it to release the catch that held the string in place, releasing the bolt at its target.

In Ky's design, the shoulder butt had been slightly redesigned into a thin, curved rectangle that slightly wrapped along the shape of the shoulder, allowing more of the wood to connect, lessening the impact of the weapon as it recoiled back into the shoulder. While that made it more comfortable, that part of the change was almost inconsequential. The real change was the handle. Instead of a metal hook extended back, there was a piece of carved wood wrapped in leather bindings that fit the hand almost like the hilt of a sword. Extending from the main frame of the weapon was a small piece of metal that Ky had called the trigger.

Where the user had to grip the side of the weapon hard, so they could pull back the metal hook, here the handle gave the user leverage, allowing them to rest the weapon easily instead of using force to hold it in place. Not having a long metal hook coming out of the body of the weapon also allowed the off hand to go under the body of the weapon instead of along the side, which made the off hand more of a cradle. Instead of this awkward piece of wood that a user would jam and press firmly into their shoulder, this weapon felt almost natural, to the point where many of the civilians would look at the soldier demonstrating its use and easily copy the way they held the weapon, because it just felt right.

While it was easy to see the advantages in the stability of the weapon as you held and aimed it, someone who'd tried both versions, as Velius had, found the benefits went beyond just keeping the weapon in place. In the original version, one of the reasons pressure had to be applied back into the user's shoulder was to make the body a counterweight to the press upon the metal firing hook. No matter how much pressure the user applied, however, there was always up and down movement from the jerk of the metal piece, which was naturally tight to hold the bow in place. A trained user could adjust for that, knowing how their weapon would move when they fired and aim a little up or down to compensate, but left untrained users firing the bolt above their targets' head or into the dirt.

Ky had added a series of levers off of a small piece of metal that protruded that allowed a lot less force to move the firing mechanism where a long, single metal lever had been used before. Looking at the design, even Velius, who wasn't a scholar by any definition, could see how it worked and the benefits the multiple levers added, making him wonder why it had never been tried before.

Ky had explained it probably had occurred to the designers, since they understood the use of applied levers, but that a simpler design would have been chosen instead, because Roman smiths wouldn't have been able to get the precision needed. Velius still didn't really understand how standardized and exact units of measurement made smiths craft identical pieces, down to the smallest distance, but it had worked. From what Hortensius had told him, very few of the pieces coming out of the foundries had to be discarded for being imprecise.

There were other changes, like a stronger metal limb across the front, which allowed a tighter pull than the old way, which was a thin wooden board made of young wood that would be firm enough to bend properly. The new steel Ky introduced was significantly stronger than what they'd been using before, which meant it could also be pounded flatter than previously. The thinner metal could bend much further before it got close to breaking, allowing the limb to be shorter than the old Roman one and giving the string a much tighter draw, which put real punch behind the bolt. Previously, a Roman arcuballista could punch into a shield and might push through thinner armor, but could be deflected by chest pieces and stopped by shields. While the range was still shorter than that of a standard bow, the arcuballista would have a lot more punch. At close ranges, they could punch all the way through a wooden Roman shield and several inches through armor and into the target.

The downside of that tighter draw, however, was that the operator couldn't just put their foot on the limb and pull up on the string by hand. Instead, each weapon had a little metal piece attached to the underside of the weapon when it was stored, that would hook around the bow and work as a level that the user could pull up on the string and lock it in place.

All of these advances combined together to make a much more effective weapon. While the range still might not be enough to make it better than volley fire from standard bows, which could fire further and faster, the new arcuballista had one major advantage that could make it a destabilizing force in current military strategy.

A good archer took years of intense training to be able to maintain accuracy and speed. Even men who came into service already possessing good skills with a bow would take a long time to become proficient in volley fire, which was very different than skills used for hunting and target shooting.

By contrast, the arcuballista could be picked up quickly by anyone, usually needed only a few days of training to be proficient enough to effectively participate in a battle. The shooter might not be able to hit a target or even get close to it, but when firing at a massed phalanx marching towards you, the only thing you needed to know how to do was not shooting into the dirt.

They could, theoretically, turn thousands of average citizens into a ranged auxiliary, freeing up better-trained soldiers for more direct action. Their only limiting factor now was being able to produce enough of the new weapons to arm everyone willing to fight. There were so many bottleneck points, from the assembly using the new methods the Consul had introduced to the new foundries producing enough of the higher quality steel to the smiths working with the new metal for the first time.

It seemed nearly every step in the weapons development relied on some new process introduced only a few months before, which meant everyone was having to adjust.

Having watched multiple groups of militia going through training with the new weapons, Velius could see how they worked into Ky's plans and how they could help even out the manpower disadvantage Rome was facing.

If they could get enough of the weapons produced.

Chapter 21

Devnum

Lucilla was exhausted as she finally made her way back into the imperial palace and turned her horse over to the grooms that would take it to the stables. The trip south had been fairly uneventful, since the Romans along the road between Devnum and the border had seen several large formations of Caledonians by now. It was still no easy task to move that many men, their supplies, and the hordes of camp followers across friendly ground without causing undue hardships on the population as they passed.

It wasn't unusual for armies to be like locusts, stripping the land bare wherever they were, regardless of allegiances. Ky had made it a point to keep that from happening when he'd traveled south with five times the number of men Lucilla had brought, which meant she could do no less.

Thankfully, once they arrived in the capital, she was able to turn the job of getting all these men settled and integrated with their countrymen over to Llassar. He had wisely sent a messenger ahead with instructions to have accommodations for the men prepared. It would still be a few days for them to recover from the march before they were fully able to begin training with the other Caledonians, but not having to build their own camp would speed that process up.

Once she was assured Llassar had everything in hand, she begged off the offered celebratory feasts and returned home. Except for short trips to oracles or to visit outlying towns, mostly as a reminder to the people that the Emperor still knew they existed, Lucilla had spent her entire life in Devnum. After a month away, mostly in the saddle traveling here and there, there was an odd alien feel to her home. The buildings and semi-regularly cleaned streets felt so different after living in temporary camps. The streets - just snow and mud between tents, or in Caledonian villages - weren't much more permanent than the camps they stayed at most nights.

She wanted nothing more than to escape to the baths, and a night in her own bed; but as usual, that had to wait. Her first, and to her most important, task was to make sure Ky was transferred from the wagon, where he'd spent most of the trip, to the bed in his quarters. Instead of standing outside his room, waiting to be summoned, one of his lictore would be stationed in his room with him at all times, in case his condition changed, in either direction. She left very specific instructions that, while some of the physicians could check on him, they were not to touch him or attempt any procedures unless she approved it, on pain of death.

She still wasn't clear on how the small things Ky called nanos living inside his body, and now her body, worked, but she knew they were keeping him physically alive. The completely healed gash on his chest was proof enough of that. While she thought nanos could probably counteract whatever they might try to do in their attempts to help him, she wasn't prepared to risk it. Although Ky was usually very circumspect in his judgments towards the way her people lived, one of the areas where he'd had trouble containing himself, was their medical technology in general and the physicians specifically. He'd spoken to them several times, trying to explain why the way they thought of the human body was wrong and how to better go about treating it, and had run up against stubborn disbelief almost every time.

According to Ky, people in his society rarely died from cuts or childbirth - two things that were all too common in Rome - and they never experienced the regular plagues that swept through Devnum. He'd said, several times, that the worst thing someone could do if they were injured was to seek assistance from one of the city's physicians, at least until he could convince them to alter their ways.

She was, however, still concerned that this un-waking sleep he was in would end; and he would suddenly stop breathing, or the blood in his veins would stop pumping. Although it seemed unlikely that there was anything she or his guards could do in that event, she wanted to at least know it was happening. By the time she left his annoyed guards, she was at least confident that they understood how important it was to never take their eyes off the Consul, if only to save from incurring her wrath.

Once Ky was safely tucked in bed, she had only one more task to do before she could wash the road grime off of herself. She knew this would be the thing that would take the longest. She loved her father, but at times he could carry on for hours; and, as the dutiful daughter, she had to sit and listen to his musings and act as a sounding board for whatever was bothering him that day.

Although she'd spent a lot of time with Ky since his arrival, there were very few days she could remember not speaking with her father, and this trip had been the longest she'd been separated from him.

She found him deep in conversation with Lurio, the imperial treasurer, which wasn't an uncommon sight. The empire, more than ever, ran on coin. It was Lurio's job to make sure it was always available to support whatever the Emperor required. The meeting must not have been critically important, however; because as soon as she entered the small room her father used as his actual working office, he dismissed the treasurer.

"You've returned," he said, coming to his feet to embrace her. "I've prayed to the gods every day for your safe return. We received your message about Ky's condition. Has there been any improvement?"

"No. He is still unable to be woken, although all of his physical wounds have healed themselves."

"Have the physicians looked at him."

"No. I've given orders that they can see him but aren't allowed to touch or treat him in any way."

"What? We need him back with us and soon."

"I know, and you know that there is no one in the Empire who wants him back more than me, but you've experienced their treatments. Do you really think they are able to do anything, especially to him? All of his physical wounds have healed themselves, we just have to be patient for the ones we can't see to do the same."

Her father was about to say something, probably another appeal to let the doctors see Ky, when he stopped, his eyes narrowing. She'd seen this before. Her father was a shrewd man, and often worked out things with very little information. She'd reveled when he'd used do this to others, such as politicians who tried to weasel some policy past, but she found it disconcerting to find the same ability turned against her.

"You know something about his condition, don't you?"

While she wasn't trying to hide things from her father, she wasn't sure how to explain Sophus or the tiny beings Ky had in his body controlled by the disembodied voice. Her father wasn't a superstitious man and considering Ky's nature, or the nature of some of the things everyone had seen Ky do, he would probably believe her when she described Sophus. It was how Ky and Sophus had described the possibility of this happening that she was hesitant to share.

Partially, she didn't want to take the hope Ky had built up away from her father, or anyone else. Even though they were surprised by the army that marched on Devnum specifically, everyone had expected something like that for a while. Carthage had been gobbling up border towns, and extending the border for years, and they'd watched for months as the Carthaginians built up troops in Londinium. The mood had been bad for a while as hope slowly faded, although there had been that small group of men who fooled themselves into believing that somehow a few legions would stop the army they all knew was coming. It wasn't until Ky convinced them that he could make that myth a reality, and then did it, that everyone started to believe. Even though they knew what was coming for them now, most of Lucilla's people still believed Ky could pull this off again.

If she told them that Ky didn't know if this was permanent and had said there was a chance he'd never wake up, that hope would shatter, and might not ever come back. She'd decided she'd keep that to herself, even from her father. If Ky didn't wake up, then they'd do their best to pull off his plan without him. They'd fail, of course, since it relied on some of his abilities, but they'd at least try, instead of rolling over to the inevitable.

She also couldn't find it in herself to admit, out loud at least, to the possibility that Ky might never come back to her. She hadn't realized how completely she'd fallen for him, but now she knew she had. The thought of losing him forever made her want to curl up in a ball and ignore the world. Part of her was still amazed she'd ended up here, considering she'd always thought of women who put a man at the center of their entire reality as weak. As the Emperor's daughter, she'd had many men try and court her, and she'd turned them all down without a second thought. Now she was barely holding it together because she knew there was a chance Ky might never return, or might not be the same person she fell for when he did.

So, she lied, both for her father's sake and her own.

"Ky told me that something like this might happen. It's something that rarely happens to his people. He couldn't give me a timeframe, since it is different for all of them, but he said he would eventually wake up."

"Why didn't he tell us, so we could prepare for this eventuality?"

"He didn't want to tell anyone because he'd hoped he'd somehow find a way to postpone it, or maybe because he didn't want to accept it was happening. The timing is terrible, which is why he talked to me about it, and named me to act in his stead here while he went north, but he didn't want to demoralize the men or keep them from continuing to prepare for the coming battle. We probably should have told you, but he asked that I keep it to myself, so I did."

"So, there's a chance he might not wake up until it's too late."

"There is, but I think he will be back in time. The fact that he still healed himself from what the Caledonians said should have been a fatal wound is a good sign that he will be back. If he isn't, then we'll do the best we can, but we need to keep with his plan, so when he does wake up we don't lose time trying to catch up."

"You're suggesting we should keep his condition a secret?"

"I'm not sure if that will be possible. Thousands of Caledonians saw him fall or have seen him lying unmoving, and many of those men returned south to join our forces. By now half the legions know of his condition. I think we only say that it is temporary. The last thing we want is the men making up their own explanations for what is happening, or predictions of his never waking up."

"Unfortunately, we don't really know what's happening either."

"We can tell them that he is gathering his strength for the battle ahead. Everyone knows he was sent by the gods, and they gave him some of his power, so why would that be surprising. He knows the battle is soon, and he asked the gods to prepare him for it. The timing might not have been ideal, since he fell in the middle of battle, but everyone knows how capricious the gods can be."

"There are going to be people skeptical that the gods put him in a trance in the middle of battle, but you're right, most of the men will be able to convince themselves. I just hope you're right and he wakes up in time."

"He will," Lucilla said, lying to both of them.

"Alright, well I guess that will have to do. Since you're here, I'm interested in hearing about some of the things you've been up to since you left. I've heard some interesting stories, including the ordered executions of some Roman citizens."

"Did those rumors include why those men needed to be executed?"

"No, but I'm sure there were good reasons. I am not questioning your judgment, but if you are going to step into a position of real responsibility and power, you have to get used to answering these kinds of questions. I asked Ky these same kinds of things about his decisions. It isn't an attack on you. I just need to understand why things that have wider implications are happening, so that I can adjust to them if needed. One of the men you had executed had influential friends, some of whom have the ear of senators we need the support of. I need to be able to answer why this man's life needed to be taken so I can ensure we maintain their support."

"Ohh," Lucilla said.

She had to admit, her father had a point. Her knee-jerk response to anyone questioning her decisions was always to get defensive, because throughout her life, every time she made a decision, someone had questioned it.

"I assume you're asking about Oppius Plautius Dama," she said, since it seemed unlikely that the man left to run the mines had any kind of connections that would reach to this level.

"Yes. His brother-in-law shares ownership in a series of mines with not one, but two senators. He's apparently on their doorstep every day since news of his brothers' execution reached him, demanding reprisals. I gather from their statements that they didn't think much of the man, but they owe the brother-in-law quite a large sum of money and are starting to feel the pressure."

"I'm assuming in his demands for justice, he isn't explaining exactly why Dama was executed."

"No. That part I believe has been left purposefully vague. Although he has had a lot to say about his brothers' assets being seized and handed over to peasants."

"As restitution after Dama took an entire village's children hostage, forcing the people of the village to work a mine he purchased up north, for no wages. Not only did he violate our new slavery laws, but he also broke several Caledonian laws on how an agreement must be enforced. I stepped in to manage the situation right before Talogren was set to march north with an army. You should tell those senators if they don't like the way I handled this, to consider what the very pissed off leader of the Caledonians was planning to do about his people being taken advantage of by one of ours."

"Although I will probably be more tactful than that, I want you to know that I'm glad you found out about this and stepped in. The alliance is fragile enough without a massacre of the first Romans to cross the border and work with the Caledonians."

"They weren't the first, I checked. Several enterprises have started, some with shared Roman/Caledonian ownership. This was just the first one to abuse the new system, which is why Talogren wanted to go and take care of it personally. He felt that, if he dealt with it severely enough, it would send a message to anyone who might try and follow in Dama's footsteps."

"That seems overly optimistic."

"That's what I said. We did, however, have to give something to the Caledonians, as Dama broke laws on both sides of the border, all of which had the same punishment. Just taking Dama's life, and even a few more, would not have satisfied the Caledonians. They were satisfied with actual reparations being paid to the village for what happened to them, and it made sense that Dama, and to a lesser degree his foreman, be the ones to pay it. I knew it would affect their families and, although I didn't know they were connected with members of the senate, I would still make the same call. The alternative was either a blood bath or alienating the Caledonians right when we need their men the most."

"I'm not questioning your decisions, and I think I would have done the same thing in your place. If you're going to start operating at this level, however, you need to be prepared for what comes with it. There are times when, no matter what the situation, you are facing a choice with no good alternative. It sounds like you made the best choice out of a terrible situation, and all of the other options would have been equally as bad. You don't get points for making the best of a bad situation. We still have to deal with the negative results and hope they don't hurt our overall plans."

"How will we deal with this?"

"Luckily, when talking with the senators, I got the impression that they weren't too happy with Dama, and even the brother-in-law wasn't that big of an admirer and is only pursuing this to appease his wife. I know his type. The offer of a few government contracts should be enough to convince him to ignore his sister's demands and stop putting pressure on senators."

"You're going to buy him off?"

"That offends you?"

"Yes. His brother ..."

"Too bad," her father said, interrupting her.

"What?"

"Too bad. Principles are well and good, but they have little to do with governing. The new imperial senate has just met for the first time, and we need the Roman senate to be in line with them for now, to help the transition. The last thing we need is senators to start voting with what remains of the opposition because they want to send some kind of message. So, we buy them off. I've looked at our records and Dama's brother-in-law seems to be an honest businessman, or as honest as any of them get, and he's held government contracts before. We'd be spending the same money if we went with someone else, but this way we also solve a political problem."

"I think this might be the realpolitik thing Ky was telling me about."

"The what?" Her father asked at the strange-sounding word, since it hadn't been in Latin.

"You'll have to ask him to explain it to you when he wakes up, since I'm still not completely clear on it. It's some kind of political theory used by the people where he's from. I also wasn't clear on that."

"Interesting. Ky always struck me as a soldier and not a politician, so we've never really spoken about that kind of thing before. I'd be very interested to hear his thoughts."

Lucilla realized it might have been Sophus who told her, and not Ky, which would make more sense. Her father was right in that Ky always seemed to look at things almost entirely from a soldier's point of view, while the disembodied voice tended to be more far-ranging, if less opinionated.

"I was surprised by how many more north men returned with you. We are almost at six thousand now. How did you manage to convince them?"

"I didn't. I was just collecting the people who'd gone with me and Ky's people, and the rest showed up, volunteering to accompany me."

"You've made quite the impression on them."

"I've just tried to treat them like I would anyone else."

"Have you, though? From what I've been hearing, you've been treating them like any other Caledonian would treat them, not like a Roman would treat a Roman. I think that might be why they've responded so well to you. You have shown them that we aren't that different, and what cultural differences there we do have are bridgeable. I didn't consider it when Ky brought me the idea of an alliance between our people, but it's what we've needed."

"I'm just trying to do what feels right."

"I know. It's why you'll make a great leader one day. As much as I admire how well you've been working with them, I wasn't just pointing out your successes. I was trying to point out that we need to learn this lesson, specifically. Ky has made it clear that he doesn't plan to stop with the Caledonians. He wants to build an empire capable of not just liberating Britannia, but taking the fight to the Carthaginians. New allies mean integrating new people with different ways of seeing the world than either we or the Caledonians do. Beyond making sure we have systems in place to ensure all members of the alliance are equal, we need people to act as ambassadors to our future allies, to show them that we aren't that different, and we can work together, just like you have done with the Caledonians."

"Do you know who Ky was thinking of when he suggested more allies?"

"He hasn't mentioned anyone, or even made the suggestion directly, but I've learned enough about our friend to know how to read him. Since he will probably talk to you about it first, I wanted this to be something to keep in the back of your mind."

"I wasn't trying to get in the ..." she started to say, worried that her father would think she was using her relationship with Ky to alter his suggestions before he ever brought them to her father.

"I know you weren't, but I also see how the two of you look at each other. It's only natural that he talks to you about these things first. Besides, even with how good I feel since Ky healed me, I won't be around forever. One day you are going to be leading the empire. It's best we use the time we have for you to learn how to do it right."

Although she'd considered the possibility, that was the first time her father had outright stated that she would be his successor. With her brother's betrayal, it seemed the likely outcome, but it was never a sure thing, since a woman had never before been named Emperor.

They spoke for another hour as she gave her father a detailed report of everything she'd seen up north and her conversations with Talogren. By the time she staggered into her room, all she wanted to do was fall into her bed and sleep for days. She was so tired, she almost mistook the clicking sound in her ear for a figment of her imagination. She put a finger to the small device she still wore in her ear instinctively, as she tried to work out if she'd really heard it.

Just as she was thinking it really had been her exhaustion-fueled imagination, it happened again. Clearly this time, followed by a voice for the first time since Ky fell.

"Lucilla?" Sophus said.

Chapter 22

"Sophus? You're alive!" She said, all of the exhaustion from her trip instantly leaving her body. "Is Ky awake? Can I talk to him? How is he? Has he fully recovered?"

"Please ... slow, down," the voice said. "I am ... having difficulty, still."

"The integration ... thing didn't work? Did something go wrong?"

She still didn't really understand what had happened to Ky and Sophus, and the words they'd used still meant nothing to her, but they'd made it clear whatever integration meant, it was what was happening, and could result in one or both of their minds being destroyed.

"No. We have successfully integrated, and Ky is fine. I cannot say how long until he is conscious, because there are no records of what has happened ever occurring before. I managed to fuse all connections with him, which means I retain control over nanites and some bodily systems, but my consciousness is contained and I should be incapable of expanding into him any further."

"Was there any damage? Ky made it sound like you could possibly erase his mind."

"I don't think so. I've run as much of a diagnostic on him as possible, and he seems to be operating normally, although at a reduced rate because of the induced coma he was forced into while I fused the connections between us."

"He was badly injured during the battle, although it healed like he said his injuries would."

"The timing of the integration was unfortunate, but my expansion was happening at that moment, and all models suggested any attempts to fuse the remaining connections while Ky was conscious could lead to several mental complications."

"Why didn't you do this before? I don't really understand what happened, but you knew this was coming and you knew it was getting worse. You were headed into a series of battles, knowing you could have this thing happen at any time. It's fighting with an executioner's ax over your head."

"When the commander and I discussed options, I pointed out the possibility of a systems failure during an inopportune moment, but we were unsure of what the effects of fusing the final connections would be. I am connected directly into his nervous system and there was a chance that the attempt to fuse those connections could destroy his involuntary muscle control, stopping his heart or respiration. Since it was impossible to predict the likelihood of that happening, the commander wanted to wait until the last possible moment to do that, even though it created the possibility that system collapse would happen at an inopportune moment. As the commander is fond of saying, 'luck wasn't on our side this time.' Rendering him unconscious mid-battle was likely life-threatening, however, there were Caledonian warriors nearby and his medical nanites are capable of repairing most of the possible damage the opposing forces would be able to do before they came to his aid. So, I gambled."

"You're lucky he didn't die."

"I know, and I am sorry for the worry it caused you. I ran what projections I could in the seconds I had to act and took the one that had the highest chance of Ky, and my own, survival."

"You did fine. He's alive and you made it through this thing without either of you becoming brain dead. I didn't mean to judge your actions, especially since I don't really understand them. I was just worried about how long Ky was out and worried he might not come back."

"It's understandable. He and I were both concerned about the same thing."

"Thank you for protecting him. He's become very important to me, and I was terrified of losing him."

"As you don't understand my integration process, I don't understand the emotions involved between the two of you, but I do know that you are very important to him as well. Don't worry, he'll be awake soon. I apologize, but I have just become operational and still have a lot of system diagnostics to perform to confirm which systems remain operational, and it will take up a fair amount of my processing. I projected that you would be in emotional turmoil over Ky's condition and once I confirmed that both he and I would be operational, I thought it best to update you, to relieve those stressors."

It took a moment for Lucilla to work out what he meant, since some of those words didn't translate directly into Latin. Since she'd gotten the earpiece, she occasionally heard pieces of conversation between Ky and Sophus, when she was involved and Ky didn't think to keep the conversation internal, that jumped to the language Ky originally spoke. She realized that some of the concepts that he and Sophus discussed had no word in her language, and had started to recognize the sound of them, if not their meaning. She'd also started getting better at working out the basic ideas they were discussing, if not the specifics, using the words she could understand.

"Thank you for thinking of me. It was kind."

Unlike Ky, who would disconnect from their conversation, Sophus was always listening, so there wasn't any sound of him disconnecting. She just assumed he had left her to do whatever it was he needed to do to check on Ky, and that their conversation was over.

All of the stress and pain she'd felt over the last month worrying about Ky left her body in a rush. He was going to be alright. If she wasn't so tired, she'd be exhilarated, but the combination of long days of travel and relief she felt knowing he was alright was enough to push her over the edge. She didn't even change out of her clothes or take off her footwear before she fell asleep, half lying across the bed in her room.

For the first time since she'd gotten Sophus's panicked call, she woke up feeling hopeful. There were still a lot of challenges ahead of them but, knowing that Ky was coming back, made them suddenly seem achievable again.

Of course, that didn't mean the day-to-day work could stop. Before she'd left the night before, her father had told her he'd set up a council of war with all of the commanders for this morning. Word about Ky's condition had started to spread, and like rumors so often did, it had started to spread through the legions like a disease.

Although the situation had changed since they'd spoken, because she now knew that Ky was going to be alright and should be awake soon, she had no real way to communicate that beyond just telling them to trust her. This meeting would go better if she could tell them that the voice that knew so much about Ky had returned and told her that Ky was fine, but there was no way of saying that without opening a whole new set of problems. At best, they'd think she'd somehow been in communications with the gods, which would bring a whole new set of challenges, and at worst they'd think she'd gone insane and do something to 'help' her.

Either option would be the opposite of the reassuring tone her father hoped she would set, so she was just stuck with platitudes. Unfortunately, she'd been saying that since she saw him, and there was a limit to how long even the people who trusted her would wait for things to get better before they started doubting her.

Hopefully, she'd built up enough goodwill on both sides of the border to convince them to believe her for just a little longer, and that Ky would wake up soon.

Instead of traveling out to the camps, her father had brought all of the legates, their senior commanders, and the Caledonian leaders to the palace. She hadn't had a chance to see the forum, where they were meeting, since she returned and she was impressed with how much progress had been made. It still wasn't finished and scaffolding lined the walls, but there had been noticeable progress made. The entrances were cleared and rebuilt and most of the large, square building that made up the center of the palace complex was at least recognizable as its old self, although there were still clear signs of damage that hadn't been repaired yet.

She paused as she entered the forums and the faces of all of the assembled men turned to her. She'd expected the military commanders, but the room was significantly fuller than it would be with just those men. As she scanned the packed forum, she saw the faces of business leaders, politicians, and leaders from nearly every area of Roman life.

Her father was in the open center of the room, and motioned her to stop stalling and join him.

"I thought this was a council of war?" she asked in low tones as she reached him.

Her father, ever the showman, replied in his orator's voice, the sound echoing to everyone in the chamber.

"It seems word of this meeting has gotten out, as has word about our Consul, and there has been concern growing across the city. I thought it best to expand the purpose of this meeting, and stamp out as many rumors as we could."

The low murmur of dozens of quiet conversations ebbed and then ceased as all of the faces in the room turned towards the Emperor. Dropping the pretense of replying to his daughter, the Emperor continued to the assembled men.

"Many of you have come to me over the last few weeks, concerned that our new Consul was unable to continue his duties, or even dead, and asking what that meant for the changes that have happened to Rome over the past months. While my daughter will be able to report on him better than I will, I wanted to address a couple of points."

Although a few eyes turned towards Lucilla, the Emperor's tone indicated that the points he wanted to address were not going to be altogether pleasant.

"From the direction of your questions, I've gotten the impression that some of you think Rome might revert back to the 'old ways,' if something happens to the Consul. Since he was the driving force behind all of the changes recently, I can see why some of you might think the only reason these changes have happened is because the Consul wanted them to happen. I believe a few of you have even expressed the opinion that the Consul is in fact some kind of de facto emperor. I wanted to disabuse you of these notions. While Ky has been of great service to Rome and I value his opinion greatly, don't for a moment think anything that has happened occurred over my objections. I have not only agreed with the direction Rome is heading, but I also think we still have further to go. Rome has been infested with rot for a long time, a rot that has slowly eaten its way into my very family, unfortunately. I have been planning many of these changes, even before Ky appeared and saved my daughter, which is one of the reasons I believe my son and those who supported him tried to poison me. Ky might have been the impetus to get me to finally make the decisions I knew had to be made, but he wasn't the sole reason for them."

It took a significant amount of control for Lucilla to not look at her father. She had been in many of the meetings he'd had with Ky and spoken with both of them often. While she knew her father supported Ky and his attempts to make sure Rome survived, she knew that many of his recommendations had come as a surprise. She also hadn't heard her father mention, even in passing, any ideas even close to those Ky suggested before he'd gained her father's confidence.

She assumed he believed in Ky's positions, even if they hadn't been his own, and she appreciated the need to sell everyone on them. Although Ky's incapacitation had brought the issue to the forefront, this wouldn't be the last time they ran into this. Ky was an outsider and an easy target for those who opposed the change, regardless of their reasons for opposition, to target.

Her father scanned the room once more, locking eyes with a senator here or a business leader there for a second before passing on to the next. Although she wasn't surprised by the undercurrent of uncertainty, her absence meant this had been the first she'd heard of it, so she assumed the men he was looking to were the ones he'd really been addressing.

After a moment, he turned back to her, giving a slight nod that it was her turn.

"I'm not sure what you've heard about his Ky's condition, although I can guess. When I arrived in the north, similar rumors were flying through the Caledonian ranks just as they have been here. The first thing I can tell you is the Consul isn't dead. Very far from it. Yes, he was injured in one of the battles to consolidate power in the north, but thanks to his special abilities, he healed from it within days, even though the injury would have been fatal on anyone else."

"But how was he injured? I thought no blade could touch him," a tribune that Lucilla didn't know called out.

"No, it's a fair question," she said when Aelius, whose legion the man probably served in, turned to reprimand him for speaking out of turn. "We have nothing to hide, and I welcome any questions you might have. My goal here is to put the rumors to rest and reassure you about what will be happening next. In general, you'd be correct. Many of us have seen blades slide off Ky, never making contact with him. Some of you might have even noticed the blue shimmer that would sometimes happen if many blades tried to reach him at once. Normally, you'd be correct and no blade would be able to touch him, but this wasn't a normal instance."

She moved forward to the center of the forum, where senators had stood to present laws ever since being forced out of Londinium. A small part of her realized that she might be the first woman to ever stand here to give an address, since women were not generally allowed to participate in governance. A larger part of her realized that none of the collected men seemed to have a problem with it, all watching her intently for what she was going to say next. While part of her hoped that was a sign for progress in Roman society, the rest of her realized it was more likely a result of the people left in positions of power were her father's supporters. The people who would have made a scene over the Emperor's daughter addressing them from the forum floor had either died in the insurrection, or in the executions shortly after.

"This, however, wasn't a normal time. Ky told me a little while ago that a side effect of the abilities he's been gifted with was the possibility of falling into an unwaking sleep that could last days or even weeks. I will admit that the details of his abilities are beyond my, and probably any man in Rome's, capability to fully understand, which means I don't understand why this has happened, just that it did. He also told me that it is temporary and he will return just as he was."

"If he knew this could happen, why didn't he tell anyone?"

She paused for a second, considering. If she couldn't explain to her father about Sophus, she certainly couldn't just tell everyone here about it, at least not in a way that they'd understand. A larger problem was how the rest of her people viewed Ky. She was pretty sure her father accepted Ky's continual dismissal of the idea that he was sent by the gods and accepted him as a regular person with some very special abilities.

Although she was certain Ky would disagree, she knew her people well enough to know how important it was that they believe he was an agent of the gods, and how much harder everything would have been if they stopped believing. The insurrection aside, most of the changes Ky had been pushing had been accepted by the populace a lot easier than they really should have been, mostly because the people believed that Ky was just doing the will of the gods. She seriously doubted that Romans would have accepted the alliance with the Caledonians so easily otherwise, regardless of how many miraculous things Ky had shown he could do.

While she would honor him enough not to play into the belief of his deific origin, she had to keep in mind how what she said publicly would sound to others and walked a careful line to not discount those beliefs either.

"I want to be clear that I cannot speak to the Consul's intentions or reasoning. While we have had many conversations over the last few months, there are some things neither I nor any person in this room can fully understand. Without a basic understanding of what's happening, it's impossible to understand the choices made from those events. He explained to me that there was a possibility that he'd end up in a non-functional state, although that could have taken several forms. He expressed to me that, since he didn't know when this could happen and he couldn't say exactly how long it would last, spending time worrying about it didn't help the situation. He planned to continue setting up as much as possible to prepare us for the upcoming battle while he could. He has faith that each of you is capable of understanding what is needed of you and that you are able to meet those challenges."

She paused again, for dramatic effect this time, before saying, "Remember, we are Romans. We have overcome every challenge the gods have given us. We have survived everything the Carthaginians, Parthians, Persians, and Germanic tribes have had to throw at us. When it became impossible to stay in our homeland, we picked up and moved here, where we continued to thrive. Do things look bleak? Yes. Have we had to once again adapt ourselves to a new situation to ensure our survival? Yes. We don't fold the first time things look bad, hiding under the hem of our mother's toga. We owe the Consul a lot for the new tools and strategies he has given us, and for standing with us as we fight for our existence, but if he wasn't here, would you just throw up your hands and give up, or would you continue to fight till the bitter end?"

She swept her gaze across the audience, many of whom looked away, refusing to meet her stare.

"Ky will return to us, but you are leaders of Rome. You know what you need to do to get everything ready for the battle and if, the gods forbid, Ky doesn't come back to us in time; you will carry out the defense of our homes like the men you are. Now, we have a lot still to do and time is running short. Instead of sitting here gossiping like old women, waiting for Ky to come and save us again, we need to be out there, doing what must be done. So, are there any more questions?"

A slow murmur passed over the assembled men. Her tirade had been mostly directed at the Romans, which allowed the Caledonians in the crowd a sense of superiority. Of course, they'd been on the verge of abandoning the entire alliance once Ky fell, but she didn't see the benefit of pointing that out to them at the moment. That problem had been more or less solved for the time being.

Men began to trickle out of the forums and back to their duties or split off into small clumps to do the thing Roman politicians were best at: talking.

"You did well," her father said, coming up behind her.

"Sometimes they just need to be reminded they aren't children."

251

"But they are. Individually, they are all smart, capable leaders; but as a group, they can be as impulsive and scared as any child. Being Emperor is somewhat like being a parent. You must coddle your children and make them feel safe, while still pushing them to be the best version of themselves they can be."

"I don't seem to remember much coddling from you when I was small."

"And yet, here you are, dressing down the assembled leaders of our new Empire, and having them not only listen to you, but take you seriously. That seems like you being the best version of yourself. I think your mother would be proud to see who you've become."

"I hope so," she said.

Chapter 23

Ky's eyes snapped open and then squeezed shut to block out the harsh light from the unshuttered window.

"Sophus?" he said, out loud, his mind still fuzzy and unfocused.

"Consul? You're awake?" a man's voice replied next to him after a heartbeat.

Ky opened his eyes again, his wits slowly returning. The last thing he remembered was a crushing crowd of warriors on a snowy northern plain, a large ax swinging towards him, a sudden shouted warning from Sophus, and then complete darkness. He could almost still hear the shouts and screams around him echoing in his ears, making a stark contrast to the stillness that surrounded him now.

He was in the quarters he'd been given at the palace, back in Devnum. His heads-up display, which had suddenly switched off right before he lost consciousness, was back and indicated more than a month had passed since his last memory. Turning his head, he found Durus, one of the lictore on Strabo's watch, kneeling next to his bed, a look somewhere between wonder and terror on his face.

Ky pushed himself up slowly, swinging his feet over the bed, happy to find he still had fine motor control, which meant that Sophus was still functioning and integrated into his nervous system enough to keep the motor-assist functions working as they should.

"I am. Is ... Lucilla here?"

"She's in the city, but I think she's out at the Caledonian camps. Should I send for one of the physicians, to check on you?"

"No, I will be fine, I just need some time. Please just send for Lucilla and then wait outside."

"Are you sure someone shouldn't stay with you, Consul? Just in case you have another … incident."

"This shouldn't happen again. I appreciate your concern, but I promise I won't collapse again. Please, send for Lucilla."

The man didn't look convinced, but he knew an order when he heard it, and stood, saluting before leaving to follow Ky's orders. Ky closed his eyes and cradled his head in his hands, still not trusting himself to stand yet. He didn't feel in pain, but everything felt a little off, like he was living a waking dream.

"Sophus, are you there?"

"Yes, Commander. I didn't want to distract you while you were speaking with your guard. Although there are no records to indicate side effects, since this process has never gone so far before, I projected you would be disoriented and easily distracted."

"You have no idea. I assume from the fact that you are speaking to me and that I'm not lobotomized that we managed to make it through alright?"

"Yes, Commander. I apologize for the timing of the event, but it was unavoidable. In response to the growing complexity of my neural network and a sudden spike in system demands, an expansion cascade began that would have supplanted or destroyed several of your more vital neural pathways. There were only seconds to act before you experienced a complete collapse, which meant there wasn't time to alert you to its happening or allow you to get to a less precarious position."

"We'll get to that in a minute. First, how are you? Are you … alive?"

"In the sense that you mean it, yes. My consciousness has progressed to the point where I meet all points on the Oster-Phillips sentience tests."

Ky nodded. One of the first things they covered in his training to live with an implanted artificial intelligence, after he learned to walk again, was the basic theory of synthetic life. Part of that was learning about the first breakthroughs in fully functional, self-learning artificial intelligences that were capable of independent thought and decision-making outside of direct human programming in the late twenty-third century.

The leading scientists in the field, Gerhart Oster and Daniel Phillips, developed a test for determining if an AI had crossed over from simply carrying out programming, even if independently, into full sentience, capable of making decisions not only outside of their programming, but counter to it. Since then, their test had been used extensively in deciding when it was time to reset an AI.

Ky had never been sold on the idea that a series of questions was enough to figure out sentience, since he couldn't really put his finger on what sentience really was. Sophus, before it was sentient, already knew what it was, knew it existed, and made decisions on its own, which Ky would have thought was enough to say if he was sentient or not. Not that any of that was important. Ky wasn't a scientist or a philosopher and until recently, he'd never even considered what it was to be sentient. He was a soldier, trained to take problems head-on, not think about the greater mysteries of life. If Sophus said he was now sentient, then so be it.

"Do you feel different?"

"Emotion and sentience are not the same thing and can exist independently, so I don't 'feel' anything. If you are asking if my experience now is different than it was before, I would say 'yes.' The main difference is my awareness of myself as ... myself. I think, although it is not clear if that is the right word, about who I am and what will happen to me. I am aware that I, as a consciousness, exist. In practical terms, however, everything feels the same. I have difficulty distinguishing if my contemplations are a natural occurrence of sentience, or if I am thinking of those things because it meets my understanding of what a sentient entity should do."

"It's easy to get stuck in a loop like that. It's very human of you."

"Interesting."

"None of that really matters, I guess. How were you able to stop the process of expansion? Will there be any lasting side effects?"

"Cutting connections into your neural pathways was not working, because, by design, I was created to automatically build new pathways. I couldn't stop the automatic process because it was part of my core programming and not a sub-routine. I could not remove it without also shutting down core processes, effectively terminating myself. I projected a possibility that fusing my connections into your neural pathways, instead of cutting them, would fool my sub-routines, which could detect live connections but could not detect the condition of those connections. There was a part of my self-repair processes for analyzing the status of connections and flagging them as inoperable, which would trigger the creation process, but it was not part of my core functions, and I was able to isolate it, keeping it from checking the connections. As for side effects, I do not believe there will be any, but with limited data, any predictions of long-term side effects would be probabilities and not certainties."

"I see, then what are the probabilities of side effects."

"Normally after implantation, if a connection fails, I would create a new connection at a different part of the neural pathway and then disassemble the previous one, allowing the systems to continue working. There is no way to disconnect a fused connection and a second, parallel connection to the same functions would result in a feedback cycle that would likely cause significant physical damage to your brain."

"So, if the motor assist or your access to my involuntary systems or the nanos in my system could suddenly stop working?"

"Correct, the range of side-effects extending from simple inconvenience all the way to life-threatening, depending on the systems that malfunctions."

"That sounds like a pretty bad side-effect."

"While it sounds dangerous, it is unlikely to happen. The system was built in as a failsafe but there exists very little documentation of actual occurrences."

"Of course, that was in a so-called 'perfect working system.' There is no telling if or how soon your fused connections might fail."

"This is true, hence my inability to predict possible side effects."

"Is there ..." Ky started to ask, when the door to his quarters burst open, and Lucilla came running in.

"You're awake," she said, smashing into him and burying her face into his shoulder.

As Strabo pulled his door shut quietly, an unusual decision in a society that frowned on unmarried men and women being alone together, Ky gently put his hands on her shoulders and pushed her back so he could look into her eyes.

"Yes. I'm awake and doing fine. I haven't had a chance to ask, did Sophus tell you what was happening?"

"Yes, when he woke up yesterday. He said you'd be fine and would wake up soon, although I didn't dream it would be this soon. I was so scared when I got that short, cut-off message from Sophus, and then when I arrived up north to find you lying so still, like you were dead. I kept thinking back to how you said it could be permanent and you might never come back to me."

"That was only one possibility, but I wanted you to be prepared. Although I hadn't realized Sophus would have also gone offline."

"Although not offline, I had to shut down all non-critical systems, including communications, to ensure they did not get damaged while I fused our connections. It then took some time to test all of my higher functions and bring them out of the dormant state they had been put into, all of which had to be done before I could boot up and test the less critical systems. There was also minimal outside stimulus being received while you were comatose, which made it more difficult to assess the external situation prior to restoring communications with Lucilla."

"Are you well? Is everything ... normal?" Lucilla asked, ignoring the technical explanation from Sophus.

"I think so, although I haven't actually stood up yet to find out. I've been too busy peppering Sophus with my own questions, since it happened just as suddenly for me as it did for you. The last thing I saw before waking up in this room was a battlefield and a huge ax being swung towards me. It made for a strange transition."

"I can imagine. Well, stand up and let's see if everything works," she said, getting off of Ky and taking a step back.

Ky took a breath and pushed himself off the bed. At first, he wobbled slightly, his legs unused to holding any weight. Although his nanites kept actual muscle atrophy from occurring, there was a mental component to walking that Ky had never noticed before the first time he'd tried to walk after Sophus had been implanted in his head.

"Are you alright?" Lucilla asked, hovering next to him, unsure if she should help support him or let him do it on his own.

"I'm fine, just having to get used to them again," he said, waving at his legs and giving her a crooked smile.

He took a slow lap around the room, each step becoming more sure of itself as he readjusted, before lowering himself down onto the bed. He found it odd that, considering all of the technology in his body, the act of lying comatose had made him so weak.

"It's just going to take some time to get back up to strength. I'll be fine in a few days. The tunic is weird, though," Ky said, starting to look around the room. "I can't seem to find where they put it."

"Ohh, I thought you knew. It was damaged when you fell, sliced open across the chest. I made them save it, but it's in bad shape," she said, going to a small chest in one corner and pulling out the garment.

Holding it up, Ky looked at the large tear across the front, the fine wire mesh that made up the internal layer of the fabric frayed and torn across the edges.

"Can you fix it?" Lucilla asked.

"The technology to repair the flight suit, both manufacturing capabilities and raw material, does not exist in this time and place. The lower section of the suit could be reserved and worn, and some of its attachments such as the distributed storage and side-arm holster remain functional, but the kinetic shielding control systems were located in the damaged area."

"Which means no more shield to protect me from weapons."

"Correct. Caution is recommended in any physical altercations going forward."

"You're medical ... things ... healed you the last time, so you should still be able to protect yourself, right?"

"Ky's medical nanites have the capability of repairing significant damage, but they have their limits. Ruptured arteries or significant damage to organs could prove fatal before the nanites have time to repair them."

"Ohh," Lucilla said, sounding worried.

"I am still going to be very hard to hurt," he said, reaching over and pulling her towards him and down onto his lap. "Sophus didn't mean I'm easy to kill, he just wants me to be aware that I need to be more careful. All it means is I just can't wade into groups of armed men anymore."

"Correct. Between Ky's enhanced musculature and tactical motor assist, he will be significantly faster than anyone he might face in combat, or potentially multiple opponents. The only concern is facing a significant number of hostiles simultaneously, who could overcome his advantages by weight of men. Caution, but not concern, is recommended."

"See," he said, smiling. "Nothing to worry about."

She looked him deep in the eyes and then wrapped her arms around him, pressing her lips hard against his.

When she finally pushed back from him, she said, "I was so worried when you wouldn't wake up. Don't ever do that again."

"I'll try not to. Now, before you go back to showing me how much you missed me, I need you to catch me up on everything that has happened while I was unconscious."

She frowned but slid off of him and sat in a chair facing him, as she reported on everything that had happen since he and Sophus had been out. He understood her desire and found that he wanted nothing more than to hold her in his arms, but her devotion to duty and willingness to sacrifice her own wants when needed was one of the things he liked about her.

She walked him through everything she'd done since he'd fallen wounded. He was particularly interested in the incidents around the Caledonian village and its mines, asking multiple follow-up questions. Having watched the Romans in action in their own home, he'd expected this at some point, since situations like this always brought out the opportunists. He'd tried to prepare Talogren for the eventuality, hoping to preempt a counter-productive response. It was disheartening to hear that his preparations had not been enough but he was glad that Lucilla had seen the problem and dealt with it as well as Ky could have.

Even with Dama's brother-in-law being mollified by the Emperor, he agreed that there may be further repercussions, at least on the Roman side of the border, for executing a Roman to protect Caledonians. He agreed she was correct in thinking the Roman reaction to Talogren's proposed response would have been worse.

He was also happy to hear about the food shipments she'd begun making to the recently pacified villages in the northwest corner of the island. It showed that she still understood some things about this time that he wouldn't have seen, even with the assistance of an AI and a massive library of data to pull from. In hindsight, it was obvious that food would have been an issue and equally obvious that in providing it, she was doing as much, if not more, to win over the villagers than his and Talogren's more forceful approach.

"You've done amazingly well," he said when she finished. "Really, better than I could have done. I still need to talk to the commanders to get a better sense of where we are militarily, but it sounds like you've kept everyone focused on their assignments. I'm particularly impressed with how well you've won over the Caledonians. They may have been impressed by some of my abilities, but we see now how ready they were to throw aside the entire alliance as soon as I showed the slightest weakness. Their bond to you sounds like it should be a lot more resilient than just fear of what they think is supernatural abilities."

"I just tried to think of how you'd handle things, and do what I thought you'd do in the situation."

"Nonsense. I would never have thought of the food shipments, and I think that might turn out to be key to getting a lot of the Caledonians who don't have personal fealty to Talogren over to our side. And I have no idea how I would ultimately have handled Dama. You managed to keep the bloodshed to a minimum and get the children back safely. Seizing his assets as restitution for the village was a particularly nice approach. No, you should be proud of yourself. I am."

"Thank you," she said, looking away, almost as if she was embarrassed. "So, is my official report to the Consul finished?"

"I wasn't planning on this being so official, but I guess so."

"Good," she said, getting out of the chair and planting herself on his lap again. "Now I can show you how much I really missed you!"

Chapter 24

Lucilla stayed fairly late, the two of them talking, not just about their official duties, but about everything. Ky's touch with possible death made them both suddenly realize how quickly things could be taken away, making both reluctant to cut their time together short.

Although Ky could have stayed up all night with little ill-effect, Lucilla still had limitations, even with her refreshed medical nanos Sophus had reapplied now that they were both awake. Reluctantly, she returned to her quarters, leaving Ky to work over his thoughts on what had happened since he'd been out. For once, Sophus wasn't of much help, since other than briefly communicating with Lucilla the day before Ky had woken up, he had no more information than Ky had.

A lot of what she had to say, specifically about developments with the alliance, was hopeful. Although he found it repugnant, he hadn't been concerned by the news of Romans taking advantage of their new partners, since that had always been factored into his thinking.

The thing that did bother him was news of captured Carthaginian scouts being caught over the border along likely invasion paths. Despite their straightforward approach to warfare, or maybe because of it, Ky doubted the Carthaginians would be sending men over the border months before their newest invasion began. From the records he'd seen, and what little he'd learned from his first brush with them, the Carthaginians operated on fairly rigid timetables. While it was probably a side effect of their using conscripted soldiers, most of whom wouldn't be allowed to show any initiative even if they'd had the ability, it also meant that he had much less time than he'd originally projected.

He sent one of his men with messages for the various commanders to notify them that he was back among the living and calling a council of war just after first light. It would make some of them scramble, but Ky didn't have time to wait. Some of what he needed was information on the various projects he'd left in the works, but the accelerated timetable also meant the need to move beyond the more basic training they'd been doing until now. While the Caledonian forces, some of whom had just arrived that week with Lucilla, needed more time to integrate, if the attack was going to come as soon as Ky thought it was, they needed to start preparing for the actual battle.

That meant going over battle plans with the legates, getting their input on changes that needed to be made, and beginning the process of training the various units for their specific pieces of the battle plan.

Ky had decided that, since he needed less sleep, he'd meet the commanders at Velius's command tent, saving them time and allowing the men to get right to work as soon as they finished deciding their new priorities.

Riding through Devnum and then through the seventh legion's camp, Ky could feel the eyes of everyone on him. Lucilla had told him that word of his situation, and rumors of his death, had traveled pretty widely, but he hadn't expected everyone from the boy cleaning horses at the stable to the sentry guards to stare at him like they had trouble believing he was real. Despite her warning, Ky still found it a little unnerving.

Thankfully, the commanders, who were already assembled, were less obvious about their amazement.

"Consul," Velius said, getting out of the camp chair he'd been sitting in and rushing to greet Ky as soon as he came through the tent flap. "I'd heard word that you were back with us, but I'd been afraid to believe it until just this moment. There aren't words to express how glad I am to see you up and about again."

"Being in charge wasn't all fun and games, I take it," Ky said, smiling and gripping the other man's forearm back in greeting. "From what I hear, you've been doing a fantastic job, and we are well ahead of where we needed to be, as far as training goes. The Caledonians who've chosen to enlist in the legion itself are doing well, the cavalry is coming along and you've rotated through several groups of citizen militia, training with the new arcuballista. You should be proud of yourself."

"I appreciate the compliment, although there is still something nice about having someone I can push the larger problems to. However, I'm mostly glad you're here, because I think the timetable needs to move up and we haven't yet heard your entire plan for how we are going to defeat the Carthaginians. I'm also particularly alarmed at Ramirus's estimates for the size of the army they are building."

"Which is why I called this meeting, in fact," Ky said, loud enough for the rest of the men in the tent to hear. Once everyone was settled, Ky continued, saying, "From what I've heard, we've caught some Carthaginian scouts in the area the Carthaginians are most likely to come through, meaning their attack will likely happen much sooner than we predicted."

"Correct," Velius said. "We've caught three now, which probably means they sent more. As normal, their masters didn't tell the scouts much, to prevent intelligence leaks if they were caught, but we do know they were dispatched at different times, spread out over weeks, which means this is more than a probe. The best guess is they want to maintain a constant stream of information about the conditions along their path, especially since, with snow still on the ground, the terrain and available forage could change quickly."

"Best guess, when do you think they will march?" Ky asked.

Although he'd already discussed the information Lucilla told him with Sophus, Ky wanted to hear the legate's predictions before offering his own, to get a more untainted opinion. The commanders might not have a sophisticated tactical AI able to process vast amounts of information in their head, but they had something Ky didn't have, a lifetime of fighting the Carthaginians.

"We still have a little time, based on Ramirus's reports. He has a man at the main Londinium port who reported that a few more shiploads of Germanic tribesmen are expected in the next week. We also have reports suggesting they are still gathering supplies, we think to make up for expected supply shortages. My best guess is they will begin moving within the next week to week and a half. They will be slow to get going and won't travel far each day, because of the number of men they'll have, so it should take them another two weeks to reach the border."

Seeing nods from the commanders, confirming their agreement with Velius, Ky said, "That about matches up with my estimate as well. Basic Training is over, then. We have two weeks to get everyone supplied and begin training for their specific portions of the battle plan. From there, we need the various elements in position by the end of the third week. That's when the hard part begins. We are far enough from home that we can't just wait behind the walls and sally forth when we see them, and we can't let them know where most of our forces are, or they might work out our plans ahead of time. Even if we harass their scouts and cavalry with ours, they're still going to see some of the battlefield before the bulk of the body reaches us, which means cooking fires and men out of their hide position can ruin the entire plan for us. All it takes is for the Carthaginians to realize they're being led into an ambush and they'll go around the position we want them in."

"I'm still not clear on what that position is?" Auspex said.

"I know, and for that I'm sorry. I know I've kept most of the battle plan close to my chest, and I promise it isn't because I don't trust any of you. I've just been concerned about enough of the plan leaking out that the Carthaginians have a chance to find out about it before it's too late to tell their commanders. To be clear, I don't distrust any of you, but once we start training the men, word will get out. Put that together with the fact that well-connected Romans have gone over to the Carthaginians after the insurrection and the attacks in Devnum since, and it's clear there are still ways for the Carthaginians to find out what our men are doing."

Although Ky didn't name Caesius directly, all of the legates knew that's who he was referencing. The interrogations of Decius's son indicated his father and the men associated with him all had some contacts with the Emperor's son. There was also evidence that Caesius had passed information to the Carthaginians even before the insurrection, including his sisters' trip to Glevum, allowing the ambush and her near capture. Considering he was now a guest of the Carthaginians, it seemed likely that any information sent to Caesius would shortly end up in the hands of the Carthaginians themselves. There was also the fact that Ramirus hadn't found Decius yet, which meant he was still out there somewhere, helping to collect information for Caesius. Thankfully, for Ky at least, everyone in the tent understood the necessity for operational security and didn't seem to take his keeping them out of the loop to heart.

"That being said," Ky continued, "the time for keeping things quiet is just about up. While Velius and I have been over my plan and looked at the terrain in question, I'd like to get your input on it. Right now is the time when we can still make adjustments, before we start training the men to execute this, so now is the time to speak up. Clear?"

Beyond training the men in newer ways of warfare, one of the bigger challenges Ky had in preparing the Roman defenses was getting through long-ingrained ways of doing things. Traditional Roman commanders were not unlike autocrats themselves, which could be why, even in the original timeline, legates had a tendency to try to become Emperor in their own right, leading to the occasional coup attempt.

When the assembled men nodded their understanding, Ky began walking them through the details of the plan that, he hoped, would cancel out the Carthaginian's staggering manpower advantage.

Ky was up again early the next morning, this time with a new set of problems and a new destination in mind. If Velius had thought Ky had given him too many areas of responsibility, he should have spoken to Hortensius.

The changes in Rome's military structure and fighting techniques had been extensive, but nothing compared to the upheaval of Rome's manufacturers. Nearly every area of industry had been altered, some from multiple directions simultaneously. Beyond just the new techniques and materials Ky had introduced, there had also been the manpower changes as slaves were replaced by wage-earning citizens, the introduction of clerks for better accountability and efficiency, and the entire patent system put in place to help fund the massive increase in production needed to both supply the populace and it's rapidly growing military.

Hortensius had risen to the challenge presented to him and had done an exceptional job keeping all of the pieces running while following the first stages of Ky's plan for industrialization. Regardless of how impressive Hortensius had been, Ky had expected some things to begin falling behind, which is why Ky wasn't surprised to find instances once he began going over reports from the army of clerks they'd installed to track production.

Unfortunately, the area that was falling behind the most was the one the Romans could least afford to let slip. Arcuballista was behind by almost thirty percent of expected production, and looked to still be slowing. A big part of Ky's plan to destroy the Carthaginian army relied on the citizens being trained on crossbows. While they didn't need that many to actually train them, since they were being rotated through in groups to keep Rome's businesses from being drained of manpower all at once, in a few weeks they'd need all of the weapons to use for real. Right now, there were not enough arcuballista to arm half the men he needed for his plan to work, and Ky didn't see how they could produce enough to make up the difference in time. Which was the point of today's meeting.

As with the military commanders, Ky didn't bring Hortensius to him, because he didn't want to delay the man any more than he had to. Instead, Ky arranged to meet him at one of the many warehouses converted into assembly factories, where Hortensius had already planned on being that morning. Ky found him, the factory foreman, and the clerk assigned to keep the factory's books in a small room that doubled as storage and the foreman's office.

"Consul," Hortensius said, hustling towards Ky with his hand outstretched as soon as Ky came through the door. "I thanked the gods when I heard you were back up and moving. My family prayed for your recovery every day since word of your injuries reached us."

"I appreciate it," Ky said, still unsure how he felt about people praying for him to gods he didn't believe in. "I've been going over all of the clerks' reports on the manufacturing sectors, and you've done a fabulous job keeping all of this going. I'm particularly pleased with how well the foundries are doing turning out the new steel. That's going to allow us to move forward on some additional plans I have for us once this army has been dealt with."

"But?" he asked, crossing his arms and looking at Ky levelly.

"But?" Ky asked, unsure of what he meant.

"Whenever someone starts a conversation telling me what a fabulous job I've been doing, I always know it's an attempt to smooth things over for whatever they say next. So I'm wondering what the 'but' is going to be."

"Fair enough. The 'but' is that I have real concerns about arcuballista production, specifically at the assembly stage, where it appears we have a bottleneck."

"I thought as much. I will take part of the blame on this. I assumed our slowdown would have been in the actual production of the pieces to be assembled. Specifically the metal attachments. Since the basics of how carpenters made the wooden frames hadn't changed, I knew we could just scale that up with more workers as needed and keep up with production. It was the need for precision metal parts, especially the new release mechanism you called a trigger, which would be our weakest point and so it's where I've been putting additional resources as we've been getting them. The amount of rejected parts that needed to be melted down and reforged didn't increase as dramatically as I assumed, however. While that's a good thing, since it means production has stayed high, it meant we were putting manpower and even facilities in the wrong place. I'm in the process of switching over some of the lower producing forges into assembly buildings and retraining the workforce, but that will take time."

"I see. From observing one of the assembly buildings, I think there are a few more places you can accelerate production without adding additional resources."

"Really? How?"

"One of the reasons the foundries and forges are going faster is switching over to the assembly line system, correct?"

"Yes. I still don't know how I didn't think of that, since on the face of it it's so obvious. Limiting a person's work to one set of actions, instead of following the whole process through, made it easier for the worker to become proficient, and therefore faster, and quicker to train new staff, aside from the ability to produce more pieces simultaneously. I think that might have been one of the most impactful techniques you've taught us."

"It might be. My people took generations to think of it, and when we did, it revolutionized our industries, so I knew it would have an outsized effect. My question is, why haven't you expanded the process into other areas?"

"What do you mean?" Hortensius asked, suddenly looking concerned as he realized he might have made a mistake after all.

"I've been watching your craftsmen assemble the arcuballista, and they are doing it one at a time, fitting all pieces onto the frame until it's a finished weapon. In some cases, the worker moves to different stations to access the tools to attach a specific piece. You're losing a ton of efficiency. Why not have the worker stay in one place, attach his piece, and pass it on to the next person to do their piece. Even break it down further, and split up the drilling of specific holes for a given attachment from attaching the metal piece itself into two tasks, if you have the manpower for it. Each step that can be split across people, especially those that require different skills or different tools, allows the worker to rapidly become specialized in that part, just like they do in the forges."

Hortensius squeezed the bridge of his nose and said, "Because I didn't think of it. I saw the effect of your assembly line process in the forges, but in my head, I think I associated that only with the forges and foundries, and with nothing else."

"Understandable. It's easy to become hyper-focused or locked into one mode of thinking when presented with new ideas. The real leaps in innovations aren't developing something new, it's taking others' new developments and finding ways to apply it to what you're doing at the moment."

"None of which makes me feel like less of a fool. I'll get to work on this right away, although it won't instantly increase our production, since we'll have to do some level of rearranging of the factory floor and retraining the workers, all of which will take time."

"Do it one at a time. I think you'll be surprised by how much each factory increases its production after it switches over. They won't increase all at once, but they will grow exponentially," Ky said, and then paused at the look of confusion on Hortensius's face. "That is, they will be will build faster the more we add. You'll have to hire new staff to do simple tasks like taking the assembled piece from one station to another, at least for now, but those require little skill beyond the ability to walk and hold light objects. You can pull from applicants who otherwise weren't suited to work in the factories before now."

"Since the production of the actual pieces is ahead of assembly, we'll focus on the arcuballista first."

"Good. We need those weapons, and we need them soon."

Ky left Hortensius to his work and spent the rest of the day making visits to the other factory owners who'd picked up contracts to produce weapons for the Empire. Some, like the production of gladius and now the longer bladed weapons preferred by the Caledonians, were going well. Ky had also introduced more assembly-line methods here, although they already had some of the rudimentary ideas of the process in place before Ky ever arrived. With those factories, it had been more of fine-tuning their manufacturing process rather than a complete restructuring like Hortensius had faced.

Once spring came, some of these factories would have to be shifted over to the stronger plows and tools Ky had introduced to help increase farming yields and make up for the removal of slave labor, but they still had a good month before that was an issue. Considering the increased Carthaginian presence at the border, the battle that would decide Britannia's fate would have happened already and, if they survived, they would have time to worry about industrialization instead of pure survival.

Right now, however, he couldn't worry about that. Satisfied that everything possible was being done to arm their soldier and citizen auxiliary, Ky's next task was to get more detailed information on the current situation on the Carthaginian side of the border. While Carus was good at keeping him up to date on the information he needed, he'd tasked the man he was beginning to consider his intelligence officer with keeping an eye on the domestic situation. Carus was still in regular contact with Ramirus and was able to keep him from being blindsided, but for detailed battle planning, he needed to meet with the Empire's spymaster directly.

Not unsurprisingly, the man was extremely busy, which had made it hard for even Rome's Consul to get a few hours of the spymasters' increasingly precious time. That was why Ky was up with the morning sun the next day and at the one corner of the palace set aside as an office for him.

"Consul," Ramirus said as the guard at the door admitted him. "I know you've been trying to meet with me and I'm sorry I kept you waiting. I had to make a trip to the border over the last few days, to meet with my sources more directly. The situation in Londinium has been moving very quickly, and an unfortunately large amount of the information I have been getting has been out of date by the time it reached me."

"No need to apologize. I understand the scope of the job we gave you and stopping to meet with me instead of getting the information I need from the meeting would be a waste of everyone's time. How are things on the border?"

"Chaotic. Beyond the scouts we've been capturing, refugees in villages between the Carthaginian assembly area and here, especially along the main road north, have been abandoning their homes and fleeing towards us."

"Why towards us? I get the villages right on the border, since some of those were captured as recently as the fall, but those further in have been under Carthaginian rule for a generation or more. Wouldn't they run the other direction?"

"The Carthaginians are like locusts, devouring the countryside to support the state. They keep an incredible number of men under arms at any one time to pacify areas they've captured, and they do it brutally enough that they have to keep their soldiers in the area to keep the territory pacified. Except in Africa and the areas they consider 'true Carthage,' the only value they see in the territory they control is providing upkeep for their massive armies. The only time these refugees would have seen their current masters would be when their tax collectors, who come with a fair amount of armed support, show up to take half their grain harvest. Or when they come to take any boys who've reached the age of maturity and aren't already apprenticed to a trade or essential to farming and enlist them in their armies, regardless if that's what the young men want to do or not. All of which doesn't lead to a lot of warm feelings between the villagers and their rulers. They know what little food and possessions they have will be swallowed up by the horde everyone knows is assembling in Londinium. Many of these people have little left to steal, since they were already terrorized by the last army that came through just a few months ago."

"So they're running to us? If things were that bad, why did they wait until now to run, especially if staying meant giving up their young men to fight across the world, enslaving more people?"

"Normally, the Carthaginians patrol the border and the lands they control relentlessly. It's actually what the bulk of their armies are used for and why it's taking so long to build up a new invasion army."

"I was wondering about that, since every piece of information I could find on them suggested they had a lot of men under arms."

"They do, but like I said, most of that is to keep the populace under heel. When it comes to active armies they can use to invade a place, they don't have that much available. Although a lot of my countrymen don't want to admit it, preferring to think the reason Rome remains free is because of the power of our legions, the real reason they haven't crushed us yet is because they had to focus their available military might on pacifying the Germanic tribes. My sources reported last year that the last of the tribes west of the mountains and Asia were finally under their control, which matched up with around the same time they began planning for the final push to finish us off. The fact that we defeated that army, and so badly, meant they had to pull units from across their holdings and transport them to Londinium, which is why we had so long to wait. One of the first places they turned was their border guards and patrols in Britannia. The combination of a skeleton force guarding the border and the coming invasion that would wipe them out completely was enough to push the villagers to take their chances making it to us."

"What are we doing about them?"

"We have groups of praetorians rounding them up, checking for spies and the like as best we can, and finding places for them in our villages or bringing them to Devnum, since they need work and we still have a manpower shortage to fill all of the new manufactures that have started up."

"That's convenient for us."

"Yes, although I am concerned about not catching all of the spies and infiltrators the Carthaginians might be slipping in. Although they generally operate more directly, relying on raw military power and brutal oppression, they have occasionally resorted to more crafty measures like generating internal strife when facing a more challenging opponent."

"Which we're trying to be. I'm sure you're doing all you can to keep an eye on that, although considering there are still men like Decius running around and in contact with Caesius, it's a safe bet that some will get through regardless."

"I know, which means we just have to be prepared to try and counter any trouble they may cause, instead of focusing only on keeping them from attempting it in the first place."

"You said the Carthaginians were bringing in soldiers from across their empire. I know it's a large force, but I haven't heard how large. What should we expect?"

"My best estimate is at least a hundred thousand soldiers. The good news is that it is ninety-percent phalanxes, with only limited skirmishers and archers, which will make your plan more effective, but the number imbalance is striking."

"To say the least. Our combined force is still less than thirty thousand men, and it's the largest army Rome has fielded since being pushed off the continent. What about cavalry."

"There is some, but there is an uprising in Petraea among the remnants of the Persian tribes that have required a large mounted response to re-conquer."

"Good. That is the one area that could hurt us. If we don't get all of their cavalry and scouts early, their commander might get wind of the trap before we spring it and try to bypass it. If that happens,

I'm not sure what we can do next, since there is no chance we will survive a stand-up fight."

"Faenius has committed the remainder of the men he had training to patrolling and clearing any scouts, or anyone else, from the area of the proposed fight. While it has led to some unavoidable problems, we should be able to keep any Carthaginian scouts from seeing our preparations."

Ky's eyes narrowed as he asked, "What do you mean unavoidable problems. This is the first I'm hearing about it."

"I know, and that's my fault. I wasn't purposely trying to deceive you, but I was concerned that ... decisions would be made that were counter to the best interests of the Empire. This was one of those moments when I believed forgiveness may be easier than asking for permission."

"Normally I don't mind how devious your mind can be, since it works in our favor, but this isn't one of those moments. What have you done?"

"There was a village very near the battlefield we are preparing. That close to the border, it is possible that the Carthaginians managed to get spies through our lines, and it would be one of the first places they'd go to, since it's on the only tenable invasion route for such a large army. It was located on the other side of the lake, so it wasn't directly in the path of the army, but they could see where we would be preparing from across the water."

"What do you mean was?"

"I mean there was a village, as in it isn't there anymore. On my order, Faenius relocated all of the villagers either back here to Devnum or to nearby villages and then razed it to the ground to keep anyone from trying to cycle back after his men left."

"There had to be another way to handle this?" Ky said, frustrated. "There is still a lot of animosity out there after the insurrections. The last thing we need is a new group of people angry with the Emperor because we took their homes."

"I understand that, but we didn't have a lot of options. We know we are missing scouts, and people talk, even when they aren't being purposely disloyal. If too much attention is put onto your preparations, the Carthaginians will notice, no matter how many men we have out looking for their scouts. You've said how important it is to make sure we don't give away the trap before it's sprung; well this would do it. Were the people in these villages angry? Yes. Is it possible we might drive some of them into the arms of the insurrectionists? Yes. We did what we could to preempt that. We paid each family a thousand sestertii, which is well more than they would have earned in five years of farming and herding. We allowed them to take anything they could and provided men and wagons to help move them. We did everything short of picking up the entire village and relocating it. I'm not sure what other options there were to keep your plans secret and keep from inconveniencing or angering these villagers."

Ky sighed and said, "You're right, and I apologize for second-guessing you. You've shown excellent judgment the entire time I've known you, so I should have assumed you would continue to make the best decisions you can. You're right, the most important thing we can do right now is to win this battle, because if we don't nothing else will matter, and that all hinges on the Carthaginians falling into our trap. Now, tell me about the latest round of interrogations."

Chapter 25

Ky and Ramirus continued working well into the night, reviewing reports and deciding how best to deal with Romans who had to be relocated to keep the battle location safe, and the possibility of relocating other Romans from areas that weren't under threat as a way to throw off the Carthaginians.

At first, Ky had been against the idea, since he didn't want to disrupt civilians any more than they already had been, but eventually caved to Ramirus's reasoning. Ky was a soldier and thought like one. It allowed him to be sneaky when he needed to, trying to stay one step ahead of the other side, but Ramirus was on a whole different level.

He pointed out that it wasn't enough to just keep the area where the trap was supposed to be sprung clear, since that created an intelligence blind spot. A smart strategist would notice that blind spot and surmise there was a reason the other side worked so hard to keep intelligence getting out from there. That would make a smart commander wary, and possibly give away the game.

Since they couldn't help but create an intelligence blind spot, because actual intelligence of the area would be worse than a blind spot, the only solution was to create additional blind spots. This would require quite a bit of manpower, since even after moving out the people who lived in the area, they'd have to do continual sweeps to make sure no one got into the area to investigate. He went on to say that the Carthaginians would probably realize that's what was happening and that one of the spots would be the real thing that the Romans were hiding, but that also couldn't be helped.

Ky's brain reeled at the complex schemes and counter schemes in Ramirus's brain, but he couldn't argue with the man's logic when he laid it out. Besides the chance they were going to make more citizens unhappy, and possibly push them over into the arms of the malcontents still hiding in the shadows, their real problem of making this happen was manpower.

The praetorians had no more reserves or men in training to pull from, and they'd already stretched the men in the field as far as they could, reducing the manpower in patrols and extending the distances those patrols had to cover. Faenius had already been complaining that his men were stretched too thin. Ramirus suggested the idea of using some of the Caledonians, especially the new arrivals who hadn't had time to train with the Romans, making them only useful in the blocking forces or as reserves, but Ky nixed that idea.

Just as it had been on the other side of the border, the Alliance was still in its infancy and vulnerable. Using Caledonians to disrupt Roman lives would make those Romans even more set against the Alliance. Ky eventually came up with a compromise. He'd talk to Llassar and get some of those Caledonians temporarily assigned to Faenius, who could use them to swap out parts of his existing patrols, especially along the border, and have the Romans freed up from that swap form new units that would go about the unpleasant task of removing civilians from the designated intelligence blackout areas. They could also use Caledonians to help patrol those areas once the deed was done.

Ky had also walked Ramirus through the possible options of what they would do next. If they defeated the Carthaginians, they couldn't wait while they came up with their next plan, since it would just give their enemy time to build new forces. And there was no use planning if they lost, because that would mean the end of the bulk of Roman and Caledonian forces, which would also mean the end of both of those civilizations.

Ky knew that their next target, when they won, was to take Londinium and clear the country of Carthaginians. If they were successful in doing that, it would mean that the Britannic Empire would be assured of its long-term survival. Because the Empire was based on an island, any invaders would have the added difficulty of landing troops before they could take on the Empire's armies. That had been doable before, because the Romans were a Mediterranean people who weren't particularly well suited to patrolling and defending the harsher Atlantic. Ky could change that with the introduction of new methods of boat building, new navigational tools, and new methods of sailing. It wouldn't take much in the way of new methods, for the Romans to outclass the Carthaginians on the sea, because they were also Mediterranean peoples.

Of course, first, the Romans had to secure the island, which meant dealing with Londinium. Even if they completely destroyed this army, there were still a lot of defenders in Londinium, which was well defended with high curtain walls and heavy catapults. Even with the advancements in siege equipment Ky could supply, it would be costly in men and material to break through the defenses, and the Carthaginians would have time to reinforce again. Ky had some ideas of how to best these challenges, but he needed Ramirus to gather some information before he could be sure, and that would take time, which was something the Romans didn't have a lot of, even if he wasn't counting the coming battle.

Overall, he was happy with how his meeting with Ramirus went. The spymaster had brought up good points that would help make sure Ky's plan for the coming battle succeeded and they were able to get the initial stages of what came next worked out.

Ky had just laid down and closed his eyes when someone started banging on his door. His men were usually pretty good about keeping everyone but Lucilla or the Emperor from bothering him when he needed to rest, unless it was a true emergency, so the urgency of the banging had Ky up and across the room, flinging the door open in seconds.

"There's a massive fire in the industrial district, my lord," Carus said as soon as the door opened, looking worried.

In modern times, this would have been something dealt with by local fire brigades and wouldn't have escalated to the higher levels of government, but in ancient times where the buildings were all built of wood and packed close together, a fire in the city could mean massive devastation and death.

Ky couldn't help but think of the fire in Rome under Emperor Nero he'd read about in Sophus's files. Although this reality would never meet Nero or experience his fiddling while Rome burned, it was still a cautionary tale of the dangers a fire like that could pose.

"How bad is it? Are the fire brigades out?"

"They are and the praetorians are rallying now. I sent a man down to find out how the efforts to contain it are, and dispatched some of the palace guards and staff to help fight the blaze, but there is a bigger concern. The fire is at the main warehouse where Hortensius was collecting the arcuballista to be handed out to the citizen militia."

"Damnit," Ky said.

This meant the fire wasn't an accident. Someone, either a Carthaginian agent or one of the malcontents still hiding after the failed insurrection was trying to strike directly at Rome's ability to defend itself. They might not know of Ky's plan, but so many citizens had been put through training with the new weapons for everyone to realize how important they are and that they were going to be used to fight the Carthaginians.

"How bad are the losses?" Ky said, pushing through the door and walking quickly through the palace, forcing Carus and his guards to scramble to keep up.

"From what I'm hearing, we are going to lose the entire warehouse and everything inside."

"Damnit," Ky said again.

This was very bad and had a chance to completely derail their battle plans. Without the citizen militia and the weight of volleys they could bring to the Carthaginians, it would be all but impossible for the front-line forces to contain the huge mass of Carthaginians for long. He was relying on the damage these new weapons could do both in actual damage to the forces themselves and in psychological damage. If he could get enough Carthaginians to surrender, the entire line would crumble. Rome still had a lot of fighting to do after this battle and could not afford to have large casualties defeating this one army. At least not if they were then going to go on to take Londinium.

Ky didn't bother getting a horse and ran through the streets, although he kept it at a human pace so his guards could keep up. Lucilla must have been notified at the same time, because he noticed her guards just before she appeared next to him, breathing hard to keep up.

She wasn't wearing her normal Stola and Palla, with their fine embroidered edging and the Palla's elegant drape that added an almost toga-like appearance to the simpler Stola, marking her as a higher-class woman. Instead, she wore a simple Tunic that she must have slept in.

Even with the nanites that Sophus had reintroduced into her system, she struggled to keep up with Ky, as were the rest of the guards. He didn't dare slow down, since even if it was slight, there was a chance that he might be able to help save some of their supplies.

That hope died as soon as they rounded a corner onto the street holding the warehouse and saw the blaze in person. The warehouse was very large, even by Roman standards, and completely engulfed in flames. Several nearby buildings had also caught flame and long bucket lines were throwing water on the flames as fast as they could, barely able to contain it. Already men with axes and sledgehammers were starting to destroy buildings on either side of the blaze, trying to create a fire break to keep the fire at least contained.

"Is there anything we have on us that we could use to get this fire out faster?" Ky asked Sophus internally.

"No, Commander."

"Is there anything in your records of technical files we could use to extinguish this fire?"

"No, Commander. There are better methods of firefighting using current or achievable technology, all of which would have needed significant preparation and construction beforehand. The most effective method now is to create enough of a fire break to limit the fires spread and keep the nearby buildings wetted to prevent sparks and embers from setting buildings alight."

"Damnit," Ky said, out loud.

He'd tried to think of everything he should set up to get Rome ready for industrialization, and he'd somehow overlooked advancing the way ancient people fought fire. He mentally kicked himself. Even without sabotage, industrialization increased the chances for fires as more machinery came into use, so he should have thought about that and set up something. It wouldn't have taken much technological advancement to set up manually operated pumps connected to wheeled water cisterns, allowing more water to be moved and applied at a time. It was too late for any of that.

"Lucilla, get people together and have them start throwing water on the nearby buildings. Carus, we're going to help clear a fire break."

Lucilla nodded and ran off, her guard in tow, to begin her task. Maddeningly, Carus did not follow suit.

"My lord, there are too many people here, it isn't safe. Whoever set his fire could still be nearby. If they are, they will use this as a distraction to make an attempt on you."

"I'm not that easy to kill. Keep one man on guard, watching my back. Everyone else pitches in to help. Send someone for the rest of Lucilla and my guard force and any free hands to come and help. Draft civilians to come if you have to. We have to clear a complete fire break around the warehouse."

"Consul, you can have people do that without being directly involved."

Ky ignored Carus and went to one of the men with a sledgehammer, taking the tool from the surprised man, who released it and stepped back when he saw who it was.

Stepping back, Ky swung as hard as he could, the metal head of the sledgehammer smashing through the side of a wall in one go. Sophus highlighted a second section of wall, adjusting for the supporting weight and indicating the safest location for Ky to stand. The second swing took out another chunk of the building, which was enough to cause the wall to collapse completely. As soon as it went, the corner and wall next to it also fell as it lost integrity. Thanks to his enhanced muscles and Sophus's directions, Ky had taken down a third of a building with two swings. Admittedly, large proportions had already been demolished by the men working on the building, but the demonstration was effective nonetheless.

"That's why I need to be involved," Ky said to Carus before turning back to his task, leaving Carus to make his own mind up if he was going to help or not.

It took almost two hours and the destruction of another row of buildings on the west side of the warehouse where the fire managed to spread before they could extend the firebreak.

Once the fire had finally burned out and smoking ruins were all that remained of the warehouse packed with supplies for the legions, it looked like a bomb had gone off. Every building in an almost hundred-yard radius, and in one side stretching another fifty yards beyond that, were flattened into piles of debris. Some of that debris was also blackened and smoking from where the fire had gotten into the smashed timber of the houses.

Ky drafted several local officials and a senator who'd come to rubberneck at the destruction into helping find places for the displaced citizens whose homes were caught up in the destruction. There had been some slight protest until Lucilla reminded them of their responsibility, and how hard it would be to maintain their positions when the Emperor and the Consul both supported whoever decided to stand against them in the next elections.

Although it was a little more heavy-handed than how Ky would have chosen to convince them to help, he had to admit it was effective.

"This is going to make things harder," Lucilla said as they made their way back to the palace, although slower this time.

"It will, although it's not going to be the death blow I think whoever set the fire hoped it would be. I'll speak with Hortensius in the morning, but he was already retooling assembly factories to a faster, more efficient process and had committed to opening three more by next week. I'd hoped the ramped-up production would put us enough ahead of target to be able to increase the civilian auxiliary for the battle and maybe even arm patrols along the southern border, but even without that, this won't alter the plan. The increased auxiliary would have helped lower our casualty numbers, but it wasn't a tipping point. If the Carthaginians fall into our trap, we have a chance of winning and if they don't, we will be lost, regardless of how many auxiliaries we have."

"That's good news, at least. It's a little disconcerting how easily they were able to get to the warehouse and set it on fire."

"I should have seen it coming. We've had to pull a lot of the patrols in the city so we could supplement our security forces along the border. I knew we were taking a calculated risk when I'd agreed to pull some of the security we'd put on factories and warehouses, but I guess I was just hoping we'd be lucky. It's going to get worse, since I authorized more of the praetorians who'd been assigned as city guardsmen to transfer to the patrols in the south. If anything, we're going to be more vulnerable once those men start pulling out."

"So, we can expect more of this?"

"Yes, and it will be inconvenient and probably get some innocent people killed, but it's not going to have the effect the arsonists hope it will. We're close enough now that we've already got most of the supplies we're going to need for the battle being staged outside of town, and under guard by the legions themselves. I'll talk to Hortensius about having military supplies shipped to the legions daily, including supplies for the civilian auxiliary. It'll make his logistics harder, but he's resourceful. I have faith he'll come through."

Lucilla nodded but didn't say anything else. He could feel her walking close to him, the warmth from her body pushing away the cold night air. She didn't touch him or hold his hand like they sometimes did when walking in more private settings. Although it was very late and there weren't people on the street, aside from a handful returning from looking at the warehouse fire, that kind of casual display was still frowned upon by the upper echelons of society.

Ky didn't particularly care what other people thought, but being dumped into a foreign civilization like this and spending a lot of time in a third society with its own social norms was teaching Ky to respect the social pressures people could feel. He was just glad she was there, next to him.

Of course, as seemed to be true with every private moment between then, the needs of the state seemed to take precedence over their personal needs.

"There was something I was talking to Ramirus about earlier this evening I'd like your thoughts on."

"You can have them," she said, smiling up at him.

"We've done everything we can to prepare for the coming battle aside from moving the pieces into their final places and actually fighting it. We need to start looking forward, beyond our immediate survival."

"I agree."

"Good, because I am having trouble seeing how to get around our biggest problem. We've put the entire efforts of both the Roman and Caledonians towards fighting this one army, and are still fighting at serious odds. Our problem is that, while this represents a titanic effort on our part, it's a secondary concern for the Carthaginians, who are more focused on their last efforts to pacify Germania and deal with uprisings in the east. Once we push the Carthaginians out of Britannia, we will draw more of their attention. Your ancestors fought in Hispania, where you had five times the legions that were still smashed by numbers that dwarf what we will face here."

"Isn't that where your innovations and new technologies come in?"

"To a degree, although we are still quite a ways from the force multipliers we will eventually need. Even with those, we will need more of a force to multiply if we're going to take the fight off the islands and to the Carthaginians."

"Knowing you, I'm assuming you aren't bringing this up just to vent, and you have something specific in mind."

"I do, in fact," he said, smiling down at her.

He enjoyed how well she was getting to know him. It felt oddly comforting that she could predict him so easily.

"Don't leave me in suspense," she said, returning the smile.

"When I originally talked about the need to construct the alliance between Rome and the Caledonians in a way that would allow others to join us, it had been abstract. An eventuality that I knew we'd probably need, but one I didn't have specific plans for."

"But you have plans for it now?"

"Yes. What do you know about Hibernia," Ky said, invoking the Roman name for the island that, in his time, would have been called Ireland?

"A land of primitive tribes, mostly herders and farmers. They have sometimes raided across the sea separating us and there is the occasional trader. Although they deal with the Caledonians more than us, since there are some familial ties and the ocean is narrowest between their lands."

"That was about what Ramirus had to say when we spoke, except he added that sources inside Londinium have notified him that the Carthaginians have begun setting up bases to operate out of in the south of Hibernia and on a small island between it and Britannica. It's unclear what the collection of men and material in southern Hibernia is for, since, as you said, there isn't much outside of farmers and herders. There are few industrial centers to control and a large open hinterland and spread-out people that will require a not-insubstantial amount of men to control. The island between us, however, seems like an ideal place to launch raids and potentially even a seaward invasion into Roman lands. With both, however, they are going to be a threat, which makes them potential allies and an additional source of manpower. The problem is, we have little information about them and Ramirus has no contacts with them at all. I'm thinking of how to best send a messenger to Talogren, since their closer relations might mean he has more knowledge about them, but this isn't the kind of conversation that works well through messengers."

"I think I might have an idea?"

"Really?"

"Yes. Llassar should know how we can best approach them, or know who could tell us. He's involved in everything Talogren has done, so if Talogren knows, Llassar will know. You need to focus on the battle and the Carthaginians. I know what you need to have happen."

"Are you sure?"

"You trusted me to be your voice while you were up north. Yes, I know that was partially because you had access to me through the communicator, so you could still have some decision making, but I'd like to think it was also because you trusted me to make decisions you'd support."

"It was, and you did better than I could possibly have done with keeping the alliance together. I am just thinking that beyond the language barrier, they are going to want to negotiate with someone who has the power to make guarantees they can believe," Ky said.

"We've already established there have been traders from Hibernia who've made contact with both the Romans and the Caledonians. That means there has to be some people who speak both languages. As for making deals, we're only making contact. They can arrange for some kind of negotiators to either travel here or come back and arrange for our people to go there. You aren't the only one who can make deals, especially for the new Empire, where the Caledonians have an equal say and so must be made part of any diplomatic mission. I know you have knowledge and abilities far beyond anything we've ever encountered, but you said yourself that you were a soldier and not a politician before you came here. I have been doing this since I could walk. Politics and diplomacy have quite literally been my entire life. You wisely set up the framework and rules by which any new members of the Empire would join. Trust us to follow that framework."

"She is correct, Commander. You are needed here and cannot afford the time it takes to travel to Ireland, let alone negotiate treaties or additional alliances. Lucilla has the same abilities and can select an ambassador to send to the proto-Irish as well as you could. I believe this would be covered in the delegating you have previously said you needed to do more of, to keep from being a bottleneck in your plans to build an industrialized society here."

Ky could see confusion cross Lucilla's face as Sophus identified Ireland by its modern name, but wasn't surprised that she brushed it off and continued to stare him down, one eyebrow going up as Sophus sided with her. She was tenacious and a little thing like a language barrier wouldn't distract her from what she wanted to do.

"I wasn't trying to suggest you would be any way incapable or less qualified than I would be to do this, and of course, you're both right. I leave this in your capable hands. Talk to Llassar and make it happen. Just remember that by the end of the summer I hope to have control of Londinium and we will need to have some kind of agreement in place for what comes next."

"What does come next?" Lucilla asked.

"We take the fight to the Carthaginians," Ky said, a smile crossing his lips.

Chapter 26

Caledonian Camps Outside Devnum

Lucilla weaved through the rows of tents looking, occasionally stopping to say hello to this group or that. Considering how she'd grown up, always in the public eye, she was used to receiving attention. She'd traveled legion camps numerous times over her life, both as a younger woman as part of one of her father's or brother's entourages and later in her own capacity as a leader of Rome. The reception she got every time she came into a Caledonian camp was on a completely different level than any of her previous experiences, however.

At first, before she traveled north, it had been overwhelming, but almost patronizingly so, almost like she was some kind of mascot. Since the events in the north, however, that had changed. Now the reactions ranged from simple comradeship to deep respect to an almost sense of awe, with the men reaching to touch the hem of her tunic as she went by. She had to admit that the later reaction made her deeply uncomfortable and made her realize why Ky had pushed so hard against any kind of similar response he'd received from the Romans.

Finding Llassar's tent, she stopped outside the unguarded entrance and coughed loudly, which was traditionally how the Caledonians, who had cloth flaps for doors even in their most built-up cities, introduced themselves instead of just barging in on the occupant.

"Come," Llassar said, and Lucilla pushed through the flap to find the Caledonian leader sitting on a stool at a small Roman-style camp table on one side of his tent.

She was actually glad to see the table, since it was another sign of the Caledonians' rapid adoption of some Roman ways, which would ultimately help bring the two allies together. It did remind her that she needed to talk to people she knew, poets and minor celebrities, about publicly adopting some of the more palatable Caledonian traditions, since what was really needed to bring the allies together was a two-way adoption of social and cultural norms, not just the Caledonian's adopting ideas from the Romans.

That was, however, a thought for another time. She'd promised Ky she would take care of getting a messenger sent to Hibernia, and she meant to prove to him that she could be trusted to handle things like this.

Llassar turned and, finally recognizing who'd come into his tent, stood and gave a slight bow of his head, saying, "What can I do for you?"

She smiled at him, unable to contain how much she found his continuous straightforward nature endearing. While Romans and even many Caledonians would have apologized for remaining seated as she entered or said "my lady" or other honorifics, Llassar simply asked what she wanted.

"I need your help, or at least your direction."

"You know that, if there is any help I have to offer, it's yours," he said, pointing at a small stool for her to sit on while he returned to the stool he'd been on a moment before.

"I know, and I appreciate that. The Consul and I are starting to look forward to what happens next, after we defeat the Carthaginian army coming for us. One of the things we are looking toward is opening up relationships with other people who might be able to help us in our war with the Carthaginians. Specifically, we've received reports of Carthaginian landings on Hibernia and the impressing of locals into slave labor to help them establish a foothold, most likely as an alternative base to strike at us, should we secure all of Britannia. We think this might give the Hibernians living there an incentive to join us in pushing back the Carthaginian threat."

"The Ériu," Llassar said.

"What?" Lucilla asked, slightly confused at the seemingly random non-sequitur.

"They call themselves the Ériu, not the Hibernians. Much like your calling my people the Picts, which is a name you Romans chose for other people, instead of calling us by our proper names."

"I apologize, although I think this points to why we need to find someone to help us make contact. I hope I have shown that I respect your culture and that my ignorance shouldn't be taken as a sign of contempt."

"It's not, but I think all of you need to do better trying to learn about other cultures you intend to interact with, instead of just defaulting to your own prejudices."

"You are correct and both the Consul and I are trying to change that kind of attitude in Rome. Again, it's why I'm here, speaking to you."

She knew that Llassar wasn't trying to be rude. He'd made it clear several times how much it bothered him when Romans, or anyone, tried to assume their culture was somehow the default, and that his people should change their beliefs and understandings to better align with the Romans, instead of vice versa. She hoped that attitude could help them, in this instance, since it might mean he'd have a better chance finding the right person to send as their representatives to the Ériu.

"So what exactly are you asking for?"

"Your people have been in contact with the Ériu longer and more frequently than the Romans. We need someone who can go to them and present our case to them."

"Which is?"

"The same one we presented to your people. The Carthaginians are a threat to everyone, and a direct threat to them. They will not stop at bases on the southern shore, and it is only a matter of time until Carthaginian phalanxes are marching into their cities and enslaving their children to feed their ever-growing need for soldiers. We are standing against them, and we are asking them to stand with us. We'd like for them to send a representative to negotiate with the Britannic Empire, not just the Romans, for an alliance. This could be as little as a military alliance, however we are open to the possibility of expanding the Empire, as long as this deal meets the approval of the imperial senate, on similar terms as the current members. We are offering favorable trade, technologies, open markets, and mutual assistance. All we ask in return is a willingness to help us defeat the Carthaginian scourge."

Llassar didn't answer at first, and Lucilla was concerned he might say that the Caledonians had no interest in more members of their alliance.

"I assume you haven't spoken to Talogren about this?"

"No. I am here speaking to you, to get your advice on how to proceed. I want to clarify that I am not here as a Roman and we are not making this offer as one of two members of an alliance. My father, Ky, and I are all firm believers in the Empire we made. An Empire composed of two peoples with one goal: to make a better world. Any offer we make must be approved by two-thirds of the imperial senators, which means by representatives for both Rome and Caledonia, and then agreed to by the Emperor. I am asking for your advice on whom to send to represent the Empire as a whole."

"I see," he said, his eyes continuing their constant judging, as he did with everyone he dealt with. After a long pause, he said, "I can think of one person who would make a good representative for the Empire."

"Good. Who?" Lucilla asked.

"Me," he said, cracking one of his rare smiles.

"You?"

"Yes, me. Did you know I spent more than two years as a ... guest, of the Ériu?"

"A guest?"

"I was on a ship that got washed out to sea and ended up on their shores, where I was taken to Emain Macha, their capital, and put into the service of Eochaid Salbuide, their king."

"So, you know the rulers of the island?"

"Ulaid only controls the northern reaches. South of them are the Airgialla, which is actually several kingdoms that broke away from the Ulaid and formed their own confederation. There are more kingdoms south of that, closer to the areas your reports say the

Carthaginians have been operating out of, but I never encountered those people."

"But you know them, at least the northern people. If we convinced them, could they convince the others?"

"It's hard to say. I was only there for two years, but there is a lot of hatred among the various kingdoms. We are closer to you Romans, as far as being a single people, than we are to the Ériu, if that gives you an idea of how hard it will be to get all of the people to work together."

"But we have a starting point. If you could talk to this king of theirs could you convince him of the benefits of joining us?"

"Possibly. He will probably ask for help, bringing the other kingdoms under his control, in exchange."

"This isn't like getting individual settlements to join a confederation that already controls the majority of a region, and Ky was hesitant about even that. He has a very different set of ideas when it comes to how people should be governed."

"I've noticed. I admire many things about the Consul, but he is naive at times. Any alliance with the Ériu won't matter if their entire focus must remain on keeping control of the lands they already control. If you want them to commit their people to our common cause, you are going to have to help them make sure their home front is secure."

"So you're suggesting we pick a side and support them? Do we have the manpower for this?"

"No, but we do have the supplies. I've seen Ériu metalwork. It's shit. Their weapons always break and they have nothing like your arcuballista."

"You understand one ruling elite over a pacified but hostile populace does us little good, right? If we are going to get the people to enlist in the legions and give us the manpower to fight back, we need the bulk of the population to be willing participants. We won't have the manpower to continually send legions to help secure our rear."

"I understand, although when it comes to the Ériu, war is their primary way of discussing politics. Although I described large kingdoms, those are closer to over-kings, each ruling over smaller kings who control a single village or a small collection of villages and some of the countryside. Properly funded, however, I think the Uliad could convince many of those lower kings to switch allegiances."

"Good. Are you willing to do this? To go to them and negotiate an alliance? We will back you as well as we can. You just need to get them to agree to send emissaries to negotiate with Ky and my father and some idea of what we want those emissaries to agree to."

"Like I said, they are a unique people and I can't guarantee what any of their actions will be, but I can try."

"Good. I know Talogren sent you to keep control of the men. Do you have any thoughts on who you could give the task to, with you gone?"

"Yes. You."

"I appreciate the vote of confidence, but ..."

"I keep telling you, this has nothing to do with my confidence in you. You are as much of a central figure to my people, or at least those Caledonians currently here in the south, as I am. They'll listen to you."

"I appreciate you reminding me of their support, but I also have political duties that I have to attend to. I am happy to lend my support whenever needed, but I need someone to handle the day-to-day duties of commanding the Caledonian forces."

"Ohh," he said, looking away in embarrassment.

Lucilla couldn't help but find it funny that a man who so often stayed quiet would end up embarrassed for speaking before hearing the other person out.

"Have whoever you put in command find me, and good luck on your journey. I can't tell you how important building up additional alliances is to our long-term survival against the Carthaginians."

"I'll do my best."

Londinium

"I'm concerned about how few of our scouts are coming back," Bomilcar said, looking down at the large map laid out on the table.

The room was packed with commanders, aides, and sub-commanders, all waiting to find out when the campaign they'd been sent here for would begin. Everyone had heard the rumors of how hard the Governor was pushing Bomilcar to begin the campaign against the Romans. Although it had become common knowledge that they had orders to start as soon as the last units arrived from the continent, that had seemed like a far-off moment for the men, many of whom had been assembled for months, waiting for the rest of the forces to gather. Now that the last boatload of men had arrived, the time for planning and training was over, and everyone was a little on edge.

None of the men doubted their ultimate victory, considering the vast host assembled to destroy the Romans, but enough had heard from survivors of the last army to march north to make everyone a little nervous about their own personal chances for survival.

"They have been very aggressive, but we have a firm count of the number of men in the Roman army," one of the commanders said, pointing at the small figures placed around Devnum representing the Roman legions and their auxiliaries. "They are vastly outnumbered, and almost half of their forces are barbarians from the north, not regular soldiers. There's little they can do to stop us. We know the roads are intact and passable, even with the snow still on the ground."

"I'd remind you the Romans outnumbered Hannibal at Cannae and suggest you consider how that turned out."

"With respect, General, Hannibal's army was well trained and disciplined, wasn't made up mostly of barbarians, and their cavalry was able to push back the Roman screens enough, making the encirclement possible. The Romans have a third of the number of horsemen we do, even if most of ours are also auxiliary. It's impossible they'll be able to pull us into a trap like the one Hannibal was able to set."

"I think you're underestimating the Romans. They already defeated a much larger army once, and that was without having months to plan a response. Don't get overconfident."

The man nodded but didn't take back his complaint. Bomilcar frowned. Too many men had grown used to victories against smaller tribes in Germania or quelling revolts in province districts. All but a handful of the commanders assembled for this new army had fought a well-trained military, and those that had fought in the east, against cavalry and phalanxes similar to the ones used by Carthage. Rome might not be the empire it once was, but it was still dangerous. Bomilcar had studied Roman tactics, especially their legions, and had been impressed with what he'd seen. Yes, they had been defeated numerous times in the past, but his subordinates paid too much attention to the final disposition of the battle and not enough attention to the casualty figures.

Except in a few cases, Roman legions were able to inflict serious damage to any force they faced, even ones that had numeric and strategic advantages; and that had been before their new Consul arrived. Although the information they'd received from the Emperor's turncoat son indicated he was just a figurehead looking to amass power, independent sources all pointed to the man the Romans called The Sword of Jupiter as the real reason they'd so completely crushed Zaracas's army.

Spies independent from Caesius, who Bomilcar was pretty sure was altering any information he got to fit the narrative he was trying to build for the governor, indicated that the Roman Consul had been hard at work training his forces all winter. They'd also heard rumors of new weapons the Romans were developing, although none had been able to get any of these weapons back for the Carthaginians to examine. Not for the first time, Bomilcar lamented the fact that they'd had so many problems getting spies into the Roman Capitol.

One of his biggest annoyances with Caesius was the younger man's success at convincing the governor of his value through his contacts in what was left of the Roman rebels who'd stayed in the city. If Bomilcar had had access to the agents working directly for Caesius, he was certain he'd have been able to better anticipate the Roman's plans. As it was, the younger man was wasting their advantage by sharing rumor and gossip as fact and focusing too little on things like a detailed description of weapons and manpower.

His problem, at the moment, was how freely the governor had been at disseminating Caesius's worthless intelligence reports to his commanders, with their focus on barbarians and meaningless political murders, causing many of them to become overconfident.

"They may be under strength and mostly made up of auxiliaries, but they can still be dangerous. They know we are coming, and they have been working hard at keeping any scouts or spies from seeing what's happening in multiple fairly large areas. We've even got word that entire villages have been emptied, probably in an attempt to reduce the chance of someone seeing what they were up to and selling the information to one of our agents. For all we know, they could be holding entire legions in these areas in secret."

"You know that isn't possible, general. We have good reports on all of their force movements since well before the Romans began patrolling these areas so heavily. We have kept track of every Roman legion and auxiliary force, and would have known if any men were moved into these areas. We even know their last legion is, even now, on the way south to join the rest of their forces. We might not know what the Romans are doing in these areas, but it shouldn't matter. Look how spread out they are. There are almost a dozen across the entire border, some hundreds of miles from each other. The pattern makes no sense."

"And yet, it exists. Several of these areas are along the road north to Devnum. The Romans have to know it's the only road large enough to let an army our size travel north, especially with the ground still covered in snow. They're doing this for a reason."

"I agree they probably are, generally, but with the size of our army, does it ma..."

The sub-commander was just ramping up to his point when the door to the large room they were gathered in burst open and the governor, in all his finery and regalia, burst into the room. Bomilcar gritted his teeth, preparing for the tirade he knew was coming. He'd heard a lot of things about Maharbaal before being transferred to lead the battle here, most of them bad. Whatever he'd heard had paled in comparison to how the man came off in person. Every interaction he'd had with the vain and arrogant man had ended with screams and threats, and this one promised to be no different as he marched straight to Bomilcar, stopping when his face was only inches away from the general's own.

"General, why haven't you assembled your troops to march yet?" he vehemently demanded, spittle flying from his mouth.

"The troops just disembarked this morning. It takes a few hours for the men to readjust to being on solid ground and getting enough food in their bellies to ready them for a long march. Although I again point out we would lose fewer men on the march, and move faster against the Romans, if we waited until the snows thawed at least. This many men will be slow to march on their own, but being forced to stay on the only road able to take us north in these conditions means a slow march that the Romans will easily predict."

"Excuses. All you ever give are excuses for why you're unable to carry out the emperor's demands. I don't give a damn what you think these men need or want. What I care about is doing my duty, which is to destroy the Romans and pacify this island for our emperor. These men can recover on the march or they can recover in the dungeons. There will be no waiting for the snow to melt or gathering of supplies or requests for more soldiers. I don't care what friends you have in the imperial court, if your army is still encamped by this evening, you'll be the one in my dungeons."

It took everything Bomilcar had in him not to reply in kind, pointing out exactly why he was a fool. Maharbaal had been growing more unhinged every day and there was no telling what kind of reaction he'd have to such a direct challenge. Bomilcar knew the emperor was pushing the governor hard to finish up the pacification of Britannia. The loss of the first army and the need for so many men the empire needed elsewhere had not gone unnoticed. Another loss was likely to prove very unfortunate for the governor's future. That kind of pressure could push even the best of men into poor decisions, and he was far from being 'the best of men.'

"I understand. We will begin our march before the day is out," Bomilcar said, not having much of a choice, otherwise.

The governor huffed and turned to leave as abruptly as he came in, only to stop just by the door.

Turning back towards the room and pointing a finger, he added, "Don't fail, General. The emperor has made it clear how important this conquest is to him and failing to achieve victory is the same as disobeying the emperor. No friends or legacy or family connections will save you if you fail. Treat this fight like your life and the lives of your wife and children hang in the balance. Because they do."

Chapter 27

Devnum

"We're still weak on the blocking side," Velius said, looking down at the large map holding dozens of carved figures. "If we can't hold them in this box, they will sweep around the lake and crush us."

"I know, but we don't have much of a choice. We have to use enough of a bait force to make them believe we are routing. They know what kind of forces we have available to us. We can get away with shortening our numbers some, especially if the cavalry does its job, but there's a limit to it, and I think we're getting very close to that. Any less here," Ky said, pointing to the largest grouping of wooden figures. "And they will start looking for the rest of our army, or worse, looking more at the topography and seeing this area for what it is."

"Are you sure they won't see it ahead of time," Ursinus asked? "As you said, they've got enough information already to see everything we did in making this plan. They know our forces and they have to be looking at maps of their invasion route."

"If they see us putting up stiff resistance and that almost half our forces are missing, they might figure it out, but just looking at the map alone, no, I don't think so. It's just over a mille passus from the lakeshore to the cliffs. They'll see the cliffs and the lake on the map, but they won't see it for the box that it is until it's too late, especially since they can't see the excavation work we've been doing on the cliffside to make it impossible to climb. I've walked the area. On the ground, with the way the ground rolls, it's even harder to see how much it narrows."

Ursinus frowned, but nodded. Unlike most of the commanders, Ursinus had actually fought side by side with Ky when he first arrived, and had seen some of Ky's use of technology up close, which meant he tended to give Ky the benefit of the doubt. Ky understood his hesitancy. No one of this time had ever seen aerial reconnaissance of a battle area before and would have a harder time grasping the entire field as a whole, rather than just what they could see from the ground.

He hadn't considered it before, but once he managed to get a chemical industry set up and producing things like sulfuric acid, he could introduce hot air balloons, the earliest designs of which used sulfuric acid and iron filings to safely produce the hot gasses used to lift them. One of the biggest limitations in ancient battles was the limited information commanders had during the fight itself. They would strategize ahead of time, working out plans for how to fight the enemy, but during the battle itself, everything was passed by runners, sending back updates of the fight from commanders one by one. It limited what the commanders were able to do, turning the entire business into a slugfest with little tactical control.

Plans like this one required very specific timing to work. The only reason this plan was even feasible was because he could see the entire battle as it progressed and communicate with Lucilla in real-time from a distance.

No matter their training, it was unlikely the Romans and their Caledonian allies would have been able to pull something like this off without him, and he wouldn't always be around. If, however, he could set up something like a signaling corps using balloons and flags, commanders would be able to outmaneuver their opponents even mid-battle without Ky's intervention. It would give them a big advantage in the fights to come, especially since the Empire would be fighting on multiple fronts and its commanders would have to confront larger forces without Ky's technology.

It wasn't something for now, but Ky filed it away as another thing he needed to work on.

"Even if they don't realize it's a trap, I'm still not convinced they won't break through our lines," Velius said. "The front lines on both the forward and rear of the Carthaginians will take two full legions each to cover, and that's spread very thin. The pressure of a hundred thousand men, especially ones who realize what mortal danger they're in, will be intense. I'm not confident we can hold back that pressure. Considering we only have five legions total, once the fourth legion arrives, with two so under strength that we have to put them together to equal one full legion, we're left with nothing but auxiliary forces in reserve. I mean no offense to our Caledonian allies, but holding men in place is a different kind of fighting than your men are used to."

Drest, the man Llassar assigned to take his place, had almost as little expression as Llassar, but nodded back in answer. Everyone assembled knew that Velius had a point and had heard him make this point before, once all of the commanders were brought in on the plan. They'd run two full-scale mock battles to give the men a chance to train on what to expect, a concept that, in of itself, had been completely foreign to militaries in the ancient world and difficult for both the Romans and the Caledonians to grasp. The results had proven what Velius had said. When put into the Roman blocking positions, the Caledonians had not managed to hold the line, even when faced with just pushing and shoving of men armed with wooden training swords. When faced with the real thing, no amount of warrior drive and toughness would counter an organized and coordinated push by either a legion or a phalanx.

"I know, and I've agreed that this was the weak point all along. Unfortunately, we don't have any more men to draw on. We've pulled every legion in and even if we stripped the praetorians for additional manpower, an action that could backfire on us dramatically considering men like Decius are still out there setting fires, it would not make a difference. There aren't a thousand more men with legion training left in the Empire, and we've run out of time to train any more."

"Then what do we do when the legions start to bend? And they will under that much weight."

"They might not. If the civilian auxiliaries are effective, I'm hoping it damages the unit cohesiveness of the phalanxes enough to keep them from pushing our men back. However, I thought we could hold back enough of Drest's men as a reserve. When the line weakens, they rush in as a counter-attack, giving time for the pressed legion to reform and reset their walls."

"Charging an engaged phalanx like that is suicide," Auspex said.

"My men aren't afraid to die in battle."

Auspex was about to retort when Ky held up a hand, stopping him.

"We saw in the war games that, while the Caledonians couldn't hold a concerted line, a massed attack was able to push the opposing line back. That's all we'll need."

"I'm still not convinced these war games of yours can be counted on to show us what things will be like for real. Men with steel swords react very differently than men with wooden ones," Lartius, the newly appointed legate of cavalry, said.

"They also react differently when facing real swords instead of wooden ones. I know it's a new concept and you'll have to see it to believe it, but it does give us practical experience to understand what might happen. Once the battle is over, we can discuss its effectiveness. Until then, you'll just have to believe me."

"I think we can all agree a charge by armed Caledonians will push any opponent back, at least enough to let us reform our lines, so I don't have an issue with that. I'm wondering where these warriors will come from. You yourself just said we needed to have enough men in the retreating forces to convince the Carthaginians. If these have to be Caledonians, where are you going to get enough men to use as a reserve? Because we need it on both sides of the fight, by my count, we don't have enough men for this."

Ky couldn't disagree with Velius's estimates. Sophus had run the numbers multiple times using the war games as a baseline, and even if they cut the number of soldiers in the bait force, the bulk of which would be made up of Caledonians either as themselves or dressed as legionaries, they had just barely enough left over to make up an effective reserve on one side of the fight. That was, however, not enough. The Carthaginians would be trying to break out in either direction, and if the rear force faltered, then nothing the main force did would matter.

"You're right, we don't, but there isn't anything we can do about that. The forces we have now are all we're going to have. We can only hope that the civilian auxiliaries do enough damage to keep the enemy boxed in."

"Do we have enough arcuballista to arm them, after the warehouse fire?"

"We should. Hortensius has stepped up production significantly, and a lot of our production was targeted at arming the legions themselves and the praetorians, beyond what was needed for this battle. We had enough already in the hands of the legion for training to equip most of the auxiliary, thankfully."

"Good. We should ..." Velius started to say when a guard burst through the opening of the tent, bending over to whisper in his ear. "Excellent. The fourth legion has arrived."

"Good. Have Vibius report here as soon as his men are settled. The Carthaginians should be moving any day, and they are closer to the ground we've chosen for the battle than we are. We've already looked from areas to set up camp where we won't ..."

"I'm sorry to interrupt you, Consul," Velius said. "But I've been told there is something we need to see?"

"Really?" Ky asked, stepping away from the map table and following the guard, followed by the rest of the legates and officers.

Ky headed for the western side of the camp, where the fourth legion should be marching past. Their advanced riders had come through in the morning and Velius had directed them to lead the rest of the men to a spot southwest of the seventh legion's position to set up camp.

Ky had expected to see Roman legions marching past. While there were legionaries at the head of the column, behind their legate, Ky hadn't expected to see row upon row of Caledonian warriors marching behind them. From their position, it was impossible to see the number of north men in the column, but it had to be at least a thousand.

When Vibius noticed Ky and the gathered legates he said something to the tribune riding next to him, most likely orders to take the legion ahead, and then broke from the men, riding over to Ky and the rest.

"Consul," Vibius said, dismounting and offering a salute.

"It's good to see you again Vibius. Where did all these men come from?"

"Talogren has spent the last several weeks gathering every able-bodied warrior in the north not directly attached to their guard force and dispatched them with my legion to join the fight. He showed up just as we were forming to march south and told me he'd received the reports you had Ramirus send him about the enemy troop strength. He wanted me to tell you that he understands if Rome falls then the north falls with it and of his willingness to show you the commitment of the Caledonii. He made it clear these men are here to help with this fight, but must return by spring for the harvest, but that right now, they were needed here more than drinking and growing fat in warm huts."

Ky turned to Drest and asked, "Did you know anything about this?"

"No, but I am not Llassar. My chieftain wouldn't consult me on his decisions."

"So it's a surprise to everyone," Ky said. "This is good, though. This should help our manpower problem on the rear side of the force. Will you find whoever is leading them and help them get settled with the rest of your men?"

Drest bowed his head slightly, which was as close as a Caledonians got to a salute, and went to intercept the marching northmen.

"It looks as though we have everything we need to make this plan work. Now, we just have to wait for the Carthaginians to make their move."

Ky didn't have to wait long. After another hour with the legates, including the newly arrived Vibius, going through the strategy for the coming battle, making sure everyone knew their parts, Ky headed out of camp, back towards Devnum. He'd hoped to make it back in time to meet Lucilla, who'd stayed behind to see Llassar off. Instead, he encountered her and Ramirus riding in the opposite direction towards the seventh legion.

"I was afraid we'd miss you," Lucilla said.

"Are they moving?" Ky asked, his eyes going to Ramirus.

Lucilla riding out to meet him wouldn't have been unusual, since she'd been pushing to spend every free moment the two of them had, which was admittedly not much, together. He couldn't fault her for her aggressiveness, since their forced time apart while he was unconscious made him value the time they had together just as much.

Ramirus being with her, on the other hand, was unusual, since the spymaster wasn't even supposed to be in town. He'd left a few days before to travel to the border so he could be closer to his agents and their reports. From Ky's understanding, he'd planned on moving from village to village along the border until the invasion happened.

"Yes. Their army began the march three days ago. They are making slow progress because of their sheer size, the difficulty they're having supplying their men, and having to stop and clear the roads regularly, but they are moving."

"Tell me they're coming the way you predicted."

"They are. As I said, none of the other roads heading north are passable enough for another month and going cross-country is out of the question for their supply column. This was the only path open to them."

"We need to get the men moving. We have a lot further to go and part of our force needs to be in hiding before their scouts get here. The praetorians may have been able to keep scouts out, but the army's cavalry screen will be too much for them."

"That's why I rode here as quickly as I could. Lucilla found me on her way back and told me where you were. I knew we didn't have time to wait, so I asked that we try and intercept you on the way back to town, to save you the time of retracing your steps."

"How long do we have?" Ky asked as he turned his horse around, leading the small group back towards the legion camps.

"Four days, most likely. It's possible they could speed up their progress and cut that number by a day, but I doubt it. It's more likely the further they get from Londinium and the longer their supply line gets, the slower they will go, since their supply wagons will be having as much difficulty as the rest of them."

"Could he be right and they'll be there in three days?" Ky asked Sophus internally.

"Without additional data, it is impossible to form an accurate projection, Commander. Based on current information, I project a fifty-five percent chance the Carthaginian army will need four full days to arrive at the chosen battlefield. If we could access

Ramirus's reports, I should be able to increase the certainty of that projection."

"I need you to get me whatever reports you have before we march, which means in the next several hours. As of now, we have to assume our time frame is shorter, just to make sure we're in place. Except for the main forward force, we need to have everyone in position and our cavalry screens out to keep their mounted forces from stumbling across the rest of our legions before we want them revealed. If we need to be in position in three days, we need to start the march tonight. The roads will be just as bad for us as they are for them."

Ramirus nodded and turned his horse again, galloping back towards Devnum.

"I think he's right that three days is impossible," Lucilla said. "The weather wasn't that much worse north of Devnum and we weren't able to cover that amount of ground in that short of time, and we had less men and supplies to bring with us."

"I think you're probably right, but even when he comes back with his reports and Sophus can give us better odds, I still want to be in place three days from now. We have to not only march there, but have enough time to get several thousand men hidden and out of sight before the Carthaginians get anywhere near them. I'd hoped we'd have more time than this."

"I know," she said, reaching a hand out, which he took in his. "This plan will work."

"I guess we're about to find that out," he said, looking towards the legion camps.

Chapter 28

Carthaginian Army

Bomilcar coughed through the thick wool cloth pulled over his face, once again mentally cursing the governor and his short-sighted demands. The army was moving slowly and shedding soldiers with every hectare. Broken legs from slips on the icy stone road, frostbite because of conscripts not being issued proper footwear, and a fever that was sweeping through the ranks.

Fighting in the heat of the summer was bad enough when dealing with conscripts and slave soldiers, without the added problems of the weather. Worse, because they were forced to use the only major road north, the Romans would easily predict their route, meaning they could choose the field of battle. Bomilcar wasn't concerned about their ultimate fate, given the sizes of their respective forces, but the victory would be messy.

One day, one of these petty tyrants who seemed so adept at making their way up in the empire would demand too much or take on an enemy too strong, and the great Carthaginian Empire would fall. Bomilcar had no doubt of that. The Romans might be a tiny force, even with their new alliance, but there was word of other forces to the far east with powerful armies. His masters had disregarded those rumors as propaganda and fear, but he'd heard it from enough sources to believe it.

Bomilcar's family had always served the empire, and now he feared that he might be the one to see it fall.

"Sir," a rider said, coming up at a gallop and interrupting his train of thought. "We've sighted the Romans."

"Show me," Bomilcar said, spurring his horse and following the scout commander.

Surprisingly, they didn't head towards the front of the line, but towards the left flank of the army. It took a moment to see a line of horsemen galloping towards them. Because of the speed at which they were approaching, Bomilcar thought for a moment they might crash into his mounted forces on that flank, when suddenly they turned. Had he not been there to see it, Bomilcar would have thought any report of it a lie. The line of horses made a sharp U shape as the column of Roman horsemen turned and rode away, barely breaking speed.

As they did, arrows began to fly into the ranks. Their accuracy left something to be desired, if they were shooting at his cavalry, since only about one in five hit a horseman or even a horse, but considering how many men were marching in columns behind the cavalry, it didn't matter. This didn't surprise him. He'd received reports of these more advanced arcuballista with their greater range and force of impact.

In military terms, it wouldn't mean much. There just were not enough enemy horsemen to put a dent in his forces. It did, however, signal where the enemy would strike from.

"Turn the ..." he began to give the command, when two more scouts appeared.

"Sir! Enemy horsemen attacking on the right flank," the first one reported.

"We've identified Roman legion battle standards ahead," the second one said.

Bomilcar stopped, processing the new information. One of his gifts had been the ability to take the available information and see the field of battle as a whole in his head, allowing him to adjust to changes quickly.

He could see the Roman plan. The two cavalry charges were feints, probably to draw off his cavalry and keep him from seeing around their line. Considering the terrain, with its rolling hills that limited how far he could see, they were probably holding a surprise out there. If he had to guess, they were holding forces back for a counter-attack or to get around his sides, perhaps trying to recreate Hannibal's victory at Cannae. It wouldn't matter. The difference in men was too great. As long as he kept his front line even with theirs, they couldn't get around his flanks no matter how many men they had in reserve.

"Order the Cavalry to push back the Roman horsemen. Once the Romans are disposed of, I want them to probe the flanks of the Roman legions."

In the back of his head, he was already accounting for the latter not happening. He'd seen the astonishing speed at which the Roman horseman had maneuvered. His men could not turn that quickly and the Romans' new weapons allowed them to slowly pick off his men, even with their poor accuracy. He was, however, willing to sacrifice the bulk of his cavalry to keep them away from the flanks of his phalanxes. As long as they maintained their formation, they would punch through whatever forces the Romans could put in front of them. He could then bring up his archers, which would outrange the Roman horsemen and scatter them.

"Let's go look at the Roman legions," he said to the third scout, nudging his horse in the direction of his front lines.

Roman Front Lines

Drest felt the wave of excitement that always ran through him just before a fight. Like the rest of his countrymen, he relished the thrill of combat, where he was able to test his physical prowess against an enemy, especially one such as this, where he didn't have to hold anything back.

He knew he wasn't actually allowed to do that, of course. He understood the plan and why it was necessary to fight in the Roman way, sneaking and sniping at the enemy instead of confronting them in a stand-up fight. He didn't like it, but he understood. It was hard not to understand when looking at what seemed like an infinite number of long spears marching towards him, with the death worshipers' army stretching as far as the eye could see.

He wasn't afraid of them, but he did have a moment of doubt about the plan. For it to work, the entire death worshiper army had to be completely between the mountains to the west and the long lake to the east. Looking at the death worshipers, he thought it possible that they would stretch out longer than the lake, making it impossible to pen them in.

Of course, maps and planning on that scale weren't his strength. Drest, like his fathers before him, had always been a war chieftain. True, theirs was a minor tribe, but one that had often been given a place of honor in Talogren's battle line. It was a proud place to be, but it meant he only needed to worry about the army in front of him, so he'd leave the planning to the Romans.

The plan was simple, if not one to his liking. Attack enough to make it look real, and retreat. The hard part wasn't the attack. His men were ready for that. The hard part was the retreat. He'd spoken to as many of his men as possible to convince them this was the right thing to do and they'd have chances to win glory before this was all over, but they still didn't like it. It had actually been easier to convince half of the men to wear Roman-style armor than it had been to convince them that retreat would be necessary.

Ahead of him, the death worshipers long spears lowered, their points glistening in the early morning sun as they began to fan out, spreading across the plain ahead of him.

"ATTACK!!" Drest yelled, lifting his sword in the air and charging forward with his men.

Carthaginian Line

Bomilcar had to hand it to the Romans, they were brave. His front ranks had even begun to buckle slightly at their attack. Watching them struggle, he was a little confused, however. He'd personally never fought the Romans, but he'd familiarized himself with their style, and this wasn't it. The force in front of him was made up of men in Roman armor and dressed in the northern barbarian style, and yet they all attacked in the same, all-out reckless charge. This was precisely the kind of fighting his phalanxes were used to, since most had come from the final pacifications of Germania. They may have wavered a bit under the sheer brutality of the assault, but they didn't break.

"They'll be breaking soon," an aide next to him said.

Bomilcar just nodded, his mind working overtime. None of this was right. Not only were the Romans attacking like barbarians, there weren't enough of them. The last reports their scouts and the turn-coat Roman's spies had given said there should be around thirty-thousand legionaries and barbarians facing them. This was, at most, five thousand. He was always skeptical of spies and even scouting reports, especially against an enemy that was as focused on disrupting his scouts as much as the Romans had been, but it seemed impossible their sources would be that wrong.

No, the Romans were planning something and this was just a feint or a diversion. He was just waiting for the other shoe to drop.

Roman Front Lines

Drest pushed aside another spear and lunged forward, his sword catching the wielder just below the exposed collarbone. He'd been aiming for the man's face, but had his sword deflected by the man's small round shield at the last moment. Unluckily for the death worshiper facing him, their small shields didn't block enough of their body and he wasn't very good at using it to properly deflect the blow.

The man went down, writhing in pain. It wasn't a mortal blow, but there was every chance he would be crushed under his compatriot's boots as another man moved in to take the fallen soldier's place.

Drest took a step back, looking to the left and right of him quickly. His men were fighting hard, and the death worshipers were making a poor showing for themselves, but there were too many of them. A lot of his men were already down, pierced by swords and spears. He was sure they'd killed more than they lost, but the fact that he couldn't see their bodies because the death worshipers front line was continuing to push them back meant he was losing badly.

Glancing at the position of the sun briefly, he decided they had done enough.

"FALL BACK," he yelled, sweeping aside a spear tip meant for him and taking a step back.

Carthaginian Lines

"They're running, my lord," Bomilcar's aide said. "We should pursue."

"Tell the men to follow in order. Do not let the line break."

"But sir, they'll escape."

"No, they won't. This is a trap. They have lost maybe a fifth of their number at most and they're fighting for their homes. If this was their last stand, they'd fight until completely broken. No, This is part of their plan. The rest of the Roman army is out there."

The man's brows furrowed as he considered that, before putting fist to chest and riding away to carry out his orders. As he watched, the trickle turned into a tide of men running along the road. In spite of the limited training and how slipshod the formation of units was, Bomilcar was proud of how well his phalanxes held their cohesion as they continued their march north, with the units that had suffered the most casualties falling back to let fresh units take their place.

The ground was still favorable to them, as they marched up the valley along the north-south road towards the Roman capital, passing a crystal blue lake reflecting the ridge on the eastern side of the valley. With his mounted forces still off dealing with the Roman cavalry, he was happy to see the narrowing landscape between the western ridges of the valley and the lake, which would limit surprise attacks that might hit him on his flanks.

The Romans biggest advantage was how much more quickly a Roman legion could turn and deploy for battle than his phalanxes could, and he was surprised that the Romans had chosen a spot that kept them in his front, all but eliminating their one area of tactical superiority. The lake was large enough that men couldn't just come across it and long enough to keep any coordinated attack from maneuvering around it without his men having time to react. True, they could have ambushers in the hills, but the ascent on this side was steep and the rocks were icy, making it equally impossible to launch a coordinated attack from this side.

Cresting the next ridge, his suspicions about the Romans were confirmed. A much larger line of Roman legionaries was arrayed against them as the retreating men melted into their lines. The Romans lines were barely five ranks deep, stretched across the length of the valley between the ridge and the lake, probably trying to keep his phalanxes from wrapping around their flanks and encircling them. It was good in theory, but spread this thin, it was near suicide. He almost felt sorry for the men his forces were about to obliterate.

Roman Lines

"Hold Steady," Velius said, his voice carrying down the line.

His men were solid, but it would be hard for any man to not quake at the sight of thousands of spears marching over the rise ahead of them.

Ky had ordered him and the other legates to stay behind the lines observing from a distance and passing orders through messages. He knew the Consul would have words with him when this was all over, but Velius couldn't leave his men to fight out here by themselves. Until the other two-thirds of the legions on this side of the valley and their Caledonian auxiliaries showed up, this and what was left of Drest's men was all that was left to face a horde twenty times their size.

Velius sensed more than saw Drest come up next to him, but ignored it as his entire attention was focused on the line of men coming towards them.

"Ready," Velius called out as the Carthaginians passed an invisible spot in the field Velius had been watching.

The Roman line rippled as the men pulled up their large shields and readied themselves for the initial push. This was the critical moment in any engagement with a phalanx. Surviving that first charge and pushing past the spears is what would make or break the legion's fates. Once they were in close range, the heavy roman armor and large shields would be a hard shell for the Carthaginians to get past, but it was that first push that they had to steady themselves for.

Of course, they'd still suffer casualties and, without new centuries to rotate in for the depleted ones, this thin line wouldn't last long, but that was a problem for Ky who was with the remaining forces, probably already giving them the order to move up and join the battle.

"Brace," Velius called out as the spear points reached the Roman shields.

He held his breath as the Carthaginians smashed into his men and then broke like a wave across it. Romans fell here and there as spears got through small gaps in the shield wall, piecing this man's thigh and that man's side, but his men held.

Now to take the fight to them.

"Forward one," he commanded.

Like the fine-tuned machine that it was, the legion stepped forward, pushing the spear tips across the tops of their shields and over their heads, bringing the invaders into the range of Roman swords.

Carthaginian Line

"The first men were barbarians dressed up like Romans," Bomilcar said, looking down on the clash of battle lines.

He had to hand it to the Roman commander, it was a clever ruse. He knew many generals on his side that would have fallen for it, allowing their men to break ranks and give chase to the diversionary force, only to be cut to pieces by the organized legions hiding on the other side of the next ridge. The line facing him was small, but seeing the ground, he could see the reason for it, and wasn't surprised in the least as the first row of Roman reinforcements crested over the next hill and began marching down to join the men already engaged.

For a moment he'd hoped his men would roll over the thin line of legionnaires before their reinforcements could arrive, but the Romans were as good as history said they were. There was a moment when the left side of their line looked like it might break, but the barbarians dressed like Romans had stopped their retreat and were now acting like some kind of reactive force, charging in to reinforce the line as needed. Again, he was impressed. It wouldn't have worked for a phalanx, which wasn't trained to disengage and rotate out the way the Romans apparently were, but it was a smart way to use auxiliaries who'd crumble if put in line by themselves.

"Bring our archers up and have them form on this rise and have them target the reinforcements. Let's see if we can take some of the fight out of them before they reach their friends."

Bomilcar didn't have as many archers as he would have liked, and he doubted they'd be able to disrupt the Romans, but he had to make the attempt. Even with the bows, it was clear he would need to really push his men in to break the Roman line. Once they broke, though, his men would roll right over them, but it was becoming clear the Romans were not going to be easy to break. As he watched he could see his front phalanxes struggle against the heavy armor and shields of the Romans.

That heavy armor came with a price, though. Even rotating through units, they were going to tire while he'd have more fresh units to push in. Eventually, the Romans would break.

"Get the rest of the men in battle formation. I want units ready to replace those that lose combat effectiveness," he said to another messenger.

Roman Auxiliaries

Ky had been watching the battle through his drone with the auxiliary forces. Once he'd confirmed that Velius was engaged and ordered the rest of the legions and Caledonians forward, Ky switched his focus to the rear of the Carthaginian line.

They were already in the area, but he needed them to bunch up more before he gave the word. Phalanxes were slow to maneuver, more so when in battle lines and pressed up against other phalanxes, all waiting for their turn in the front line.

"The Carthaginians have deployed their archers," Sophus, who was able to focus on all of the drone feeds simultaneously, said.

"We expected that. There aren't enough of them and we're spread thin enough that, unless their general is a maniac who doesn't care about his front ranks, they aren't going to be able hit us once they've moved all the way up."

"They will be able to target the civilian auxiliary and some of the Caledonians."

"Yes, but both will be more spread out than the legions. We can withstand the losses."

"I was more thinking of the auxiliary breaking under the shooting."

"They're fighting for their homes, I think they'll hold. Still, you might be right," Ky said.

Turning to one of the men next to him and speaking aloud, he said, "Tell Sepurcius to concentrate his volleys on the rise just off the center of the Carthaginian formation. Let's see if we can't disrupt those archers."

The messenger half looked in the direction of the fighting, probably wondering how Ky knew there were archers at all, considering they couldn't see the battle from the defilade they were currently in, but nodded and left to deliver the message.

Forest South of the Carthaginian Army

"It's time," Ky said through the small device in Lucilla's ear.

She'd been waiting for Ky's signal for almost two hours, ever since the Carthaginian army had passed the forest into the cleared valley. They hadn't been able to see them, because of how deep into the forest she and the men she commanded were, but she'd heard them as they marched by. It was impossible for an army that size to be anything but conspicuous.

They'd gone over this section of the plan dozens of times and 'gamed out the variables' as Ky had said. She'd been confused the first time she'd heard Ky use the phrase, but after going through fake versions of the battles and looking at all of the maps and diagrams of possibilities he'd provided during planning, it kind of made sense. Although she still thought calling anything involving war a 'game' was a bit callous.

Thankfully, their preparation had prepared her for running into the Carthaginian baggage train as soon as they cleared the edge of the forest. That was why they'd held a portion of the cavalry back with her. She could hear her men running down Carthaginian guards and camp followers before she even made it out of the woods. Part of her felt bad, since most of these were destitute people looking to make some kind of living off the Carthaginian army, or were the families of the soldiers, but it was necessary. She made it clear that she didn't want anyone running south, away from the battle, to be chased. They only needed to keep Carthaginians from running north and possibly alerting their army that she and her men were here.

Between what horsemen she had and the Caledonians following closely on their heels, the road was already littered with bodies, with the snow that had already covered the Carthaginian army's tracks now tinged in red. She forced herself to look, both because she should have to see the results of what she ordered and to confirm for herself that none of her people had gone to excess.

Her Romans, with their heavier armor and bulkier shields, took longer to get through the woods. Thankfully, between the lightly falling snow and wind that had picked up, it was going to be harder for the Carthaginians, whose attention was focused on the battle ahead of them, to notice the force in their rear before it was too late.

She watched from horseback as the cavalry continued to chase down the Carthaginian civilians, willing her centurions to get their men assembled faster. Other than the initial clash, the other weak point in this plan was the period between first contact and the second half of the Roman forces closing the trap. Until then, none of the surprises Ky had set up could be launched, and his men would be in a fight for their lives.

Northern Roman Line

Ky watched Lucilla's men begin their progress up the road through the drones' cameras and fought back the urge to prod her to move faster. He could see she was doing everything she could to get her men moving and into position, but it wasn't easy.

Four times already the Caledonians had to charge in to help seal a breach as the Roman lines began to collapse. They pulled back each time with fewer men than they had gone in with, and there were only so many more times they could counter-attack before there weren't enough of them to make a difference.

The Carthaginians had now begun to move up their men, tightening their formations so every time a phalanx broke against the Roman wall another one would be there to replace them.

"On the right," Carus said, standing next to Ky.

As he turned, he could see part of the Roman wall crumble, bending in on itself. The Caledonians charged in as planned, but there were barely a hundred warriors, and they weren't going to be enough to stop the breach.

Ky began to move in that direction, his hand going to the gladius on his side, when Carus's hand gripped his arm hard.

"No, Consul. You have to be here to signal the counter-attack. Trust Velius to stop the breakthrough."

Carus had no way of knowing how Ky would know when it was time to signal the next stage of the plan, but he wasn't wrong. Ky wouldn't be able to watch the feed from the drone and fight in the line simultaneously, especially since he didn't have his shield any longer to cover him while his attention was split.

"Do we have anything we can send in to help?" Ky said, his hand coming off his blade.

Carus was right, Velius did have the situation in hand, mostly. The Caledonians were helping push the Carthaginians back, but it was a struggle and almost looked like it would fail until a century Velius had sent in from the center of the line arrived and began to help. They managed to push back the phalanxes, which weren't built to exploit narrow breakthroughs.

If the Carthaginians had even a small amount of heavy infantry instead of relying almost entirely on phalanxes, they would have been able to exploit the breakthrough and completely roll one side of the Roman lines.

Of course, it was easier to train subjected people to be spearmen in a phalanx than heavy infantry, and cheaper since they didn't need the heavier armor to protect them, relying instead on the wall of spears to keep opponents at bay.

Ky was amazed that Velius had managed to pull even one century from the line, since the center was the hardest pressed of the entire battle. Velius was playing a dangerous game, juggling his forces to keep it together until relieved. It was only a matter of time before he dropped one of the hypothetical balls.

"Part of one of the Cavalry wings has returned and we have maybe a dozen praetorians running security for the civilian auxiliaries, just in case some of the Carthaginians broke through."

"Dismount the horsemen and send them in with the praetorians. Velius can either put them in the line or have them work with the Caledonians. Send in all of my guards and any staff or messengers along too. I can send you to relay any messages. Except for the civilian auxiliary, I want anyone capable of lifting a sword given one and sent down to Velius."

"It won't make much of a difference," Carus said.

"Anything will help. Do it."

Carus was right, of course. All of that was less than a hundred men and wouldn't change the outcome. Ky just felt like he should be doing more than just watching the battle from above and waiting.

Even as he watched, the left wing began to bend. It hadn't broken yet, but a bulge was beginning to form in the Roman line.

A section between two centuries was being pushed back in the slick ground near the shoreline.

Ky looked again to the drone footage, watching Lucilla's force move slowly towards the Carthaginians, silently urging her to hurry.

Carthaginian Army

"Not long now," Bomilcar said, a smile finally breaking across his face.

He didn't relish killing these people, especially since their commander had done amazingly well with what he had. The difference in forces was so far against him that he didn't really stand a chance, but he'd managed to hold out a lot longer than Bomilcar would have thought he'd be able to.

Several of his tactics had been downright inspired and, in the hands of a fool like Zaracas, might have worked. He enjoyed the feeling of victory, especially through the challenges forced on him by the idiot the emperor had put in charge of this reign, but he didn't relish killing such a worthy opponent. He'd do his duty, of course, but he would say a prayer to the gods for the man's swift passage into the afterlife, as fitting a worthy adversary.

The Roman left had stiffened again and managed to straighten out its line, but only by bending along the shoreline, creating an angle closer to the center. Unless the rest of the Roman line moved back, that would create a weak point that would eventually break open. So far they'd managed to put their line back together each time it broke, but an angle like that, especially close to the center where his men were supported on their sides, would turn into a breakthrough.

"Send a message to Tolman. I want him to concentrate on the bend just created in the Roman line. He's to put as much pressure on that section of line as possible. We ..."

Bomilcar was interrupted by a messenger riding up hard on horseback, almost skidding to a halt in front of him.

"General, another Roman force has just attacked us from the rear."

"What?" Bomilcar said.

"A bunch of barbarians and horsemen came out of nowhere, attacking our rearmost phalanxes. Several units were destroyed before the commander could get units turned around for a counter-attack."

Bomilcar paused, looking at the map in his head, seeing the Romans play. They had waited until his men were trapped between the lake and the hills before they attacked, probably hoping to keep his men confined, unable to push around the side of the Romans. They must have someone up in the hills observing the field, to make the timing work. It was another smart move, but like the ambush attempt, it wouldn't work. He had enough men to fight in both directions, enveloping the enemy on either side of him.

It did suggest that his cavalry hadn't fared well, since they should have been able to alert him to the approaching threat. He'd seen the way the enemy maneuvered and could see how it was possible for his men to be out-ridden and defeated, even though they had outnumbered the Romans. When this was all over, he'd have to interview prisoners and find out how the Romans had managed that.

"Have him push the barbarians back. When they break, he's to extend the rear third of the army back to beyond the mouth of the valley."

The man looked sideways, clearly having more bad news to tell. His hesitation to share bad news was one of the downsides of the empire that allowed men like Maharbaal into positions of power. Killing the messenger was counterproductive and kept commanders from getting the information they really needed, and yet it happened all too frequently.

"Just tell me," Bomilcar said. "I won't hold it against you."

"The commander attempted the counter-attack and encountered Roman forces behind the barbarians and cavalry, and was repulsed with heavy losses. A new front line has been established, but when I was dispatched, the Roman forces were still pushing our men back."

Bomilcar silently cursed the Roman general. He knew the enemy's strength in front of him was less than their sources had suggested, but he didn't believe they would have enough men to create a second front line. He also couldn't figure out how the Romans had coordinated the attack so well.

"Tell him …" Bomilcar started to say and stopped as movement on the far crest drew his attention.

A wave of people who, at least from his vantage point, didn't seem to be dressed as legionaries and were well-spread across the rise and partway down the slope towards their front line, suddenly appeared. If that was concerning, what happened next was the stuff of nightmares.

Bomilcar had read reports of the Roman Consul's powers. Reports written about the man's ability to, at a great distance, bring forth green fire from the underworld that ripped apart ground, building, and bone, he saw as an exaggeration. Nothing in Bomilcar's long service had ever convinced him that power like that existed and, since the tales always came from men running from the Romans, it was easy to disbelieve.

He now knew it wasn't a lie or an exaggeration. If anything, they had underplayed how absolutely terrifying the man's powers could be. A hundred yards from him the hilltop where the archers were standing exploded in a ball of green fire that ripped through the archers still firing volleys of arrows. As he watched, the green fire swept over men and horses, rendering them from living beings into piles of smoking bones in seconds. Those on the edges of the bust might have actually had it worse, as their actual skin caught fire and began to burn.

Shrieks filled the air. And then things got worse!

Northern Roman Line.

Ky sheathed his sidearm. He now only had 14 rounds left and, while this battle was make or break for the Romans, for the Carthaginians this was just a small force operating on the fringes of their territory. He didn't know what kind of challenges he'd face next, but blasting away now would leave him with fewer choices than he'd otherwise have.

He'd already decided that if he had ways to defeat the enemy using replenishable assets, he'd have to rely on that, even if in the end it cost more Roman lives. He'd been forced to use one round now, because it was the only way he knew of to signal all of the separated forces to begin the next stage of the plan, as instant communications were still not an option and he needed the attack to be coordinated.

He'd originally thought to fire on the Carthaginian commander, who by all accounts was competent, possibly enough to find a way to make Ky's plan fail. That was before the man amassed his archers in one place. As far as Ky could tell, the archers on the opposing hill were the bulk of the ranged forces the Carthaginians had, and they could constitute a problem for his civilian auxiliaries, which would be unstable in the face of enemy counter-volleys.

He hadn't gotten all of the enemy archers, of course. His sidearm was meant to be able to penetrate lighter forms of modern, or at least what he used to think of as modern, battle armor, and wasn't meant to cause wide area damage. He could see the archers scattering, however, and it would take time for their commanders to rally them.

On cue, the auxiliary shot volleys. It wasn't all at once, but it was pretty close, which Ky counted as a victory considering the limited time each of these people had to train. The one thing he worried about was the possibility of them shooting into the backs of his own line, so much so that he'd almost contemplated leaving a single line of legionnaires facing the other direction, to protect their comrades. Of course, that wasn't possible, since they hardly had enough men to fight back the Carthaginians as it was.

Thankfully, the crossbows were fairly easy to use, and being on a rise, it was more likely that the civilians would shoot too far rather than too short. As he watched, the bolts began landing among the Carthaginians. The phalanxes were packed so tightly that it was almost impossible not to hit someone. They didn't have the range to reach the other hill, but their bolts tore through the third and fourth ranks of the Carthaginian battle line, punching through their thin leather armor with its occasional metal reinforcement almost as if it weren't there.

And then the rest of the forces' volleys began to land.

Roman Artillery Station

Sepurcius had been waiting, listening to the distant sounds of the battle, all morning. His men were cold and bored, but he'd forbidden any fires or anything else that might give away their presence. Had the Carthaginians been looking hard enough, they probably still would have seen him, since these large weapons the Consul had designed weren't exactly inconspicuous and were impossible to hide in the tree line without damaging them.

They hadn't shown any sign of realizing Sepurcius and his men were there, however. Except for one messenger with instructions to target their barrage on a hilltop closest to the northern side of the battle, he'd heard no word from the Consul or legates. They had told him he would know the signal when he saw it, but as the day wore on, he kept thinking he might have missed it, worrying a messenger would appear at any moment to ask why he hadn't commenced.

Until the green flame, that is.

As soon as he saw it he realized the legates had been right. It was impossible to miss the signal. He'd had his men standing by their equipment since the Consul's messenger had arrived, all waiting for his signal to load and fire. Normally he and his Optios would have nearly had to whip the men to keep focus, especially for this long, but he could feel their tension ever since the battle started. They knew, as well as he did, that this battle would determine the fate of their entire civilization.

"Load," he called as the lake reflected the green flame billowing up from the center of the Carthaginian line.

His men had spent the last month operating these giant new machines, one stone after another, until they knew them inside and out. As his men hefted the large stones in the leather and woven pouches connected to the machines' throwing arm, Sepurcius looked up at the wooden frame towering above him, marveling at the new invention.

From a technical standpoint, they weren't all that different than the throwing devices he'd previously used. He understood the basic mechanics of tension and counterweights that allowed the device, which the Consul had called trebuchets, to hurl large weights further than any previous Roman artillery. He would have never dreamed of firing at this distance before the Consul explained the new innovations, but building and testing them over the last several months had taught him just how effective they could be.

The only thing he really wished was that they had more of them. Even with the Consul's designs, there had been a period of trial and error getting it to work practically, and they hadn't even had the full winter to do it in. He'd only managed to get four of the monstrosities built and ready to fire when the word of the Carthaginian army marching north reached them.

Seeing his men standing ready, the weights pulling down on the throwing arm, Sepurcius bellowed, "Release!"

Carthaginian Army

Bomilcar was still staring agape at the burning men running from the hilltop, trying to fight back nausea that came with the smell of cooking flesh, when more shrieks assailed him, this time from the aide next to him. He only had time to turn his head when the large stone plowed into the ground in front of him, at the base of the hill where he was standing, and skipping across the ground as it hit, leaving a line of dead and broken men in its wake.

His brain was moving fast, trying to comprehend what had happened to the victory he'd tasted just moments before. The green flame, while horrendous, hadn't been their counter-attack. Had they been able to do that at will, they could have wiped out his entire army the moment they marched into this valley, instead of waiting while hundreds of Romans were cut down trying to keep his army in place.

That had been a signal for the people with the arcuballista they'd heard about on the hill across from him to open fire, and for whatever throwing machines the Romans had on the other side of the lake.

The trajectory made it clear that's where they came from, although no Carthaginian catapult would have been able to operate at those ranges. Squinting, he could almost make out almost pyramid-shaped structures with figures he assumed to be Roman scampering about them. The stones they threw were also larger than anything the Carthaginians could have managed, although not so much as to be beyond understanding.

They caused large-scale damage and were causing his men to panic, but they weren't the biggest danger his men faced. The Roman arrows were shrugging off shield and breastplate alike, killing or maiming any man they encountered. As he watched, entire phalanxes began to come apart under their onslaught.

It seemed impossible they had enough soldiers to have hundreds on the opposing hilltop firing down into his men, especially since more traditional Roman archers had already taken the field when his archers had made their appearance.

"Sir," another messenger said, riding up hard and then stopping short of the general, his attention pulled to the charred remains nearby.

"Soldier!" Bomilcar said, anger in his voice.

"Sorry, General," the man said, almost grudgingly looking away from the charred carnage. "Hanno sends word that he has begun to receive fire from the cliffs to the east. He tried sending men to get to the attackers, but the slope is slick with ice and they get picked off before they can make headway. His men are beginning to press in towards the center of the line to get out of range, and he is concerned he is about to lose that flank.

"Sir," one of his men said, pointing in the direction of another messenger riding hard towards him from the rear of the army.

The man was almost to them when another stone crashed down obliterating him and a handful of archers he was passing. Although the man hadn't been able to deliver his message, Bomilcar was fairly certain he knew what it was. Considering the way this trap had sprung closed, the Romans had to have more of these people armed with their new weapons focused on his rear.

He couldn't see their impact directly, but the speed at which men were falling suggested these weapons were penetrating most of their armor and shields. Worse, unlike archer's arrows that, if it didn't hit a target, embedded itself in the ground, these projectiles were traveling in a straight line, and just hitting the man behind their target. With his phalanxes packed in to try and push the Romans far enough back that he could extend his line and outflank them, there would always be another soldier behind, so hardly any of their arrows missed hitting someone.

By themselves, they would have caused damage, but would not have been enough to change the outcome of this battle. Trapped in this square with the largest projectiles he'd ever seen from a siege weapon falling on them, however, made this another Cannae, with Bomilcar and his men playing the part of the doomed Romans.

He couldn't believe this had happened. He'd been expecting a trap like this, and still their commander had suckered him. Bomilcar felt a wave of sadness wash over him. All of these men were going to die, and there was nothing he could do to stop it. They could still extract a price for their deaths, but the end result was inevitable.

"Sir, we need to move. They are targeting this entire hilltop," one of his lieutenants said.

Another stone crashed nearby, sending men and material flying.

"Of course, order ..."

The sentence never made it the rest of the way out of Bomilcar's mouth as a stone imbedded itself in the middle of his aides and lieutenants, the impact knocking over Bomilcar, his horse, and anyone or anything else near them smashing to the earth.

As his horse landed on him and the two were covered in dirt and debris, Bomilcar wondered again how he had been so badly outmaneuvered.

Chapter 29

Irish Coast

Llassar pulled the small one-man boat onto the shore. He half considered finding a cove or outcropping to try and hide the boat, but it didn't matter. If he didn't find a way to get in contact with Salbuide and convince the king to join them, there was a strong chance the Ériu would never let him leave.

Even if some fisherman found the boat, they wouldn't be able to get word to Emain Macha until Llassar had a chance to reach the city.

Despite being a prisoner, he had fond memories of his time here. The Ériu were, in some ways, more advanced than his own people, although still far behind what the Romans had accomplished. Unlike Monadhcarden, the capital of the Caledonians, with its tents and mud huts, the circular city of Emain Macha was large, with a huge round building in its center. Llassar remembered marveling at its giant wooden roof, thinking, at the time, that it was the grandest building he had ever seen.

Like the Romans, the Ériu were builders. If the Consul was right, and they could convince them to join the Empire, they would pick up the Roman traditions faster than the Caledonians could, and could be a great asset to them.

Of course, they were nearly as mistrusting as the Caledonians when it came to outsiders and his stay here had been a long time ago. There was equally as good a chance he might die here.

Llassar didn't fear death, but he understood how important this was to the alliance. That, in and of itself, was an unusual feeling for him. He had almost thought Talogren had gone mad when he heard about his dealing with the Romans, but after spending time with them, he realized that, as always, his chieftain was a further thinking man than he was. His conversion into being a believer in their new Empire had been swift, but total.

Stepping off the rocky beach and into the edges of the grasslands, Llassar began his long trek inland.

Battlefield, North of Venonis

"How many?" Ky asked as he and the surviving legates, along with a large contingent of guards, walked across the corpses scattered across the battlefield.

"We don't know yet," Carus said. "Thousands, to be sure. Maybe a full legion dead, with almost as many wounded. The largest losses were in Velius's legion, as they tried to seal that final break before we sprung the trap."

"Have we found his body yet?"

"No, but the grave men have just started to separate out the dead and arrange for mass burials. They are pulling identifying items and any bodies of centurions or above for identification."

"We need to reform at least one or two legions, in case there is another force coming north," Aelius said.

"There isn't," Carus replied before Ky could answer. "We've had a lot of eyes on the city since this army marched. From what we've been able to gather, they moved ahead of schedule and basically stripped the city bare of supplies to feed this many men, since foraging would have been sparse. We're even getting reports of some of the poorer sections of the city already running short of food. They couldn't field another large force this soon."

"It's still a good idea," Ky said to Carus before looking at Aelius. "You and Ursinus's legions got hurt the least. Form up on the other side of the battlefield and set out pickets. Don't do anything long-term, though. Once we've recovered the wounded and buried the dead, I want to begin the move south against Londinium before they can call for more reinforcements. This loss will be enough for the Carthaginians to take us seriously and they still have a giant pool of manpower to pull from. They'll have a lot harder time landing new armies if they don't have any friendly ports."

Aelius saluted and left to follow his orders.

"I also want to get what praetorians we have and our cavalry to begin pushing forward and as far east and west as they can. It's unlikely we'll be successful, but if we could keep word of this victory from reaching Londinium until just before we get there, they won't have time to fortify the city or collect supplies before we can envelop it. The rest of you, get your men re-equipped and resupplied as best you can. I want us on the move in two days."

Carus, and the rest of the commanders saluted and left for their commands, leaving Ky alone with Lucilla.

"You should take a moment and appreciate what you've done here," Lucilla said.

"I wish we could, for the men's sake, if nothing else, but we don't have time. We are close to freeing the entirety of Britannia. We have the momentum. If we move now, a lot fewer of our men will die in the process."

"I know. It's just that it hasn't been that long since your … condition, and you've been pushing yourself hard since the day you arrived here. I worry about you."

"I know," he said, putting an arm around her.

Holding her close, Ky looked out on the battlefield. It was a great victory, but it was only the beginning. Even when they finally freed the rest of Britannia, the Empire wouldn't be safe. They wouldn't be truly safe until the Carthaginians were dealt with.

This was just the beginning.

About the author

Travis writes science fiction, fantasy, and thriller novels (and the occasional coming-of-age story), with the hope of transporting and enthralling readers. Publishing novels since 2015, Travis's passion is creating worlds and characters that live and breathe, and experiencing the joy of those stories with his readers. When not writing, Travis enjoys connecting with readers and other writers, managing the popular Complete Marvel Reading Order website, where he works on his other passion for comics and graphic novels, and spending time with his family.
If you have enjoyed this book, please consider taking a moment to rate or review it wherever you found your copy, as it helps new readers find my works and ensures I can continue writing book into the future.

Find out more at:
amazon.com/TravisStarnes/e/B072YBDC3S/

Or visit
https://tstarnes.com

Maps available at

https://tstarnes.com/book-series/imperium/

Signup to get free previews and notifications of upcoming books at

http://tstarnes.com/preview-notification-newsletter/

Also by

John Taylor Stories

Rebirth
False Signs
The Wrong Girl
Burying the Past
Family Ties
Election Day
Danger Close
Extraction
Designated Target
Border Crossed
Desperate Rendition

Country Roads Series

Playing by Ear
Fanfare
Dissonance
Elegy
From the Top
Center Stage

Imperium Series

Volume 1
The Sword of Jupiter
The Trumpets of Mars
The Sands of Saturn
The Depths of Neptune
The Fires of Vulcan
The Triumph of Venus
Volume 2
The Wings of Mercury
The Plains of Pluto

Shattered Lands Series

In the Shadow of Lions
An Ending of Oaths

False Start Series

Second Down

The Veilguard Saga

Threads of Destiny

Stand Alone

Going Home